Some Days Are Diamonds

Some Days Are Diamonds

A Theatre On Main Novel

Stephanie Surma

Published by Tablo

ACKNOWLEDGEMENTS

Thank you, thank you, *thank you* to all of my wonderful friends who read my novel in its early drafts, and who helped me turn it from a disjointed mess into the vision I had in my head. Your support and love and guidance is everything to me, and I love you all so much.

A special shout out to Hannah, for being my first hardcore fan, and for your wonderful fan art. It's the first time my characters had come to life visually— I didn't even draw them— and I cannot express the amazement and gratitude and joy I felt getting to see my babies' faces for the first time.

For Pioneer Hall.
Let's Raise the Roof.

1

The Theatre On Main had always been Elle's home. From the moment she'd stepped into it, a fresh-faced college kid with big dreams and big shoes to fill, she'd felt a bone deep, soul filling sense of *belonging*.

Perhaps that was why she spent all of her time here, Elle thought, staring out at the empty seats and tables of the dinner theater. Her little two bedroom apartment hadn't felt like home in months; not since the fighting had started with her roommate. At least work offered some stability. Besides, the people here were her family— the chef in the back, the waitstaff, the performers, the other techs. Greg, the resident director, had been like a father to her, inviting her to work here before she'd even finished college.

Elle sighed and dropped her *Kingdom Hearts* backpack to the floor of the tech booth, kicking it under the sound table. Gina had announced that she was leaving almost two weeks ago, which Elle was still pretending not to feel relieved about. It left Elle in need of a roommate, and she was running out of time to find one. Her lease was up the second week of August, and July was nearly over. She didn't even have anyone in *mind*. She couldn't afford the place on her own, and it was too late to cancel the lease. All around, it was an impending disaster.

"You look mopey," said a friendly voice behind her. Elle's tech booth partner-in-crime shuffled in, dropped his saddle bag beside hers, then wrapped his arms around her shoulders. "We're only three days into this run. You shouldn't be moping yet. Why are you moping already?"

Elle returned his hug and squeezed. "Hi, Ben." She sighed as he moved away to sit on his rolling chair. He was a sweet kid; a little mousy, maybe a little overweight, with thinning brown hair and beetle black eyes behind thick square glasses. Still, he gave the best hugs, and sometimes brought her tacos, and really, he was just a *nice* person.

"Hi, Elle." Ben grabbed the bin of microphone packs out from under the sound table and slid it her way. "So again, why are you mopey? Usually you're singing by this point."

"I'm not *mopey*." Just to prove it, she started to hum the title song of the show—*Oklahoma*. It only lasted a few seconds before she trailed off, sighed, and ran a hand over her face.

"You are, but I'll let that little lie slide." Ben took to switching on the stage lights from the control panel. "Is it your roommate? Is she still being a bi—"

"*Antagonistic,* " Elle cut him off. Even if Gina *was* being horrible, it wasn't fair to talk shit about her.

"Right," Ben said, one eyebrow hiked up over his glasses. "That."

The mic packs needed new batteries before every show, so Elle hopped up onto her stool and popped the back off the first one. It was a soothing, familiar routine, taking out the old batteries, putting in new, and closing the pack up again. "It's fine. I just…"*don't want to go home,* Elle thought, but she couldn't say that aloud. Ben was great, but on a list of things he didn't need to know, that qualified.

"It's a lot to put up with." Ben jiggled open the top drawer of the filing cabinet under the table and pulled out two tootsie pops. "Want one?"

Elle smirked. Ben would solve *any* problem with candy, if it was up to him. "No, thanks."

"Come on, you can crunch on it and pretend it's your roommate's head."

"Are you two talking about the banshee Elle lives with?" Despite the scathing tone, Elle found herself smiling as her best friend came in, filling the tiny tech booth to bursting. Logan was a tall beanpole of a man, with copper hair that stood in tufts from his square head, and a sharply hooked nose. He planted a loud kiss on her cheek which brought giggles up her throat like soda bubbles.

"Hi, Log—*oof!* " His enthusiastic greeting nearly knocked her over, and her stool swayed underneath her. Ben steadied it, calm as ever, with one foot pressed against the seat of the stool, snorting as Logan proceeded to squeeze Elle in a rib crushing hug.

Logan grabbed Elle's face and squished it between his hands. "You tell Gina she can come talk to me, personally, about whatever she's been on you about, so that I can tell her to shove it up her ass." He narrowed his eyes and scrutinized her face, no doubt noting the exhaustion she was wearing underneath her eyes like designer bags. "What was it this time, Doll?"

"Oh, god," Elle groaned, residual laughter fluttering out of her throat. She took Logan's hands in her own, squeezing them before getting back to her mic packs. "Spin a wheel and throw a dart. I think it was the trash last week."

"Has she ever taken the trash out?" Logan demanded.

"She should take herself out," Ben muttered behind Elle.

She reached back and swatted his arm. "Be *nice.*"

With a snort, Ben said, "Absolutely not. If she's gonna be a nuisance over stupid shit—"

"I just forgot what day it was," Elle insisted, trying to focus on what her hands were doing. Open pack, old batteries out, new batteries in, close pack. Rinse and repeat. "Apparently yelling at me was more important than just taking it out herself." And the fight that had ensued had been long and grueling, Gina's words still ringing in her ears. Even now, it soured her mood. Elle closed her mic pack with a little more force than necessary and winced at the sharp *crack* of plastic against plastic. "I think it was the microwave a few days before that." The rest of the sentence got caught somewhere between Elle's brain and tongue, coming out strained. "The dishes were what started it."

Logan's hand fell gently onto her shoulder, and squeezed.

"What, does she have a kitchen fetish?" Ben joked, sneering. Elle's laugh sounded forced even to her own ears.

"Hey, guys." Just outside the door, Logan's roommate, John, waved.

Elle waved back, glad for the brief distraction from the conversation. "Hey, John!"

At over six feet tall, trying to come into the room would have ended in tragedy and possibly broken limbs. There was just too much of *him*, and not enough *room* , which he'd learned pretty quickly when Elle had nagged at him during the last show they'd done together. He stopped outside the booth window, instead, running a hand through his golden hair. "Where am I, Elle?"

"You're in for Curly, tonight. Davy's out today."

"Ten-four." And with that, John strolled away into the dining area toward the door to the back rooms. He looked almost comically large amidst the small square tables with their plain white tablecloths, the matching wooden chairs. It was a wonder he never tripped over them.

"Does she ever consider maybe just doing things," Ben asked as John slipped from view, "instead of bitching at you?"

Probably not. Elle shrugged, dropping her eyes to her mic packs. "I don't know."

Two batteries fell into her trembling hand, and then dropped right out of it to the floor. Elle just sighed before leaning down to pick them up.

"So, when is she leaving?" Ben continued, testing each row of lights one by one from his lighting board.

"I don't *know.*" When she tried to close the pack, it stuck. Frowning, she opened it back up, and—*oh.* She'd put the batteries in backwards. *God* .

Elle closed her eyes. She was better than this. She was actually *good* at her job. *Get a grip, Elle.*

Logan scoffed. "Come on, Ben, even Gina probably doesn't know when she's moving out. I can't imagine anyone wanting to live with her, let alone letting her move in on short notice. Where would she even *go?*"

"*I don't know.*" Elle snapped, almost before he had finished speaking. She didn't want to *talk* about this. She wanted to be left *alone.*

No. No, she didn't.

Elle dropped the mic pack to the table and put her head in her hands.

"Oh, Honey." Logan's arms came around her shoulders. His weight against her side grounded her, giving her something to focus on. She clutched the arm he wrapped around her and sighed, leaning her head against his chest. "I'm sorry for pushing. I know you're stressed."

"It's fine," Elle said. Really, it was. "I just want to know what's going on. She's given me *nothing* to go on, not when she's leaving, not how. She doesn't have a car, and she hasn't asked me to help her—"

"I doubt she will," Logan said. "She's being a bitch on purpose, Doll."

"She needs to sort herself out," Ben added.

Logan patted her arm. "It's not your responsibility to anticipate her needs."

"I know." Elle combed her fingers through her hair, nails scraping against her scalp. "I *know* that. I do. I just feel so…"

"Guilty." Logan nodded, understanding in a way that only her best friend could. "It's how she wants you to feel." He stepped away, and placed the mic pack back into her hands.

Elle steadied herself with a breath, fixed the backwards batteries, and moved onto the next pack. Talking with Logan usually calmed her down, but right now, she really wished he— and Ben, and anyone else who even *thought* about talking to her about Gina— would just drop it.

"Have you thought about moving out?" Logan asked at length, just when she thought he'd decided to let the subject go.

Damn. "I can't," Elle said, finishing with the battery packs. "It's too late to break the lease without getting a fine." She tried to open the drawer under the counter, the one with the condoms they used to protect the mic packs from sweaty performers. It stuck, and she gave it a frustrated wiggle, popping it open with a horrible scraping sound of wood against metal. Pretty much the sound her brain made whenever she talked about Gina. *Ugh.*

"Well, you *could* pull a fast one on her and just leave."

Elle turned to Logan with open mouthed horror on her face. "I absolutely could *not* do that, unless I want to see Gina in court—"

"Nevermind!" Logan held up his hands in surrender at her look, taking a step back.

"Yeah, *nevermind*," Elle said, scooping up a handful of condom packets and dropping them beside the bin of mic packs. "Trying to get me thrown in jail. Some friend."

"Hey, I'm just trying to explore all of your options."

Elle threw a condom wrapper at him. "Don't you have ten layers of makeup to put on?"

"Sadly, I do," Logan said, and with another noisy kiss to her cheek, he sailed out of the room. He was halfway to the stage when he called over his shoulder, "See you at warm ups, Doll!"

Elle shook her head and started to test mics, plugging a wire in, turning the battery pack on, and then listening to the snap of her fingers as it rang through the auditorium.

"So if Gina's—"

"Ben," Elle said softly, closing her eyes. This was all too much. She felt tired, all of the sudden; like she hadn't slept in *weeks*. "I really don't want to talk about it, right now."

Ben patted her thigh. "You'll be okay," he said, in that firm, confident tone he used on her sometimes. Anytime her anxiety hit, it seemed, he knew to pull the *no nonsense* voice out. "You're so much stronger than you give yourself credit for. Things will turn out alright."

Elle met his warm, dark eyes. He *meant* it. A little bewildered, she gave him a grateful smile, and then focused on her mics.

People slowly trickled in, filling the space with life. The servers, in their black dress shirts and slacks, began cleaning and setting their linen draped tables with their shiny wooden chairs. Old-fashioned lanterns sprang to life on the tables, as did the enormous chandelier above, casting the entire place in a homey yellow glow. People called good-naturedly from the balcony— nicknamed the Shelf, though Elle had never asked why— down to those on the main floor. Dishes and silverware clattered onto tables beside cheerful blue checkered napkins. Chef Rossi, the head chef, came in to greet them in his booming, jovial way, and several minutes later, swung by the booth with snacks from the kitchen, which Elle and Ben eagerly attacked. Performers and stagehands waved as they crossed through the dining room to the green room backstage, some warming up vocally as they went, others chattering amongst themselves, and a few sneaking treats from the front window of the tech booth, to amused but weak protestations. Before long, the whole auditorium was alive with movement and sound.

"Mornin', y'all!" A young woman stopped at the tech booth, her shiny black hair in two loose French braids down the sides of her head.

She dropped her bag on the ground beside her and propped her folded arms onto the edge of the booth window, the picture of effortless grace.

"Morning, Haley," Elle said, offering her a muffin from the snack tray. "How goes?"

"Movin' right along," Haley said, with her pretty New Orleans accent, grinning. "I'm late, of course."

"Not just yet," Elle told her, eyeing the clock on the wall above the booth window. "You will be if you don't get a move on."

"Has your terrible tramp left yet?" Haley asked around a mouthful of muffin, making no move to leave. At least she looked mostly put together— her pretty, oval face already made up, her hair done, and no doubt, the bloomers and corset from her costume already on beneath her sweatpants and over-sized tee shirt.

Elle laughed despite herself at the nickname, though she really hoped they could keep this conversation *short* . "Gina? No, not yet."

With a nod, Haley straightened up from the booth, pointing a finger at Elle with the same hand holding her muffin. "Sugar, you tell me the minute she's gone," she insisted, already scooping up her bag again. "I'll bring over the whiskey and the beignets, and we'll celebrate."

God, Elle thought, past a bittersweet tightness in her chest. Between Haley, Ben, and Logan, she had enough love and strength to get through anything. "I will."

Haley blew a kiss as she scooted her way past the cluster of servers having their pre-show meeting. Something heavy settled in Elle's chest. She *really* didn't want to think about her roommate, but everyone else seemed to want to *talk* about her.

"I've got to get these mics up to the green room," Elle said, at about ten minutes to warm ups, propping the bin of mic packs under her arm as she stood up.

Ben looked up from whatever game he was playing on his phone, a bit dazed, like he hadn't even realized what time it was. "Uh?"

Elle jiggled the bin under her arm a little, mics rattling around inside it. "Mics. Green room." Ben's expression cleared, and he nodded. "Try to save some of that fruit for me, would you?" She teased. Ben just rolled his eyes at her, picking up a rather large strawberry and stuffing the whole thing into his mouth at once. He immediately choked, coughing. She could see the regret on his face as soon as he realized his mistake. She was so busy laughing at him, she didn't look where she was going— not that anyone ever came to the booth, anyway. It was the only feasible explanation for why she didn't expect to find the giant wall of person she promptly plowed into.

"Oh!" Startled, she backtracked, her head craning up— up, *up*, to meet sharp jade eyes. There had always been an underlying sharpness to John, not just in his eyes, but to the rest of him, as well. Something about him had always struck her as slightly intimidating. It didn't help that he was so much *larger* than her, large enough to fill the tiny tech booth to bursting, to move the air until it felt like there wasn't enough left for her to breathe.

That wasn't to say he wasn't attractive. Elle would be lying if she said she hadn't noticed the clean cut of his jaw, or the leanness of his muscles. Which, in the tank top he wore with the neckline cut nearly to his naval, there were a *lot* to look at.

"John! Hi." She gave him her usual, professionally friendly smile, the one she kept solidly in place whenever she was at work. "Come for your mic?"

John's eyes dropped to the bin in her arms, then rose back to hers. "Logan told me you've been having roommate troubles."

Of course he did, Elle thought wryly. Logan told John everything, the same way she told Logan everything, like a lifelong game of telephone. They'd all been friends for years, anyway, but it still felt weird— John was more of an extension of Logan than anything; *his* college buddy, *his* roommate. It had always been like that between the three of them; whenever the lines blurred, it never failed to throw her for a loop.

"It's been a time," She said, hoping her smile didn't look too forced. "Would you like to tape your mic yourself, or—"

"You know, if you need a place to get away, you're always welcome to come to our place," John continued, then blinked at her, apparently realizing that he'd spoken over her. "Sorry— I mean, yeah, you can tape me up. That's fine. Thanks."

"Right," Elle muttered, setting the bin back onto the sound table. In her peripherals, Ben was determinedly staring at his phone, pretending to be invisible. "I appreciate the offer," she said to John, rooting through until she found his mic pack, "but for now I'm just looking for a roommate to take over Gina's part of the lease." She finally found his mic— god, why did so many people have mics in this show?— and pulled it out.

"Ah, she's leaving?" John took the proffered pack from her hands and unwound the mic wire, clipping the battery case into the back pocket of his jeans.

"Yeah," Elle said flatly. "I have no idea when she's leaving, or where she's going, so that's fun." She snapped off two pieces of mic tape, then hesitated at the sight of John's back. "Kneel down, you monster, I'm half your height."

"Oh, right—" Like a half-hearted attempt at origami, John knelt down on one knee, folding himself awkwardly into the cramped space. Somehow, he seemed to fill it up even more, like this. "Sorry."

"After all these years of towering over me," Elle teased. "It's like you *forget.*"

John chuckled while she set up his mic wire, handing him one strip of tape to put on his cheek, while she taped up his neck. "Hey, it's not *my* fault you're vertically challenged."

"Or that *you're* part *tree,*" Elle countered, grinning despite herself. "Really, though, thank you for the offer. It's nice to know I have somewhere to go, if things get dicey."

"Anytime." John stood (and stood, and stood) and then faced her again, giving her a half smile. It would have been condescending, if she didn't know it was just how his face looked. "I mean it. You let me or Logan know if anything changes, or you just need to get away."

Honestly, even if the offer had come from Logan— her very *best* friend, since forever—she'd have probably said no. The thought of imposing on someone so nice, and in Logan's case, so important to her, made her skin crawl. Not that she could tell John that, though. So instead, she smiled up at him again, and said, "I will. Thanks."

John gestured to the mic bin. "Want me to take those back? I'm headed that way, anyway."

"Oh—" Elle tucked the mic tape into the empty slot left by his mic, and then handed him the bin. "That would be great! Thank you."

The bin seemed so much smaller in John's arm than it had in hers. With one last salute to Ben, he turned to go. "Later, guys."

"Have a good show!" John waved at her without looking back, smiled and nodded politely at a few of the waitresses who stopped to bat their eyelashes at him, and then disappeared through the door beside the stage.

"That was nice of him," Ben said, the first real words out of his mouth in the past hour.

"Yeah," Elle agreed. It *was* nice. Even if it meant Logan was running his mouth back in the dressing room. She'd have to talk to him about that.

"He's a nice dude," Ben continued.

Elle nodded without really looking at him, giving the sound board another quick once-over to make sure everything was in working order.

"I think Logan's right," Ben added. "You should ditch Gina and move in with them—"

"Ben," Elle sighed, not bothering to look up, "I *will* kill you."

Something was *off*, when Elle got back to her apartment that night. She could sense the tension the second she opened the front door. It was like a friction in the air, charged up and ready to— to— to do *something* . Something big.

Her stomach dropped.

It took Elle at least thirty seconds to convince herself to step through the door and close it behind her. All the lights in the front room were on. Boxes were stacked neatly by the door, taped shut and labeled *kitchen, living room,* and—

Oh.

Oh, *no.*

Elle— she really should have seen this coming, shouldn't she?

"Gina?" There was no response, which— fair. Elle wouldn't want to be around for this either, if she had the option. "Gina?" She tried again, poking her head into the master suite with a polite double-knock on the half-open door. Gina's cat, Bast, raised her head from her perch on Gina's unmade bed, and— honestly, it was a wonder anyone could live in the amount of trash littering the entire floor, and the dirty clothing, and just... everything else going on in there. Which was a *lot* .

Still no answer. Elle swallowed and backtracked, looking around for some sort of sign of life, of something to explain what was going on. There was nothing to go on, here, except the empty solarium that had previously held all of her sewing stuff, where only her sewing table and its chair stood now, and the notably empty kitchen. Elle couldn't decide if she was relieved or not by the fact that all of her stuff had clearly been packed away— and, she noted, a few things that hadn't been hers, though that wasn't really an inconvenience.

Nevertheless. Nothing to go on out here. Resigned, Elle opened her own bedroom door.

Her heart sank down to join her stomach at her feet.

Flat boxes lay in a haphazard stack on her neatly made bed. On top of them was a sheet of paper, on which Elle could make out Gina's impossible, cramped handwriting.

Elle,

I've decided to keep the apartment. I have a new roommate lined up. She gets here in a few days. I want to clean this room before she gets here. Please be out with your stuff by Thursday. I'll be in Michigan until then. Everything of yours from our shared spaces has been wrapped and packed for you, and there should be enough boxes here for the rest of your stuff.

It was too difficult for me to find a place to live within my price range on such short notice. Seeing as you're financially better off than me, and have parents who will actually send you money, I'm sure you'll have better luck. I hope you understand.

Good luck,

Gina.

P.s. Please feed the cat while I'm gone. You can leave the keys with the front office when you're all moved out.

It took... an embarrassing amount of time, really, for Elle to read through the note. Her hand was shaking so violently that she could barely track the words. Halfway through, she ended up having to stop and rub her eyes, telling herself firmly that crying could wait, she just had to *think* , to plot out all the things she had to do— wash all of her clothing, pack it up. Wrap and pack all of her knickknacks and pictures, box up her books, her linens, her bathroom—

The first sob came as a surprise. The second, less so. Before she could stop it, Elle found herself openly weeping, standing in the middle of her bedroom with fat, hot tears rolling down her face.

There was too much to sort through at once. Too much to *do* . And there, underneath all of the panic and shock, was a horrible, boiling anger, welling up in her chest until she could barely breathe. All because *Gina* decided it was too *hard* to find a new place.

"Okay," she muttered to herself, forcing herself to breathe. Her nose was so stuffed up it was nearly impossible. "Okay. I can..." She could do this. She could keep it together long enough to get her shit together before Gina got back from Michigan. Today was Sunday. She had to be out by Thursday. She had three whole days to get her stuff together and get out.

Get out.

God, where would she even go? And on such short notice? Her Mom lived up in Pennsylvania, she hadn't seen her dad in person since her college graduation and didn't intend to, her brother... She loved him to pieces, but she didn't want to live with him and his weird, chain smoking roommates. Honestly, she could probably sleep in the tech booth, or the costume room in the back of the theater. Not like anyone would expect to find her anywhere else, she basically already lived there...

John's words sprang into her mind so suddenly and vividly, she actually gasped, the sound shaky and loud in the empty apartment.

You let me or Logan know if anything changes.

Her phone all but lived in her left pocket, which was probably *not* healthy, but at a time like this, she found she didn't really care. Her hands were still shaking, making it twice as hard to unlock her phone and pull up Logan's name in her contacts. Except no, Logan had a date tonight. It was bad enough she was about to ask if she could mooch a place to live off of him, let alone interrupting whatever the two of them were in the middle of to do so. Besides, it had been *John's* offer. Technically.

She switched to John's contact info, and before she could worry her way out of it, she pressed *call*.

The sheer stupidity of her life's choices hit her before it even rang. She couldn't— she couldn't just *move in*, in three days, with her best friend and his roommate. God, what would they think? Her roommate was kicking her out. They'd probably ask why. Logan already basically knew. They'd realize she was a *garbage* roommate. They'd ask her to leave. They wouldn't even let her move in. They'd laugh in her face. They'd realize who she really was as a person, and they'd *hate* her for it—

John picked up on the second ring, just as Elle felt herself tip from shock and anger into crippling panic. "Elle? Are you okay?"

"I'm—" She'd been planning to say *fine*, but her voice sounded so hysterical to her own ears that she stopped herself before the lie could even come out. She sucked in another sharp breath as her throat began to close up.

In the background, she could hear more masculine voices; first Logan's, with a noticeably alarmed pitch, saying her name, and beyond his, the gentler, more confused voice of his boyfriend, Tyler, saying something indecipherable. John's voice went muffled as he shushed them.

God, this was *ridiculous*. She should have just gotten a hotel until she could find an apartment of her own, instead of expecting her friends to—

"Elle?"

Elle sucked in a shuddering breath. She didn't really have many options, right now. Throat tight, she swallowed, and then choked out the only words she could come up with.

"Is that offer still on the table?"

2

"Turn left here, Doll."

Elle nodded silently and made the turn, trying to keep herself grounded while she drove. If it weren't for Logan giving her directions in a calm, patient, firm tone, she'd have probably driven herself into a tree at this point.

She'd never come through the back way to their place, before. John and Logan lived in a cozy suburban neighborhood about ten minutes from Main Street, and no more than half an hour from her old apartment. The houses came in all different shapes and sizes and colors, a far cry from the faded, cookie-cutter houses from her childhood neighborhood. Tall oak and maple trees stood in a few yards, casting their proud shadows onto the road and over her car as she passed them. There were even *people* in this neighborhood— a man mowing his lawn, a woman walking her dog. Kids played out in the early August heat, as the warm golden rays of a summer afternoon sun stretched over them.

It should have been a cheerful, heartwarming sight. Happy and summery. And yet, all she wanted to do was sit in total silence and decompress. It had already been a rough day, both physically and emotionally.

"Right here," Logan said a few moments later, pointing vaguely through the windshield.

"I know," Elle said mildly. "Blue mailbox, obnoxiously long driveway. Can't miss it. Almost like I've been here before. *Weird.*"

Logan chuckled, while Elle turned into the— god, it really *was* an obnoxiously long driveway. She'd never really noticed. The house at the end of it was massive, and a little daunting, but it was also rather pretty. She'd always thought so, ever since she'd helped Logan move in with John right after college. It had a sort of rustic feel to it, stones climbing up one side and slate grey siding on the other. Dark blue window shutters stood out against the house's facade, as did the enormous wooden front door. The effect was almost face-like, but somehow, more welcoming than creepy. There were so many slants and angles, a tall chimney standing proudly in the back.

"There we go," Elle murmured, putting her car into park. She looked out the window, past Logan, to the red door of the garage. "This really is a pretty house." And now she was going to live here, too.

"Ask John about it, some time," Logan told her, already opening his door. "It's got a lot of history." As they both got out, Elle heard the front door of the house open in the distance. "Ah, looks like he's home already."

Elle's stomach somersaulted. She really didn't want John knowing how stressed out and anxious she was about moving in with him and Logan.

It had been bad enough, having Logan— as well as Ben, and Haley, and Haley's boyfriend Jack— listening to her cry while she'd tried to explain what had happened with Gina. She'd been so incoherent, they'd each ended up reading Gina's letter, all with carefully blank expressions. It had been a level of mortifying she hadn't really been prepared for. Nor, she thought, would she ever get over it.

"Here we go," Logan grunted, hoisting her enormous and ancient black suitcase from her trunk. "Hey, John!" Elle felt her heart sink even further and shut her eyes, bent into the back seat with a bag in her hand. She could do this. "You're just in time. Here, take this suitcase, would you?"

"Sure."

Still. They'd gotten her stuff put together and carted to the storage place on Main in only a few hours. Ben and his truck had been a godsend, and Haley and Jack had kept the ball rolling while Logan kept Elle focused on her packing checklist. She didn't know how to thank them enough.

Elle straightened up on the other side of the car and forced herself to smile. She watched as John took the suitcase from Logan, lifting it like it weighed next to nothing, and waved when he glanced over at her. "Hi," she said.

He smiled at her. It wasn't weird, in and of itself, but seeing his usually stoic face break into a grin at the sight of her— it was like something in her chest unclenched and relaxed.

She *could* do this. She could look John in the face and gracefully accept his kindness, and *not be weird about it*. They were friends— they *were* friends, right?— and he wanted to help her, as much as Logan and Ben and Haley did. If he didn't, he wouldn't have offered her a place to stay while she glued the scattered pieces of her life back together.

"Hey, Elle!" John took the bag Logan shoved into his arms. "You guys got done earlier than I thought. I was about to text and ask if you needed help."

"Haley and Jack and Ben came," Logan explained, already playing the mother hen and taking things from Elle's hands. She didn't have too many, but since she hadn't been sure how long it would take her to find her own place, she'd just brought a little of everything. A couple of duffels, a plastic bin of all of her toiletries, a box of pictures that she probably wouldn't even bother unpacking but couldn't bear to leave in storage. "Besides," Logan continued, as they closed up her car and started toward the front door, "Gina had most of her stuff all packed up for her, anyway. All stacked up by the front door."

John turned to frown at Elle over his shoulder. Whatever had loosened in her chest tightened right back up, seeing that his smile was gone. "Can she do that?"

Elle shrugged, her duffel shifting against her shoulder. "She already did, so..."

He stopped to open the door, stepping back to let Logan through. "But isn't *your* name on the lease, too?"

"Honestly, as long as I don't have to live with her anymore, I don't care."

"Well, *I*, for one, am glad you're here." Logan's voice carried from the stairs near the back of the house, where bright golden sunlight filled the room. Elle had been to their home several times over the past few years to hang out with Logan, and it had always felt warm and welcoming. The two men had decorated every available surface with movie and game paraphernalia, pictures of them and their family and friends, and— her particular favorite— colorful string lights. There were even two bookcases along one wall that Elle had browsed time and time again with Logan, looking for music for auditions, or borrowing whatever book he had recommended to her. It could use some colorful curtains, and maybe a few flowers, but overall, it was homey.

Elle followed Logan to the stairs, glancing longingly into the living room. The long, dark leather couch was calling to her after hours of moving boxes. She could go for a nice cup of tea and a book, right now. Or, really, anything that involved not standing anymore. Maybe a movie on their enormous TV— men and their electronics, *honestly* — would help her settle a bit.

Maybe she'd just lay face down on the guest room floor.

"Right up here, Doll," Logan said, already halfway up the stairs.

Elle glanced back at John, who gestured for her to lead the way with a nod of his head. She'd never been upstairs before. It felt almost like an invasion, even now, but she forced her nerves down as she followed Logan up.

"I hope you're ready to cook all the time," Logan continued merrily. "John's a beast on the grill, and he does okay with breakfast food, but otherwise, he can't cook for shit."

"Hey!"

Elle's face cracked into a smile at John's indignant remark behind her. She paused on the landing halfway up and shot a teasing smile over her shoulder. "Noted."

John rolled his eyes at her. "Come on, Logan, I'm not *that* bad a cook."

"You forgot about your pasta and burnt it."

Elle bit her lip as John reached the landing with her. "I've done that, too," she whispered, once Logan was out of earshot. "Don't tell him."

"I don't think he'd believe you." John grinned down at her, and...

And suddenly, this whole situation wasn't so weird. She was still sore, and still had a headache, but... Yeah. Maybe Ben had been right; things *would* be okay.

Elle paused as she reached the second floor, looking around. It was an empty, open space, with a decent amount of light from two skylights above her head. The walls had some pleasant, classy art, but otherwise, there wasn't much by way of decoration. There were two doors to her right, one tucked further back behind an angled hallway. The walls to her left were angled slightly as well, each with their own door.

"You have a lovely house," Elle said, glancing again at John. "Thanks for letting me stay."

John's look was puzzled. "Of course. I'm glad you called me."

Elle blinked, startled. He was...*what?*

Logan's voice echoed through the second floor before Elle could work her way through her own thoughts. "Back here, Doll."

Still a bit dazed from John's statement, Elle adjusted the bag on her shoulder and followed Logan's voice through a door in one of the angled walls.

The room—*her* room, she supposed— was just as pretty as the rest of the house. The bed had maybe half a dozen pillows, sunny yellow and pale peach, propped up against a downy white comforter. There was a nightstand with a lamp that matched the pillows, a big chest of drawers across the room, a vanity with a mirror, and a sparsely filled bookshelf. The ceiling was slanted down at an angle on one side, giving the whole place a lofted feeling.

"Logan decorated," John said, already moving past her.

"It's lovely." The bed looked like the most inviting thing she'd ever seen. She just wanted to lay face down on it, completely immobile, for the next sixteen hours or so, until her muscles loosened up and her head stopped hurting.

"I hope you like sunlight," Logan said, eyeing the giant, arched window over the bed. "You'll never have to worry about seasonal depression, here."

"Speak for yourself." But she still chuckled, dropping her bags at the foot of the bed.

"You can rearrange whatever you want," John called from the closet. "Logan and I will help."

"And redecorate however you want." Logan took the bags from Elle's feet and dropped them, instead, right in front of John, just as he made to leave the closet. John rolled his eyes and took them in, while Logan danced over to press a kiss to Elle's forehead. "I want you to be completely at home, here—"

"It's perfect," Elle cut him off, pulling his hands from her face and squeezing them. She wouldn't be staying long enough to bother, anyway.

"And when you're ready, we can—" Logan cut off at the sound of a phone buzzing.

Elle's hand instinctively shot to her left pocket, but her phone was still and solid against her thigh. "It's not me."

"It's me," John said, finally emerging from her closet, scowling at his buzzing phone in his hand. "I'll be right back." With that, he disappeared through the bedroom door with a firm but kind *hello,* and then he was gone.

Elle felt herself relax, marginally, the moment John's voice had faded. Strange.

"Right, anyway," Logan said, steering Elle by the shoulders. "Come look at your closet! It's nice and roomy."

He was right. Even with all her stuff in it, there was still plenty of space. All of her garment bags were already hanging from the rail on one wall, and there was a wooden dresser in the back of the room. The room, by itself, was almost as big as her bedroom back at the apartment.

The apartment. Just thinking about it made her skin crawl, and her heart jerk painfully in her chest. The hopefulness that had started to spread through her dissipated like steam in the air.

"Logan, I love you with all my heart," Elle said, wringing her hands, "but I've got to be honest. This is *really* overwhelming."

Logan turned back to face her with a frown, a plastic garment bag in his hands, clearly intending to hang its contents for her. "The... closet?"

"What? No." Elle blinked, and then played the conversation over in her head. Yeah, actually, she could see how he might have gotten to that conclusion. It *was* the biggest closet she'd ever seen. She shook her head, though, continuing. "No, I meant... Living here. Moving in with you two." She shrugged, at a loss for how to put it into words— the crippling fear that she was being a burden, the tension from being around John as more than just *Logan's Friend Elle*, but as actual roommates. "It's just... weird, I guess. I feel like I'm..." She ran a hand over the back of her head, the word clogging up her throat. "Intruding."

Her words caught Logan's full attention, causing him to re-hang the bag and face her fully. "Elle, no," He cooed, coming forward to grab her shoulders. He gave her a little shake, craning his neck down to look her in the eye. "You are *not* intruding. You're our friend. Ask John, he'll tell you the same thing. We wouldn't have offered you a place if we didn't want you to live here with us."

I'm glad you called me.

Right , Elle thought, though the tense knot in her chest remained just as tight and uncomfortable. Logan was right. She was being silly. What he was saying made more sense than her ridiculous self-doubt. Elle sucked in a breath and let it out slowly, nodding at him.

He gave her forehead a kiss. "Come on, Doll. Let's get you unpacked." He went right back to the garment bag, unzipping it to pull out the clothing that hung inside it. "When you're a bit more adjusted, we can go back to the storage place and get the rest of your stuff."

"The... rest?" Elle continued to stand there, her body struggling to catch up with her brain, while Logan continued to unpack her things for her.

"Yeah, your books and pictures and stuff," Logan said. When Elle didn't respond, opting instead to get her ass in gear and help unpack things, he nudged her. "Elle?"

She swallowed. "I wasn't planning on moving in permanently."

"Elle." The disapproval in his tone shook her, especially when he turned to cross his arms at her.

"What?" She unzipped the second garment bag, avoiding his gaze, and started pulling dresses from it. "Logan, eventually I'll need a place of my own. Even if I do adore you."

"That could take *months*, Elle," Logan insisted. "You can't just leave all your stuff in storage while you wait."

"Why not?" She didn't mean to sound so defensive. She couldn't even look at him, inwardly cringing at the tone of her own voice. "That's the point of storage." He still watched her with disapproval on his face; she could see it in her peripherals. Elle sighed, maybe a little more harshly than necessary, but *god*. This was getting frustrating. "It's not that big a deal, Logan. With any luck, I'll be out of your hair in a couple of months, and then—"

"You're not *in our hair*, Elle—"

"You can't expect me to just stay here and be a burden—"

"Oh, come *on* , Ellie—"

"*Don't 'Ellie' me*," Elle snapped, and then froze.

They stared at each other, the silence stretching between them, like a rubber band about to snap. Logan's face was wide with shock, and Elle felt the guilt start to seep into her core.

This was *exactly* what she'd been afraid of. Being — being *her*, being like *this*. Impossible to live with, too sensitive, overly emotional.

This is why Gina kicked you out, a snide little voice in her head spat. *You push everyone away.*

This was it. She was barely moved in, and now he was certain to kick her out. *Great going, idiot.*

Elle took a deep breath, and then swallowed. "I— I'm sorry," she started, voice shaky. "I didn't mean—"

"No," Logan said, shaking his head. "No, I crossed a line." He laughed, the sound almost humorless. "God, I sounded like your *mom*. No wonder you snapped at me."

He may have had a point, but still. Elle rubbed at her face with her hands. Then just left them there.

By some miracle, she didn't immediately cry when Logan came to wrap his arms around her. It didn't particularly help when he squeezed her around the middle, one hand sweeping down her back in a comforting motion. The tension in her chest and throat cracked, just a little, around the edges.

As he rocked her a little, she pressed her face into his lean, solid chest, trying to hide the impending tears. "I'm sorry, Doll," he murmured, still rubbing her back. "What I *should* have said was, since you'll probably be here for a while, we should at least get you a few things to make you feel more at home. A few pictures, maybe some of your books?" He pulled back to look down at her, and she propped her chin on his chest, sniffling a little. "We can unpack what you've got here, then go grab one or two boxes from storage. How's that sound?"

She nodded, the movement stiff against his chest. "I don't want to be a—"

"Burden, I know. You said that already." She winced and nodded again. "We wouldn't have invited you to stay if we didn't expect you to actually live here. That includes eating, sleeping, showering, watching TV, *all of it*." He tucked her head back against his chest. "We're not Gina. You don't have to be all quiet and invisible here."

Shit, that stung. But he had a point. She'd been watering herself down around Gina for months, trying not to set her ex-roommate off, tip-toeing around the ever-impending explosion that seemed to happen whenever Gina remembered Elle existed.

"Okay." When she leaned away, Logan let her go, but not without squeezing her one more time first. "Okay. You're right. I…" Elle glanced around the mostly barren closet. "I think it would be… nice, to have some books and stuff."

"Atta girl," Logan said, patting her arm.

Elle finished the bag she'd been unpacking before she continued. "I want to pay my way, though."

Logan actually slapped a palm to his face. "Elle."

"That's not negotiable," She insisted, already lowering her suitcase to the ground to open it. "If I'm going to be using water, electricity, wifi, whatever, I want to pay my share. And rent, too."

"For Pete's—"

"You guys okay?" John stood at the closet door with a brow arched, looking back and forth between Elle and Logan with concern.

Logan pointed at Elle like a child, and before she could say anything, whined, "Elle's trying to pay us *rent* ." Elle rolled her eyes at him and continued putting clothing into the dresser in the back of the closet.

"Why?"

"What do you mean, *why?*" Barely sparing John a glance, she gestured vaguely around her. "If I live here with you, I should pay rent, too!"

"We don't pay rent." John stepped over to where Logan was examining the contents of a duffel. "Bathroom?"

"You don't...?" There was no way, *no way*, these two were living here for free. That wasn't possible.

"I own the house, Elle," John explained flatly when he caught sight of her expression, taking the duffel from Logan.

Elle just stared at him, mouth open.

John straightened up and froze, visibly startled. "What?"

Without thinking, and though it may have been an enormous *faux pas*, Elle looked him up and down. Was it possible that she'd misjudged his age? He can't have been *that* much older than her. They'd been at college together for a couple of years; if she remembered correctly, he wasn't even thirty yet. "How do *you* own a *house?*" Then, realizing she sounded more jaded than shocked, she added, "Why aren't you starving and poor like the rest of us Millennials?"

John laughed at that. *Thank god.* "It was my grandparents' house. I inherited it after my grandad passed."

"Oh." Okay, so she wasn't *completely* stupid. A true miracle. Still, her hand automatically came up to cover her heart. "That's... sad. Sweet, but sad."

"So no rent," John continued, slinging her bag over his shoulder, "but if you're dead set on paying your share, we can just split the bills evenly between the three of us."

"I am, in fact, dead set," Elle insisted, pushing the last drawer shut. She reached up to take the bag from John. "It's only fair."

"I can take—" John started, but his phone cut him off. He rolled his eyes and sighed. "For Chrissakes. These idiots are going to give me an ulcer."

Elle started to laugh. "Well, that's just rude."

"Wh— oh, no, not you." John waved toward Logan, already turning away. "Could you...?" Logan nodded as John answered the phone. "*Yes,* Mrs. Henderson?"

"The country club," Logan explained, while John's voice faded away out of the room. "He took over running a lot of the events when his grandparents died."

"Ah." It was just like John, she thought, to lead the community. Something about him screamed *leader*. Probably his height.

"Yeah." Logan huffed, looking around at all the work they had left to do. "Hey, you hungry?"

"Always." Elle gestured with the bag in her hand. "Let me toss this in the bathroom, and then we can take a break from all this *moving*. Besides," She continued, heading to the only closed door left in the room, "I want to put on sweatpants."

"Fair enough."

John's head came around the door frame. "I have to head over to the clubhouse to help Mrs. Henderson set up her dinner party," he said, sounding resigned. "I'll be back in a little while."

"Have fun," Logan said, waving him off.

"Bye," Elle murmured, then turned to Logan. "Should I go back to feed the cat? Gina won't be home til—"

"Elle, you already turned your keys in," Logan reminded her, watching her toss the duffel of towels into the bathroom with a dull *thud*. "And you gave that cat enough food for the next month."

"I was nervous!" But Logan's expression brooked no argument. With a sigh, Elle changed the subject. "What do you have in your fridge? Maybe I can pull something together for us."

"Funny you should ask."

Several minutes later, after a refreshing change of clothes, Elle stood basking in the middle of the most impressive kitchen she'd ever stepped foot in. It was practically the size of her old apartment, with gleaming wooden floors, glistening granite counter tops, and enough space that she could have cooked four separate meals at once and had space leftover.

"*God,* I love your kitchen." Logan started to laugh, watching her reaction from somewhere behind her. "I'm going to live in this room. I don't even need a bed. I could fit on the counters. That breakfast bar alone could hold all of my belongings." She shook her head. "What do you even *do* in a kitchen this big? Roast entire animals on a spit?"

"John and I don't do much of anything in here," Logan said. "I burn water, and his skills are limited to TV dinners, pasta— also burnt— with jarred sauce, breakfast food, and anything involving the grill out back."

"This kitchen is mine now," Elle declared. She ran a hand over the smooth counter top beside her, eyeing the sparkling steel sink. "If you ever lose me, I'm probably in here, crying tears of joy."

"*Well*, you sentimental slob," Logan said, taking her by the shoulders and steering her toward a door across from the fridge, "then you won't mind breaking it in tonight. I had a craving while I was at the dentist the other day, so I hope you're in the mood for lasagna." As he opened the door for her— revealing what turned out to be a pantry the size of her closet upstairs— he added, "There's also pineapple cider in the fridge."

Delighted, both by that and the pantry, Elle grinned up at him. "You remembered."

"*Duh.*" Logan watched her raid the pantry for a split second of silence. "I bet you could cook for us instead of paying *rent*, or whatever."

Elle rolled her eyes. "Logan."

"I'm serious! John will be overjoyed when he finds out how well you cook. He'll probably ask you himself. Hell," Logan stepped out of her way, wisely not trying to remove ingredients from her loaded arms, "when he finds out you can bake, he might straight up propose."

As she passed him toward the counter, Elle pinched his arm.

Later, with their drinks on the pretty glass coffee table and plates of food balanced in their laps, Elle shook her head at the painfully fake monster slinking down a flight of stairs after the leading lady. "Please don't go in the basement," she said, belatedly, as the woman did exactly that. "Don't— oh, you absolute *idiot*. Can't you hear the ominous music?" Logan burst out laughing beside her, while Elle scrunched up her face in response to the awful fake gore and overdone sound effects. "*God.* Serves her right."

"You have *no* tolerance for the tropes," Logan teased, poking her in the thigh.

Elle was about to respond that, no, she really didn't, but the sound of the front door opening cut her off. The realization that John actually *lived* here struck her, as though somewhere along the lines, she'd managed to set that fact aside in her mind. Anxiety rippled through her, a slight tremor starting up underneath her skin.

"Welcome home," Logan called.

"Hey." John strode into the room, immediately frowning at the TV screen. "What... *are* you two watching?"

"Poorly done CGI with a garbage plot," Logan answered flatly. "There's lasagna in the oven."

"Oh, nice." Distracted, apparently, by the prospect of food, John strolled into the kitchen, which suddenly seemed much less enormous with him taking up so much of the space. Amazing, Elle reflected— and then realized she was staring. She snapped her attention back to the TV—*Ugh,* no, horrible fake blood everywhere, *abort mission.* She picked up her cider, intent on hiding behind it for as long as possible.

"How was being a charitable human being?" Logan asked.

"The usual." John emerged from the kitchen and dropped into an armchair, his plate piled high with food. "Mostly old people droning about HOA. Jackie was there being—" He hesitated, looking down at his plate. "Well. Jackie."

Elle frowned. She'd heard that name before. Where had she heard that name before?

She didn't get a chance before John scowled at the TV. "God, this movie is *awful.*"

Welp, that moment had passed. "Honestly, I think that's what they were going for," Elle decided, setting her cider back down, and trying not to look at John.

"I don't know if that's better or worse than just being honestly terrible." He finally took a bite of his lasagna, and then nodded. "Great lasagna."

"Thanks," Elle responded, knee-jerk, "it's dairy-free."

"No kidding?" John looked at Logan, waving his fork in Elle's direction. "Jesus, Logan, you should have asked her to move in *years* ago. We could have been eating real food all this time."

It felt a lot like puzzle pieces falling into place, Elle mused, and smiled. "I can bake, too."

John's eyes widened. "You can?" Elle nodded. "You wouldn't want to pay your way with food, would you?"

Logan poked Elle in the thigh as she began to laugh. "I told you so."

3

Elle lived in his house.

Elle lived in his house.

John lay awake and stared at the ceiling, trying and failing to get the image of Elle out of his head. Elle with her miles of coffee brown hair braided down her back, and her sleepy eyes as Logan started up another god-awful horror flick, her head resting on Logan's shoulder. Elle in sweatpants at least two sizes too big, and a cozy-looking knit sweater over a *Bye Bye Birdie 2008* cast tee shirt.

It wasn't too much different having her here now than it had been the few times she'd come over in the past. Hell, it wasn't that much different than seeing her at work. Well, no; in some ways, it was. At work, she was smart as a whip, efficient and organized. She was always chatting with someone, or so intently focused she didn't notice anything around her, or sassing performers about their lack of punctuality and sloppy dance work. All work and no play, that was Elle. So put together, all the time.

Even in what was clearly a state of panic, she held it together. She did a good job hiding it, for the most part; until something tipped the scales. Whatever conversation she and Logan had been having while he'd been on the phone had upset her, enough that her face was still red when he got back. It was unsettling, seeing her anything besides smiling and warm, or snarky, which he almost preferred.

Even more unsettling was the fact that he'd immediately wanted to comfort her. Which was, honestly, not new, so much as a weird, bone deep impulse he'd been ignoring since the day he'd met her.

John scrubbed his hands over his face, wishing for sleep to come and take him. He'd tried to keep from staring at Elle the whole night, with only marginal success. The cheesy horror movie didn't exactly hold his attention—too cliché, and *way* too gory—but Elle obviously hadn't been watching it for the scare factor. She'd done nothing but flat out *roast* it, going barely two minutes at a time without a scathing comment. From anyone else, it would have been annoying, but from her, John found it downright charming.

Charming and *hilarious*.

Prim and proper Elle, all put together, even outside of work clothes, and slightly tipsy. It was almost jarring to see her there, actually *in* his home, as though someone had cut her out of the tech booth and pasted her on his couch, sarcastic commentary and all.

God, he wanted to see her disheveled. Early morning, hair tousled, eyes still heavy with sleep. He wanted to see her underneath the makeup, when her hair wasn't neatly pulled back from her pretty face. He wanted to mess her up a little himself.

Stop that, he chastised himself. *She's your roommate, not your girlfriend.*

His very attractive roommate.

His very attractive, *single* roommate.

God, he had it bad. He'd had it bad since he'd met her— before that, maybe. She and Logan had been friends forever, and the second John had seen her in pictures on Logan's Facebook—

Yeah. He'd had it bad since the first time he saw her, and it was getting worse by the day. By the *minute*.

With an aggravated sigh, John rolled onto his side. Living with Elle couldn't be that different than living with Logan, right? He just had to pretend everything was normal. He'd get used to her— or she'd be out in a few months, and things would actually go *back* to normal. Still, for now, Elle— living in *his house* — was the new normal.

Right, John thought, just as far from sleep as he had been when he'd turned out his light. Everything was normal.

Things were definitely *not* normal.

John dragged himself out of bed at seven, after a fitful night of off-and-on sleep, interrupted by dreams of aquamarine eyes and musical laughter. He jogged through the blue light of early morning to the neighborhood fitness center, forcing himself to focus on the chill in the morning air, on keeping his breathing even, and not on the fact that Elle would inevitably be there, at his house, when he got back to it. He pushed himself a little harder than usual through his workout, trying to escape the images of a sleepy and unkempt Elle from his mind. The run home was just this side of hell, and it did nothing to distract him.

The house was still and silent when he returned, the palest rays of sunlight beginning to peek through the back windows in the living room. John had to bite down on the disappointment that ebbed up inside him. He shouldn't want a quiet, early morning moment alone with Elle. That was all sorts of weird of him.

Maybe a nice, cold shower would help him clear his head.

Logan was up and brewing coffee when John came back downstairs. He turned with his hand on the cupboard door, his coppery hair sticking up in tufts, in just a tank top and pajama pants so old and worn the pattern was no longer recognizable. "Good morning, stud."

"Morning." John ran a hand through his wet hair and tried to discreetly glance into the living room as he passed it. Elle was noticeably absent, either not awake yet, or still— probably— pulling herself together. It did weird things to his brain, thinking of her doing her morning routine. He wished he was there to—

Get a grip, *John.*

Clamping down on that line of thought, John opened the fridge and frowned. "Why don't we have eggs?"

"Because *someone* neglected to stop by the grocery store on his way home, yesterday," Logan accused, giving John a pointed look.

Oh, crap. He'd completely forgotten. He'd just wanted to be home to help Elle move in. "Shit."

"Yeah, well," Logan grumbled, opening the pantry behind John. "We have bagels, so you're in luck."

"I'll order grocery delivery," John said, pulling his phone from his pocket.

"You could have done that yesterday, you big lug." Logan's voice was waspish, but he turned a teasing grin at John before popping a bagel into the toaster.

"Do you want cereal?" John asked, already on InstaCart. "They're having a sale."

"Get Honeycombs if they have them," Logan said. "Elle could eat her body weight in them. I got almond milk the other day, in case she had to escape Gina for a night."

"That paid off nicely," John muttered. He had a strange feeling he'd met Gina at one point, but he couldn't conjure up an image of her in his head. Not that it mattered— whether or not he knew what she looked like, he disliked her. "Anything else?"

"For the love of god, John, buy us some *fruit*."

John rolled his eyes, added a few kinds of fruit to the cart, and hit *checkout*.

"I'll probably take Elle grocery shopping on Monday," Logan said, already spreading peanut butter on his bagel. "She'll stock us up on food, and then all you have to worry about is giving her breakfast."

"Right," John said, grabbing a mug for his coffee. "I am capable of more than just breakfast food, you know."

"Keep telling yourself that, stud." John took a breath to defend himself, but Logan kept right on talking. "Poor Ellie's probably upstairs having a mild panic attack. I'll have to go up and get her if she's not down here in ten more minutes."

Ellie? John thought, frowning up at the stairs. No one called her that. The name alone sounded too cute for her. More importantly, though—"Why would she be having a panic attack?"

"She's got pretty bad anxiety," Logan explained. "She hates telling people about it, but honestly, they're so much more accommodating when they *know*."

"She doesn't seem like the type," John found himself saying. "She just seems so put together."

"She's had her whole life to perfect that."

Fair enough, John mused, as the coffee finished brewing. Except the idea of Elle upstairs, freaking out over— what? Him? No way she'd freak out about Logan, right? They'd been best friends forever. Something about her being nervous around him, though, darkened his mood. He didn't want her to be scared of him, for any reason. He wanted her to *like* living with him.

Maybe even enough to stay, instead of—

"Good morning, Sunshine!"

John almost spilled the damn coffee. That'd be fun to explain. *Sorry, I scalded my skin off thinking about you living in my house for the rest of time. No big deal.*

Christ. He *really* needed to pull himself together.

"I hope you like bagels," Logan continued merrily, oblivious to John's near-crisis. "This idiot forgot to go shopping yesterday."

"I didn't—" John started, scowling over his shoulder, but Logan cut him off.

"We've got peanut butter, jelly, butter, and if you go for the cream cheese, I'm gonna have to hurt you."

John turned at that, alarmed, only to find Elle grinning at Logan, her hands in the air in surrender. "Yikes! Okay, then; good morning to you, too." With a soft chuckle, she took up a seat at the breakfast bar, beside Logan, who kissed her temple.

She still looked so… collected, John mused. Hair in a sleek ponytail, in her clothing from the night before. *Strange,* the pang of disappointment that shot through him at the sight of her already pulled together. Strange and silly.

Without thinking, he filled the mug he'd gotten out for himself with coffee and slid it toward Elle, looking for signs of anxiety or stress. Her expression was closed off, practically shy, until the moment the coffee reached her. Then she blinked at it— and blinked even more when John set the almond milk and sugar in front of her.

"Oh," she said, clearly surprised. "Um. Thank you." With that, she looked up at him, the cloudiness of her expression clearing into a sunny smile.

Christ, John thought, feeling himself smile back. He was really hopeless.

"No problem," He said, and then turned decidedly away from her to start over with his coffee.

Walking into the tech booth that afternoon was like coming home after a long and harrowing workday. Elle hoisted herself up onto her stool, more content than she'd been in days. She couldn't wait to run sound tonight, to follow her steady, comforting routine of replacing mic batteries, to test the sound board.

God, if work was her happy place, she probably needed therapy.

"We'll be back in a bit," Logan said, kissing her cheek before he followed John through the dining room. Ben ambled in about five minutes later and, true to form, dropped into his chair with his saddlebag at his side.

"So, how's the new place?" He asked it with a grin, nudging her thigh with the toe of his steel-toed boot.

"I've only been there one night," she reminded him, already swapping out batteries in the mic packs. "It's nice, though. I love their house; always have."

"And now you get to live there!" Ben straightened in his chair and started his own routine. "Plus, you have roommates that aren't garbage." His words should have been funny, or at least a relief, but Elle flinched at them.

"Yeah, now *I'm* the garbage roommate."

She was so focused on her mics, it took her several seconds to realize Ben hadn't responded. When she glanced over, he was frowning at her, brow deeply furrowed.

Heat began to creep up her neck. "What's that look for?"

"Don't start that shit up," Ben snapped. "You need at least two whole weeks of excitement before your depression is allowed back."

"That's not how this works!" Nevertheless, she found herself giggling. "I should be allowed to wallow in my self-deprecating humor as much as I please, thank you."

"Not until two Thursdays from now." Ben opened a drawer in the booth and pulled something from it. "Here."

Elle yelped as whatever he'd thrown landed in front of her, and then her laughter doubled. She picked up the tootsie-pop and tossed it back at him, watching him fumble it. "Lollipops don't solve emotional crises, Ben!"

"They do, and you know it." He gestured out toward the dining room with the candy. "Ask Chef Rossi."

Elle snorted and opened up the next drawer down, full of unlubricated condoms they used to protect the mic packs from sweaty performers. "Chef Rossi would say *food* is the cure to emotional crises, and then bake us something."

"I absolutely would."

Figures, Elle mused, watching the Chef struggle to sidestep a few tables to get to the booth, a plate of cut fruits and veggies in his plump hand. Chef Rossi had always been one of those people who materialized the moment anyone spoke about him. Greg called it his *sixth sense.*

"Here," Chef Rossi said, setting the snack plate down on their table through the booth window. "Eat these to fuel your body, and I will bring you something sweet that will ease your soul."

Elle laughed. Chef Rossi was the best baker in town, and being pure-blooded Italian, one of the best pasta makers, too. If anyone knew comfort food, it was him. "I'm happy with strawberries," she told him, plucking one up from the plate. "Thank you, Chef."

"A sad heart needs a sweet treat!" The chef insisted in his thick accent. "You are quiet and stressed all week. You need chocolate."

"You're absolutely right, Chef."

Elle jumped at Logan's voice. How had she not seen him coming? "Can you all please stop sneaking up on me?"

"It's good for you," Logan said, already wriggling his way into the booth behind her to wrap his arms around her shoulders. "Keeps your heart going." When Elle struggled, giggling madly, he just tightened his arms and propped his head on her shoulder. "Am I wrong, though?"

"Yes!"

Logan ignored her in favor of talking to Chef Rossi. "No dairy treats for Elle! It makes her sick."

"He knows that," Elle told Logan, worming her arm free to poke him in the stomach. He yelped.

"Bah," Chef Rossi said, throwing a hand up, and then pointing at Logan with clear accusation. "You think I don't know how to care for our little *stellina*! I'll make a roast pig for the cast party, just to spite you."

"Hey!" Logan whined, pouting. Elle couldn't suppress her squawk of laughter. He'd never been a strictly Kosher Jew, except on holidays, but the chef's meaning was clear nonetheless.

Ignoring Logan's protests, Chef Rossi gave Elle an adoring smile. "I come back with dessert, and you will feel better." With that, he turned and, brushing several chairs with his hefty belly as he went, made his way back to the kitchen.

Elle gave Logan a gentle shove about ten minutes later, sending him back to the green room with the mic bin. "No treats for you, heathen," she told him, earning herself a pout and a whine in response. "I'll save one for you if you don't paraphrase your line tonight!"

"You're *mean*, Elle!"

"You have *one line!*"

"Yeah, Logan, you have one line." Elle watched Logan stick his tongue out at John as they passed each other. John just gave him a shit-eating grin. Before he even reached the booth, he jerked his chin at Elle. "You need extra manpower?"

Elle turned to Ben. "We good up here?"

"We could use you on spot," Ben called to John. "Come on back."

"What happened to Hank?" Elle asked. An unusual blinking caught her eye— something was weird with her soundboard. *Shoot,* she thought, looking underneath the tech table to the web of wires behind it. One of her cords must have come loose. *Damn.*

"Called out." Ben flicked his eyes to her. "And Jim's unreachable."

"*Good*," Elle said, sneering despite herself. "Keep that greasy shitbag out of my way."*Aha.* Good thing she'd found the wire now. Half of her soundboard would be useless without it.

John's voice came from somewhere behind her as she unplugged the cord to disentangle it from the others. "What, you don't like Jim?"

Elle felt her expression sour. She leaned out and waved the cord accusingly at John. "If I have to hear him call me *Elodie* for the rest of my life, I'm going to cut out his tongue and give it to Chef Rossi."

"And probably feed it back to him later," Ben muttered above her.

"Damn straight." Elle went back to her task, giving the plug a nice little shove back into its appropriate port. "With the state of these wires, I'd be surprised if he hasn't been messing with my soundboard. Ben, are my lights all on now?"

"Yeah."

"Why would he call you *Elodie*?" John asked.

Elle unfolded herself from under the counter to find him propped against the door frame, arms crossed over his chest, watching her emerge.

Weird. She shrugged and went back to her board. "It's my full name. I hate it, and I think that's why he uses it." She hoisted herself back onto the stool with a scowl, grumbling, "I haven't gone by Elodie since the sixth grade."

John nodded thoughtfully. "It's pretty, but Elle suits you better."

Elle felt her lips twitch. "That was very polite, and somehow not offensive at all. I'm impressed."

"It's a talent," He replied dryly.

She put on an exaggerated, posh accent, turning up her nose haughtily. "Part of your country-club upbringing."

John snorted. "Right. Well, I'm going up."

Elle waved him off. "Have fun!"

Act one almost ran smoothly, until Haley's mic popped during one of her last lines in the act. Elle sighed and pulled out her emergency mic wire and an extra set of batteries.

"I'm going back," she said, as soon as house lights were fully up for intermission. Ben saluted her as she ducked out, hidden in the shadows at the edge of the dining room, while everyone's food was delivered.

She could get to the back without crossing through the dining room by going up to the Shelf, which was sparsely filled for the week night show. As she climbed the stairs, she caught sight of John in his little hidden booth behind the spotlight, reading something on his phone.

"Hey, you good?" she asked. John looked up from his phone, eyes wide, like she'd startled him. She gestured to the spotlight. "You doin' okay?"

"Oh. Yeah." He gave the spot a dark look. "Heavy thing, isn't it?"

"Well, you're doing great," Elle assured him. "I've got to go check Haley's mic."

John saluted her the same way Ben had, and Elle crossed the Shelf, smiling at anyone who looked at her, using her customer service voice to ask if they were enjoying the show. The overwhelming positivity she got back put a spring in her step as she entered the second story server station, waving at the girls who were pulling trays of drinks together. She was so distracted she didn't notice the person standing at the bottom of the stairs until she almost bowled them over.

"Oh!" Elle stumbled back, damn near tripping backwards up the steps. "Davy! Hi. Sorry."

Davy, to his credit, looked just as startled to see her as she was to see him. He'd always been quiet, somewhat shy, despite his good looks and natural Southern charm. He pushed a hand through his thick gold curls and stepped back, out of Elle's way, with a soft, "'Scuse me, Ma'am."

Elle nodded at him, then gestured to the wire taped onto his face. "Your mic okay?"

"Yes, Ma'am."

"Good." Poor Davy, she thought. He was a damn good actor, but as himself, he seemed like he didn't know who to be. It was as though he was always on the verge of saying something, but couldn't figure out what the words were.

Relatable, when she stopped to think about it.

Elle patted his arm as she started past him. "You sound great today. The kids love you."

"Thank you, M—"

Chuckling, Elle glanced back at him. "You can call me *Elle*, Davy. You've known me long enough." Davy clearly didn't know what to do with that, so he just nodded at her.

Poor Davy, Elle thought again. She knew exactly how he felt. Strange, how her people skills managed to exist only within the walls of this building. The moment she was out of it— in Logan and John's place, namely— she was a social disaster.

Maybe she really *did* need therapy.

Pushing those thoughts aside, Elle poked her head into the green room. "Can someone get Haley from the dressing room, please? I need to check her mic."

4

On the following Friday, Elle got to the theater almost two hours before her usual call time of five-o-clock, called in by none other than Greg himself. A call from Greg wasn't exactly out of the ordinary, but they were only three weeks into the ten-week run, and auditions for the next show weren't until next week. That could only mean a crisis— and if Greg had a crisis, *Elle* had a crisis.

The moment she walked in the door, she could feel something was off. "Greg?" House lights were already up, which wasn't unusual if someone beat her there, but the stage lights were *also* up, which was *highly* unusual. Elle reached the tech booth door and peeked into it. "Greg?"

"Elle!" Greg, a portly, dark skinned man in a classy navy suit, smiled the moment he saw her, bouncing on his toes just outside the booth window. "Just the young lady I wanted to see."

"I kind of figured that when you called me in," she told him flatly, but— as was their routine— went to hug him anyway. He seemed to need it, practically vibrating at a low level as his arms came around her waist.

Inside the booth, Ben was sitting on her stool with mics already started, and loitering beside him was Hank, a wiry college kid with a red face and a ballcap. In Ben's chair, a greasy looking man with thinning yellow hair and aviator sunglasses turned to leer at her.

"Elodie," Jim drawled, by way of greeting.

"Jimothy," she replied, her disdain for him loud and clear in her voice. Jim scowled at her, but she ignored him, one hand still lingering on Greg's shoulder. "What's the panic? You sounded upset on the phone."

Greg didn't exactly smile. It was really more like a grimace. The second Elle stepped away, he pulled a dark red handkerchief out of his breast pocket to wipe it over his brow. "Sarah's still out sick."

Right, Elle thought. Poor Sarah had caught the plague, as they liked to refer to illnesses in the theater. She had been hoarse as a frog last Friday, and out the following two days. "So, Bridget tonight?" Although, Elle mused, Bridget had been a little rusty herself, last night. Elle glanced back at Ben, who was decidedly *not* looking at her. "Are we going to run the lifts? Logan and John were right behind me—"

"I know you're incompetent, Elodie, but Greg wouldn't have called me in with both Hank *and* Ben here, if you were gonna be in this booth."

Instantly, Elle's entire body went tense. She turned her gaze onto Jim with the most patronizing expression she could manage, and said, "So, two weeks ago, you just, what— turned into a corn stalk backstage?" She gave a reflective hum, looking him up and down. "Explains why they were crooked."

Jim's face went red. "I—"

"Bridget called in," Greg cut in, before they could continue to bicker.

That got Elle's attention. "What? Oh no!" Oh, shit, they'd have to refund a whole *load* of people. "With the same thing?"

Greg nodded. "I could barely hear her. She was crying something awful."

"Poor thing!" Elle put a hand on her chest. Behind her, the theater doors swung open, and John and Logan strolled in. "Hey, Bridget and Sarah are both down for the count."

"Oh, shit," Logan said. He stopped at the threshold with his hands on his hips. "Well, I guess I can finally play Laurey."

John nudged Logan further in, until they were both standing with Elle in front of Greg. "If you say I'm playing Curly, I will quit," he said, his face and voice both devoid of expression.

"You're Jud, actually."

"I stand by what I said." Logan swatted at John, breaking his stoic facade into a smile.

Elle snorted. "I think you're safe, big guy," she said. "Logan looks sallow as a blond." Despite Logan's dramatically offended expression, she smiled patiently at Greg. "So what's the plan?"

Behind her, Ben coughed, the sound noticeably forced. When Elle glanced back at him, he looked like he'd rather sink into the floor than look at her. Hank was right there with him, scratching the back of his head and staring at the ceiling. Jim sneered at her, his feet propped up on the table.

Elle narrowed her eyes, and slid them back to Greg.

"Well, Elle..." Greg meticulously began to fold his handkerchief. "You've done the show before. You know all of the lines. You practically put this show together with me." He waved his arm up and down at her. "You've even played Laurey. You could do it."

Elle blinked. Her mind was surprisingly blank. Probably a side effect of the shock that was rapidly replacing all of her other emotions. "You want me to *what*."

"Just until one of them is back!" Greg said. "It's only one show tonight, you'll be fine."

Elle looked Greg up and down. She'd known him for years, now; ever since he took over the theater from the last director. He'd talked her into joining the theater while she was in college. She'd done several shows with him, at this point. She'd even been known to fill in for dancers after she switched to tech a couple of years ago, anytime he asked.

Besides, he'd seen the terrible YouTube video of her as Laurey in high school. She'd drunkenly forced him to watch it when they were deciding on this season's lineup, so it wasn't like she could *deny* knowing the show. He was right— she knew the show so well, she could step in for *Curly* if she really wanted to.

Except that she didn't want to.

"No." Decided, Elle spun on her heel, fully intent on walking out of the theater. Maybe she could go get lunch before—

"Oh, *please*, Elle," Logan said, looping his arm around her waist and swinging her around to face the rest of the group again. "You haven't performed in *ages* , and you're so good."

"I can't remember the last time you were actually *in* a show," Ben supplied, propping his arms on the counter, and his chin on his joined hands.

"You stay out of this," Elle snapped at him. "And it was *Bye Bye Birdie* , two years ago, thank you."

"God, no wonder you stopped," John muttered.

"I miss performing with you," Logan continued, his best puppy dog eyes trained on her as he propped his chin on her shoulder.

"We wouldn't even interact!" Elle said. She shoved him gently off of her and turned for the door again, only to find her way solidly blocked by John.

"I've actually never performed with you," he said, folding his arms over his chest.

"Yeah, because you spent two years performing at the Opera House uptown instead of here with me," Elle reminded him. She'd had enough of this. "Look, I'm sure any of the girls would be *ecstatic* to take over, but—"

"I told you she'd flake," Jim cut her off.

Silence fell. It was as though the entire group had collectively sucked in a breath and held it, waiting for her response.

Elle turned, very slowly, to face Jim. She could feel heat spreading up her chest and into her face, not from embarrassment, but from sheer rage. It coiled in her throat like a cat about to pounce. Her voice, however, was deceptively soft and even. "Say that to my face, Jimantha."

"I don't recall *ever* seeing you in a lead," Jim sneered, leaning forward over his propped up legs toward her. "High school doesn't count for shit."

Her anger went icy cold.

Logan opened his mouth, probably in an attempt to defend her, but Elle grabbed his arm and squeezed. *Hard.* The rest of the men were, wisely, silent, waiting for her reaction.

Eyes slitted dangerously, she slid her gaze back to Greg, then beside herself, to Logan. "How fast can you get my dance bag and my makeup and get back here?"

Everyone exhaled in unison. "Thank god," Greg muttered, wiping his brow again.

Logan's lips curled into a smug grin. "Give me half an hour." With that, he turned on his heel and sailed back out the door, nabbing the car keys from John's outstretched hand as he went.

"God bless you, Elle," Greg said, reaching for her hands. Elle let him take them, pressing both to his lips in reverent gratitude.

"Yeah, yeah," she said after a moment, shaking her hands free from his grip. "While you grovel, I have a last minute costume to pull together." Greg, at least, had the decency to look sheepish. Elle threw a look over her shoulder at John. "You should go get ready while I find myself something to wear. I wanna run scenes when we're both set."

"Why not wear one of the other girls' costumes?" John asked, following her.

Elle made a disgusted noise. "And catch the plague?"

He grimaced. "Fair point."

They crossed through the empty kitchen into the back half of the theater, across the hall from the green room, through the servers' break room with its enormous TVs and scattered, cheap table and chair sets. In the back of the break room was an extra door, and beyond it—

"Welcome to Narnia," Elle said, staring at the enormous room full of racks upon racks of clothing. "Ever been back here?"

John looked like maybe he'd rather be *anywhere else,* staring at the racks like they might suck him into the mass of fabric, never to be seen again. "Once or twice."

"They don't bite, I promise." She turned a sweet smile to him, then went back to surveying the room. So much *junk* had been crammed into such a small space. Hat and shoe boxes lined an entire wall, so high they almost reached the ceiling. The other wall had almost the same amount of boxes, filled with wigs. Poor John stood out like a sore thumb, with all of the racks almost half his height, not even as tall as Elle.

It occurred to her, like getting hit in the face with a brick, that she'd actually be *performing* with John. She'd have to dance with him, to talk to him, to—

Her shoulders tensed. She'd have to kiss him. And not just once, nor in a sweet romantic way.

Oh, no. Oh *no*. She'd never— she didn't— this was—

God, they were friends. If anything, that should make her feel *better*. He would never do anything to intentionally hurt her, and the scenes where they— where he had to—

"Right," he said, clearly doubtful. His voice jolted Elle from her brain's panicked rambling, and she shook herself, forcing her focus onto him just as he gestured over his shoulder. "I'm gonna go get ready. Yell if you need anything."

"Will do." Elle waved him off, and then faced the room as a whole. She'd personally organized this room two years ago, and since then, it had fallen into chaos. Kind of like what her mind was doing right now, thinking about— about everything.

Definitely about that kiss.

Yikes.

"Right," she said into the empty room, her voice strangely loud in the solitary silence. "We'll just— deal with that later."

God, her mind was racing. There was so much to think about. Lines, songs, choreography, costumes. Rubbing her hands over her face, Elle ran through the costume basics— she'd need a wig, and some underpinnings, before she did anything else. Best to start with that, then.

Not bad, she thought, once she had the wig in place, about fifteen minutes later. The fluffy, honey-blonde bangs and sweeping sides did a great job of hiding her hairline. Once she dolled up her face, it would look close to natural. It hung in fat sausage curls down below her shoulders, a little heavy, but nothing a few extra pins couldn't handle. Or, actually, she thought, grabbing her purse, one of the enormous claw clips she kept for her real hair.

It was certainly a look, she decided on her way back out, regarding her reflection in the mirror. The only things she had so far were her corset, bloomers, tights, and boots, all in white. It wasn't even the weirdest look she'd sported in this theater. *Wild* .

No sign of Logan yet. Elle strolled back into the costume closet, humming through one of her songs. She needed a dress for most of act one, a party dress, a wedding dress, one for the dance sequence. There was a dress she'd seen in here a few months ago that—

"Hey, Bridget." Elle jumped at Davy's deep Southern drawl, whipping around toward the door as he came through, in his usual flannel and jeans. "Greg said—" His eyes found her amidst the sea of fabric, and he faltered. "Oh. 'Scuse me, Ma'am." He looked around at the racks, like he was considering getting to her to greet her properly, but apparently thought better of it and lifted a hand to wave at her instead. "You must be covering for Laurey tonight. I'm Davy, I'll be—"

"Davy," Elle cut him off, trying desperately not to laugh. "You have known me for two years. I've been giving you a mic every weekend for the past month."

Davy's smile dropped. The shock on his face was downright comical, as was the way he blatantly looked her over. "*Elle?*"

Laughter swelled in her chest despite her best efforts. "Did Greg forget to tell you?"

"He said he wanted me early to run some scenes," he said, rubbing the back of his head. "I figured he wanted me to practice the lifts with Bridget, since she keeps doing the thing—"

"Where she just doesn't jump?" Elle nodded. "Yeah, that drives me nuts. Is it better or worse than launching Sarah into the catwalk?"

Davy shrugged. "Six in one, half-a-dozen in the other." He had yet to stop looking her up and down like a swimsuit model. It would have been uncomfortable, except Elle had the sneaking suspicion he was trying to find *her* amidst all the period-clothing and blonde curls. "You look…" He cleared his throat, looking at his feet. "Blonde looks nice on you."

"Thank you." Elle felt herself blush, touching one of the curls that slipped forward over her shoulder. "Listen, I've still got costumes to find," she told him, gesturing to the room at large. "Give me, like, ten more minutes, and I'll come out to run scenes, okay?"

"Sure thing, Ma'am."

"*Elle*," she reminded him, smirking, and then went back to browsing the racks.

"Right." A beat, and then, "Can I ask you something?"

"Sure, as long as you don't mind me not looking at you." Not that she'd be able to see him from where she was headed, anyway.

"You just moved in with John, didn't you?"

"Yeah." Weird question. "He and Logan gave me a room when my ex-roommate pulled a fast one on me." And in the week since she'd moved in, they'd already created a routine between the three of them, one that felt natural and steady. She was honestly pretty floored by it—but then, that was Logan for you. Always trying to make safe spaces for her. "Why do you ask?"

"Just heard it through the rumor mill."

Elle hummed a response and ducked behind one of the racks, which proved to be filled with several bright pink monstrosities. "They've always been really good friends," she said, when nothing else came to mind.

"Y'all have known each other for awhile."

"Yeah, since college." She could almost see Davy now, as she worked her way back toward the front of the room, not finding anything resembling the dress she wanted to find.

"That's mighty kind of them, taking you in." Again, Elle hummed her answer. Davy was silent for a moment, and then—"Miss Elle?"

Elle sighed— eventually, she *would* find her damn dresses— and turned to Davy with a droll expression. "Drop the *Miss*, and then ask me whatever you want to ask."

Davy swallowed, nodded, and then swallowed again. "M—*Elle*, would you... um... would you go to dinner with me?"

"I—" Elle blinked at him stupidly, as his words slowly sunk in. Clearly, she'd used too much hairspray to set the wig. It was ruining her brain cells by the second. "What?"

Davy had exactly the look of someone who had made it all the way to the vet and then realized they'd left their pet at home: some mixture of horror, shock, and embarrassment. Clearly, he was just as surprised at his question as she was. "Um..."

"Like…" Elle intertwined her fingers in front of herself, flexing them nervously. She found she couldn't look at him for more than a few seconds at a time, her eyes dancing sideways as she worked through his words at a snail's pace. "Like… a *date?*"

He ducked his head. "Um. Yes, M—" He caught himself before he could call her *Ma'am* again, and cleared his throat. "Yes."

Well. That had come from *nowhere* . Davy barely even spoke to her on a regular basis. He was just so *shy* . Though, perhaps that was the reason behind his shyness… he *liked* her.

Wild.

"I've been…" Davy was having trouble looking at her, too. "I've been meaning to ask, but I didn't know if you were…"

He didn't finish the sentence, but Elle could pretty much guess one of the several things it could be. *Straight* , for one, since theater people were notoriously *not*— though, honestly, she had no particular preference. Not that he needed to know that. *Single* was probably another, except the only people she consistently hung around outside of work were her roommates, Ben, and Haley. Logan was gay, Ben had a girlfriend, and John… well, he clearly wasn't interested. They'd been friends for ages, and he'd never made a move.

Dinner. It wasn't a marriage proposal. Just a nice date with a nice guy from work. Besides, it wasn't like she was getting any other offers right now.

Davy shifted on his feet, visibly uncomfortable. "You don't have to—"

"I'd love to."

They both spoke at once, and Davy cut off sharply with a strangled noise.

What she'd said appeared to sink in after a few seconds of him just staring at her. "I— really?"

Apparently. Elle smiled at him, and nodded. "Really." Maybe this show would be… testing the waters, or something. Not that she could put stock into how he treated her in character, but maybe it could help her put him into perspective a little easier.

Oh, god, she thought suddenly. She'd have to kiss him, too. Though at least with Davy, the kisses were supposed to be loving, happy moments in the show, and not—

Gah. She was overthinking this.

"Oh." Poor Davy looked so relieved, Elle almost laughed at him again. Pretty flattering, really. "Okay. Uh, how about... next week? Tuesday?"

"Sure— no, wait, *Little Shop* auditions are next Tuesday."

Davy frowned. "You're auditioning?"

"No, I'm stage managing, but I'm on the casting committee." She bit her lip, running through her schedule in her head. "Wednesday?"

He smiled. A *real* smile, which showed the dimples in his cheeks. It was actually pretty attractive. "Alright, Miss Elle. Wednesday."

"One condition." Davy's face fell at her tone, but Elle wasn't feeling particularly serious. Her lips twitched at the corners as she said, "You stop calling me *Miss Elle* or *Ma'am* ."

"Can't do that, Ma'am," Davy said— and, she realized from his sly smile, he was *teasing* her. "It's in my blood."

Elle rolled her eyes at him. "Yeah, yeah, Tennessee blood, and all that." She waved him off. "Go get yourself ready; I'll be out in a little bit to run scenes."

With a nod, Davy left her alone to her sea of costumes. Elle sighed, her heart fluttering in her throat with... excitement? Anxiety? She wasn't sure, really.

Still. A date. She hadn't been on a date in... god, *years* . Since college. For the past two, at least, she hadn't wanted to deal with Gina's reaction, or trying to explain anything regarding her apartment situation to a potential lover. Though now she had roommates who, so far, actually seemed to *like* her, and to enjoy living with her. People she was comfortable spending time with.

Speaking of, Elle thought, finding— at long last— the dress she'd been looking for on one of the racks, crammed into so much taffeta and tulle she had to fight to get it out. She should probably tell the boys that she might, potentially, have a...*thing*. A thing going on, with another man. Logan, she knew, would be ecstatic about her developing a social life beyond work, but John... who knew what he'd say?

God, the thought of him being upset with her about it— or, worse, *annoyed* by it— made her heart stick in her throat.

"Hey, Doll, Davy said you were back here?" Logan's voice preceded him; he breezed in with her pink dance bag over his shoulder, scanning the racks to find her. "Sorry I took so long; there was an accident up the—" The moment his eyes landed on her, his jaw dropped. *"Wow!"*

Elle felt heat rising in her cheeks and chuckled, touching the side of her wig gingerly. "It works, right?"

"Again: *wow*." Logan gave her an approving nod. "Girl. I'm *shook*."

"Thank you." Elle wiggled the dress by her face. "You're just in time to help me finish finding dresses."

"Ooh!" Logan dropped her dance bag by the door and began to work his way in toward her. "I know exactly what I want you to wear for the party scene."

"Of course you do." While Logan wiggled his way over to another rack, she held up the dress she'd found. "Do we like this one for act one?"

"Isn't it one *you* donated?"

Well, yes, Elle thought, but that hadn't answered her question. It may have been hers once, but it wasn't like she was going to wear it anywhere outside of the theater. The thing went down to her ankles, white cotton dotted with red and blue flowers, trimmed with yellow ribbon. The pillowy sleeves went to her wrists and cuffed there, and the collar was high and lacy.

Not exactly high fashion, unless it was early twentieth century America. "I'm going with it."

"At least you know it will fit."

"And come off easily for *Many A New Day*." Though, why Greg had decided to have Laurey change in that number, when she just had to change into yet another dress later in act one, was beyond her. "Isn't there a gray dress from *Wizard of Oz* I can use after that?"

Logan huffed a dry laugh. "Somewhere. How about this for your party dress?"

Elle looked up as pale lavender checks became visible over the rest of the costume hoard. The front had a bib-like structure, dainty lace encircling the neck and wrists. When he turned it for her, she grinned at the big, matching bow snapped to the waist. "I love it."

It took them what felt like another year to find the other dresses she needed, though it was probably no more than a grueling five minutes. Time seemed to be slipping away from them faster than Elle could keep track of it, and she still needed to run blocking.

"I think that's it," Elle said, finally freeing herself from the confines of fabric.

"*Finally.*" Logan came out of the clothing wall beside her and looked her over. "God, John and Davy are going to have a stroke when they see you dressed like that."

She snorted. "Davy basically did. He was in here talking about running scenes before the show."

"I bet." Realization lit up Logan's face, brightening his eyes. "You have to kiss him!" He draped an arm— the one not holding half of her costumes— over her shoulders. "You gonna be okay?"

"I mean he's already asked me on a date," Elle announced with a shrug. Logan's jaw dropped. "So at least he's covering his bases."

"Girl, *when?*" Logan demanded.

"Just before you got back."

Logan pulled away from her, putting a hand to his heart in mock distress. "And that wasn't the *first* thing you told me?"

"I was preoccupied!" She pushed into the green room, finding the ancient leather couches still empty. What a relief. "Besides, I have to kiss John, too, and you don't seem too hung up on that."

"He never actually kisses the girls," Logan says dismissively, a comment that made Elle frown. Logan, of course, didn't give her a chance to ask about it. "Girl, back up to the Davy thing. I need details!"

"Oh my *god*. You're *blonde*. "

Haley breezed into the cramped little dressing room like a summer storm, her makeup and hair already done as usual. "You're awfully early," Elle noted. They still had a good hour until call time.

"Greg called me in to practice with you." Elle watched her, a human tornado, as she dropped her purse under the vanity beside Elle's, fell into the next chair over, and placed two mic packs on the vanity between them. "When Ben told me to bring your mic back, I just about *died*. I'm so excited!"

"Thanks." Elle sighed at her reflection in the vanity mirror. "How do you *do* that, with your makeup? I look like a clown!"

It was true and there was no denying it. Compared to Haley's effortless, natural olive complexion, Elle looked like an escaped mime. Or maybe a ghost with blue eyelids.

"It's all about blending," Haley said, spraying down her braids with Aquanet. As Elle regarded her makeup brushes with increasing panic, Haley sighed. "*Lord,* Elle, you've been off the stage for too long." Shaking her head, Haley capped her hairspray can and set it down with clatter. "Here, let me help you." She snatched up a sponge and began to dab at Elle's face, holding Elle's chin firmly in one hand. Elle tried not to grimace as the sponge stretched and smooshed her skin. "Where's Logan? I thought for sure he'd have put you together already."

"He's giving John stubble," Elle mumbled, despite Haley smearing her face beyond recognition.

"What's John need stubble for?" Haley asked. "He's perfectly yummy the way he is."

Was he? Elle attempted to shrug. "I think that's the point. The stubble makes him look rugged, or something." Elle scrunched up her face as a brush sent powder up her nose. "*Bleh*. We're running scenes as soon as you're done mutilating my face."

"Oh, hush." Haley leaned back to observe her work. "You've been practicing your lines, right?"

"Haley, at this point I could do this entire show by myself."

"Fair." Haley nodded, apparently pleased with the outcome. "You're all set, sweet pea."

Elle looked in the mirror, turning her face from side to side. Everything was smooth, just a hair more defined than her natural makeup. "God bless, I don't look like a French whore from the nineteenth century."

Haley snorted. "My work here is done."

"Wait, not yet!" Elle stood, gesturing to the gaping zipper of her dress. "Could you zip me, please?"

A moment later, assembled and with her dance shoes in hand, Elle stepped back into the still deserted greenroom. She'd been in the sound booth for so long, she hadn't really seen it since they'd redecorated. The vanity along the back wall had new lights, though the clutter of donated stage makeup was the same as always. The leather couches had seen better days, maybe back in the nineties. Above one of them was a bulletin board filled to bursting with pictures and newspaper clippings from their shows.

One newspaper article caught her eye, and she grinned, bending over to read the text below the picture. *Elle Williams, "Chava"*. From when she'd done *Fiddler on the Roof.* It was one of her favorite pictures of herself, a candid snapshot of her reading on the set during their downtime, in full costume.

"Hey, have you seen—"

Elle straightened to face John when she heard his voice. He stared at her, lips parted, and... did nothing. If she didn't know better, she'd say he was struck dumb by the sight of her.

The thought was just ludicrous enough to bring a smile to her face. "Hi. Ready to go?"

"What?" John's gaze snapped up to hers. He seemed to shake himself from wherever his mind had wandered. "Oh. Yeah." He cleared his throat, and then moved past her to open the door, holding it for her. "You look... pretty."

"Thank you." Elle flashed him a grateful smile as she strolled out past him. "I prefer being brunette, though."

"Dark hair suits you better." She didn't know what to make of that, or how to respond, but he thankfully didn't give her a chance. "You nervous?"

"Not really," Elle said, and meant it. They still had plenty of time before the rest of the cast would even get here. They could run practically the entire show before they even opened the dining room to guests.

As she climbed the stairs into the wings, she caught sight of Davy waiting, checking his props. He looked over at her as she approached and smiled. She waved back. "Ready, Davy?"

"Yes, Ma'am." He nodded over her head at John, then gestured for her to lead them out to stage.

"Elle, you look *stunning.*" Greg's voice boomed from the narrow pit, where he stood with the only two people he could apparently bring in early: Tommy, a bald, hooked-nosed pianist, and Anthony, a grinning, heavy set banjo player with enormous square glasses.

"Thank you," Elle said, and then waved excitedly at the musicians. "Hi, guys!"

"Welcome back," Anthony said. "You've been off the stage for too long!"

"She'll stay on it, if I have my way," Greg said. Before Elle could protest, he waved his arm at the stage. "Alright, start from Laurey's entrance— actually, Davy, your line before it— and we'll go from there."

He had to kiss Elle.

He had to kiss Elle.

John locked himself in the men's room and started to pace. They'd just finished the run of the first act, which had been a combination of Greg lamenting Elle's refusal to audition and Elle muttering her lines while John or Davy herded her around like a sheep. Or, in Elle's case, it was more like herding a cat. The dream sequence had been right out of a horror story, what with John having to manhandle her the entire time, to sneer and snarl at her like some sort of deranged, rabid dog.

He didn't even really get to kiss her, either. Just one aggressive, villainous lip lock, and then otherwise, he basically just buried his face in her neck or against her chest. Really, a lot of antagonistic, one-sided action.

Oh, god. He needed to talk to her. Ask her if she'd be alright with him pawing at her like a bear. She was so *tiny*, and he was a monster in comparison, so big he could easily hurt her if he wasn't *exceptionally* careful.

God, she'd hate him after this, if he didn't take care of her.

He *had* to talk to her.

John stalked out of the men's room, fully prepared to pull her aside and double check with her about all the ways he was probably about to traumatize her. He was headed back toward the green room when he happened to glance through the stage door, catching sight of her standing backstage.

With Davy.

John could see them through the door to the back of the stage, just on the other side of the glass windows. Elle was smiling, that sweet, heart-melting look she gave people she enjoyed being with. He'd been on the receiving end of it once or twice, and it was her baseline expression whenever she was with Logan, but Davy? He barely even *talked* to Elle, let alone saying anything worth getting that look from her.

The man was practically on top of her, too. Close enough to—

Oh. *Oh.*

John immediately felt like an asshole. Of course, Davy would need to talk to her. He had to *actually* kiss her. She had to pretend to be in love with him. And he—

Well. From the look on his face, he wouldn't need to do much pretending.

The thought put a bitter taste in John's mouth.

"Hey, John." John turned sharply away from watching Elle and Davy and tried not to glare at his roommate. Logan merely raised his brows. "You good, buddy?"

"Yeah," John lied. "No problems here."

Logan's eyes slitted, and then roamed over John's face. "You wanna try that again?"

Not really. But this was Logan, and one way or another, he'd get the truth eventually. Even if it meant getting John shitfaced and then nagging at him until he spilled his heart out like a heartbroken teenager. No use putting it off.

"What's up with Davy?" He asked, jerking his head toward the doors.

"What, you mean with Elle?" Logan shrugged. "She seems pretty okay with it. I didn't even realize he had a thing for her."

"No kidding." *Do not scowl. Do not move your face. Stay completely calm.*

"Still, she seems excited. She hasn't dated anyone in *years* ; not since Gina went off the deep end about her having people over and spending time with anyone that wasn't her. How she managed to live with that for three years, I'll never know."

"God, Gina sounds—" John's thoughts cut off like a scratched record. "Wait. Dated?"

"I know, right?" Logan shook his head, almost in a disapproving way, but he was smiling. Weird, *weird,* this whole situation. "Bold move, asking her out before the show. As though she wouldn't be nervous enough."

John couldn't feel his face anymore. He was grinding his teeth so hard they'd crack any moment.

"Though she seems like— John?" John swallowed, fully intent on answering— whenever his voice came back— but Logan gasped, realization dawning. "Oh my god, she hasn't even told you yet, has she?" He clapped a hand over his eyes when John mutely shook his head. "Great, now I'm the shitty best friend."

"I'm sure she won't mind," John mumbled. Maybe he should sit down.

"It's not my news to tell." Logan glared at him. "Don't tell her you know. She'll hate that. Make sure she's the one to tell you before you talk to her about it."

"Why would I need to talk to her about it?" John snapped. At Logan's utter lack of reaction— save a singular raised eyebrow— he closed his eyes. "She's a healthy, consenting adult. She can do whatever she likes."

"You have got to be the most air-headed man on this earth," Logan told him.

John laughed bitterly. "Apparently."

With a sigh, Logan patted his chest. "Don't worry, big guy. Things will work out."

What things? John wanted to ask, but he knew. Logan knew. The waitstaff passing them to go set up knew. Chef Rossi *definitely* knew. Everyone who had ever seen John probably knew.

Everyone except Elle.

He couldn't... he couldn't talk to her. Not right now. Not feeling like this.

It was... fine. It was really...fine. He'd just talk his way through act two with her in a few minutes, and then during the show, he'd do his best not to get too handsy while still giving a decent villain performance. Maybe when this weekend was over, he'd even manage to be able to look at Elle without his brain cells evaporating on him.

But probably not.

5

John was acting kind of... *weird*.

Elle assumed it was just a method-acting thing, or something. A way to keep himself in character throughout the show. But he had barely looked at her since before warm ups, except to leer at her in-character during the dream ballet, or to guide her through the *Farmer and the Cowman* polka. Even now, waiting for their next entrance, he was avoiding her gaze.

Maybe he was just uncomfortable with having to kiss all over her neck and chest. He hadn't even wanted to physically run it, just talking her through it and assuring her he wouldn't get too rough or touch her anywhere he wasn't supposed to. Like she would have been worried about it.

She wasn't. If she knew anything about John, it was that he was respectful to a fault.

"You okay?" She whispered, as Haley and Nathan danced their way through their duet as Ado Annie and Will Parker. John just nodded curtly, and kept watching the show from their spot in the wings.

He didn't seem okay. Elle tried not to sigh. Everything, so far, had gone swimmingly. The audience didn't seem the least bit bothered by the sudden change in cast— they were actually more involved today than they'd been the last few shows. What with everyone else bringing their A-game to make up for losing both of their leading ladies, it was like opening night all over again.

Even John was giving his all. *Lonely Room* had been haunting and vicious in a way Elle had never heard him sing it before. Though maybe it just sounded different from backstage.

No time to analyze, she realized. They were on.

John took her hand and her waist, and she gave him a fleeting smile, before focusing on where her feet were going.

It wasn't hard to play scared when John's lines grew steadily more vile, as he reached around her from behind and pressed his face into her hair. He'd always played Jud as cunning and evil. Not like the versions she'd seen before, where Jud was just stupid and unfortunately unattractive.

Definitely not the case, with John. Even the stubble Logan had given him couldn't detract from his good looks. If anything, it made him *more* appealing.

Elle knew how to convince an audience, though. She brought up her arms when John grabbed her, burying his face in her neck, and—

She went stiff as a board. Instantly.

John's lips barely even did anything on her neck, but they were there nonetheless, soft and gentle, as he muttered lines she was supposed to be frightened of. Except, for a split second, Elle forgot to be frightened of him.

Something warm and liquid melted through her belly. Her heart stuttered, and then began to canter in her chest, racing so fast she could hardly breathe. The spots John kissed, around her neck and then across her collarbone, began to tingle, as though she'd had a brush with an exposed wire. As he reached the edge of her blouse, her breath hitched.

It terrified her.

Panicking, Elle shoved John away. She must have used more force than necessary, because John stumbled back, staring at her with open shock. There was a very heavy, tense pause, both of them staring at each other, before his face settled back into the nasty expression he wore as Jud, and he continued his lines.

She screamed her own lines, shaking so hard it was the only way she could say them without stuttering. Moments later, she found herself sitting on the stage, desperately trying not to cry.

Davy came in and delivered his lines in his usual snarky manner, smirking right up to the moment he saw Elle's face.

He hesitated for a second, and that was all she needed.

She flung herself into his arms, and oddly enough, it eased her. Davy was strong and steady and solid against her. So long as he kept holding her like this, she would be fine.

Elle felt herself calm as Davy held her, murmuring his lines while she stumbled through her own, and then she looked up at him, and...

Davy's lips were soft against her own. Perfectly gentle, perfectly sweet. No tongue, no roaming. Just a nice, simple kiss.

Elle felt nothing.

Nothing.

Oh, *no.*

The rest of the scene went by in a blur. Exactly *none* of Davy's kisses made her body react the way it had to John merely speaking against her neck and collarbone. It helped her ground herself for the scene, make it through the song, until she could get off stage. And promptly panic.

Logan caught her the moment she came flying off, his and Haley's hands flying to get her out of her party dress and into the wedding dress. His words were barely audible over the scene change music, a hushed murmur of concern. "Elle, are you okay?"

"I need to talk to you later," she whispered, in a breathless rush, jamming the veiled headband onto her head.

Logan nodded, his eyes wide. Elle turned around at Davy's hand on her back, pasted on a smile, and sailed onto the stage for the title song.

After the wedding scene, she was offstage, pulling off her veil, when John appeared, panting, looking actually stricken when he saw her.

"Did I hurt you?" He demanded, in the same harsh whisper that Elle had used on Logan. He strode toward her with his arms out, as though he needed to touch her, to make sure she was unharmed and intact.

Elle shook her head as his hands came up to her arms, his touch gentle. "Did I push you too hard? Are you—"

"I'm fine." John didn't look convinced as he looked her over. "Will you be okay for the next scene?"

God, Elle thought. Another kiss. She nodded. "I'm okay." Then, because he looked like he needed to hear it, "We're okay."

Barely a breath passed before he nodded, but she could see the relief in his eyes.

She stepped out of his grasp and turned. "Will you get my zipper?"

There was something… oddly intimate, she realized, about him helping her change. He made quick work of her zipper and dutifully took the dress once she was out of it, his face back to— god, that *mask* he'd been wearing this entire show. It made her want to scream. Was it that awful, pretending to kiss her?

She was left in her chemise, petticoat, and corset. Davy tossed her his shirt, and as she yanked it on, she gave John the most reassuring smile she could manage. A true feat, considering how shaky she was herself.

This scene was a nightmare to do sound for, and, she realized, even *worse* to be in. The noise around her surged, and she grabbed Davy's arm with both hands as they were dragged onstage by two ensemble men. She was clinging to him like a koala as they climbed onto a picnic table. The noise only surged further, the entire cast, save John, swarming them like a mob. She had to at least *pretend* to find this funny, but it was all too *much*.

It was only a handful of seconds— dragging, *grueling* seconds— and then all sound cut out except for John's lines. He seemed to materialize in the heart of the crowd out of nowhere.

Elle scrambled off the table and started to back up. She knew this blocking perfectly well, but something about John actually creeping toward her, predatory and focused, a sinister expression on his handsome face, had her brain scrambling.

Focus, she told herself. She had directions to follow.

His lines ended, silence stretching, tense and thick, across the entire auditorium. She grit her teeth and turned her face, giving him her cheek, while the audience got to see her closing her eyes and wincing. Waiting for him to turn her head.

His grip was firm, but gentle, and she somehow still didn't expect it. Elle jumped upon finding herself facing John. She gasped, and then—

John's lips pressed, ever so gently, against hers. He kept one hand on her chin, the other in her hair, and made a good show of forcing her to kiss him, without hurting her in the slightest.

Elle would be psychoanalyzing this for the rest of her life. She was sure of it. Her body went rigid, but she could still feel *it*. The same thing that had swept through her when he'd kissed her neck, not even ten minutes ago. And, horrifyingly, she didn't want him to stop.

Elle reared back when John got pulled off of her by Davy, and then, forgetting her blocking entirely, took a step forward.

It was a stupid move. An *immensely* stupid move.

John's elbow came back as the fight sequence started, when he wrestled it free from Davy's grip. Elle miscalculated the distance between them so badly she ended up catching it directly in her solar plexus.

Pain shot through her in a jolt at the contact. With a grunt, she tumbled backwards and hit the ground, the wind leaving her lungs in a rush.

Chaos erupted. Miriam's face appeared above her first, shrewdly made up for her role as Aunt Eller, then Logan's beside hers. Elle could barely catch her breath, a hand on her middle where John had nailed her. She couldn't even force herself to stay in character, too busy struggling to get air back into her lungs. It took an enormous effort, but she reached up when they took her arms and tensed enough for them to pull her to her feet. Fresh pain throbbed in her stomach as she did it, and she almost sagged right back down.

At least six people surrounded her, clamoring to ask if she was okay, all blatantly ignoring the actual blocking of the show. Elle nodded, more and more frantically, and eventually just shoved her way out of their grip, just in time to see John fall to the ground for Jud's death, clutching the prop knife against his chest. She screamed on cue, grabbing ahold of Logan, who had yet to fully let go of her.

John met her eyes, his back to the audience. She could see the panic in them as he looked her over, the relief when he realized she was generally okay, and then the way he slipped back into character as two of the ensemble men went to turn him over.

Her hand went to her lips, and she watched the rest of the scene as though from a great distance, clutching onto Logan.

"Thank god it's over." Elle dropped onto the worn leather couch, back in her own clothing, and then just stayed there, an arm flung over her eyes. "I'm never doing Greg any favors again."

"Save yourself the trouble and just *audition* for things." Greg's voice came from somewhere beside her, but she was too tired to bother looking at him. "Are you okay?"

Elle nodded. "Winded, that's all. Might have a little bruise. John's elbows are *sharp*."

"Yeah, well, as long as you'll be okay for tomorrow's performances." Elle groaned. "You were magnificent tonight, Elle. You should have been Laurey this whole time."

"Don't tell the other girls you said that," Elle warned. "I'm not auditioning for anything again until you do a show I haven't been in, or until you promise to cast me as the role I want and not just the lead."

"Other girls would *die* to be the lead." Logan's voice was accompanied by him lifting her legs up from the couch and settling himself underneath them.

"Exactly!" Elle finally lifted her arm from her face, if only to wave her agreement at Logan. "Give it to one of them."

"Honestly, Elle, you're going to give me an aneurysm." Greg shook his head at her. "I'll go get the dining room sectioned off at Hollywood Grill," he announced, and turned to go. At least a dozen other people emerged from the dressing rooms, as though summoned by the prospect of food, and swept out of the green room with him, all arguing about carpooling and Venmo.

Elle couldn't help but smile. This was the part she actually missed about performing. Dancing was fun, singing made her happy, but in the end, it was the sense of family, of *belonging* , that she really loved.

"Elle, are you okay?"

Elle peered up at John and gave him a faint smile. "Relax, big guy," she soothed, patting her middle where his elbow had met her body. "You didn't get me that badly. Besides, it's my fault I was in the wrong place."

"Jesse said I knocked you down." He knelt down beside her, bringing his face level with hers. She could see the concern in the piercing jade, and found it almost overwhelming. Their kiss flashed through her mind, and she snapped her gaze away.

"Yeah. Winded me, too." She chuckled. "Nothing a little ice couldn't help. Smart of Jesse, too, wrapping it in one of the napkins from the kitchen." *Leave it to the Stage Manager*, she thought wryly.

"Nothing says early twentieth-century America like blue and white checks." Logan started to lift the hem of Elle's tee shirt. "How's the bruise?" Elle slapped his hand away, and he just laughed.

"It's black, thanks." Elle glanced at John to find him panic-stricken, staring down at her stomach. "Relax, John. I bruise like an old apple. I'll have this for about a week, and then everything will be perfectly fine." She sat up and swung her legs off of Logan, and then reached out to pat John's face. His skin was smooth, most of his makeup cleaned off, and—

Elle snatched back her hand. Clearing her throat, she said, "We should head to the diner."

"I'm going to eat my body weight in French Toast," Logan announced. He hopped to his feet, then reached down and hauled Elle to hers by her arms. She groaned dramatically, but the sound dissolved into laughter.

John was on her in an instant, wedging himself between Logan and Elle and looking her over with a deep set frown. Elle's laughter swelled, and she started swatting him away. "John! I'm fine!" To prove it, she pulled up her tee shirt, baring her stomach. John froze, his eyes trained on the bruise under her sternum. "Look. It's not even that big." She pulled her shirt back down and reached up to pat his arms. "You're just sharp, big guy. Sharp elbows, sharp collarbones." She squeezed his jaw in one hand, shaking it a little. "Sharp jawline—"

"Yeah, okay," John said, pulling her arm away, his eyes rolling so hard they'd probably stick. "I get it."

"You're a regular Adonis." *God*, Elle realized, the truth of her words hitting her squarely in the chest. He really... he really was attractive. Extremely so.

Oh, no. No, no,*no*.

She snatched her arm out of his grip and ran it through her hair, crimped and frizzy from being trapped under her wig in braids for so long. The green room seemed too small, all of the sudden. Grabbing onto Logan, she started out of it, dragging him with her. "Do we all want to carpool to the diner?"

John's face went blank the moment she glanced up at him. He somehow managed to avoid her eyes and hold the door for her at the same time. "I think I'm actually gonna go home."

It shouldn't sting, but Elle felt her own face fall. She recovered as quickly as she could, but she knew Logan had seen her face before she managed to focus on where she was walking. "Tired of us already?" She chuckled and barrelled on before he could respond. "Or just exhausted from all this hard work, elbowing your poor costars in the ribs—"

"Hardy har." John pulled open the door to his Lexus and shot Elle— no, shot *them* a dry look. "I'll see you both at home."

"Bye, stud!" Logan waved with just a little too much enthusiasm before he joined Elle in her car. The moment both of their doors were shut, he turned on her, hawk-eyed and serious. "Bitch, *spill*."

Elle pressed her palms together, and touched them to her lips. "John kissed me."

Logan stalled out at her words. She didn't dare look at him. There was too much swirling around in her head to sort through, and looking at him— she'd probably say something *stupid*.

"I mean, Davy also kissed me, which was..." Not as good, really. Not even close. "It was fine."

"That bodes well for your date," Logan commented.

"I don't—" Oh, *no*. She didn't want to think about that right now. "That's not the point."

"Then what's your point?"

"I can hear you laughing at me," Elle said, reaching out to swat Logan's arm. She glanced out of her car window and watched John turn out of the parking lot. Something in her chest tightened. "The point is— the point is that he's my roommate." Yes, that was it. The panic in her chest was because she'd still have to live with him, now that they'd kissed. "I can't just kiss my roommate."

Logan shrugged. "It's acting, sweetie. He has to kiss Bridget or Sarah every time he performs."

Elle started her car and began to back out. "I know. I *know* that. But— wait, you said he doesn't kiss the other girls."

"Not really," Logan said. "It's just a peck on the lips. Isn't that all he did to you?"

Other than kissing my neck until I forgot my lines? "Yes, it just..." Elle made a frustrated sound. "I don't know. It's just weird, okay?"

"That bad, huh?"

She almost closed her eyes, before she remembered she was driving. "No, actually. That's the problem."

Logan gasped. Elle spared him a suffering glance. "Girl, you *enjoyed* getting kissed by John!" Helpless to deny it, Elle nodded. "Ellie, oh my *god!*"

"Oh, *no*," Elle groaned.

"Elle, this is— this is so *big!*" Logan was outright laughing at her misery. He didn't even have the decency to hide it. "You're gonna tell him, right?"

"*No!*" If she weren't focused on getting them to the diner without crashing the car into a streetlight, she'd have buried her face in her hands. "I haven't even worked up enough courage to tell him I'm going on a date!"

"You—" Logan sputtered through his own laughter—"you're still gonna go on the date with Davy?"

"Stop laughing at me!" Elle wailed. "Of course I am, he's a sweetheart, he's perfectly nice to me—"

"You just said kissing him was, and I quote, *fine,*" Logan reminded her. "And then you said John kissing you— without you even kissing him back— was something you enjoyed."

"I didn't say that—"

"Oh, *sorry,* " Logan teased, rolling his eyes. "It just wasn't *bad.*"

Elle stopped at a red light and sank lower in her seat. "This is terrible."

"This is hilarious." He ignored her glare to continue, "Ellie, just tell John you'd like to try kissing him outside of the stage and see what happens. I bet he'd let you."

"I bet he wouldn't." God, she could imagine it too well. The friend-of-a-friend he'd offered a room to, hitting on him in his own house. *Yikes.* "No, I'm gonna tell him about Davy— at some point— and then I'm gonna go on the date, with Davy, and have a perfectly nice time."

Logan sighed at her, his expression... disapproving. Maybe a little disappointed. Heck if Elle knew. "Green light, Doll."

Elle straightened up and started the car forward again. "Look, just— please don't tell John I've got a— a *thing*, or whatever. I don't want to make him uncomfortable."

It was a few long, nail-biting seconds before Logan responded. "On one condition."

Elle groaned. "What condition?"

"If you turn out not to have any feelings for Davy, you kiss John— off the stage— before you decide not to pursue him."

Elle's jaw nearly dropped out of the floor of her car. "What kind of condition is *that?*"

"The kind where you get to kiss someone for once in your life," Logan insisted, poking her arm. "It's been *years* since you've dated. At least say you'll kiss the man if you get the chance!"

"Alright, alright!" Elle turned into the diner parking lot, relieved to have a way out of this... everything. The car, the conversation, the entire train of thought involving John and— and *kissing* him. "If things fall through with Davy, I'll lay a hot one on John, and prove to you that, despite his kisses distracting me tonight—"

"*Ha!*" Logan danced in his seat, pointing emphatically at her. "I *told* you—"

"He's definitely not into me," Elle finished over Logan's sentence. "You'll see. It'll be weird, and then we'll never talk about it again. If it even happens." Elle yanked off her seatbelt and threw open her door. "Which it won't, since I'll be dating Davy."

Logan smirked as he also got out of the car. "Yeah, okay. We'll see."

The front door opened and closed, accompanied by Elle's soft giggles and Logan's loud cackle. John paused *Resident Evil 2*, which he'd been playing in the hopes of distracting himself from— really, the entire night, if he was honest. Instead he'd found himself obliterating zombies at a truly cathartic pace, imagining each one was Davy, and trying to feel guilty about it.

He couldn't stop his eyes from drifting to Elle. Still done up in her stage makeup, her mile long hair swinging around her arms, back in her black tech clothes from before the show, a takeout box in her hands. She was even more beautiful like this than in the fancy dresses he'd seen her in earlier.

They were laughing about something John didn't catch, but Elle elbowed Logan in the side over something he said. "You can't *say* that, Logan, it's not— oh!" She smiled the moment she caught John's eye, and it hit him like a spike to the chest. "You're still awake!"

"Yeah," he said, resuming his game. "Couldn't settle."

"It was an eventful day." Elle strolled into the kitchen to put her leftovers away.

Logan narrowed his eyes at John, who pointedly ignored him. "Hmm. Well. I'm going to bed." He made a beeline for the stairs. "Goodnight, you two."

"Goodnight!" Elle sang, while John mumbled the same. He was already watching her again, admiring the sweep of her spine as she pulled her hair up into one of those messy knots she liked to put it in.

Hopeless, that's what he was. A hopeless train wreck with an unrequited crush on his roommate.

Grinding his teeth, John focused on his video game. *Davy* was going to get to put his hands on her back, to bury them in her long hair. To kiss her soft, gentle lips—

The zombie he shot at didn't stand a chance, blown to smithereens by a dead-on head shot.

"Ugh, zombies." Elle dropped down right next to him, folding herself up like a cat.

"I thought you liked horror." John commended himself for keeping his eyes off of her, but he could still *feel* her, like a sixth sense, sitting so closely to him.

"Not zombies," she admitted. He felt the blanket draped over the back of the couch shift, and leaned forward so she could take it. Always cold, his Elle. Always seeking out warmth from people who weren't him.

He took another zombie's head clean off in one hit.

"They're... unsettling," Elle continued, oblivious. "Dead things should stay dead."

"Fair enough." John tried to focus on his game, but he could see Elle's reflection in the dark corner of the TV screen, looking at him with a furrowed brow. He swallowed and forced himself not to look at her. "So. Davy laid a hot one on you, huh?"

He heard Elle huff, and knew she was rolling her eyes at him. "You're turning into Logan, I swear. A couple of gossiping busybodies, you know that?"

John shrugged and convinced himself to smile, though he still couldn't bear to look at her. "Comes from being friends for so long."

"Yeah, tell me about it." She chuckled, and John almost sent Leon Kennedy into a wall at the sound. "Pot, kettle. I'm just as bad when he riles me up."

"I wasn't going to tell you, but—" The blanket went over his head, and he laughed. "Hey! I'm trying to save Raccoon City here!" He flung the blanket back at her, catching her playful grin, and—

Nope, nope, *nope*, mayday, abort mission. He snapped his focus back to his game before he could focus on her face. Maybe if he didn't look at her, he wouldn't feel compelled to kiss her again, to see if that— that *whatever*, that spark from earlier, hit him again.

God, kissing her on stage. With Davy standing right behind him. Davy, who she was going on a date with. Davy, who had won Elle over before John had even figured out how to try.

Torture of the purest form.

"So how was it?" John prompted, and then spared her one more glance.

Elle's face had gone completely blank. She stared at the TV, where John was loading up on ammo and med kits.

Tell me, he urged her silently, watching her face in the still-dark corner of the TV. *Tell me about Davy. Tell me why you chose him .*

Elle shrugged. "It was a kiss."

John missed the zombie he shot at by a mile. It felt like his own brain had taken the bullet instead, thoughts scattering in so many directions he couldn't catch any of them. And, like an absolute asshole, he said, "No fireworks on your end, huh?"

"It's just been awhile since I've kissed anybody," she said. Not a confirmation exactly, but not a denial either.

John shouldn't feel smug about the idea of Elle not enjoying kissing Davy, but— well. He shouldn't be curious about how she felt kissing him, either. And yet, here he was. Curious. "Damn, I should have put more effort into it. Then you and Logan would have *loads* to gossip about."

"Hmm. You should have," she agreed. "We'd be upstairs comparing the two of you—"

"Oh, so you didn't do that on the drive to the diner?" John flicked his eyes to her, and saw the flash of guilt that crossed her face. "Ah, you did!"

Elle regained her composure by clearing her throat. "Not much to compare. Neither of you put any effort into it." She sighed, the sound just a bit too dramatic. "I suppose kissing me was *such* a chore—"

"Hey!" John's head whipped around, and he opened his mouth to tell her *exactly* how much he'd like to kiss her, until he saw the grin she was trying to hide behind her hands. He scowled. "No fair, Elle." To prove his indignation, he yanked the blanket off of her. "No blanket privileges for you."

Elle's laughter followed the blanket's path as she launched herself after it, almost toppling into John's lap as she went. "Give it back, you giant! Some of us don't radiate heat like a furnace!"

"Yeah, you're basically part reptile," John teased. Elle was— she was *very* close to him, all of the sudden, one hand on his shoulder to brace herself as she reached across him for the blanket. It brought her chest dangerously close to his face. For the *second* time tonight.

Panicking, John tilted himself to the side, sending Elle toppling backwards to where she'd been sitting, and tossed the blanket over her head. "Next time I'll be sure to give you something to write home about." With that, he resumed his game, and promptly— and embarrassingly— flung Leon into another wall.

"I'll hold you to that." She stood up and threw the blanket over the back of the couch. "I expect it to be uncomfortably long. With tongue."

That image, in John's head, went directly between his legs. "I'll keep that in mind," he choked out. And then he remembered: Davy.

Shit.

Elle muttered something that sounded suspiciously like *I'll bet*, rolling her shoulders. "I'm going up to shower off the sixteen layers of makeup Haley put on me." With that, she sent John one last smile and headed toward the stairs. He put a valiant effort into not watching her, and failed miserably. "Goodnight!"

When he went to bed tonight, he'd dream of her soft neck under his mouth, her lips against his. He knew it as well as he knew his own name. "Night."

6

Either their schedules had somehow magically fallen into opposites, or Elle was avoiding him. John couldn't decide which option was more annoying.

It had only been a couple of days since she'd been drafted into the role of Laurey, and he hadn't been pulled for any of the other shows she'd been in. He kept telling himself his disappointment was that of an unused performer, and not based around Elle. Though he did see Paul's rendition of Jud's death scene— Paul barely got a chance to put his lips to Elle's before Davy hauled him away and started the fight scene up.

John had left the moment Greg had dismissed him tonight. He really couldn't justify standing around the tech booth watching Elle— again. At least last night, they'd needed him for the spotlight again.

Seeing Davy put a bitter taste in John's mouth, but as Elle still hadn't told him about their date, he kept pretending to be indifferent. Though if he spent any more time slaughtering zombies in various horror games, he'd go become a zombie himself. Not exactly helpful.

At any rate, Elle had her last show as Laurey this afternoon, so she wouldn't be home until suppertime— or, if everyone dragged her out to celebrate, even later. Logan was supposed to go to Tyler's to do sickeningly cute couple things, which left John alone for dinner. Thank god Elle had made a point to binge cook her body weight in meals. The woman could feed an army with the amount she cooked.

Honestly, bless her. He hadn't eaten this many home cooked meals, this consistently, in years. Probably since living with his parents. Logan wasn't exactly hopeless, but he wasn't great. John himself had a track record of setting the stove on fire, and grilling was too much of a hassle to do with great regularity.

He ended up planting himself in his usual spot in the middle of the couch, with a bowl of Elle's homemade beef stew on the coffee table in front of him. For once in his life, the idea of playing *Resident Evil* wasn't even remotely appealing. Time for something different, then. Maybe a game with a different atmosphere.

He didn't realize what time it was until the front door opened, and Elle's voice called out.

"Hey," he said, distracted by his game. "How was the show?"

"Well," Elle sighed, "Paul almost flung me into the catwalk, so pretty normal." A beat, then—"Though I haven't developed any more mysterious bruises."

John rolled his eyes. "Hardy har."

"It's almost gone, actually." She paused on her way to the kitchen to glance at the TV, and delight warmed up her face. John almost fumbled the controller at the genuine smile— he hadn't seen her smile like that in days. It felt like an eternity. "Bioshock!"

"The first one," he told her. He really shouldn't have looked at her. The delight on her face turned wistful, and he sent his character past the turn he needed to take and into a wall. God, he hoped this wouldn't become a habit.

"The best one," she said, making her way to the kitchen. "Have you eaten?"

"Yeah," John said, backtracking in the game. "Great stew."

"Thanks!"

He was promptly attacked by enemies, his health knocked down drastically low. *You're better than this,* he reminded himself. *Get a grip.* He could hear her humming as she made herself a plate of food and put it in the microwave.

"Savior or genocide run?" she asked over the hum.

As he was actively in the middle of saving one of the Little Sisters, he said, "I wish I could say I was a ruthless murderer, but here we are."

"I feel that," Elle said. "I used to watch my older brother play this when we were kids. We would load up on junk food and try to out-massacre each other in different games."

"Sounds fun," John said. "My sister wasn't really into video games." He healed his character and stocked up on ammo as the microwave went off. "Hey, if you're coming over here, would you mind grabbing me a beer?"

She didn't respond. For a moment, he thought she hadn't heard him— or had somehow ignored him and left, without him noticing at all— but a moment later, a beer settled on the coffee table in front of him, along with a bottle of Elle's favorite pineapple cider, and her plate of leftovers.

"Thanks," he said, finally back on track in his game.

"No problem," Elle sang. He spared her a glance, only to find her sitting cross legged on the floor, between the couch and the table.

"We have an entire couch," he reminded her, "and a chair."

Elle just laughed. "I like the floor." She watched him play as she ate, the silence somewhere between tense and companionable. John wondered if she was thinking about Davy, and tried not to scowl. "Have you weaponized the bees yet?"

"Haven't gotten that far," he said. And again, like Friday night, he felt that silent urging begin in his head. *Tell me about Davy. Tell me about the date.*

They sat there in that same tense silence again, until Elle set her empty plate on the table and reached her hand up toward him. "May I?"

"Sure," John said, handing over the controller and picking up his beer instead.

She wasn't bad, really. It was obvious she'd played the game before, but it was equally obvious that she was out of practice. John watched her in silence, willing her to start up a conversation, to bring up the one thing they were both avoiding talking about.

Or maybe she just didn't care enough to tell him.

Though she must have gotten tired of the silence, after a few minutes. "So if your sister wasn't pestering you to play your games, how *did* she pester you?"

Not what John wanted to talk about, but better than nothing, he supposed. "She didn't really pester me. We used to lay on the floor and watch cartoons in here. Gran would knit, and Pop would do the crossword puzzle."

"Is that, like, a *grandfather* thing?" Elle asked, laughter in her voice. "The crossword puzzles in the newspaper?"

"I guess so." She laughed, the sound both soothing and frustrating. "Yours did them, too?"

"Religiously," Elle said, "while Grandma read murder mysteries, and both of them ignored *The Price is Right*."

"Yeah, why did they even turn that show on?" John started to laugh himself. "They never actually watched it!"

"Exactly!" Elle looked up at him, her grin sweet and open, like sunshine washing over him, to hand back his controller. "Here. Thanks for letting me play."

"No problem." John took the controller and went right back to the grind of defeating enemies. "Sometimes you've just got to mass murder some weird, masked maniacs, right?"

Elle laughed, but the sound was hollow. "Yeah."

John's eyes narrowed. "So Paul almost sent you into the flies, huh?"

"Yep," Elle said, and took a long pull from her cider. "Thanks, by the way, for knowing how to do a lift. I didn't think it was that difficult to pick a girl up and put her back down."

John forced himself to chuckle. "Glad to know I got one thing right."

Elle's elbow met his shin in a playfully light jab. "Come on, the elbow thing was an accident. *I'm* the idiot who forgot my blocking."

"Yeah, yeah." There was something bothering her, though. He had a sinking feeling he knew what it was, but he hoped he was wrong. Clearing his throat, he hedged, "And... Davy?"

Her face went blank, and then twitched, minutely. John would have missed it if he hadn't been stupid and looked directly at her when it happened.

When Elle neither responded nor looked at him, he frowned and paused his game. "Did Davy do something, Elle?"

"What?" That got her attention, in a deer-in-the-headlights sort of way. She looked up at John as though she'd only just realized he was there.

"You've been acting weird," he told her, trying not to let his irritation bleed into his voice. Judging from the slight shift in Elle's face, he failed. "If Davy did something, or upset you, or whatever, you can tell me." *Or maybe if you two have been getting friendly backstage.* "Do I need to start throwing punches, Elle?"

"No!" The word came out too quickly, but rather than relaxing him, it just cranked John's irritation up another notch. Elle turned away from him again, gathering up both of their dishes. "No, it's nothing like that. He didn't upset me."

As she walked away from him, John found himself standing, following her toward the kitchen. "Then what happened, Elle?" *Tell me. Tell me now. Tell me about the date.*

Elle set the dishes in the sink with a sort of half-hearted laugh. "Actually… we're uh. We're going on a date. On Wednesday."

If John thought hearing her say it would be a relief, in any way, he was sadly mistaken. Exactly the opposite, really. He was more— more—

God, he wanted to go find Davy and give the man a black eye.

"He asked me out, so we're going to dinner." She didn't look particularly happy about the ordeal. In fact, she rinsed out the dishes like they might bite her if she didn't do them quickly enough, and then put them in the dishwasher, closing it a little too forcefully. "I know I didn't seem all that…*enthusiastic*, about him kissing me," she said. She hadn't even looked at him yet. "It's just…" Her eyes wandered to the couch, then back down to her own hands, toying with the latch on the dishwasher. "I don't know. It might be fun. It's been… god," she laughed, "*years*, since I've been on a real date." She shrugged. "Maybe I'm just out of practice with the whole… kissing thing."

There were so many things he wanted to say to that, but they all got stuck somewhere between his vocal cords and his mouth, so he said none of them. He felt like his heart had just strolled out on him, and a pool of misery was rapidly filling the crater left in his chest. Elle and *Davy* . Confirmed by her. Not just gossip from Logan anymore, but honest to god facts.

God, *god*, Elle and *Davy*, going out on a date, when John felt— when he felt—

It doesn't matter.

It didn't matter, he realized. Elle wasn't into him like that. Elle didn't deserve him forcing his feelings onto her. She didn't need to know what was going on in his head, or in his— in what was left of his heart. He wasn't going to guilt her like that. It wasn't fair to her.

This whole garbage fire situation wasn't fair at all.

Still. Something in him surged forward, words coming out of his mouth unbidden. "If you don't feel anything for him you don't have to go."*Please don't go.* He shoved the thought aside. "You shouldn't have to settle just because it's been a while, Elle."

She— she *laughed*. Bitter, resentful laughter, that twisted her face into a painful mockery of a smile. The sound, and her expression, tore the hole in his chest even further open. "Come on, John," she said, barely holding his eyes for more than a second."You live with me. You've known me for years. You know what I'm like."

White hot anger flashed through him. "What's that supposed to mean?" The words came out more harshly than he'd meant them to, and Elle's face snapped up, her eyes meeting his. Yes, he *did* know what she was like. She was kind, and caring, and *wonderful*, and she deserved to be *happy*. Not to settle for the perfect Southern Gentleman *Davy*, who she obviously wasn't even emotionally attached to, just because he'd asked her out.

Elle recoiled at his expression. "Nevermind."

"No, I—" John was fully prepared to ruin his own life, apparently, ready to tell her *exactly* what he knew of her, what he thought of her, how completely and utterly *gone* he was for her, but the front door opened, cutting him off.

John had never been so furious to see Logan and Tyler in his life.

"Oh!" Logan grinned at them, clearly oblivious to the tension between John and Elle. "You're both still up! I expected her to be passed out by now."

John swallowed down at least six different threats, and took a step away from Elle. She leaned over the counter and waved at the men. "Hey guys! I thought you were going to Tyler's tonight?"

Tyler waved at them from behind Logan, calm and collected in all the ways Logan was wild and dramatic. "A water main burst at my place, so the whole complex is SOL as far as water goes." He looked up and gestured to the makeup still on Logan's face. "He still looks like he broke out of the circus, so—"

"Hey!"

"We really need running water."

"I bet," Elle teased. She looked almost normal, as though they hadn't just been borderline fighting. The same couldn't be said for John, he was sure.

Logan pouted. "This is what I get for dating a lawyer." He looked down at his short, stocky boyfriend, and scowled. "See if you get to join me *now*."

"Oh, *oh*, more information than I needed." Elle grimaced, covering her ears.

John watched the entire exchange happen as though from a great distance. Elle's friendship with Logan was so smooth, so easy. She probably never kept anything from him. She had no reason to. But with him— she acted like telling him something so simple as getting a date was the most difficult thing she could possibly do.

Though, given the way he'd reacted so far, perhaps it was.

He forced himself to say goodnight to the happy couple, and watched them go upstairs, bickering affectionately like they'd been married for years. It just drove it further home that Elle didn't share his feelings. How utterly cruel, that she would never see him as anything but a friend. Maybe the most painful thing he'd ever experienced.

Now he was just being dramatic. *God.*

John shoved the thought aside and swallowed, forcing himself to breathe, to be calm. Elle still wasn't looking at him, but she hadn't tried to move past him. So he stepped up beside her instead, and ran his hand lightly down her ponytail. It seemed to startle her, that one gentle, friendly gesture that he'd done countless times before.

"You deserve to be happy, Elle," He whispered.

He almost didn't hear the catch in her breath as he went upstairs.

"I deserve to be happy," Elle repeated to herself on Wednesday evening, winding a lock of hair around her curling wand. "I don't have to settle."

Things had been... tense, with John. They hadn't exactly been avoiding each other, but... between him spending all of Monday at the country club doing community services or whatever, and her being trapped at *Little Shop* auditions all day yesterday, and then neither of them managing to be in the same room for longer than a handful of minutes today... they'd certainly spent less time together. She didn't know why that made her feel so uneasy.

No, uneasy wasn't the word for it. She was *sad*. She missed her friend.

Elle wondered if— no, actually, she wondered *why* John disapproved of Davy so much. He wasn't interested in her, that much was clear. He'd known her for years and never said anything, never even hinted at having romantic feelings for her. He treated her more like a sibling than anything— and before she'd moved in, she'd been like an extension of Logan anyway, only around John when Logan was present. So what made him so uptight about her going on *one* date?

It was just so *frustrating*. She already had an older brother, thanks, and at least Garth minded his own goddamn business about her dating life unless she asked him not to.

Still. She'd taken John's words to heart. They echoed in her head— that one strange, tender moment before he'd gone upstairs, where he'd brushed his hand over her hair. Like a friend would.

You deserve to be happy.

Her heart squeezed in her chest.

"It's okay," she breathed to her reflection as she finished curling her hair and unplugged the iron. If she didn't feel anything for Davy after tonight, she'd let him down nice and easy. Simple as that.

Or something.

Logan, of course, had spent the afternoon picking out her outfit for her—*Nothing too fancy for a first date, Ellie*— and she went back out to her room to slide on the pretty, turquoise sundress, dotted with hot pink flowers. Perfectly summery. He'd pulled out a pair of pink heels she hadn't worn since college, tossed a light white cardigan onto her bed in case the late August evening turned chilly, and then laid out her jewelry on top of it, a pair of gold and pink teardrop earrings and the gold locket Garth had gotten her for Christmas several years ago.

All in all, she looked… pretty. Meeting her eyes in the mirror, she gave herself a once over, did a little twirl.

And felt like a complete idiot.

Why couldn't she just put on a nice blouse and jeans? Maybe her cowboy boots, to spice the look up. Why was she getting all dressed up for a first date, anyway? Especially for *Davy* . He'd seen her in primarily black for the past… god, since she'd met him. Except for this past weekend.

None of the other shows had proven any better than the first. Kissing Davy wasn't uncomfortable, it wasn't weird, but neither did any of his kisses make her want to kiss him again. She hadn't even bothered with lipstick tonight, just a tinted lip balm. In case he wanted to kiss her again. Maybe better than he had during the shows.

Paul hadn't even kissed her. Davy had yanked him away before he could even grab her properly.

Not like it would have been anywhere near as staggering as John kissing her.

God, not now, Elle inwardly groaned, and swallowed. No reason to think about kissing one man right before going on a date with another.

Her deal with Logan hadn't left her alone for days. She found herself thinking more about that than her date. Worse, she found herself *planning* for it, as though it was an inevitability, which— of course not. She'd probably find herself enjoying her time with Davy so much, she went on a second date. A third.

Or she'd hate it, and get to kiss John again.

With a sigh, she turned off her bedroom light.

She could hear Logan and John chatting downstairs, their voices echoing through the high loft ceiling. The sound of them made her pause, staring up through the skylights at the twinkling stars.

Her own name came up, and her heart sank. Not really a conversation she wanted to walk in on, but Davy would be here to pick her up any minute, so she didn't really have a choice. No time to wait for a subject change.

As the light from the kitchen spilled, gold and warm, over her, she plastered on a smile.

"And, unlike you, Elle hasn't attempted to burn the house down by boiling water, so—" Logan cut off the moment he saw her and gasped. "Oh, Elle! You look so pretty!"

Elle did a little twirl before joining him by his bar stool at the breakfast bar. "You chose my outfit, so really, it's all your fault."

John hadn't looked at her yet, already pulling out the frozen leftovers for himself and Logan. Elle kept the smile on her face by sheer force of will, but—

Look at me. The thought came unbidden to her mind. *Look at me, John.*

"Well, I'm sure you'll have a great time," Logan insisted. He reached out to brush dust off of the hem of her dress, looking her over like a proud mother on Prom night. Elle certainly felt the part, like a timid schoolgirl going out for the very first time. Which was ridiculous. She'd been on dates before. She'd even enjoyed them before. She'd had one night stands, for god's sake. Hell, she managed to date *Gina*, once upon a time.

Then again, look how that had turned out.

"I don't see why I can't just wear jeans," Elle said. "I feel ridiculous, all dressed up—"

"You look great."

Startled, Elle looked at John. His expression was unreadable, but he stared at her with the Tupperware clutched in his hand, looking just past her shoulder. Her heart started to skip beats.

"Uh—" *Very eloquent, Elle.* She put the smile back on, just because— he couldn't know how much that had surprised her. "Thank you. I—"

Whatever idiotic thing she was about to ruin her life by saying never came out, interrupted by a knock at the door. *Thank god.*

Elle turned on her heel, relief sweeping through her at her chance for escape. This wouldn't be so bad, anyway. Davy was perfectly sweet, and a real gentleman. "Wish me luck!" she called over her shoulder.

"Have fun, Doll!" Logan called back.

Please let this work, Elle prayed, and opened the door.

It wasn't working.

Elle had known from the moment Davy had bent down to peck her lightly on the lips, once she'd locked the door behind her. She'd known when he brought her to a perfectly nice, family owned Italian restaurant in downtown Middleton. She'd known when he'd held her hand and asked to walk with her around Main Street, near the college campus that was so familiar to her. She knew now, as they passed Theatre On Main on their way to nowhere.

It was too much like going on a date with her brother, she realized. They could talk, sort of, mostly about the things they had in common. They both loved theater, he had a music degree from the same college she'd gone to— the campus they were on right now, actually. She found out he was in a folk/country band, which was neat, and she told him about how she liked to cosplay and go to conventions. The conversation was stilted and slow.

I'm sorry, she found herself thinking, on their way back to his car. This wasn't fair to him at all. It wasn't fair to either of them.

He had done a decent job of keeping the conversation going all night. One more thing that wasn't fair to him. He did so now, while Elle was struggling to think of something other than how unfair she was being. "So did you make those dresses you wore for *Oklahoma*, or were they a lucky find?"

"Most of them were pieces I'd worn before in other shows," Elle told him. She inched closer to him around the crowd of college kids and bar hoppers, and he didn't seem to mind. "Though the first dress was one my aunt and I made that I ended up donating." Elle chuckled at the memory of her eccentric aunt. "She's really the reason I'm into theater at all." *There,* she told herself, *see?* A nice, easy conversation.

"Does she do theater stuff around here?"

"Nah," Elle said with a shrug. "She lives in New York City with her wife now that they're both retired. We used to volunteer for stuff together when she lived here, though. I guess it's what brought me here."

"That's nice." The conversation tapered off, but they still had a few blocks to go before they reached his car.

I'm so sorry, Elle thought again. Rather than making a fool of herself, she asked, "Does your band play this side of town often?"

"A few of the bars have had us," Davy said. "Mostly Cowgirls." He chuckled and ran his fingers through his golden curls. "Pretty cliche, I know."

"Hey, cliche pays the bills." Elle couldn't even bring herself to look at him. Poor, sweet Davy, who deserved a girl who loved him with all she had. Not this half-assed attempt at feeling something Elle was giving him.

They made it almost to the parking lot before he threw her a curve ball.

"I'm sorry, Elle."

Frowning, Elle glanced up at him. "For what?"

Davy, with his sweet, boyish face, smiled at her. "You're trying mighty hard, Elle, and I appreciate it, but when you think I'm not looking, you look awful sad. A little guilty, too."

Shit. *Shit.* No. Elle scrambled for words, opening and closing her mouth like a fish while her face turned red hot. "That's... it's not—" But she really didn't know what to say, because none of it was really true, anyway. She closed her mouth instead.

Davy took it in stride. "I figured asking you out was kind of a long shot, anyway. I was surprised you said yes."

"You were?" Elle felt her brow furrow. "Why?"

It was Davy's turn to shrug. "I figured you and John would have gotten together by now."

That stopped Elle in her tracks. She dropped his hand as he kept walking. "Why do you say that?"

Davy turned back to face her and shrugged, his hands going into his pockets. "John's had a thing for you for years. I figured he'd have asked you out by now."

"John's had—" *What?* Clearly, Elle was hearing things. "I..." she shook her head. "He... definitely doesn't have a... a *thing*, or whatever. For me." God, how horribly *skewed* that was. "I think he sees me as a kid sister, or something. An extension of Logan. Someone he feels responsible for."

Davy snorted. "Elle, he's been scowling at me all weekend."

Well, Elle was the one scowling, now. "He's barely even been there, why would he— oh, because he knows you've been kissing me?"

Davy's expression was one of pity. "Elle."

"No," Elle said, "no. I— he's just over protective. It's definitely not romantic." Davy still looked doubtful, and Elle sighed. "John's... a really great friend. He has been for years. He's had...*so* many chances to make a move, or... I don't know, ask me out, or whatever." She looked at her feet, studying the silky pink heels, the little bow above the open toe. "He never has, so."

Chancing a glance up at Davy, Elle saw his kind eyes, a soft smile. He gave her a patient nod.

"I'm *so* sorry," she breathed. "You're wonderful, Davy. I really like you." Her lips quirked up in a smile. "You know how to show a girl a good time." With a sigh, she added, "I... really wanted this to work."

"Elle." Davy came forward, laying gentle hands on her shoulders, while her own hands came up to cover her face. "You don't have to rush into anything. You deserve to be happy."

The words, inexplicably, brought a smile to her lips.

Elle wrapped her arms around his waist in a hug. "You do, too, Davy. I'm sorry I can't make you happy right now."

"Don't say that." Davy hugged her right back, his hand coming up to rest on the back of her head, fingers threading through her hair. "Now we can be friends."

Elle laughed, cheek against his chest. "We were already friends, Davy. Even if you do call me *Ma'am* all the time." His chuckle rumbled through her cheek.

"Good," he said. He stepped away and offered her his hand, which she took with a smile.

Maybe this whole John misunderstanding was actually a blessing in disguise, Elle mused. This silence was so much less awkward than before. More companionable, now that she wasn't trying to figure out how to turn him down.

"Thank you," she murmured as they reached his car. "For understanding."

Davy squeezed her hand. "Thank you for giving me a chance." With that, he opened the door for her.

Elle smiled to herself as she buckled up. This really wasn't that bad.

"Just one more question," Davy said, once they were on the road.

"Shoot."

"Would you want him to?" When she gave him a puzzled look, he continued. "You said John has never made a move. Would you want him to?"

It was an innocent enough question. Elle went back to looking at her shoes— god, poor Davy, trying to psychoanalyze his date. What a night. "I..." She had no idea. She literally didn't know. "Um."

"He's an idiot," Davy breathed. Elle whipped her head up, taken aback. "He's an idiot if he doesn't return your feelings. If you get the chance, tell him I said that."

Elle started to laugh. "I never said—"

"You didn't have to."

Elle winced, but laughter still lingered in her throat. "Ouch. Fair, I guess."

Davy chuckled. "Take it from someone on the outside of all of this: you two are a pair of heart-eyed fools."

Yeah, right, Elle thought. Sure. She pressed her lips together for a moment, to keep from snorting. "I'll keep that in mind, I guess?"

"Great," Davy said. "Then I can't wait to see you get John's attention."

"You *what?*"

"I want to see you and him get together." Davy sent her one of his boyish grins, and a dimple appeared in the corner of his lips. "Come on, Elle, don't you want to give it a shot?"

Elle covered her face and groaned. "Logan made me swear that if things didn't work out with you, I'd kiss John. You know, off the stage."

"See?" He paused at a stop sign, almost to her— to *John's* house. "Even Logan knows." With another wry smile, he added, "Maybe we can start a betting pool."

Ridiculous, Elle thought, laughing outright. This sweet man, with his boyish face and his dimples, who had tried to win her over, was backing her up. Even though she didn't return his feelings, he wanted the best for her.

What a sweetheart.

He parked in front of the house, and the moment he did, Elle threw off her seatbelt and leaned across the car to kiss his cheek. "You're good people, Davy."

Davy's laugh— a real, full laugh— eased any lingering guilt from her mind. "So are you, Elle."

God. *God.* What an awful night.

John should have expected this, really. Laying in his bed, staring at the dark ceiling, wishing he could have what he didn't deserve. It wasn't Elle's fault he was completely head over heels for her. It was his own damn mess to deal with.

It also wasn't her fault she was into Davy, and not him.

He'd been so close. *So close.* He should have kissed her when he'd had the chance during *Oklahoma*. He could have wrapped his arms around her lithe, little body, and kissed her the way he wanted to.

What a stupid, idiotic move. She'd smelled like vanilla. She'd fit like a puzzle piece against his chest. She'd been so warm, and solid, and *real*—

Pitiful people often indulged in fantasies, John reminded himself bitterly. That kiss— that glorified peck— he'd given her had been better than kissing Sarah or Bridget by miles. By leagues. By *lightyears* .

And here, he had to go and want *more*, like the pathetic mess he was.

He scrubbed his hands over his face, but all it did was block out the ceiling. Immediately, he saw her starstruck expression from the moment after he'd kissed her, a split second before Davy had initiated the fight sequence. He heard the catch in her breath, from when he'd buried his face in her neck, as though she were in the room with him right now.

"Cut it out," John rasped to himself. His brain played the two scenes over and over and over, like a movie specifically designed to torture him.

Growling with frustration, both from the images in his head and the effect they had on his body, John rolled out of bed and all but stomped to the en suite master bathroom to splash cold water on his face.

It didn't matter. Elle could date whoever she wanted to. She was his roommate, not his girlfriend.

The bitter reminder made him want to throw something.

He thought about Davy, about the sweet Southern charm and easy manners the other man possessed, and scowled. Perfect Davy, calling the women *Ma'am* or tacking *Miss* in front of their names. Holding doors and pulling out chairs, and all that—

Now, that wasn't fair, John told himself. He swallowed, sighed. Davy was a perfectly nice man. Easy to talk to. Fun to work with. Reliable, for the most part, and very committed to his jobs, and the people he worked with.

He also happened to have Elle's attention.

John looked into the mirror, observing his reflection— scrutinizing himself, really. He was big, broad, somewhat bulky. He'd always been tall for his age, and he was still taller than everyone he knew. His hair needed to be trimmed. His nose was too big, his mouth too small.

No wonder she preferred Davy's good looks and easy charm. The man had charisma. John couldn't even look at his own reflection.

Ridiculous.

Maybe he was *too* bitter about this. It wasn't like Elle had ever shown interest in him. Actually, she'd never shown interest in anyone, until Friday. She loved her work, loved her friends, but he'd never heard her talk about being *in* love. She might not have been the white-picket-fence, marriage and family type, which was fair— depressing, but fair— and completely her choice. It was her life. She could do whatever she wanted with it.

Which, judging by the whole Davy situation, didn't involve John kissing her. Unless it was on a stage.

The one thing he didn't get was— why had she stepped toward him after he'd kissed her? Elle knew her blocking. She'd been there for every rehearsal, choreographing the big dances, taking notes for Greg. She practically ran the show when Greg wasn't there. It didn't make sense that she'd put herself literally in harm's way. She'd come out with a bruise from it. Just yesterday he'd seen her show Logan— when she hadn't realized he was there— and the bruise he'd given her was still a mottled cloud of green and yellow on her soft, pale skin.

Just one more torturous image to add to the rest.

As he stepped out of his bathroom, he heard Logan and Elle's footsteps on the stairs outside, accompanied by Elle's hushed laughter. He glanced at the clock— just after eleven. He'd been up here hiding from her, like a coward, for over an hour.

He heard them bid each other goodnight, and then two doors shut.

At least he had her as a roommate. He could hold onto that with everything he had. Maybe he could even become a sort of brother to her, rather than just an extension of Logan. Another shoulder to cry on, an ear to listen to her problems, someone to support her and build her up.

And love her.

With a weary sigh, John crawled back into bed. Having Elle as a roommate wasn't ideal, but it could be enough. It *would* be. Even if it meant staring miserably at the ceiling through the nights.

7

"It's so nice to eat real food and not just breakfast food," Logan said the following Monday morning, pouring himself a cup of OJ. He glanced over his shoulder at John, who gave him an arch look above the pan he was frying eggs in. "No offense."

"You can make your own eggs, if *that's* how you're gonna be," John told him.

Elle watched the exchange from the other side of the breakfast bar, an amused smile on her lips as she ate her bagel. She wondered if they realized how much they acted like an old married couple.

"At least I don't eat mine still *runny*, like a *heathen*," Logan said, jabbing John in the side with his elbow. "Move over, you big galute."

"Make me, beanpole."

Elle snorted, hiding her grin with her coffee cup. Adorable, both of her boys.

"What are you laughing at?" Logan snapped. "*You* eat your eggs runny, too!"

"I'm staying out of this," Elle insisted. Her phone buzzed on the counter beside her plate, but she ignored it.

"Elle eats them sunny side up," John said easily, "which means she's on my side by default. Over-easy eggs are better than scrambled."

"At least you can *cook* eggs."

"Hey!"

"*Little Shop*'s cast list went out last night," Elle told them, interrupting their bickering. "Did you look?"

"You already *know* the cast list, Elle," Logan accused, and Elle grinned.

"I do. Do you?"

"Yeah, and John's still on a villain streak." Logan stirred his eggs until they were unrecognizable in the pan. "Congrats, big guy."

"Can't wait to be cut up and fed to a giant Venus fly trap," John drawled, before sipping his coffee.

"Hey, I never said we were going with the Venus fly trap design," Elle told him. Her phone buzzed again, so she picked it up, expecting some sort of panicked text from Greg about one of the shows. "Though I hope you look forward to looking like the Joker. We're going Neon."

"Oh my god!" Logan spun around with a delighted grin on his face. "I get to have weird hair."

"What, ginger isn't weird enough?"

Logan mimed hitting John with the spatula.

Laughter filled Elle's chest, right up until the moment she read who she'd gotten a text from.

Mom.

The smile dropped from her face.

No. No no *no.* Not her. Not now.

The world around her dimmed, just slightly.

"Elle?"

Her head snapped up, finding twin frowns aimed at her. Startled, she jerked back. "What?"

"I asked if you wanted eggs," Logan said slowly.

"I..." Elle swallowed. Did she want...? "Uh..." She shook her head, because it seemed like the right thing to do, and said, "No, thank you. I..."

This was probably nothing. Her mom texted her little check-ins every once in awhile. They hadn't spoken since before the move, she realized— no, once, when Elle sent her the new address, but they hadn't actually talked *about* the move. The why behind it. The way Gina had kicked her out on short notice.

Her mom would have *loads* to say about that, she was sure. Just *loads.*

The thought alone made Elle begin to shake.

"Do you want more coffee, Elle?" John asked. His voice sounded far away, or maybe softer than usual. Elle wasn't paying enough attention to tell.

"She's already shaking," Logan said flatly. Curse his attention to details. "She doesn't need more caffeine." He slid his mangled egg onto a plate and promptly tossed the frying pan into the sink with a clattering racket.

Elle flinched.

"Elle?" Logan had seen. He had to have. He set his plate on the counter— much more carefully, she noticed— and then sat down beside her. "What happened, Doll?"

"Nothing," Elle muttered, too quickly. "Just… Mom. She texted me."

Logan leaned over to kiss her temple. "Did you read it yet?"

"No." And she didn't want to. But she also didn't want to try to explain to John why a text from her mom would make her shake like a leaf and want to throw up what little breakfast she'd had.

"Do you want me to check it for you?" Logan set down his fork, mouth full, and reached for her phone.

"No!" Elle snatched her hands away from his. "It's probably just one of those bitmoji things. She sends them every now and then when she thinks of me." Actually, that was a fair point, Elle realized. Her mom was prone to weeks of radio silence followed by a day of cheerful, enthusiastic catching up. No reason today should be different.

Swallowing her anxiety, and another bite of bagel, she opened her messages.

The world receded even further around her.

"So?" Logan went right back to eating, but his eyes stayed on her.

Do not panic, Elle told herself. *Do not let this get to you.* "She wants to come visit."

John's back was to them, topping off his own coffee. "We have an extra room she can stay in."

"*Fuck,* no," Logan spat. His expression told Elle exactly how far from on board he was with seeing her mom. "We are *not* keeping Karen under the same roof as Elle. Ever."

Bless Logan. Elle set her phone very carefully onto the counter, face down, and just as carefully slipped her hand into Logan's, pulling it into her lap and cradling it in both of hers. Anything to ground herself from the mild buzzing that had started in her ears.

John turned to scowl at Logan over his shoulder. "Elle's allowed to have guests," he chided. "She lives here."

"It's okay," Elle tried to say, but the words came out airy and quiet. The buzzing in her ears got louder. She didn't want her friends to fight over her.

"No, you don't get it," Logan said to John. "You haven't met Karen."

"She's Elle's *mom*." John set his coffee cup down with a sharp *clink* , and Elle's grip tightened on Logan's hands.

"Yeah, that's my point," Logan spat. "She's a narcissistic, guilt-tripping, manipulative—"

"You can't *say* that in front of— Elle?" John's voice switched from irritated to alarmed in a heartbeat. "What's wrong?"

Elle stared at her coffee cup. Her face was numb. The world around her was blurry. She couldn't tighten her grip to squeeze Logan's hand anymore, both of hers shaking too hard to control.

John hadn't met her mother. Karen hadn't met *him* . The moment they encountered each other— when Karen found out how Gina had kicked Elle out— when John found out what Elle's family was like—

She couldn't breathe.

"Elle?" Logan reached up with the hand she'd previously been holding, heading for her arm. Elle flinched the moment it made contact. Logan, to his credit, snatched his hand away instantly.

"I—" Her throat closed before she could manage more than one word. There weren't any words, anyway, to explain this— the walls closing in around her, the way Logan and John's worried gazes felt like spotlights on her, the knowledge that they'd *hate* her, if Karen came here—

Oh, god. She was gonna throw up.

Elle leapt from her stool and, ignoring her roommates, her phone, and her breakfast, sprinted up the stairs to her bedroom.

What. The *fuck*.

John watched Elle turn green in the face, and then scramble out of the room, his jaw hanging open.

"God *dammit*," Logan said, wiping his face with one hand. *"That's* why we can't have Karen stay here."

"What just happened?" John demanded. He didn't intend for the words to come out so harshly. Truth be told, he was more worried than confused. Not to mention Logan's gatekeeping attitude toward Elle's mom had rubbed him the wrong way.

"Elle's never had a panic attack that wasn't somehow based around Karen or the shitty beliefs Karen's instilled in her." Logan scowled at Elle's phone and picked it up, entering her passcode as though it was second nature.

"I still don't get—"

"You know that feeling you get every time Jackie's at the country club?" At Logan's question, John felt his entire body stiffen. Logan nodded, his point made. "There you go."

John remembered the morning after Elle moved in, and what Logan had said. *She's probably up there having a mild panic attack.* But how could that be in any way related to her mom? Something there didn't add up.

"So…" he hedged, *"that* was a panic attack?"

"A bad one," Logan said. "She's probably gonna be hiding in her bathtub in a nest of blankets when I get up there." He curled his lip as his thumbs went wild on Elle's touchscreen. "I'm telling Karen that Elle's talking to us about it first. But I swear by all that is holy, if that woman sleeps in this house, I will smother her." As he typed up the message, he all but snarled at the screen. *"God,* I hate that woman. Ellie deserved a better family, and what she got was one decent step brother, college tuition from her dad, and an anxiety disorder."

None of this made a damn lick of sense. John gathered Elle's breakfast dishes and started to wash them while Logan finished up the message. "You really have a shitty opinion of Elle's mom."

Logan set Elle's phone down with a scowl and went back to his own breakfast. "When I met Karen, the first thing she said was how amazed she was that Elle could even make friends. We were freshmen in high school."

It was John's turn to scowl. "Elle? She could make friends with a gang of armed robbers. *Everyone* likes Elle." *Especially me.*

He put the dishes in the rack to dry, and then headed for the pantry. If Elle was out of sorts, there was one thing he knew would cheer her up.

"Everyone loved her at school. She basically lived in the auditorium with the other theater kids."

"So much has changed," John drawled, scanning the pantry shelves for—*aha.* A pack of Elle's favorite chocolate, which Logan had hidden a few days after Elle moved in, *for emergencies.* This, John decided, counted.

"Yeah, really," Logan said, his tone more amused than it had been moments earlier. "Garth was there for the first year of high school, and then he went to college. Her dad lives in— somewhere foreign, I think, though you'd have to ask her where, if she even knows. He left the States somewhere in the middle of junior year to find himself, or something. It was just Karen, three divorces in, raising Elle by herself."

It sounded cozy, really, with it just being the two of them. John couldn't really relate to the single-parent life. His parents had been wonderful. He'd never known a moment when they weren't loving and supportive. They didn't really fight, even when they disagreed, and they rarely, if ever, raised their voices. They'd been kind to their children, their extended family, their community.

John also grabbed a packet of hot chocolate before emerging from the pantry. "I still don't get why that's a bad thing, though she sounds kind of condescending."

Logan's expression went sour, his tone icy. "I have heard Karen, in no particular order, lose her temper about—" he began to count off on his fingers as he listed— "Elle asking to buy fruit, Elle asking to go to a friend's birthday party, Elle making herself dessert while Karen was on some fad diet, and Elle not doing dishes."

Something clicked into place in the back of John's mind. He set the chocolate bar by Elle's phone and frowned, turning Logan's words over in his head. "Is that why you always insist on doing the dishes in front of her?"

"Well, I was also raised to clean if someone else cooked," Logan explained. "But also that, yes." He glanced at Elle's phone when it lit up with another notification, and sneered at it. "She liked to yell at Elle in front of people whenever possible. I have no idea how much worse it was when I wasn't around, but she's hinted at some things that..." he trailed off and shook his head. "If I ever see that expression on Elle's face again, I'll gladly go to jail for murder."

Jesus. No strong feelings on Logan's part, obviously. John turned on the stove and started to set up the teakettle and a mug for Elle's hot chocolate. "So keep you away from Karen. Got it."

"No!" Logan cried. "Keep *Elle* away from her! As much as possible!" The urgency in his voice wasn't exactly unusual, but considering the topic, it had John's shoulders tensing. "If we leave Elle with Karen for too long, I can guarantee you a full meltdown on Elle's part, that can and will include her trying to leave."

John whirled around to gape at Logan. "She'd leave?"

Logan laughed, but there was no humor in the sound. "Elle was raised to believe that every bad thing that happened, especially to herself or Karen, was directly her fault. She still believes that, sometimes, right down to her core. And she thinks she *deserves* it."

John opened his mouth, and then closed it. His eyes wandered to the stairs Elle had just run up. "I still don't see how that would make Elle leave."

"Because she'll think she's ruining our lives by living here." Logan shook his head. "We had that argument the day she moved in. She's so afraid of being a burden, she automatically assumed living here was temporary."

She was afraid—*oh*. Maybe that was why she'd been crying that day, when he'd come back from talking to Mrs. Henderson.

"I think we've managed to convince her she's actually *welcome* here," Logan continued, "but Karen can pull that rug out from under her at any moment."

Maybe meeting Karen would help him understand, John mused. He could hardly believe that Elle could have turned out so— so *her*, charming and kind and delightful, after being raised by someone as cruel as Logan had described Karen. Nevertheless, he nodded, turning back around to pour the hot water into Elle's mug, over the chocolate powder. "Distract Karen and keep Elle happy, then," he said. "Got it."

"And don't let Karen stay here."

"Right." John reached back to hand the cup to Logan. "She probably doesn't want to see me right now, but I think she'll need this."

"She probably doesn't want to see me, either," Logan admitted, but took the mug, and put Elle's phone in his pocket before taking the chocolate bar. "Good thinking, though. I'll tell her it was your idea."

John shrugged. "Just keep me posted. I hate to see her upset."

Logan smirked, already on his way to the stairs. "I know you do, big guy."

John listened to Elle's bedroom door open and shut upstairs, and scrubbed his hand over his face. There was nothing he could do, right now, but wait for her to decide she wanted to see him.

He wondered if she'd want to see Davy. Though maybe their— their *thing* was too new. It had only been a week since their date, anyway. Maybe she wouldn't trust *him* with the anxiety yet, either.

None of his damn business, John told himself, and started to load up the dishwasher.

An hour passed before Logan emerged from the second floor, his face drawn in tight lines. John looked over from where he was wiping down the bookshelves in the living room and arched a brow at him as he approached. "I'm going to Tyler's for the night. I'm sure you can keep an eye on Ellie."

"Sure," John said, though he was anything but sure. "She okay?"

"As okay as she can be." Logan's eyes narrowed. "What are you *doing?*"

"Stress cleaning," John answered flatly, and continued to wipe the shelves down. "It'll keep me from checking in on Elle every ten minutes like a nervous mother hen."

"At least you're honest with yourself." Logan patted his shoulder. "She'll probably sleep for most of the day, anyway, so you won't have to worry. Panic attacks really wear her out."

That did nothing to ease John's concern. "Was she in her bathtub nest?"

"Closet," Logan sighed. "The benefit of a walk in. Small, dark, secluded, and has a door. Took me ten minutes to get her out."

God. Poor Elle. John finished up the bottom shelf and straightened up to actually face Logan. "Anything else I should know?"

"Comfort food," Logan said. "If she doesn't come down for dinner, feed her. Make some pasta."

"It's all I can make," John muttered.

"Good, it's what she'll want later. Good idea sending her chocolate, though. It helped."

Like that, relief swept through John. He pictured Elle curled in a ball of blankets with the mug of cocoa, and wished he'd been the one to give it to her. "I'm glad," he told Logan, and started for the laundry room.

"Anyway," Logan sighed, hot on his heels, "I'm off. Text me if you need anything."

"Right," John muttered. "Have fun. Say *hi* to Tyler for me."

"Good luck, big guy."

With the house silent, it took John about ten minutes to get too restless to just sit around. Even the thought of playing video games made him antsy. He ended up stress cleaning the entire house, doing laundry, and— mortifyingly— pressing his ear to Elle's bedroom door every so often, hearing only the muted murmurs of some video she'd turned on. No sounds of her crying, or even speaking.

He wondered if she'd told Davy about her mom. About the panic attack. About anything. He wondered if he'd ever stop feeling the bitterness that filled him up anytime he thought of Davy.

God, he hoped so. Elle deserved to be happy with whoever she wanted. He'd never even bothered asking how her date went— and he wasn't sure he was emotionally ready to find out.

Hours passed, and still Elle didn't emerge from her bedroom. Realistically, John knew she was probably still sleeping, or watching a movie, or reading. Not like she didn't have plenty to entertain herself with. But as dinnertime crept closer, his concern got the better of him.

A soft light flickered from the crack under her door when he reached her room. Again, he heard the muffled voices of movie characters, a soft strain of music he didn't recognize. He tapped lightly on the wood with his knuckles, the sound jarring to his own ears in the quietness of the evening. "Elle?"

No response.

He waited a few seconds, and then knocked a little louder. "Elle?"

Still nothing. Frowning, John carefully opened the door and poked his head inside.

The first thing he noticed was the mountain of pillows and blankets. If he hadn't known better, he wouldn't have thought Elle was even in the room, despite her laptop playing an animated movie on her bookshelf, and her phone laying dormant beside it. But the nest on her bed was moving slightly, clearly breathing, and the long, dark waves of her hair sprawled over one of the pillows. She had to be asleep.

He hated to wake her. But she'd barely eaten all day, and Logan had told him to get her up and feed her if she hadn't come down by now. So, steeling himself against the nerves coiling in his belly, John called her name again.

She hummed in response, barely a sigh of acknowledgement.

"Do you want something to eat?" For a long moment, she didn't respond. No noise, no movement. Just the even rise and fall of the blankets on top of her. John had resigned himself to letting her sleep, and even made to close the door, before she finally shifted.

She sighed, her arm appearing from underneath her blankets to push them away, and then her face came into view. Her eyes were barely open. "Yeah," she mumbled, her voice thick with sleep. "I guess I should eat."

"I'm making pasta," he told her, and saw the glimmer of a smile appear on her face.

"It's all you can cook." She pushed herself to sit up, then frowned and craned her neck around to look out her window. "It's raining?"

"Yeah," John said. "Started about an hour ago."

"Huh." Elle pushed a hand through her hair, shaking out the tangles. "I hadn't noticed." Then she smiled at John, and— god, he'd never get tired of that sleepy, soft smile. The same one she gave him in the morning when he put a mug of coffee into her hands. "Pasta sounds great."

"Sure—" John almost bit off his tongue to stop himself from talking. He'd almost called her *sweetheart*. He swallowed and nodded at her. "Okay. I'll go..." he waved behind himself, before remembering she wasn't looking at him. "Uh... get that started."

Ten minutes later, while the pasta cooked, he heard footsteps on the stairs. He didn't bother pausing *Bioshock*, focusing on the game rather than on her. *Everything's normal,* he thought. No need for Elle to be anxious. Just another normal night of staying in.

"I could have brought food up to you," he started to say, and glanced up to find what might as well have been an animated bundle of pink fabric making its way to the couch.. "Are you... cold?"

Elle hummed, but it didn't sound like a confirmation or a denial. She sat down in the corner of the couch beside him, her pale pink blanket squishing around her, and then curled into a ball.

Okay, then. John focused on his game again. "Want me to turn on one of those horrible horror movies for you?"

"No!" Elle's answer was immediate— a little too sudden. "No, that's— I'm fine. You just... do whatever."

Right. John nodded, but her answer felt a lot like a deflection. Though, hadn't she mentioned watching her brother play video games when they were kids? Maybe she just needed to watch John play, as some kind of comfort.

Man, she really *did* see him as a brother. How depressing.

"So," he said at length, when her silence became unnerving. "You and your brother used to load up on snacks and play games?"

"Yeah." Elle shifted beside him, getting more comfortable in the plush cocoon she'd made for herself. "Sometimes we'd take turns, but usually I'd just watch him play. Co-ops and heavy stuff like this weren't my thing." She inclined her head toward the TV. "Other times he'd watch me play something less intense, like *Spyro* or *Kingdom Hearts* . Or we'd just watch someone else play games on YouTube." The memory brought a smile to her face— and John tried not to lose his focus on the game. "I liked Markiplier's *Five Nights At Freddy's* and Jacksepticeye's *Until Dawn.*"

"You really do like horror."

"I really like ghosts and mysteries," Elle corrected. "I've never been a big fan of torture porn. *Saw, The Purge—* " She made a face, sticking out her tongue in disgust. "That's all too gross for me."

"But you like *Until Dawn?*" John held the controller out to Elle when the pasta timer started to beep. She took it without comment and began to play.

"I loved the atmosphere," she said while he went to the kitchen, "very murder mystery, like *Nancy Drew.* The twist at the end really got me."

"So what's your favorite game?" John checked the pasta, then picked up the whole pot and brought it to the sink to strain it out.

"*Spyro.*" He could barely hear her over the water pouring into the sink, steam billowing up into his face. "I think *Enter the Dragonfly* is the best, but the first one was my very first video game, so I'm pretty fond of that one, too."

"Both great games." John plated the pasta, poured some sauce over it, and grabbed forks. "I'm sure you'll be shocked to know that *Resident Evil* is my favorite series."

"I'm so surprised," Elle said dryly. She grinned up at him as he set food on the coffee table in front of her.

At least she sounded like herself again. She didn't look as tired as she had, even just a few minutes ago. John plucked the controller from her hands and waved it toward her plate. "Eat," he told her. "You can play when you're done."

"Bossy." But she picked up her plate and fork nonetheless.

"Yeah, yeah," he said. This was, honestly, okay. The companionship between them was— okay. Maybe… maybe not how he'd envisioned his friendship with Elle going, but it was… good. Really…

Yeah. Good.

"Thank you for cooking."

John looked over at Elle— pink blanket, plate in her lap, hair messy— and a part of him melted. He chanced a smile at her. "I'm ninety-nine percent sure that won't kill you."

Elle laughed, and like that, the world relaxed.

8

Elle was anything *but* relaxed.

She was miles from relaxed. *Lightyears* from relaxed. In fact, at this point, she was convinced that she'd never been relaxed in her entire life, and that any time she *had* felt relaxed was actually just a convincing hallucination. Or maybe a fever dream.

At any rate, she'd left any vain hope of being relaxed completely in the dust the moment she'd agreed to let her mom come visit. Or rather, the moment she'd resigned herself to the fact that the visit was happening, whether she wanted it to or not. On the bright side, Logan had convinced Karen (while pretending to be Elle) to book a room at one of the family owned hotels on Main for the night. He'd been lucky to find one for her on such short notice, just ten days before Karen came down from Pennsylvania.

Logan, of course, was prepared for Karen's visit, and the wall of blind panic that Elle had turned into. He *should* have been at Tyler's, celebrating Rosh Hashanah, but he'd insisted on staying with her instead— which just added another fun layer of guilt-ridden gratitude over her anxiety. As she watched her mom's car drive up the road, he draped his arm around her shoulders, rubbing her arm. Behind them, John radiated tranquility, in that easy, unaffected manner he had, as though nothing could possibly ruffle his feathers.

Of course, the prospect of John even *meeting* her mother was driving her anxiety to new heights, but that was beside the point. If he didn't want to kick her out after meeting her mom, she'd probably weep with joy.

If she didn't cry before that.

Yikes.

"You ready?" Logan asked her, as though reading her spiraling train of thought. He squeezed her shoulders, which helped ground her, if only for a moment.

"Absolutely not," Elle said, and stamped a smile onto her face. "Too late now."

The ancient, faded white suburban snarled to a stop in the driveway, and a moment later, the driver door opened.

Karen Williams climbed out of the car with a delighted squeal, her blonde beehive solid and unmoving despite the early autumn breeze. For a moment, Elle felt a bone deep contentment, a joy that could only come from seeing the woman who had raised her, who had loved her for over two decades. It filled her heart up, made her wonder why she'd been worried in the first place—

"Elodie!"

Ah. Right. That.

Elle kept the grin on her face by sheer force of will. The pitch of Karen's voice alone grated down Elle's neck, but hearing her full name? The brief glimmer of contentment inside her popped as suddenly as a balloon bursting, replaced immediately with the slight tremor Elle had grown accustomed to in her mother's presence.

Trying desperately not to grind her teeth, Elle opened her arms. As she folded Karen's shorter, frailer body into her embrace, she let out a deep breath. "Momma! I'm glad you made it."

"How are you, Cupcake?" Karen pulled back, all pink lips and square glasses. She looked like maybe the eighties and fifties had come together in an angry fashion battle, and lost on both sides.

Nervous was the word on Elle's tongue, but she managed to stop herself. "I'm good." She touched the chain hanging down from Karen's outrageously large glasses. "I like your beads."

"Oh, this old thing!" Karen tittered loudly. "I found it in the attic!"

I have no doubt, Elle thought. Stepping to the side, she yanked Logan into her mom's path. "Say hi to Logan before he gets jealous."

Karen's squeals went up a full octave as she hung from Logan's neck. Elle took a steadying breath as her ears rang, and chanced a glance at John.

So far, so good. He didn't even look affected. Politely detached, a smile that he probably used at community functions gracing his lips. Not a trace of panic.

Talk about small blessings.

"Look how tall you've gotten!" Karen pulled away from Logan and pushed her glasses back into place with a hot pink nail. "I bet the boys are falling all over you."

"Something like that," Logan said. Over Karen's head, he met Elle's gaze and rolled his eyes.

Sorry, Elle mouthed, grimacing.

Karen finally disentangled herself from Logan. "Oh, and you must be John!"

Elle felt as though she'd been doused in ice water. Her chest tightened dangerously, her brain spiraling into an erratic mantra of *no, no, don't talk to him, he'll hate me, please, you can't—*

Logan's arm came back around her shoulders and squeezed.

Watching the scene unfold was somehow both relieving and horrifying at the same time. John reached out a hand, but Karen was already going in for a hug, a delighted grin on her face. "It's so nice to finally meet you! Ellie's told me plenty about you. All good, I promise!"

"It's nice to meet you, too," John said. His smile as he looked down at Karen was charming, and— to Elle's surprise— sincere.

He doesn't know, Elle reminded herself. He hadn't spent much time with Karen yet. But he would. He'd know soon. He'd find out. And then he'd hate Elle, and realize she wasn't worth the effort of living with, and—

John held the front door for Karen, and with a wink at Elle, followed the older woman in. Elle's chest tightened even more.

"Oh, what a lovely home you have!" Karen's voice bounced off the walls and shattered in the space, filling it in a way that had Elle tensing and speed walking after her mother. Karen had already made it to the living room, looking around at all the cleverly arranged, subtly nerdy decorations, and the wall of books, with blatant approval.

A small sliver of relief inched its way into Elle's chest. Maybe this actually wouldn't be so—

"It's so nice of you to let Ellie stay here while she finds her own place," Karen continued merrily.

Nevermind. "Mom," Elle said weakly, closing her eyes. She felt rather than heard Logan behind her, but stepped out of his reach when she felt his hand on the small of her back. She couldn't bear to be touched. Not now; not while she was trying to conduct damage control.

John's frown was so innocently puzzled, Elle had to wonder whether he was genuinely confused by her mother's statement. "This *is* Elle's place," he said, a touch firmly—*ah.* It was an act. He knew damn well what he was doing.

Just wait, Elle thought miserably. *You'll change your tune in about two hours. If that.*

Karen just waved a dismissive, clawed hand at John, and made herself comfortable on the sofa, in the opposite corner to where Elle usually sat. "I know what Ellie wants."

Christ. Now she *wanted* Logan's safe, grounding touch, but it would be too obvious that she was losing the battle with her anxiety. Instead, she dropped down beside her mother in the center of the couch, pulled up her legs to sit cross legged, and resigned herself to a day of torture.

As Logan sat down beside her, Elle caught a glimpse of John as his expression hardened.

Here we go, she realized, her heart sinking.

"I'm glad she finally found more friends as weird as she is," Karen continued, reaching up to touch Elle's hair. "Logan was always a bit of a geek." She cackled at the memory. "You two were always traipsing off with your theater group to do one thing or another."

"Elle has so much talent," Logan said, adjusting so that Elle was tucked safely into his side, his arm going around her in an affectionate— and blatantly protective— manner. "More often than not, Mickey and Marge were always sticking her places. Costumes, lights, even on stage."

Elle smiled, thinking of the drama and music teachers fondly. She hadn't realized how much her school days would end up being her whole adult life, but she wouldn't change anything about it. The theater had always been her safe haven.

"If you'd actually tried, you'd have gotten leads," Karen sniffed.

Frowning, Elle said, "I *did*, Momma. I was Belle in *Beauty and the Beast* my junior year, I was Laurey senior year, *and* I did all of my college shows." Elle gripped her hands in her lap until they hurt. She would *not* chew her nails. She'd gotten over that habit years ago. "That's how I got my job, anyway. Greg saw me do *Matchmaker* in the revue freshman year of college and offered me a role in *Fiddler* the same day."

"He *begged* you to join the cast," Logan corrected.

"And now you're just another techie," Karen sighed. The obvious disappointment in her voice brought a familiar heaviness to Elle's body. She sank further into Logan's arms.

"Elle's the best we've got," John said, settling into the leather recliner. "Everyone thinks so. She even managed to get a boyfriend out of working for the theater."

"What?" Elle frowned. "I don't—" Oh, god. She hadn't told John how the date with Davy had gone. Clearly, neither had Logan.

She didn't get to finish her sentence before Karen, who apparently hadn't registered what he'd said, cut in. "Ellie could be on Broadway, if she really wanted to."

"I don't," Elle repeated. She couldn't feel her face anymore.

"How's the salon, Karen?" Logan seized the brief sliver of silence and redirected the conversation. Elle's shoulders relaxed marginally as Karen launched into a rant about something other than Elle's failures as a person. She could get through this day, and tomorrow, in one piece, if they could just keep Karen distracted. Though listening to her shrill voice in her friends' home was *agony*.

"...And now Mrs. Dawson looks like a bright blue poodle," Karen finished, and then grinned pointedly at Elle. "I'm amazed you two handle Ellie so well!"

God, *god*, could the woman find *anything* else to talk about?

"How so?" There was a faint edge to John's voice that grabbed Elle's attention. Their eyes met briefly, and then Elle snapped her gaze away. She couldn't bring herself to look at him again.

"Oh, just a few of her habits." With a giggle, she swatted at Elle's thigh. "Is the sink empty, Ellie?"

Something akin to a laugh escaped Elle's lips. She began to fantasize about taking shots. Preferably of Jameson, or something else strong and smooth that she wouldn't be able to taste. Many, many shots. So many she wouldn't remember today happening. This entire *week*, if she was lucky.

Logan was saying something, Elle realized, a little guiltily. She stared at the coffee table, eyes roaming over the smoky swirls in the dark wood, and forced herself to at least *listen* to her best friend.

"We almost fought over it, I was so determined," Logan was saying. His hand rubbed over her arm, slowly up and slowly back down. "John and I are firm believers that whoever cooks shouldn't be the one to clean up, and you know what a great cook Elle is."

It was true, except she wouldn't call it a fight. Logan made absolutely sure that Elle never touched a dish unless she was eating alone. The one time she'd bothered protesting, he'd simply said: *You don't have to do everything by yourself, Doll. Let us take care of you.*

"It's for the best," John agreed, pulling Elle's attention back. "I burn water."

"Oh, Ellie and I used to fight about chores all the time!" Karen's tone was— of all things— cheerful, a little nostalgic. As though the memory was warm and fuzzy to her.

Elle's stomach turned over. "Yeah," she managed, smiling vacantly straight ahead. "Good times."

"She learned to cook from her grandmother, you know," Karen continued. Elle shut her eyes with relief. She'd rather think about her family than her childhood. "Oh, that reminds me! Ellie, I brought down Nana's chest."

Elle's heart leapt. "You did?" Her great-grandmother's chest, filled with her twice-great-grandmother's knitted and crocheted blankets, tablecloths with needlepoint embroidery, baby blankets from the past four generations, including Elle's—

"I brought *lots* of stuff," Karen continued, already unfolding herself from the couch. "It's in my car. Come help me carry it in."

"How much is *lots?*" Panic had Elle on her feet before she registered choosing to stand.

"Oh, a few boxes," Karen said. "Some knickknacks, some pictures, books of yours…"

"I'll help," Logan volunteered, already snagging Karen's arm, wedging himself between her and Elle. "Karen, did you frost your hair? It looks stunning!"

"Oh, you noticed!" Karen patted her beehive as Logan walked her out of the room. Elle watched them go, her feet rooted to the spot. Half of her begged for her to stay inside, to get herself together, to take a damn break and *breathe*. The other half was screaming at her to go save Logan, to distract Karen from the boys for the rest of the visit. And a tiny, quiet part of her brain that she hadn't heard from in years told her to get into her car and just drive to nowhere. None of the options were winning, since all she was doing was winding herself up into a panic attack—

A hand landed on her shoulder, jolting Elle back to the present. The shift was almost painful in it's suddenness, one moment drowning, the next hyper-aware of her own body and her surroundings. She tensed and flinched away, throat closing.

John put himself firmly in between Elle and the door, completely blocking her view of Logan and her mom leaving the house.

"*Hey*," he said, insistently. She wondered how many times he'd already said it. "Do you want to sit back down? You look pretty pale."

God, yes. Please. Elle sucked in a breath, mortified to find that she was shaking even harder than before. "No, thanks."

"I can help them—"

"I'm fine," Elle insisted. She even managed to smile in a way that didn't feel entirely fake or manic. "I do need to go rescue Logan, though, before he decides to off himself to get away from Mom."

"Logan's fine." John's no-nonsense tone had Elle's shoulders tensing even further. "She's easier to handle than a puppy, and we both know he's had one of those. It's you I'm worried about." His eyes did a quick once-over on her, and Elle— she'd never felt so exposed in her entire *life*. "If you need a break, take it. We can handle her."

"She's *my* mom," Elle snapped, and then regretted it instantly. Pressing her lips together, she inhaled deeply, shutting her eyes against the vague shock on John's face. "Sorry. She can just be... a lot. Sometimes." She looked down at her feet, because looking at John was infinitely harder than she'd like it to be. "I wouldn't want to stick the two of you with her."

"You don't have to handle her by yourself," John insisted.

Yes, I do, Elle thought bitterly. "It's fine," she said.

"Right," John said flatly. "Obviously."

"What?" Elle's head snapped up. "What's that supposed to mean?"

John's expression was grim. "You can pretend you're fine all you want, Elle, but at the very least, don't *lie* about it. Not to me."

Elle gaped at him. How dare he— of all the— he was— he was—

He was *right*. The words hung in the air between them, like stage lights casting onto Elle, showing her who she truly was.

Ungrateful, her brain scolded her. *After all he's done for you. You're a liar and a failure.*

"I..." Elle started to say, but Karen's voice rang through the entryway, startling her.

"Elodie, are you coming to get your stuff, or are you going to make Logan do all the work for you?"

Nausea swept through Elle, eliminating anything else she might have felt. "Coming," she called, closing her eyes.

John's arms around her made her open them again. Startled, she just stood there, letting him hug her, unsure as to whether she should—*could* — hug him back.

"I meant what I said," he told her, his hand in her hair. "You don't have to do this alone."

Tears prickled at Elle's eyes. When John let her go, she swallowed, willing them back. "I've done this all my life," she admitted. Then, making her way past him, she said, "I can handle it."

Handling it probably wasn't how John would describe Elle, standing amidst the boxes the three of them had hauled up to her room, her face drawn and tight. He'd seen her wrangle children and rewire an entire light-up set with less stress than this. He'd also seen her ream Greg over an unsafe flight rig, *publicly*, and watched the man silently take it, despite being at least twice her age and significantly larger than her. Yet, facing off with her mother—

Yeah, no. Not handling it. Not at all.

"You're lucky you have friends who like you so much," Karen griped, sitting on the bed and checking her nails. The sneer hadn't left her face since she sat down (which had been almost immediately after she'd first entered the room), shifting between condescending and openly disdainful.

John looked away from his task of hanging Elle's fairy lights across the curtain rod over her window, catching her resigned expression in her mirror before it shifted back to a carefully neutral mask. "I really am," she agreed. She'd been "arranging" the candles and pictures on her vanity for nearly ten minutes.

Logan finished putting books on her bookshelf and broke down the empty box. "This is lots of fun," he said, his cheerful tone sharp.

"Higher on the right, John," Karen instructed. John saw the lightning fast flash of irritation on Elle's face just as he went back to fixing the lights. "At least this is better than when you lived with Gina."

"Hooray for not living out of boxes anymore."

Elle sounded exhausted. John's hands tightened on the string of lights.

"What time do you need to be at the theater?" Karen asked, her mood finally shifting back to the grating cheeriness that John was starting to recognize as fleeting, at best. "We should get dinner!"

Elle looked into the mirror just as John looked over at her. Their eyes met for barely a heartbeat before hers flicked back down.

"Elle and I usually get there at five," he said. "She's got to set the stage up, and I need to know where I'm filling in."

"But you need to eat." Fleeting, indeed; Karen was back to disapproval like flipping a light switch. John tried not to roll his eyes as he came down off the step stool and closed it up.

"Well, *Ben* sure as hell isn't going to run checks," Logan snapped, gathering up the flattened boxes. "The one weekend Elle stepped in as Laurey, he waited until the last possible second to do anything."

"Actually that was Jimberly," Elle corrected.

"Oh, I *loved* watching that," Karen said. "I'm so glad you filmed it for me, Logan."

"Actually," Elle said again, the faintest little wry smile appearing on her lips, "*that* was Ben."

"I really wish you'd get a job at a real theater," Karen began, promising a long winded sermon about Elle's vocation. John opened his mouth to deter her, but Logan beat him to it.

"Anyway, *I* don't have to be at the theater until five thirty, so if we leave now, we'll have just enough time to swing by Panera and get some sandwiches." He tucked the boxes underneath his arm and offered the free one to Karen. "Why don't you and I go have ourselves a date?"

Karen stood, but John lingered, keeping one eye on Elle. She was still staring down at the candles as though they were pieces in a puzzle she couldn't sort out.

"I wanted your opinion, anyway," Logan continued. "After *Oklahoma*, I want to dye my hair the most outrageous color possible for *Little Shop*."

"Oh, Sweetie, of course!" Karen cooed, allowing Logan to usher her out of Elle's room.

John hung back, watching Elle's mask fall away to reveal her exasperation. She sighed heavily before she turned around, and then startled at the sight of John. "Oh!" She put a hand on her heart. "I thought..." She swallowed, steadying herself against the vanity. "I thought you'd gone downstairs."

Clearly. "Wanted to be sure you're alright."

Elle nodded, but her eyes were weary. "I'm... handling it."

No, John wanted to say, *you're not.* Instead, he nodded.

At Karen's sudden and enthusiastically raised voice, Elle heaved another sigh, this time with thinly veiled irritation, and then practically sprinted down the stairs. John didn't need to sprint to keep up, glad for once that his legs were so freakishly long. Logan was in the midst of describing a bizarre combination of turquoise and purple dye to Karen, the pair standing in the entryway, clearly waiting to say their goodbyes. John kept his eye on Elle's back— her shoulders were so tightly drawn she could probably hold a pencil between them.

"Hey, Momma," she said, the second Logan paused for air, "could you touch up my hair, too?" She smiled as John came around to join them— a *genuine* smile, for the first time all day— and continued, "You're so much better at roots, and I keep having to redo the entire thing from a box and getting mixed results—"

"Absolutely not," Karen snapped.

It was as though every cell in Elle's body had been put on pause.

Logan gaped openly. Even John had to grit his teeth to keep his jaw from dropping.

"I hate that color on you," Karen steamrolled on. "I wish you'd just leave your hair its natural color. You had such *pretty* hair."

Elle's face fell.

Now John understood why Logan would willingly go to prison over this woman. Intentional or not, she'd ruined the only real joy Elle had shown all day. That alone put John on a dangerous edge.

With a careful smile in place, John dropped a hand onto Elle's shoulder. She flinched at his touch. "I think it suits her," he said, squeezing his hand lightly. "It brings out her eyes." With that, he passed Elle, reaching out to clap Logan on the back. "You two go have some fun, now. Elle and I need to get going in a little bit."

The hostility melted off of Karen's face, and to John's complete shock, she *laughed*. As though this was all a big joke to her. "I'm sure you do, early birds." Her smile was downright sickening. Giving him a cheerful little wave, she turned on her heel.

John met Logan's eyes, and read the same mixture of shocked confusion and annoyance he felt mirrored in them. When John made to step forward, to follow them out and close the door behind them, he felt a light tug on the back of his shirt. It rooted him to the spot.

"Break a leg tonight," Karen sang. "I can't wait to see the show!"

Logan shot Elle a concerned glance as he followed her mother out the door, shutting it firmly behind him.

And then they were alone.

John felt Elle's hand drop away from his shirt. Slowly, so as not to startle her, he turned around to face her. She stared at the floor, her face red. By some miracle, despite the fact that she was shaking like a leaf in a hurricane, she was holding it together.

At a loss, he swallowed. "What do you need, Elle?"

It was, apparently, the wrong thing to say. Whatever tether had been holding her temper back snapped, and she scowled up at him, her eyes wet. "I *don't* need you jumping in to rescue me every time my mom's being a bitch."

Yes, John thought with clenched teeth, *you do.*

Elle stormed around him, over to the coat closet, and pulled out a long knit cardigan, yanking it on over her black tech shirt. "I am *perfectly* capable of handling her," she snapped, her voice pitched in just a way that it was almost hysterical. If she hadn't been dangerously close to crying before, she certainly was now. He said nothing as she pushed past him and into the kitchen. She pulled two tubs of leftovers from the fridge, and then pulled two paper bags from under the sink. "I don't need a— a *hero* , swooping in to save the day," she said, the words broken by a sharp gasp, her voice too tight. "I need a goddamn *backbone.*" She produced a sharpie from a drawer, writing her name on one bag, his on the other. Still scowling, she stormed past him again, muttering under her breath. "*Men,* and their inflated *hero complexes.* I can't even—"

He didn't mean to respond, but the words fell out of his mouth anyway. "At least I don't wear tights."

Elle froze at the door, one hand on the knob. Completely silent.

Shit. He hadn't meant to upset her. Honestly, his humor was so poorly timed, even *he* hated himself for it.

John pressed a hand against his eyes, trying to figure out what he could say— if anything— that wouldn't just dig him into a deeper hole.

Elle huffed.

Then she giggled.

And then, her musical laughter, albeit a little wet, filled the hallway.

John lowered his hand, only to find Elle right in front of him, wrapping her arms around his waist. His hands came up of their own accord, just like that awkward, uncomfortable hug he'd given her earlier today, one hand threaded through her soft hair.

"I'm sorry I snapped at you," she murmured.

"I'm not," he said, before he could stop himself. "You're right about the hero complex. Side effects of having a kid sister, I guess." Elle chuckled. It was a welcome change from her tears, honestly. "I'll try to keep the swooping to a minimum."

Elle tilted her head up to smirk at him. "No, you won't," she teased, and turned back to the door.

"No," John agreed, a strange pressure in his chest. "I probably won't."

"So, what was John saying about you having a boyfriend?"

Perhaps post-show ice cream had been a bad idea. So far, all Karen had done was gush about Davy and John's performances, tell Elle that she was a better Laurey than Sarah, and casually remind Elle that she could do better than the Theatre On Main. Elle could do without the backhanded compliments, but she supposed Karen's unshakable faith in Elle's performing skills was a comfort. In a way.

Elle shrugged, swirling a fry in ranch dressing. "I don't actually have a boyfriend. I went on *one* date with Davy, and it felt like having dinner with Garth. We decided to keep it platonic."

"Aw." Karen's sympathy was, of course, short lived. "John's single, isn't he?"

Here we go. "I guess," Elle said with another shrug. "I haven't asked, but he hasn't mentioned seeing anyone recently." She bit into her fry, pretending not to know where this conversation was headed. "Why do you ask?"

Karen gave her a pointed look over her bowl of mostly melted chocolate ice cream. "Don't you know these things? You live with him."

"His personal life isn't my business." Elle dipped the rest of her fry in the ranch. "He'll tell us if he starts seeing someone, I'm sure. Or Logan will announce it loudly enough for you to hear up in PA." She popped the fry into her mouth. "Until that happens, I don't particularly care." Not entirely true— especially with her deal with Logan hanging over her head. She wasn't sure if it would be a relief or a disappointment, if John found someone else to date before she could kiss him again. She honestly didn't want to think about it.

"Oh, but *Ellie,*" Karen simpered. "He's just your type. He's talented, and gorgeous, and *straight.*" She slurped up a spoonful of ice cream and wiggled excitedly in her seat. "Why haven't you made a move?"

"Mom," Elle sighed, faintly amused. "When have I *ever* made the first move?"

"True enough." Karen swirled her spoon around the ice cream soup again. "Though I know when you met Logan, you went on that free-spirited sexual awakening binge. You were all about being bisexual, or whatever, in high school."

Elle almost bit off her tongue. She wasn't even going to *start* on that one.

Speak of the Devil, Elle thought, as her phone buzzed. She read Logan's message—*Staying at Tyler's, you okay?* — and smiled as she typed a quick response.

We're fine. Have fun. Happy Rosh Hashanah. Love you!

"Deep down, though, you're straight," Karen continued cheerfully. Elle tried not to roll her eyes. "Maybe John's the right man for you!"

"John's a great person," Elle said, pushing away her fries, "but he's my roommate. I really don't want to compromise that by flirting with him— or worse, sleeping with him."

Karen hummed, the sound somehow condemning. "Well, what, are you going to date a girl instead? Decide you're gay?"

"I literally dated a girl in college," Elle reminded her.

"And look how poorly that went," Karen snapped. "Just how *did* you end up moving in with Gina after you two broke up?"

"The other apartment was infested with roaches." They'd moved in together in the middle of two different crises, Gina to get away from her horrible, animal hoarding roommates, and Elle to get away from the *bugs*. "It worked for three years. I'd say those are pretty good odds, all things considered."

"I thought you were going to keep the apartment." Karen slid her bowl of mush to the side. "What changed?"

It was bound to happen. Elle felt her eyes unfocus above her mom's head. All she'd wanted was one meal— a short slice of time, just the two of them. Things were usually so relaxed when Karen wasn't putting on a show for someone, pretending to be a stern parent and a doting mom all at the same time, and invariably coming up short on both fronts. Still, this was her *mom*. That had to count for something. Didn't it?

"Gina changed her mind," Elle said carefully. "With her job streak and family issues—" *Pot, kettle*— "she had too much trouble finding her own place, so she asked me to leave instead."

"She kicked you out?"

Shit. Yes, but—"No, not exactly—"

But Karen had heard all she needed to hear. "This is what I'm *talking* about, Ellie!" Her voice hit *the pitch* , the one she got when she was getting angry at Elle's stupidity. "You need to learn to take care of things yourself, instead of waiting around for other people to do it for you. What are you going to do if you get married?" She threw up her hands in exasperation. "Who would want to marry a slob who can't even clean up after herself?"

Elle opened her mouth to speak, and nothing came out. Because really— her mom was *right*.

"This is why you need to find your own place," Karen continued, either oblivious to Elle's attempt at speaking or ignoring it. "Maybe once you've learned how to live by yourself, you'll be able to keep a boyfriend for longer than a few months."

"I'm looking for a place," Elle stammered. It wasn't true— yet. But it would be, as of— as of tonight. As soon as she got home. The very second she walked in the door.

"Good," Karen said, nodding her head with smug pleasure. "You let me know if you want help looking. I'll come down to help you move, and bring the rest of your furniture from home."

Elle nodded, resignation sinking into her chest. "Okay, Momma."

"Welcome home," John said when he heard the front door open. "How was ice cream?"

Silence.

John paused *Resident Evil 3*, frowning. "Elle?" When she still didn't respond, he figured he must have heard something in the game. Though he could have sworn he heard the door.

It was just as well, he decided, hitting *resume*. He'd been so worried about Elle spending an extended chunk of time with Karen that he couldn't settle. He'd stress-vacuumed most of the upstairs before convincing himself to just wait for her to come home and check in with her when she got there. The diner was closed at this point, but as Karen had insisted on driving Elle to the diner and back home, he wouldn't put it past them to stay up for the rest of the night chatting. Or at least, for Karen to talk Elle's ear off, and for Elle to come home and immediately crash.

Maybe that's what he'd heard. Maybe Elle had gone right upstairs—

Movement by the stairs caught his eye, and he looked up— and froze, sending Jill Valentine headfirst into Nemesis, killing her instantly.

Elle looked like she'd just witnessed a death. Possibly her own, judging from how grey she looked. He'd never seen her so tired, even during tech weeks for any of the shows he'd worked with her. Dark circles had taken residence under her eyes, making her look vaguely like a Tim Burton character come to life.

She clearly hadn't seen him yet. After their *impasse* earlier, he wasn't sure whether to go to her— maybe hold her long enough to put her back together— or let her go do whatever she needed to do to recover from what was obviously a traumatic event.

God, had something happened, he wondered? Other than Karen's usual bullshit— which, he realized now, was probably the root of so many things Elle did that he'd taken for granted— had someone been hurt? Had *Elle?*

She looked like she was, physically, in one piece, as she slowly made her way to the couch. It didn't help John feel any less alarmed, but it was a start.

"Elle?" John said, when she came to stand in front of the couch. "What's—"

He might have finished his question, except that Elle stunned him right out of words by planting herself directly into his lap.

"Whoa—" John grabbed her, wrapping his arms around her as she curled in on herself. Her arms went around his neck, and then she pressed her face into his shoulder. She was trembling, like she had been all day, but somehow worse. "Hey. It's okay. I've got you."

Elle said nothing, but her arms tightened marginally around his neck. Carefully, so as not to dislodge her, John reached back to grab the blanket from the back of the couch, and managed to wrap it around her.

She seemed like she had no intention of going anywhere, just sitting there, unmoving, in his lap. "You're okay," he murmured, arranging his arms to hold the controller around her back so that he could still play while she went through whatever she needed to go through. "It's okay, Sweetheart."

For several minutes, Elle did nothing but cling to him and shiver. John bit back all of his questions— what had Karen said to make Elle, who hours ago had insisted she didn't need a hero, sit in his lap like a cat and not even budge? Any ideas he got were unsettling at best.

It took him... honestly, an embarrassing amount of time, to realize that Elle had started to cry against him. Which is what really did him in.

John stopped his game and chucked the controller to the other side of the couch. His hands were much better suited to holding Elle, feeling her shake as she silently wept. He could feel his shoulder growing wet from her tears. A strange, primal part of his mind wanted to make sure she never saw Karen again, which was *ridiculous*— he wasn't going to keep her away from her mom, if she wanted to see the woman. But hell if he wasn't going to do just as much heroic swooping as he'd done today, if not more, from here on out.

"Do you want to talk about it?" he murmured, when Elle's hushed sobs seemed to taper off. Elle shook her head against the front of his shoulder. "But it was your mom, right?" A slight hesitation, and then a nod. "Something she said?" Another nod. John nodded, too. "Okay." And, even though he was probably pushing all kinds of boundaries, he pressed a kiss to the top of Elle's head.

He wondered if maybe she wanted to talk to Davy. Were they close enough for that? Though as much as John wanted to make her happy, he couldn't bring himself to make the offer. Maybe that made him selfish, but in the end, he didn't really care.

Several more minutes passed before Elle drew a deep breath and sat up slightly. Her breathing was still shaky, but she seemed calmer, overall. Rather than meeting John's eyes, she looked at the spot on his shirt she'd just been crying into. "Sorry about your shirt."

"I'm not worried about that," he said. The way she'd sat up, his hands were around her waist, holding her in place in his lap. "I'm more worried about whatever Karen said that set you off so badly." Elle tensed, but he continued. "You don't have to tell me, but I want to make sure I never say anything like it, even by accident."

"You won't," Elle said instantly, *insistently*, shaking her head. "I don't think you could."

"Fair enough." Though he had a feeling that, whatever it was, it ran deeper than just tonight's conversation, whatever it had been, between the mother and daughter. "Was it more of the bullshit she was spouting earlier today?"

A smile flirted with Elle's lips at his word choice, but faded before it could take hold. She nodded.

"Good thing it's all garbage," John said. The smile almost came back. He slid his arms back, grabbing her waist more firmly. "I mean it,

Elle. It's nonsense. She made it sound like having you here is some sort of burden—" Elle winced—"but it's not."

Apparently, he'd hit the nail on the head. Elle grimaced and turned her head, avoiding his eyes entirely. "She thinks I should move out."

"What?" John scowled. He didn't even notice his grip on Elle's waist tightening. "Why?" Elle clammed up, her mouth clamped shut. "Because you live with two men?"

She shook her head. "I don't think that bothers her, really."

"So, what, then?" She didn't respond. John forced himself to relax back into the sofa, to loosen the grip of his hands, but it took effort. "Do you... want to leave?"

Elle was silent for *way* too long for comfort. "I don't know."

Right. Maybe she wanted to move in with Davy and get away from John being clingy and heroic. Or maybe she felt compelled to leave, since her mom had filled her head with crap about how hard she was to live with. Over stupid shit, too—*chores.* Who the fuck cared about *chores?* Sure, they had to be done, but in the end, that was a tiny thread in a huge tapestry. Life was so much more than that. *Elle* was so much more than that.

"Well," John said at length. His fingers flexed, fidgeting with her tee shirt. "Whatever you decide... Logan and I will support your decision." It killed him to say it, but it was true. "But Elle?"

Finally, *finally,* she looked him in the eye. "Hmm?"

God, he hated the thought of her leaving. She'd only been there for a little over a month, and yet, he could hardly bear the thought of living here without her.

John swallowed. "Just... know that we love having you here." Then, because he sounded dangerously close to saying more than he should, he added, "And not just because you can cook."

Elle huffed a laugh. "Are you and Logan ever going to let that go?"

John grinned up at her. "Absolutely not."

At last, Elle grinned back at him. It was weak, but it was there. She leaned over, half off of John's lap, and he figured she would go to her corner, but once again, she surprised him.

"Here," she said, settling more squarely into his lap and putting the controller in his hand. "Kill some zombies, so that I can pretend they're my mom and inevitably feel guilty about it."

John laughed. "Catharsis it is."

9

Logan's deft, skinny fingers tightened the braid down the back of Elle's head. "You should have texted me," he insisted, adding in another section.

"And interrupt your holiday with Tyler?" Elle watched the performers begin to gather on stage for warm ups, while Logan did her hair in the tech booth. She tried not to let her eyes linger for too long on John, and failed miserably.

"Tyler adores you," Logan said. "He'd have come over, just to make sure you were okay."

"John handled it fine, actually." And handle it, he really had. Last night had been something else entirely. She still had no idea what had possessed her to drape herself across John like a melodramatic Shakespearian heroine and lose it completely. Nor did she have a clue why he'd been so accommodating of her emotional distress. He hadn't complained about her crying into his shirt, or taking up residence in his lap, even when she fell asleep there, watching him play *Resident Evil* until almost two in the morning. He'd been completely nonplussed when he'd shaken her awake, softly telling her it was time to go to bed. It was all pretty weird, to be honest.

Weirder still was her reaction to it. They'd gone to breakfast with her mom as a send off, and Elle had purposefully planted herself across from Karen, tucked into the inner part of the booth with John at her side. Whenever Karen had gotten back on her bullshit— as John was now referring to it— he'd put a hand on her knee, just for long enough to ground her, as he steered the conversation toward safe topics. Elle had depended on that contact— and, by the end of breakfast, actively sought it out. It made her wonder if maybe he had a point about her mom filling her head with crap.

Someday, she'd go get therapy for all of this. She really would.

"I bet he did," Logan muttered, yanking her hair to keep her from turning her head. She hadn't realized she'd been watching John so intensely. "Did he tell you that you're not allowed to leave, no matter how much Karen wants you to?"

"He said the two of you would support me either way, but that you loved having me around." Elle watched Sarah, with her Barbie-blonde hair in a messy bun, as she sidled up to John with a coy smile. He ignored her.

"He's absolutely right," Logan said, tying off her braid. "But I'm not letting you move out over Karen being a bitch."

Elle sighed. "I thought about leaving."

Logan's arms came around her shoulders, his chin settling on her shoulder. "I know you did."

"Remember Kacey, from Middleton U?" Logan nodded. "She still lives in the area. We used to get lunch every week or so, before our jobs got in the way, and then it became whenever we had time."

"Right."

"Well, turns out she and her girlfriend— sorry, *fiancée*— are moving in together. Which I found out when I asked when her lease was up."

"That escalated quickly," Logan noted. "I didn't even know she was dating anyone."

"Yeah, but Heather's an actual *delight*." Elle touched her hair, checking for strays and finding none. "She looks like Luna Lovegood, too."

"Isn't Kacey the four-ten goth girl with every kind of piercing imaginable?"

"And green and black hair, yeah. They're quite the couple." Elle watched Sarah say something to John, who smiled politely, and then promptly turned his back to her. "How long has Sarah been on John like that?"

"What? Oh." Logan wrinkled his nose. "Since the beginning of this show, why?"

Elle frowned. She hadn't noticed that at all. Then again, she hadn't really been looking for it. "No reason." Sarah scowled at John's back, clearly dejected.

"Right," Logan said flatly. "Well, I'm going up for warm ups. And Elle?"

Elle looked at him as he leaned in the door, arching one ginger brow over his piercing blue eyes. "Hmm?"

"I'm glad you're not moving in with Kacey."

Elle smiled, because she couldn't help it. "Yeah. Me, too."

Behind her, Ben nudged her stool with the toe of one steel-toed boot. "You good, champ?"

Elle shrugged. "You know, one existential crisis after another. The usual."

"I can't see you moving anytime soon," Ben said, propping his feet on the table in front of them, his chair tilted dangerously back. "You haven't been so happy since you were in college."

"Really?" Elle hadn't thought about it, really, but Ben had a point. She *was* happy living with John and Logan. Despite her mom's visit, living with them was better than any place she'd lived before. Maybe it was for the better that she hadn't been able to room with Kacey.

"Yeah."

Elle wanted to respond, but Davy caught her eye, standing just beside John. She stalled, watching the two with a slight frown. Had John always been so tense around Davy?

Ben nudged her with his foot. "What's got you staring at your roommate like you don't know him?"

"Nothing."

"The holes you're staring into his head are proof of that."

Elle smirked and shook her head, forcing herself not to look at John or Davy, or to over-analyze. "You are entirely too observant for your own good, Ben."

Ben smirked right back. "That's part of my charm."

She didn't have much chance to explain herself, though, since Anthony started warm ups— on his banjo, no less— and she had to focus on balancing the stage mics. Ten minutes later, after the usual pep talk and announcements from Jesse, everyone scattered, save for those who had mics on. Elle ran through her sound check with practiced efficiency, watching the leads scamper away to finish with their costumes and makeup. Everyone except John, who strolled out to the tech booth, weaving through the servers double checking their tables. He leaned patiently against the door frame as Elle finished up, his plaid shirt over one arm.

"What's up?" she asked, switching off the handheld she'd been using to call names.

"You've got an emergency sewing kit in here, don't you?" He asked, stepping further into the booth. The tiny room suddenly felt full to bursting, no room for either of them to go that wouldn't end in them touching. Not that she'd mind, though; he had on that cutoff, deeply v-necked tee that showed off miles and miles of his smooth skin, his broad shoulders, his strong arms—

Oh, no. No way. She was *not* going down that road.

"Yeah." Inwardly shaking herself, she reached under the tech booth and opened the largest drawer of the filing cabinet underneath. "Here you go," she said, hoisting the full toolbox onto the table.

For reasons unknown, Ben looked between the two of them, patted Elle's shoulder, and squeezed his way out of the tech booth, mumbling some excuse she didn't catch. It freed up a little space, but it also left her there alone.

With John.

Elle swallowed and flipped open the top compartment of the toolbox. "What happened to your shirt?"

"Lost a button," John muttered. Elle did her best not to laugh at him as she pulled out the tiny pink sewing kit.

"You're too swole," she accused, teasing him. "You're practically bursting at the seams."

"Yeah, tell me about it." John handed his shirt over once Elle had pulled out the needle and threaded it.

She wondered what had made him so tense around Davy. Did it have to do with her? Was John's Big Brother Hero complex going to transfer

over to him now, instead of focusing on her mom? From what L
told her on their date, that had already happened.

"Do you have—" he beat her to her question, holding the tiny bre
button out to her. It was almost comically small in his enormous paln
Elle plucked it up and tried not to notice how tiny her own hand was, in
comparison. "Thank you."

She hummed softly as she worked, eyes zeroed in on the tiny holes
in the button. The last thing she needed was to stab herself and bleed on
his costume. She was already shaking just trying to hold the needle.

"I saw you giving Sarah the cold shoulder," she said after a while.
"She giving you a hard time?"

John snorted. "You could say that."

"Hey, you could always fling her up into the catwalk like Paul does."
Elle smirked up at him as she pulled the thread through the button.

"You *do* have a vindictive side," John teased, grinning down at her. "I
thought it was a myth."

"I'm secretly very petty," Elle informed him.

"Someone better warn Davy."

Good thing Elle had already knotted the thread, or she'd have
stabbed herself with the needle. Her head snapped up. "What?"

"He ought to know," John said with a shrug. "It might keep him in
line."

Oh my god, Elle realized. He *did* still think she was still seeing Davy.
And his brother complex was in full swing. She couldn't believe it.

She laughed, snipping the thread on the finished button. "John, I'm
not—"

"*Stellina!*"

Chef Rossi's voice made Elle jump. In a feat of utmost grace, she
dropped the scissors, sending them to the floor with a clatter. With a
muttered curse, she hopped off her stool. "What is it, Chef?"

"Benjamin tells me your mother was in town." Elle scowled, which
was apparently enough of an answer for the portly Italian. "I bring you
torrone . I expect them to be eaten before intermission."

Elle's scowl melted away into a grin as Chef Rossi set the plate by
her soundboard. "Feeding my soul again, Chef?"

"*Si, signorina.* Always." With that, he saluted her and headed on his way. "And do not let little Ben snatch them away from you!"

"Thank you, Chef," Elle called, grinning despite herself as she bent to pick up the scissors.

Clearly, her sense of spatial awareness was on the fritz. As Elle straightened, holding the closed blades of the scissors in one hand, she found herself almost pressed against John's chest.

Startled, she froze. She could feel the heat from his body, standing this close to him. His eyes bored down at her, more intense than she'd ever seen them before, a piercing jade blue that seemed to go right through her.

He swallowed. She watched his throat work, her eyes dropping down the length of his neck, down to where his tee shirt was split wide open over his chest. "Elle, I—"

"John!"

This time both of them jumped. Elle whipped around to face Jesse, the stage manager, a tall beanpole of a man with long blond hair and square glasses. She didn't even realize she was clutching both the scissors and John's shirt to her chest.

"What are you doing here?" Jesse asked. "We're about to open house."

"Lost a button," John said. Elle realized she was still, in fact, holding his shirt hostage, and forced herself to relax. "Elle's a better seamstress than Debbie is— but please don't tell Debbie I said that."

"Wouldn't dream of it." Maybe the lack of intonation was a stage manager thing, Elle thought, setting the scissors on the table. "Now hurry it up."

As he disappeared, Elle faced John again. "Uh…" she held his shirt out to him. "Here you go."

"Thanks." He took the shirt without looking at her. Not that she could look at him, either. She wasn't entirely sure what just happened— or almost happened— but she wasn't sure she wanted to know, either. "See you after the show."

"Have fun," Elle said. Her voice sounded breathless to her own ears. She swallowed as John stepped out of the room, suddenly able to breathe again once she had space. "Try not to accidentally-on-purpose drop Sarah."

"Ha."

Elle put a hand on her chest as Ben came back in, barely filling the empty space John had left in his wake. "Looks like you two were having fun," he said, a *torrone* already in one hand, with a shit-eating grin that made Elle want to punch him in his button nose.

"Oh, bite me," she snapped, and snatched the pastry from his hand to put into her own mouth.

Oklahoma closed the next weekend, and October arrived in its wake a week later. Two weeks of rehearsals passed in a blur of neon colors and experimenting with green hair spray, and then *Little Shop* opened. The leaves turned to fire, bright colors painting the skies and the streets as John drove home from the grocery store on a late Friday morning. October had breezed in, quite literally, and was gearing up to breeze out just as fast. Elle had been living with him for long enough that he could no longer imagine a time she hadn't lived there. She'd been there for most of the ten-week run of *Oklahoma*, actually, now that he thought about it. He'd never be able to hear those songs again without thinking of her.

John pulled into the driveway, thinking about nothing, really— what Elle was making for dinner, what time they needed to head to the theater. Elle's sleepy smile that morning, when he'd handed her a mug of— of all things— pumpkin spiced coffee.

Most of his thoughts were centered around Elle, nowadays. He'd gotten used to her being his first thought when he woke up, and his last before he fell asleep. Sometimes she'd go out— with Davy, he figured— and still, he wouldn't be able to sleep until he heard her come home, no matter how late it was.

Not having Davy in *Little Shop* was... a relief, really. Though now he had nothing to gauge their relationship by. It was strange, how Elle never spoke about their dates, or about Davy in general. Maybe she'd figured out that it was a sore spot for John? The thought made him cringe. He didn't want her to have to hide a part of herself from him.

It didn't matter, he reminded himself, opening the front door with the grocery bags over his arm. When he reached the end of the front hallway, he drew up short— and then burst out laughing.

Autumn had exploded *inside* his home, just as boldly and brightly as it had outside. Yellow and orange leaf garlands decorated the mantel, the front of the breakfast bar, and the handrail of the stairs up to the first landing. The kitchen table they used for dinner had a vase overflowing with marigolds, sunflowers, and those enormous red daisies, as did the coffee table in the living room. Scented candles filled the air with musky cinnamon and apple, and something spicy he couldn't place.

Amidst the chaos, Elle sat on the floor in the living room, looking like some sort of autumnal fairy princess. She'd even dressed to match the color scheme, wearing a dress for the first time since her first date with Davy, a brick red number that flowed in a circle around her legs. She had a tan cardigan on over it— he was *certain* she had an identical sweater in black— and a halo of flowers, glimmering ribbons cascading down with her lovely dark hair. In her hands, she carefully held a wreath of twigs, sparsely decorated with more leaves. As she tucked fake flowers into it, she sang along to the indie rock music drifting from the TV speakers.

"You're a decorating demon," he told her over the music, setting the grocery bags on the bar top counter. "I was only gone for an hour."

When Elle looked up at him, her eyes were glowing, her smile bright. "Logan helped. He's in the laundry room, I think." She gestured to the doorway behind John with the marigold in her hand, before looping it through her circle of twigs. "Though, if it hadn't been for Mom coming, I'd have had this place decorated on September first."

"Oh, good," Logan said, swooping into the room with an armful of candles, a lighter clutched in one hand. His newly colored hair practically glowed under the kitchen lights, bright turquoise and purple streaks that Elle had helped him dye. "We've been decorating," he announced, opening his arms across the counter from John, sending candles everywhere with a clatter.

"I see that." John arched a brow at him, plucking up an orange candle. "What do you call it? *Autumn Explosion?"*

From the corner of his eye, he saw Elle's smile fade, and watched her bite the nail of her forefinger. "You're not... mad, are you?"

"What— no?" He hadn't really meant for that to be a question, but that's how it came out. "Why would I be mad?"

The wreath sat abandoned in her lap as she looked past him at Logan, biting her lip. "We did... kind of overrun the place..."

"And?" John shrugged, turning his attention back to the groceries to get them put away. "I've had to deal with this idiot decorating for the past two years. At least your decorations resemble organized effort and not a Yankee Candle store."

"Hey!" Logan gave John a friendly shove as he passed. "Candles are great."

"Logan's right," Elle said. "But as long as you're sure."

"I'm sure," John insisted.

Elle held up her wreath and turned it back and forth, gold and copper ribbons sparkling in the sunlight, woven into the flowers. "Logan, should I add more spoop to this?"

"More *what?*" Not that her question was directed to him, but John frowned at the wreath anyway, halfway to the pantry with a bag in hand.

Logan waved him along, squinting at Elle's wreath. "Nostalgic spooky things, like glitter skulls and purple bats, as opposed to actual scary things, like lifelike spiders—" Elle visibly shuddered and gagged—"or gore."

"Got it," John said, even more confused.

"Ellie, my love, leave this one as it is," Logan continued, ignoring John. "We can leave it up through Thanksgiving. The black one needs more spoop, though." His opinion stated, Logan returned to his task of lighting tea lights in tiny pumpkin-shaped candle holders on the bar.

"I have never been more confused in my life." With that, John disappeared into the pantry.

"Did you get lunch meat?" Logan asked. John heard the fridge open behind him. "You did! Hey Ellie, he got roast beef!"

"Ooh!" Elle's muffled excitement put a smile on John's face. "I should probably eat more than a bagel." Her laughter followed a moment later. "God, this whole house is going to have glitter all over it, for the rest of time. I smell like pumpkins and—*oh my gosh!*"

John stepped out of the pantry, only to draw up short, milliseconds before he bowled over Elle. He hadn't realized she'd made it to the kitchen already.

She smiled pleadingly up at him, bouncing on her feet. "John, can we carve pumpkins?"

Between the delight on her face and her smile, John sincerely considered buying her a thousand pumpkins and helping her carve them himself. "Um, yeah," he said, running a hand through his hair. "Sure. I'm game."

Elle squealed, and then spun in a circle, reaching for Logan, who was in the middle of putting sandwich fixings onto the kitchen counter. "We're gonna carve *pumpkins!*"

Logan laughed and scooped her into his side, kissing her cheek noisily. John tried to skirt around them without interrupting the affection, but he barely made it half a foot before Elle descended upon him.

"Thank you!" She wrapped her arms around his waist and squeezed. "I miss pumpkins. They didn't let us have them at the apartment, and they're my favorite part of Halloween."

"Anytime," John said, squeezing her back for a brief moment before disentangling himself from her— or else he'd be just like Logan, showering her in an amount of affection that *definitely* went beyond roommate levels. Or even pseudo-brotherly love.

Ugh.

"We should just have a Halloween party," Logan suggested. He gave John a loaded look, over the three sandwiches he was preparing. "It's on a Tuesday, in a few weeks. We could have the cast over. Their datemates. A couple of other friends." He shrugged when John arched a brow, and concentrated on layering meat on bread. "Nothing too overboard. Elle will want to give out candy—"

"Correct," she agreed.

"But the kids are usually done before seven. The second it gets dark out, parents pull them inside." Logan's attention went to Elle, who was standing beside John, deeply inspecting one of the ribbons from her flower crown. "What do you think, Ellie?"

After a beat, Elle shrugged, not looking up from her ribbon. "A party would be... nice," she hedged, and then cleared her throat. "It could be fun."

John narrowed his eyes at her, propping himself up against the counter. "We don't have to have a party," he told her. "Just because this idiot is King of the Extroverts—" but Elle's face had scrunched up into a grimace, her lip between her teeth. "What's that look for?"

"I... may have texted Haley this morning and asked if she wanted to come here for Halloween to give out treats," she admitted. "Which I was going to tell you, but I hadn't gotten that far yet."

"Okay," John said, shrugging. "That's fine. It's not like you designed invitations or created an itinerary."

"Don't give her ideas," Logan warned.

"So, Haley can come over, and we'll invite the cast of *Little Shop*." John shrugged. "Logan can bring Tyler, you can have Davy, and maybe Sarah won't throw herself in my path every few seconds."

Logan stopped cutting sandwiches to shoot an arched brow at Elle. "Davy, huh?"

Elle ignored him to look at John instead. "No one from the country club would want to come?"

John grimaced. "I'll see enough suburban white soccer moms and their kids when they trick or treat, thanks."

"Yeah, Elle," Logan said, handing her a plated sandwich. "Don't wish that kind of negativity on us on the best day of the year."

Elle laughed. "What, you don't want to bob for apples and play *pin the tail on your friends and pretend it was an accident*?" With a suitably witchy grin, she took the plate, and winked at Logan.

"I think I'd rather spike some punch and eat my body weight in pizza dressed in drag," Logan told her, shoving a plate into John's hands. "I'll make a beautiful Morticia Addams."

"With those chicken legs of yours?" John goaded, biting into his sandwich.

"Quiet, you."

"I think I'll pull out Snow White," Elle said, inspecting her sandwich as though it might give her an opinion. "Maybe Haley will do a princess theme with me. I know I have it in one of my cosplay bags in storage—"

"Hold," John said, swallowing his bite of sandwich so fast he almost choked. "You still have stuff in storage?"

Elle looked at him with an expression he couldn't really name, something between shock, confusion, and a grimace. "Yeah, why?"

Frowning, he said, "I thought you brought all your stuff here already."

"I..." Elle looked at her plate. "There's... a lot. Most of it is furniture."

"We have a whole extra room upstairs," John reminded her. "Not to mention the sun room, which is basically empty. Unless—" it occurred to him as he was speaking, his heart sinking at the thought. "Unless you're still looking for your own place."

God, he'd gotten so used to her being here. What would he do if she left?

"No," Elle said, the word rushed. John could hit himself for the relief he felt at the one simple word. "No, I'm not looking anywhere else. I just... it's mostly my sewing stuff."

"So use the spare bedroom as a sewing room," John suggested, getting back to his sandwich. "There's a whole closet for cosplays. We can keep the twin bed in there for guests, just in case." Before she could protest, he forged on. "Hey, if we get your stuff before next weekend, you can fix the hole in my Joker vest, and I'll use that for Halloween."

"Wait, is that the one you wore last year?" Elle asked, perking up.

"For Comic-Con," he blurted, and then winced. That was— of all the things he could have said—

God, what a nerd, he thought, wishing he could melt into the floor. *Never say anything to her ever again. Just stop talking now.*

Elle didn't laugh, though. She grinned excitedly. "I saw it on your Facebook! I can't believe we didn't see each other."

"We might have," John said. Though he felt like he'd remember seeing Elle, no matter what she was wearing, unless she was somehow completely unrecognizable. "Why, what did you cosplay?"

Elle smirked. "A very extravagant genderbent Jack Skellington."

Yeah, John thought, that would do it.

"You and at least six other women," Logan said, "And John was *definitely* not the only Joker. Now, can we get back to party planning, please?"

"So John," Logan asked one morning, dropping down beside him with a bowl of cereal. "When exactly are you going to tell Elle that you're painfully in love with her?"

John promptly sent his *Fallout 4* character off the edge of a wall, killing him from the fall damage. "I used to be good at games," he said mournfully, and then sent Logan a reproachful look. "Between you and Elle, I'm losing my touch."

"We are pretty distracting," Logan agreed around a mouthful of Cheerios. "So, when?"

John hit *continue* on the game over screen and feigned obliviousness. "I have no idea what you're talking about." Honestly, he thought he'd done a pretty decent job of maintaining indifference toward Elle and Davy's relationship. He wasn't about to stop that now. Though it helped that she just... never spoke about it around him.

"Oh, Honey." Logan had a particular talent for sounding sympathetic and amused at the same time, even while spooning more cereal into his mouth. "If you'd seen your face yesterday when she hugged you, you'd have known. You're lucky Elle's the most oblivious person on the planet." He swallowed, regarding John levelly. "Well, aside from *you*."

John kept his attention on his game. One of these days, he'd manage to play without Elle—physically *or* hypothetically— distracting him. "You can't tell that much from my face," he said.

Clearly, Logan took it as a challenge. "I mean, I knew you had a thing for her— pretty sure everyone and their mother knows— but I didn't realize it ran *that* deep." It was hard to understand him past the crunching. "Ellie is gorgeous, there's no doubt about that, but that's not it." Swallow, clatter, crunch. "At first I thought you were just protective of her because we're all friends, but that's not it, either. You didn't stop glaring at Davy for the entire run of *Oklahoma* after he asked Elle out, even when—"

"I was *not* glaring at Davy," John insisted, even though he knew damn well he had been.

"Right. And you clearly haven't talked to Elle about him, either."

"What's there to talk about?" John demanded. "She's dating him. Not me. Which is perfectly fine." And maybe he'd actually believe that, one of these days.

"John." At this point, Logan just sounded exasperated. "She smiled at you, and you went heart-eyed. Then she asked you if we could carve pumpkins, and I watched you consider her, all five feet of her, *coated* in glitter and pieces of fake flowers, and decide that putting her anywhere near a giant, goopy vegetable was a good idea. Since you're clearly not sane, you have to be in love."

John's character fell to a valiant second death, and the game menu came up.

"How long has it *really* been, John?" Logan asked softly, reaching one long arm over to lay a hand on John's leg.

John sighed. "I don't know. Since the beginning, maybe?"

"Since Jackie?"

John shrugged. "Things were already falling apart with Jackie by the time I realized how I felt about Elle."

"That's a long time," Logan pointed out. "You never asked her out."

It probably wasn't meant to be an accusation, but John shrugged. "She was dating someone for awhile, and we really weren't all that close until you moved in— and then she moved in."

"So you kept it to yourself." John nodded at Logan's assessment. "Oh, John, you absolute fool."

Yeah, John thought, he really was. "Too late, now," he said, shrugging. "She's with Davy, and eventually that'll move forward, and she'll..."*leave*. She would leave, eventually.

"How can you be so sure?"

"Because that's who Elle is," John sighed. "Loyal to a fault. Committed." And smart, and funny, and witty, and passionate— and not his.

"John," Logan said, shaking his head, as though in pity. "You really are clueless."

"What's that supposed to mean?"

Whatever Logan was about to say was cut off by a door opening upstairs, followed by the sound of Elle humming, cheerful as ever. John gave Logan a loaded look and hit *continue* on his game again.

10

Snacks were fine, drinks were fine, music was playing, people seemed to be enjoying themselves. There hadn't been any costume mishaps. Nobody was blackout drunk. In fact, Elle hedged, sweeping into the kitchen, the Halloween party seemed to be going really well.

Between her and Logan, they'd put as much effort into the house as they usually put into shows. Maybe more, between her cooking every kind of thematic treat she could manage, and him decorating every available surface within an inch of its life. John had even helped carve the pumpkins the night before. Though, in all honesty, putting her near messy, impossibly large vegetables had probably been a bad plan— but they'd ended up with half a dozen pumpkins, both spooky and silly. She loved them all.

The effect was delightfully spooky, borderline tacky. In other words, festive and fun. And, amazingly, the place was still intact, already a good hour into the party. So was her slightly modernized Snow White costume, even after handing out candy to children with Haley before the party even started. The guests didn't disappoint, either; they'd all come in costume. Not surprising, for a bunch of theater people.

God, they really didn't know anyone outside of work, did they?

At any rate, she could maybe, *finally* relax. She'd had food, and half a cup of punch that she'd set down and immediately lost track of. It was only right that she get herself a nice, heavily alcoholic drink, maybe mingle a bit—

"Ellie *please* sit down," Logan said, catching sight of her the moment she started to fill a plate with snacks.

"Hmm?" She turned, popping a devilled egg into her mouth, careful not to smudge her lipstick. Logan really did make a stunning Morticia, even *with* his chicken legs. The heels actually helped a great deal with his posture. She'd already caught Tyler— dressed, naturally, as Gomez Addams— unabashedly staring at Logan's ass in the dress.

"I know you're dressed as Snow White, but you're not *actually* Snow White," Logan said, grabbing her by her bare shoulders. Elle snagged an extra brownie as he guided her out of the kitchen.

"I was just getting snacks," she insisted, once she'd swallowed.

"After checking everything for the fifth time." Logan ushered her into the sunroom and onto a couch beside Haley, dressed as Princess Jasmine. "You're giving me an ulcer. For the love of god, let someone else handle it."

"You and John are hopeless," Elle said, munching on one of her brownies. Beside her, Haley snorted her agreement, turning her attention to them at the first sign of drama.

"Yeah, well," Logan grumbled. "I might be… a little bit tipsy, but John should be fine."

Elle hummed her vague agreement. "At least one of us is having the punch."

"You had punch," Logan recalled, frowning.

"A while ago," she said, watching Haley snag a chip and scoop up some three-layer dip from Elle's plate. "*Someone* decided to manhandle me away from it before I could get more, so I'm only marginally tipsy."

"Oh my *god*," Logan said. "Wait here, I'll get you more." With that, he turned on his heel, his long black wig flying as he sailed out of the room.

Elle smirked as she watched him go, and then turned to Haley, holding the plate better between them. "He'll get distracted by four other people and then his boyfriend, and I'll never get my punch."

"You sure won't," Haley agreed, passing over her own cup. "Here, I'm not sick. Share my germs."

"Thanks," Elle said, taking a sip. Sweet enough not to taste the alcohol. "God, this is dangerous," she said, and then took another full gulp.

"Hell, Elle, you drink like a fish!"

"Here, quick, take it back," Elle said, after another large gulp. "I'm a lightweight."

She did, with a laugh. "How's the *Little Shop* run going?"

"You know, it's creepy, it's neon, half of it is uncomfortably sexual." Elle shrugged. "Is it better or worse than getting your Masters?"

"Oh, *so* much better," Haley groaned. "I don't want to think about it. Tell me more about the show."

"Why don't you just come *see* the show?" Elle took the cup from Haley's hand before the other woman could take a drink, and took one of her own, winking.

"Hey!" Haley scowled, and snatched her cup back. "If I didn't know for a fact that Logan is standing in your hallway with your drink, talking to someone that's *not* you, I'd be offended."

"No, you wouldn't," Elle said, nudging a cookie toward her. "Not as long as I keep feeding you."

"Bitch," Haley said fondly, and took the whole plate. "I can't come to the show until I stop drowning in my own workload. I'm already having regrets about this party."

"But you came for the free food." The alcohol was certainly setting in, Elle realized, winking at Haley again. God, she'd always been a shamelessly flirtatious drunk.

"No one cooks like you, Elle," Haley said, with a blissful expression as she chewed on her cookie. "I'd skip an exam for your cooking."

Elle didn't even respond. She just laughed and laid her head on Haley's shoulder. God, she *loved* having friends over. Why didn't they have more parties? "John looks like Orin tonight."

Haley's shoulder shifted under Elle's cheek. "Elle, he's the *Joker*."

"Hmm. Yeah." And damn if his costume hadn't gotten under Elle's skin the moment she'd seen him come down the stairs earlier. "I felt bad for the kids. I don't think they recognized him as *Nice Mr. Ebner from the country club*."

"So how does he look like the Dentist from *Little Shop*?"

"The green hair, the leather jacket, the skinny jeans—" Elle sighed. "Those girls are so lucky. They basically crawl all over him during his first song."

"Alright, no more punch for you," Haley said, setting the cup down on the end table on her other side, out of Elle's reach.

Elle pouted. "Spoilsport."

"Hey, Miss Elle." Elle looked up to find Davy perching himself on the arm of the couch beside her. "Great party."

Struggling not to laugh, Elle regarded him. "A cowboy, Davy? Really?" She couldn't help giggling. "*Oklahoma* ended like, a month ago."

Davy did a very good job of not rolling his eyes at her, in Elle's humble opinion. "Someone tell John that."

"What's John got to do with anything?" Elle asked. She frowned up at Davy and rested her chin on his leg.

Davy blinked, clearly startled by her show of affection, but Elle didn't much care. He was a sweetheart, and apparently had a feeding tube of *respect-women* juice going right into his system. She *really* liked him.

"Uh…" Davy looked over at Haley, who chuckled.

"She's drunk. Take everything she says and does with a grain of salt."

With another wary glance at Elle, he said, "Yes, Ma'am."

"Hey," Elle said, poking his knee. "John. *Oklahoma*. What's that all about?"

"He's been glaring at me all night," Davy explained. "He glared at me all the way through the end of our run, after the first night you filled in as Laurey."

Elle hummed thoughtfully and started to play with her flowery yellow skirt. "I think that might just be the Joker makeup, my guy."

Davy shot Haley a perplexed look, and then shook his head, apparently deciding not to say whatever he'd been planning to. "Didn't you tell him we're not dating, Miss Elle?"

"Wait," Haley interrupted, around a mouthful of— whatever she'd stolen from Elle's plate this time. "You never said you two weren't dating!"

Elle lifted her head to scowl at Haley. "We never said we *were* dating!"

"You went on a date!" Haley's shock was downright comical.

"Yeah, one!"

"This is why John keeps glaring," Davy groaned.

"But why would he glare at you?" Elle propped her chin on his leg again, pouting. "I thought the two of you were friends."

Davy gaped, and then his expression grew piteous. "Oh, Elle, you can't be *that* drunk."

Elle gasped, perking up. "Davy!" She grinned, patting his knee excitedly. "You called me *Elle* without putting *Miss* in front of it! I'm so proud of you!"

With a heavy sigh, Davy closed his eyes. "Right." Then he chuckled softly, and patted her head. "You're a darned mess when you're drunk, Miss Elle." She really would have argued, but he was right, so she just grinned up at him instead. He shook his head at her. "Try to remember to tell him, when you're done nursing your hangover tomorrow."

"You know, *you* could tell him." Elle glanced back to find her plate of snacks empty. Haley grimaced apologetically, but Elle just rolled her eyes.

"No, thanks," Davy said, holding up his hands. "I'm fairly certain John would deck me if I said anything that might be misconstrued as a breakup."

Elle huffed, taking Haley's cup from her hand. "He *does* have a major big brother complex, doesn't he?" Even Haley's cup was empty. How rude.

Davy's sigh came back. "Elle."

"What?" She handed the empty cup back to Haley. "I swear the man adopted me the minute I moved in here. Maybe before that, but I wasn't really paying attention to him then, you know?" But boy did he have her attention now. Maybe he was around somewhere nearby, and he could have more of it. "Here, I'll go talk to him so you can stop worrying." Elle stood, surprisingly steady, since her entire body felt sort of light and woozy. God, how much alcohol had Logan put in that punch?

"You should probably have some water," Haley advised. "Davy, make her get water."

"I can get my own water." Elle smiled at Davy and patted his knee again. "Sit, chat, have fun. I'm fine."

With that, she strolled out of the room— or she was about to, until John came in, looking a bit pained underneath his extreme goth-clown makeup. He glanced over his shoulder, just in time for Elle to make a beeline for him.

"John! Hi! I was just—" She wasn't sure why she lifted her arms in the first place, but she stumbled, ending up halfway plastered against his front with her hands on his chest. His arms came up to steady her, holding her waist. "Whoops! Sorry. You good?"

John frowned at her. "Are *you*?"

God, what a *gentleman*. What a stand up guy. And he was pretty, too, wasn't he? Elle had never really thought about it. "I might be tipsy. But Logan owes me another drink, which he said he'd get me— um." How long had it been? "A while ago, I think."

"I think you've had enough," John said. "He put at least two bottles of flavored vodka into that punch. Malibu, too."

"Oh!" Elle said cheerfully. She hadn't bothered to step out of John's arms yet, and honestly, she wasn't particularly inclined to. "Is that why I'm already drunk? I didn't have that much." Though she did drink it kind of fast. She pouted up at him. "Why were you frowning just now? Aren't you having fun?"

"What?" He looked puzzled, but then—"Oh. Yeah, I'm— Sarah's here. I was just…"

Elle giggled, leaning into him. "Running away from her?" He grimaced, which she took as a confirmation. "Hmm. Well, we could always sacrifice her to the Halloween gods."

John barked a laugh, his smile only slightly distorted by the jagged red lines stretching out over his cheeks. "You would. Is Logan helping you make this sacrifice?"

"He'd better," Elle decided, playing idly with the zipper to John's jacket. Wasn't there something she was supposed to be telling him?

"You'd get blood all over your dress," John told her. "It's too pretty to ruin it like that."

"Aww!" Warmth rose up from Elle's chest, and she leaned back in his arms. They tightened around her, supporting her full weight. "You think I'm pretty?" She was fairly certain John's face went blank, but it was hard to tell with the makeup— and the fact that her head was swimming a little. She didn't exactly give him time to answer her, however, distracted by playing with the studs on his jacket. "I love this jacket. I love this whole aesthetic. It really works for you."

There was a beat of silence. "You really are drunk," John said at length.

"Hmm? Oh." Elle shrugged. "Yeah, I'm a lightweight. I'll probably want to die tomorrow, but oh well. I'm enjoying myself." To prove it, she grinned up at him, all teeth.

John rolled his eyes. "Alright, Princess Lightweight, let's get you some water." With that, he turned her around with his hands on her waist, and guided her through the crowd. "It's almost late enough to kick people out, and then you can be drunk and watch a Halloween movie with us."

"I've never seen *Halloween*," Elle confessed, misunderstanding him completely.

"What?" Elle laughed outright at John's outrage. "Elle, it's a *classic*. How can you not have seen it? You *love* horror."

"I love terrible effects and a good mystery," Elle corrected him. "Really bad acting, cliche plots, and painfully fake props are my jam."

"*Halloween* has at least three of those," John told her. "We'll watch it later."

"Alright," Elle sighed, letting him pick her up and put her on a bar stool. She really did feel like a princess in that split second she was in the air, her curls bouncing, her corset stealing her breath. Or maybe that last one was just John being John. Once she was settled on the seat, she continued, "Only if you hold my hand when I get scared."

John paused, his eyes wide. Then his expression softened. "If you're that scared, I'll just let you sit in my lap again."

Elle giggled. "Deal."

As he rounded the counter to get her water, the girl sitting next to her turned to grin at her. Elle recognized her from the ensemble of *Oklahoma,* one of their dancers, Penny, currently dressed as Columbia from *Rocky Horror*. "You two are so cute!"

Elle blinked. It hadn't even occurred to her that there were other people around that could see them interact. Though living with the man probably wasn't doing anything for her reputation, anyway. And it *had* been sweet, the way he'd been taking care of her just now. Glancing at John she sighed. "Yeah. Yeah, I guess we are."

If only it were less familial on his part.

11

"Ooh, don't *you* look cute!"

Elle caught Logan's eye in her mirror as she put her earring in and sent him a slightly harried smile. "Thanks! I'm going out with Haley tonight for a girls' night."

"Fun, fun," Logan said, propping himself against her bathroom door. "Love the shorts-stockings combo."

"Isn't it fun?" Elle did a little twirl. The stockings were thick enough to keep her warm, even though her shorts were probably scandalously short. "I was thinking my burgundy cardigan and suede boots with it?"

Logan pursed his lips and thought about it. "Keep doing your makeup while I look in your closet."

Elle frowned at her reflection. "I've already finished my—"

"Mascara and lipstick," Logan called from her closet, voice muted.

Right, Elle thought. At least one of them had any makeup skills. She whisked on her mascara, managing somehow not to get it onto the rest of her eye makeup, and then examined her painfully eclectic collection of lipsticks. "What color lipstick?"

"Got a dark pink?" Logan asked, his voice getting louder as he came back. "Actually, no, scrap that."

"It's fine, I don't think I— oh, wait, I do have one." Elle spotted it in the back of her makeup drawer. "Why do I have more stage makeup than regular makeup?"

"Occupational hazard." Logan returned with two cardigans in his arms, a dusty pink and a tan. "Girl, you have *way* too many cardigans."

"I live for comfort." Elle waited patiently for Logan to hold up both sweaters over her brown camisole.

"Maybe that's what I'll get you for your birthday," Logan said, and then froze.

Elle knew he was doing math in his head, but held her breath. Maybe he wouldn't remember. "Are you sure the burgandy one—"

"Don't try to distract me," Logan snapped. "I know what day it is."

"Sure," Elle said innocently. "It's Wednesday."

"Wednesday the *eighth.* " Logan draped both sweaters over his arm and scowled at her. "Your birthday is in two days, and you haven't said a *thing* about it."

"Well—" Logan tossed the tan cardigan at her and she yelped, scrambling to catch it. "Hey!"

"*That's* why you made pot roast last night!" He cried. "You're making yourself soup again!"

"It's a tradition!" Elle pulled on her sweater and then checked herself out in the mirror. The tan actually worked, brightening the whole outfit. "I love this. Great choice."

"Yeah, yeah," Logan said, waving her words away. "I'm still on your birthday. You're gonna make soup, which I can't stop you from doing, but if you try to make your own cake, all the eggs in this house will mysteriously go missing."

Elle snorted. "Noted." She swept on coppery lipstick and nodded at her reflection. "Alright, fashion guru, what shoes are you putting on me?" The second she stepped out of her bathroom a pair of brown suede booties landed at her feet with twin *thuds.* "Ah. Nice. Thanks."

"Shoot, we work on Friday," Logan said, pacing while Elle struggled to get the boots on without falling. "We'll have to celebrate after the show, then."

"I mean I guess," She said, bracing herself on the wall. "As long as you're not planning a party or anything. I don't think I can handle two hangovers less than two weeks apart."

"Fair enough."

Shoes on, Elle sailed out of her room past Logan. "I mean, that's why Haley wanted to celebrate tonight. Since we work."

"Smart," Logan said, following her down the stairs. "Why didn't I think of that?"

"Think of what?" John asked. Elle glanced over from the stairs to find him in his usual spot on the couch, but rather than playing video games, he had a book in his large hand.

"Look at you, changing things up," she said, leaning against the banister. "I may die of shock."

"I might say the same to you," John said. "I didn't know you owned clothing that wasn't black, or a cosplay."

"It's an optical illusion," Elle said as Logan passed her, patting her ass as he went. She returned the gesture out of habit. "This is actually all black. You're just going blind."

John watched their exchange and snorted. As Elle reached the bottom of the stairs, he asked, "What's the point of wearing leggings under shorts?"

Elle smirked and started for the front door with an exaggerated model-strut. *"Fashion."*

"Elle's birthday is Friday," Logan announced, heading the opposite direction. "Wear a hat, Ellie. It's cold out."

"Wait—" Elle could hear John standing with a rustle of movement. "Your birthday?"

As she opened the coat closet, looking for her hat and scarf, Elle spared him a glance. "I'm making soup. Logan's making cake. Please don't buy me anything."

"But if you want to, she lives for infinite comfort items," Logan added.

Elle snorted. "You're not wrong." She pulled on her beanie, trying to convince it not to just slide off her hair. "I'm not super fond of presents anyway."

"Just for that, I'm buying you something obnoxious." Logan's voice was muffled, coming from the kitchen. "John, do you want a sandwich?"

"No, thanks. You're twenty-five this year, right?" Elle looked over, and— yep. John was walking toward her, his brow furrowed in thought. "That's a big birthday."

"Not really." Now to find her scarf—*aha*. "I'm not really expecting a lot. Mom will call and talk my ear off, Dad might remember to send

a card— which, since it's coming from Bavaria, will probably be late—
and Garth will send a text. *Maybe* also a present." She wound the scarf
around her neck, and immediately had to fix her beanie, with a huff.
"Aunt Roxy and Melanie will send something wildly extravagant and
expensive that I will have no choice but to accept, and I'll stress about it
until they send something even worse for Christmas."

"They love to spoil you," Logan said.

"We can do someth— oh, no, we work." With gentle hands, John
pulled Elle's hair out of her scarf. She couldn't tell if his fingers lingered
there, or if it was just her imagination.

"That's why I'm going to dinner tonight," Elle said. She felt John
stiffen behind her, but then caught sight of the time on the ornate clock
hanging just above her head. "Which I'm gonna be late for, if I don't get
out of here." She turned and, without thinking, wrapped John in a hug.
"I'll see you guys when I get home. Goodnight!" With that, she sashayed
around John and out the door.

John heard Elle come in and, like a coward pretended to be asleep on the
couch. As if he hadn't been waiting up for her to get home from dinner.

Dinner. For her birthday. Probably with Davy. He hadn't really
thought about it since Halloween, which had been weird in and of
itself. Davy had barely been around Elle— though, in the same vein,
Tyler hadn't been all over Logan. Who the hell was John to judge their
relationship?

You can't avoid talking to her about this forever, his brain pointed out.

Maybe they'd spent this dinner talking about the future. Maybe Elle
was considering moving out and living with him eventually. Maybe they
were getting *serious*. It had been— what, almost three months, now?

He didn't want to think about it.

Stomach churning, John waited, listening to see if she'd brought
Davy home with her. It was only a matter of time. How many dates had

they been on, anyway? He hadn't been keeping track. He'd been too busy trying not to feel the ugly, biting jealousy that seemed to spring up whenever he saw Davy nowadays— or when he talked to him, or thought of him, or remembered his existence at all.

All he could hear was the hushed dialogue of one of the *Batman* movies, and the slight squeak of the coat closet door. Elle's heels clicked on the wooden floor, and then she cursed under her breath.

Right, not waiting up. Just listening to *Batman* and not contemplating the emptiness his life would hold once Elle left.

Soft footsteps grew louder. Only one set of them. Then, inexplicably:

"John?"

Her voice was so soft, and so tender, he almost recoiled. He hadn't heard that tone from her... ever, he didn't think. Not directed at him, at least.

"John?" She said again, shaking him gently by the shoulder. He forced himself to open his eyes and found her lovely face level with his. She'd crouched down on the floor in front of him, a concerned frown narrowing her pretty blue eyes, her light, flowery perfume tickling his nose. It was the same one she'd worn on Halloween, when she'd sat drunkenly in his lap and watched the horror movie with him and Logan.

His heart felt sore.

"Why aren't you in bed, darling?" She asked, rubbing her hand down his arm. The endearment made his heart clench. "Are you feeling alright?"

No.

He should say yes. Pretend everything was fine. Ask her about her date, and then go upstairs to wallow in the privacy of his own bedroom.

He didn't.

Shaking his head, John closed his eyes, hoping she might let him stay right where he was and work out his ridiculous jealousy on his own. Maybe he'd grab a few beers and drink away his sorrows. Unlikely, since he had no intention of moving from the couch.

The next thing he knew, a blanket fell over his body, and then Elle's tiny, delicate hand stroked his hair back. "Sit up for a second, my love."

Love. How utterly, depressingly ironic.

John obediently propped himself up, giving her room to sit. He was none too surprised when she pulled him back down, arranging his head in her lap, her legs criss-crossed underneath him. Hating himself for it, he looped his hand around her thigh, his hand spanning most of it. He felt her tense, but she said nothing, simply running her hand through his hair.

They stayed like that for several long minutes, Elle petting him like a cat, and John trying not to be painfully, desperately in love with her.

"How was your date?" He had no idea how much time had passed, when he spoke. He wasn't sure he cared, either.

Elle hesitated, and then, clearly confused, answered, "It wasn't a date."

John's eyes snapped open.

"I thought you went out with Davy," He said, his voice strained "For your birthday?"

"No," Elle said. He turned his head toward her, awkwardly, and saw her frowning at the TV. "I was out with Haley, and a couple of my college friends. We had a girls' night."

"Oh," John said, settling back into her lap. "Sorry, I just assumed—"

"Davy and I aren't dating."

"*What?* "

Elle chuckled, still calmly threading her fingers through his hair. "We went on one date and mutually agreed that it was weird. I felt like I'd gone on a date with Garth." She shifted slightly, dropping one of her legs— the one he wasn't holding onto— down to dangle off the couch. "He's a sweet man, and a gentleman, but in the end, it was strictly platonic."

John stared at the TV. He couldn't believe— there was no *way* he'd been that oblivious. And yet.

"And you, sir," She said, poking his upper arm, "need to stop glaring at him every time you see him." Her tone was teasing, but John grimaced nonetheless. "Remember what you promised me when Mom was here? About the hero complex?"

"No tights," John deadpanned, still in shock.

Elle's musical laughter rained over him. "You're impossible," she told him, and leaned down to kiss his temple. John screwed his eyes shut as all of his focus zeroed in on that spot. Warmth began to spread through his chest—*hope*. That was hope. Fragile and fleeting, maybe, but hope nonetheless.

"So," he ventured, trying not to let his relief show. "No Davy?"

"No," Elle murmured, her hand resuming its trek with his hair. "No Davy."

John tightened his grip on her leg.

According to Logan, nothing said "birthday breakfast" like chocolate chip waffles. So, the moment he got back from his morning run and showered off, John settled into the kitchen to make the one meal he knew he could cook.

Since Wednesday night, John had been in a *spectacular* mood. Now that he wasn't avoiding her, or obsessing over her, things had really smoothed out. He hadn't even realized how weird things had gotten until he ran into Davy, who'd come to the theater Thursday night to fill in backstage. The shock on Davy's face when John had talked to him was nearly comical. Even Elle shot him two thumbs up and an approving grin when she saw them talking together.

Apparently, since it was Elle's birthday, Logan had decided to stay upstairs and play fairy-godmother with her. He'd told John as much after coming down to pour Elle a mimosa, at just after nine. Like she needed any alcohol in her system.

"The birthday girl is getting the spa treatment," he'd said, going a little heavy-handed with his champagne pour. "Try not to swallow your tongue when we come down." John had just rolled his eyes and started mixing waffle batter.

Coffee poured itself into the pot, ready to be mixed with obscene amounts of chocolate. Bacon sizzled in the pan, and an aluminium tin of hot waffles sat beside the waffle maker where John stood, a pitcher of batter in his hand. He deliberately kept his back to the stairs when he heard Elle's laughter floating down them. For once, he thought as he poured waffle mix onto the hot iron, he wanted to prove to Logan— and himself— that he wasn't completely gone for Elle. Even if she was, officially, single again. Besides, making Logan eat his words would be *so* worth it.

"Happy Birthday," he said brightly, glancing over his shoulder. He almost put his hand down on the waffle iron.

Elle floated down the stairs in a delicate pink dress and a denim jacket, and— of all things— bedazzled cowboy boots. Logan had really outdone himself with her, leaving her lovely, long hair falling over her shoulders in soft curls, and her face glowing like it was lit from the inside.

John was going to scoop his jaw off the floor and say something, any minute now. He was going to grab her the second she was in arms reach and kiss her, right in front of Logan, the smug bastard. He was going to haul Elle back up the stairs over his shoulder and spend the rest of her birthday showing her how happy he was that she'd been born.

He was going to burn the waffle on one side, if he didn't close the damn lid.

"Nice dress," He croaked. He even managed to close the waffle iron, like a functional adult.

"Thanks," Elle said, a little breathless as she reached the bottom of the stairs. She twirled, and tiny sequins in her skirt caught the sunlight, making it glimmer and gleam. "I made it!"

"It's..."*stunning. Perfect. Dazzling. Better suited for my bedroom floor while I—* "beautiful."

Pink dusted her cheeks, and John had to turn away, trying to discreetly adjust himself.

Get a grip, he demanded of himself, checking the waffle— and, yeah, the bottom was noticeably darker than the top. *You have better control than this.*

Then again, he'd been losing his goddamn mind since the day she moved in, and she didn't even seem to notice, so. Maybe he didn't.

Since he'd apparently forgotten how to form a complete, coherent sentence worth saying, John decided to cut his losses, and just went about putting waffles on a plate for her.

"Alright, birthday girl," Logan said, and John could hear him settling onto a bar stool behind him. "It's time for you to open your fan mail."

John turned to slide Elle's breakfast across the bar to her, only to damn near trample her. When had she even gotten this close to him? As he reared back, defending himself with the plate, she let out a delighted gasp. "Oh, you made waffles!"

John felt ten years shave off his lifespan as she took the plate from him and practically danced over to the counter, setting her plate down and then immediately coming back to him. "Thank you!"

When she flung her arms around his neck, John acted on instinct, lifting her up and whirling her around in a circle. Her peal of laughter rang throughout the room, her arms tight around his neck. Once he set her down, he happened to glance at Logan— Logan, the jerk, who was smirking at him over his crossed arms, one eyebrow up in an annoyingly smug expression.

John felt himself blush like a schoolboy, and turned pointedly back to his dangerously dark waffle.

"Oh, they're chocolate chip!" While Elle ate her waffles in contented bliss, swinging her legs like a child, John tried not to imagine strangling the grin off of Logan's pointy face. Elle focused on her small stack of mail, opening cards from her family one at a time. "Mom says hi," she sang, setting aside a gift card and a lacy pink card that almost matched her dress. "Dad sent me a necklace, how sweet! And on time, too. How nice."

Circling the breakfast bar, John set his own breakfast aside so he could unlatch the necklace— a thread-thin silver chain with delicate, tiny pearls in the center— and drape it around her neck. Logan arched a brow at him, but John ignored him, carefully pushing Elle's soft hair off of her neck. "Why is there so much glitter on that envelope?" He asked. The manila envelope in question was almost completely covered in sparkly rainbows, swirling handwriting, and cat stickers.

"My aunts go all out," she explained as he clasped the chain. "Thank you, love."

Anything, John thought, sitting down beside her.

"They're delightful," Logan said, helping her peel a few of the stickers off of the lip of the envelope so she could open it.

"They're what you might call *extra.*" As if to prove her point, more glitter fell out of the envelope the moment it was open. Elle sighed and shook her head, grinning.

Logan snorted. "If it hadn't been for them keeping you in the theater community, I think you'd have cracked before you graduated high school."

"You say that like I'm sane now," Elle teased. The card she pulled out— accompanied by a small cloud of glitter— was even more ostentatious than the envelope, and obviously handmade. Out of the card slid three pieces of paper, which Elle fumbled to catch, and then frowned at. The moment she'd read the first, she shrieked, dropping everything on the counter beside her empty plate, her hands clapping over her mouth.

"What?" Logan asked, jerking away from her. John burst out laughing as Logan knocked his elbow into his mug, coffee splashing over the edges. *Payback.*

"Oh my god," Elle breathed.

"What?" John parroted, reaching over to lift up one of the papers.

"Oh my god," Elle repeated, as John's jaw dropped. "We're going to NYCC."

John gaped, floored, as Elle snatched the papers back up, shuffling through them. "We?" He hedged. "As in—"

"*As in ,*" Elle said, waving the papers at him, "my rich gay aunts got the three of us tickets to New York Comic Con. Top tier, VIP tickets." She gazed down at the papers with shining eyes, shaking her head at them. "We get first access to like, *every* panel and event, meet and greets—"

"So let me get this straight," John interrupted. "Your two lesbian aunts, who have never met me or Logan—"

"Speak for yourself," Logan muttered.

"— sent you three VIP tickets to NYCC?" He met Logan's eyes over Elle's head, and then looked back to her. "Is this what you meant by extravagant and expensive?"

Chewing on her fingernail, Elle flicked open the card, effectively dusting all three of them with glitter.

"Hey!" He started brushing off the glitter, but it just seemed to sink into the denim of his jeans.

Logan sighed. "It'll be there forever." He didn't even bother to dust his own legs off. "Glitter, the herpes of art and theater."

Elle cleared her throat, and John indulgently returned his attention to her. *"Hoppy Birdy to our little Starlette,"* She read, ignoring the glitter fiasco entirely. *"Bring those two roommates of yours up for some fun! Can't wait to see you all. Love, Aunties Roxy and Melanie."* By the time she finished reading, she was beaming. "In case you didn't catch that," she said, nudging John's leg with her own and dousing it with even more glitter, "that means you, too."

"Well, hell," he said, brushing some of the glitter off of the counter and onto her lap, delighted by her squealing giggles. "I guess we're going to Comic Con."

Elle tilted her head toward him, a sly smile on her face. "I can dig up my Harley Quinn cosplay, to go with your Joker."

John blinked. She could—*what?*

"Though I'm really more of a Harley-Ivy shipper," she continued, either missing his surprised look or ignoring it. "Joker may get an A for aesthetic, but he's really a garbage boyfriend. Besides—*lesbians.*"

"Bisexuality strikes again," Logan said, smirking. "I'd make a lovely Catwoman."

"You would," Elle agreed, then glanced over at John again. "Though if you didn't want to do Joker, I'm sure you'd look stunning with green body paint and a red wig—"

Rolling his eyes, John swept the rest of the glitter off the counter and onto her lap.

12

Winter arrived in much the same way that coffee came out of the pot: slowly at first, and then in a chaotic spill. All Elle knew was that, one morning, she opened the door, expecting a chilly autumn breeze, and instead she found a good two inches of snow already on the ground. It fell in blissful silence, coating the world in soft, fluffy comfort.

It was a day to stay inside, she decided, breath huffing in white clouds in front of her. Maybe a good day to bake a little. Mail in hand and snow dusting her hair, Elle came back into the toasty warmth of the house, and decided that a little redecorating might be in order, too.

Since John was off being a good community member, hosting some event or another at the country club, and since he'd roped Logan into lending him manpower, she was alone for the day. Elle busied herself with pulling down and putting away a few of the brighter autumnal decorations, singing showtunes to herself. Somewhere, probably in the laundry room, she knew Logan had a box of Thanksgiving decorations that were *just* this side of tacky. With a bin of orange and yellow leaves on her hip, she ventured into the laundry room to hunt down turkeys and gourds instead.

Her mom had always been the decorator during holidays. It was, perhaps, the most steady part of Elle's childhood, a constant and predictable progression of colors and themes from one month to the next. Elle herself was still a sucker for fun holiday decorations. Though her mother lacked the skill to really bring it all together, it was still a comfort even now, all these years later, to see some ridiculous stickers on someone's windows, or a festive banner outside of a house.

Turkeys and gourds, Elle reminded herself, peeking into a couple of bins until she found them. Maybe while she decorated, she'd get something baking for later. Something warm and cozy to combat the cold outside.

As she carried the box out, she rooted through the recipes in her mind, until— oh, *yes*. Ginger scones and wassail (did people even call it that anymore? God, she sounded like her grandmother), both festive and delicious, just the right kind of warm and comforting. Plus, she was pretty sure she had the ingredients for both, after her adventure with Logan to the farmer's market a few days ago. Apple cider, some oranges, cloves, ginger...

The house smelled like sweet spices when she heard the front door open, a couple of hours later. Elle arranged a pair of wine-red candles to frame a wicker cornucopia on the dining table, filled to overflowing with tiny pumpkins and apples and leaves. "Hi, boys," she called over her shoulder. When she didn't get any response, she frowned over her shoulder. Maybe she was hearing things? But no, the boys were, indeed, back, hanging their coats in the front closet. "How was the country club today?"

Logan grimaced at her, and jerked his head toward John. As he waved his hand in front of his throat, John marched toward the stairs, avoiding her eyes, his expression— Oh, *god*. What the hell had happened to put *that* look on his face?

His entire body was tense as he gripped the banister like a lifeline and surged up the stairs. Within seconds, he was out of sight.

Elle opened her mouth, but before she could ask Logan anything, he held up a hand to stop her. They both waited, listening to John's heavy footsteps, until a door shut firmly— but not, she noticed, violently— upstairs.

Logan sighed, dropping his hand. "Jackie."

Elle blinked. "Um... no." She pointed to herself. "Elle."

"What?" Logan frowned at her, and then seemed to realize what she'd said. "Oh! Ha. Yes, you're Elle. Jackie, however, is the reason for John's shit mood."

"Is this the same Jackie from the night I moved in?" Logan nodded. "She sounds like a suburban mom with frosted hair who says *I want to talk to your manager* until you want to crack a vase over her head." Elle snorted and gathered up the empty storage bin and all the smaller boxes that had lived in it to take back into the laundry room.

"She probably would be, if she'd married John like she wanted to."

Elle's jaw hit the floor. She almost dropped the bin, but Logan scooped it up out of her arms, and she ended up gaping at his back as he walked down the hall. "I'm sorry, if she had *what?* "

"You heard me," Logan said. "She and her family have been members of this country club since the ice age. She's an accountant or something— and yes, her hair *is* frosted, but at least she doesn't have an asymmetrical bob with bangs— and she thinks that, between her desk job and her acrylic nails and her family money, that she's better than everyone else."

"Delightful," Elle remarked, trying to distract herself from what Logan had just told her by stirring her wassail.

"She's got an entire tree up her ass." Logan returned and swiped a scone off of her cooling rack. "Shit, these are delicious."

"Thanks," she said. "Ginger scones. They're my favorite."

"Light, fluffy, spicy." Still chewing, Logan nodded. "I dig it."

Elle ladled some wassail into a mug for him and handed it off before making a cup for herself. "So, backtracking," she said, watching the steam rise in gentle clouds. "What I'm hearing is, this snobby bitch of an ex showed up at the club and put John in a mood." Her eyes flicked to the stairs. "Relatable, to be honest."

"Oh, no, she didn't just show up," Logan explained, plopping down on the couch and dragging Elle down with him. "Though, really, that was enough to make me want to throw hands."

"You always want to throw hands," Elle sighed. "Tyler's the only reason you've never ended up in jail, and you know it."

"No, it's you *and* Tyler." Logan sipped his wassail and then paused, looking into the cup. "Mulled cider?"

"Is that what people call it?" Elle asked, looking into her own mug. "I've literally only heard of it as wassail."

"Huh." He nodded thoughtfully at it. "Well, whatever it's called, it's great. But anyway, Jackie."

"Right, the bitch with the tree up her ass."

"Yeah, she decided to drag her new beau into it, gush about him like he shits gold, flaunt her million karat diamond ring in front of John, and then pick a fight about John not being good enough."

"*Bullshit.*" The word fell out of Elle's mouth before she could stop it.

Logan leaned back against the couch with his mug lazily gripped in one hand. "Babe, you know it. I know it. The damn mailman knows it. But John just calmly agreed with her and walked away, as he is wont to do when she does this— and that's alarmingly often, mind you."

"Poor John." Elle glanced at the stairs again. Maybe he'd like a scone. It couldn't possibly put him in a worse mood, if nothing else.

"It gets worse." Logan washed the announcement down with more wassail. "She decided she didn't like him playing nice, and chased him down."

"Oh, *no.* "

"And then slapped him across the face." Elle gasped, and Logan nodded. "Hard enough that the whole room heard it," he continued, his jaw setting. Elle hadn't seen him this angry since her mom had come— and that was saying something, since he usually *only* got angry around her mom.

"Jesus Christ on a crocodile," Elle breathed. "Why would she—"

"Spoiled bitch," Logan reminded her. "She hates being told *no.* Which is rich, since she's the one who dumped John."

Elle gasped again. "I remember her!"

Logan nodded. "His first year of grad school."

"We were— what, freshmen? Sophomores?" God, she hadn't thought about that in ages. "She dumped him during *Seven Brides for Seven Brothers*. He almost dropped out of the cast."

"Yep," Logan said. It was surreal, remembering this with him. "Two weeks after, she came crawling back, and couldn't fathom that he didn't want her back."

"It's been— what, five years since that?" Logan shrugged at that. Elle shook her head. "What the *fuck* , Jackie?"

"God, Ellie, preach." Logan patted her leg. "I can still see her ugly cake-face, mysteriously not streaked with tears as she wailed her way out of the club."

"She should go into theater." Logan barked with laughter at that. Elle laid down against him, sighing. "Poor John. He deserves better."

"He deserves you."

Elle snorted. "He deserves whoever he wants."

"I haven't forgotten our deal," Logan said.

"Oh, shit," Elle groaned and threw her hands over her face. "I did."

"I'm sure you'll have plenty of time to lock lips with him," Logan assured her, rubbing her arm gently.

"Now is *so* not the time." She sighed. "Alright, what's his favorite meal?"

Logan burst out laughing again. "Oh, Elle, you just want to fix everyone with food!"

"You're damn right," Elle said, jabbing Logan in the rib. He yelped. "He took care of me that night Mom gave me a panic attack. Not to mention after my panic attack when she told me she was coming. I owe him."

"You are, without a doubt, the most ridiculous two people I've ever met," Logan moaned. "Fine, Betty Crocker, it's chicken fried steak."

"Oh, I *love* chicken fried steak!" Elle clapped her hands together, remembering the dish with wistful nostalgia. "I have a family recipe— I think it was my second step dad's mom's recipe?" Shaking her head, she threw that train of thought away. "Whatever. It's a family recipe, it's homemade gravy, the whole works."

"He'll love it." Logan pressed a kiss into her hair. "I have a date tonight, so if you decide to finish our deal and seduce him with food—" He cut off laughing when Elle swatted his arm.

Hours passed. Logan left, the snow let up, and the sun set. The smells of ginger and wassail faded from the kitchen, replaced with the savory aroma of frying meat, roasting vegetables, garlic, and potatoes. Elle resumed her humming from earlier as she dipped steaks into the flour;

an egg, milk, and Tabasco mixture; then into the flour and spice mixture for the crust. The first four pieces were already on a plate, covered in tinfoil to keep them warm. When she was done with these last two pieces, she'd make herself some gravy out of the leftover drippings in the pan. The soothing, reliable task of cooking centered her, grounded her, made her feel both useful and fulfilled, all at once.

As she laid the steak into the pan to fry, Elle heard a door open upstairs and smiled. Food could lure anyone out of the worst funk. She should know. Even if he didn't want to talk about today, or if he didn't want to talk to her at all, at least she would know he was well fed.

She snuck a glance over her shoulder as John's footsteps reached the landing. He looked... mostly like he didn't want to kill anyone. More like maybe he'd like to throw himself over the banister. Too bad it would be a short drop. Considering how tall he was, he probably wouldn't even break a bone.

Well. Misery wouldn't do, would it?

Still humming and pretending not to watch him, Elle pulled the last steak from the pan and covered it in the foil. From the corner of her eye, she watched John, apparently oblivious to her existence, as he sulked over to the bookshelves in the living room.

Hmm. Reading. She felt that on a spiritual level. Escaping into someone else's bullshit to avoid her own.

He was still standing in the same spot when her gravy had thickened and she began to plate. She put the leftovers into topless containers to cool, then put her dishes in a neat stack in the sink, rinsing each of them.

Not clean enough, never clean enough, some nasty part of her brain told her. Gritting her teeth, she told it to shut up. Tonight was about solving John's problems, not wallowing in her own.

By the time she looked up from her existential crisis, John had relocated, staring down at the set dining room table with a lost expression. Not exactly promising.

Elle picked up his plate and a glass of water for him. Either John had the presence of mind to sit at one of the place settings, or he'd chosen the most convenient chair. Either way, he didn't look up, even when she set the plate and glass in front of him. Silently, she gave his shoulder a squeeze, and then walked away.

When she returned with her own food, he was staring down at his plate as though it might be an illusion, or a particularly vivid hallucination.

Been there, Elle reminded herself as she sat. It was an awful emotional backlash, when someone ripped open old wounds and left you bleeding and raw, teetering on a razor edge between fury and depression. As though a single word stood between a meltdown or an explosion.

Elle casually cut into her steak, which— by some timing miracle— was just the right shade of pink, and took a bite. "Do you remember when we still had that horrible wire system, before Greg finally came to his senses and got us a real flight system?"

John jerked his face up, eyes wide, and blinked a couple of times. "Um. Yeah, when we had that window washing harness." He seemed to regain control of his fine motor skills and picked up his fork and knife.

"We did *Charlotte's Web,* " Elle said. "When we had that summer camp for kids, and none of the adults auditioned. Greg, surprise surprise, drafted me as Charlotte." She watched John cut into the steak and take his first bite, and then just... freeze. "Um. There was a night that they couldn't get the hook off of the harness when they pulled me up. Tommy and Anthony had to vamp the scene change, Jesse was doing that weird whisper-scream he does, telling Ben not to bring up the lights. I almost missed my next cue, and Jesse almost pushed me back down to keep the wire on til act two."

John was *so* not listening to a word she was saying, even if he did nod politely. He still looked worried that the food may vanish at any second. Elle waited patiently as he finished chewing, and watched his throat bob as he swallowed.

"This is... really good," he said at length.

Elle released a breath she hadn't realized she'd been holding. "Thank you." She swallowed. "I made it to cheer you up. Is it working?"

A faint smile appeared on his face. "Yeah. Yeah, it's working." He cut a larger piece off of the steak. "My Gran used to make this on my birthday. I have no idea how you did it, but your gravy tastes *exactly* like hers."

"Family recipe," Elle said with a smile. "I made it from scratch."

"It's perfect," he mumbled. More to himself than to her.

Elle felt heat sweep into her cheeks and grinned down at her own plate. "Thank you."

They were both silent for a moment, and then: "So, who managed to free you from the flight hook?"

Elle laughed, and cut another piece of her steak.

13

"I'm pretty sure this is how obstetricians feel." With her arms elbow deep in turkey, Elle tilted her head back and blew the hair out of her eyes. She was almost certain that tucking the ends of her hair into the hair tie was supposed to keep it *out* of her face, but here she was, nonetheless. "Logan, could you—" His hands came up and pulled her hair back, securing it once again in the elastic. "Thank you." He pulled one of the legs back for her once his hands were free. Elle carefully slid her arms out and grimaced at the sticky moisture on her arms. "Ugh, this is the *worst* part of Thanksgiving."

"Stuffing is soggy and nasty," Logan said, watching her reach back into the giant bowl of it sitting beside the bird. "You could bake it in a casserole dish, Elle. You could make it bearable."

"We're doing both," she told him. "If you don't want to help, just send John in. Give him something to do other than pace at the door."

"You did the same thing when your mom showed up." He gave her his most dejected look, and then held the turkey open for her again.

"No, I went outside and contemplated laying down in the road. So he's already doing better than I did."

"Elle, this oversized chicken is *sticky*."

"Hold *still*." Her arms went in with a squelch, and Elle sighed. "*Ugh.*"

The air was thick with scents, both savory and sweet. The minute they'd finished breakfast that morning, Elle had kicked the men out, insisting that they either help her cook or clean something, so long as they made themselves useful. By noon, she had a full menu in the works. Two casseroles waited in the fridge to be reheated later. Potatoes and vegetables roasted in the oven. Her pies waited in the fridge, too, and she'd put those in to bake once dinner was on the table. Everything looked, smelled, and *felt* like Thanksgiving.

With her arms occupied, to put it mildly, Elle couldn't do much more than jerk her head toward the front of the house when the doorbell rang. "Go help John play host," she told Logan. "I've got this."

"There's no way that's John's family," Logan said, frowning and making no move to leave her side. "They're much louder than—"

"Logan," John's voice called, "I think this one's yours."

Elle twisted around awkwardly to see who had come, and grinned at the man that walked into her kitchen, accompanied by a frazzled John. "Hi, Tyler! Glad you could make it."

"Hey, Sugar," he said, coming around to plant a careful kiss on her cheek. "Smells great. I brought wine!"

"You're an angel," Elle told him. "Pour me some so I can have it when I'm done impersonating a midwife."

John snorted, coming over to hover while Logan greeted his boyfriend properly out of their line of sight. "That looks... intricate," he observed.

Elle rolled her eyes. "Do *you* want to be elbow deep in a turkey?" A strange, pained expression passed over John's face, and she nodded. "I didn't think so. Instead, you can hold these legs open for me, since Logan's hands are otherwise occupied."

"Thank god," Logan said behind her somewhere. "Save me from the overgrown chicken."

John examined the turkey, and Elle's mostly submerged arms, and nodded. "Looks like you've got it under control."

She had to crane her neck to glare at him, seriously considering throwing the stuffing she'd just crammed into the bird at his face. "Don't be mean."

John smirked down at her, then wrapped his arms around her, carefully opening the legs of the turkey with two fingers on each. "Sorry," he murmured into her hair.

It would have been a cute moment, she mused, in any other situation. Just to freak him out, Elle tugged her arms out, the quick motion causing another awful squelch. "Thanks," she said dryly, when

John jerked away. "Serves you right for attempting to abandon me." She headed directly for the sink jamming the heel of her palm into the faucet to turn it on. "You can go back to your pacing, now, love. I've got it from here."

"I wasn't pacing," John said, a touch petulant.

"We could hear your footsteps in here," Logan told him. He rested his chin on top of Tyler's head, arms around the stocky man's shoulders. "You'll lose ten pounds before we even get dinner cooked."

"I—" He had the decency, at least, to look sheepish. "Okay, maybe I was pacing. A little."

Elle took pity on him, soaping up her arms. "Logan, why don't you and your beau go sit? You've been a great help. John, you can keep yourself from pacing by taking the potatoes out of the oven for me, please."

"Where do you want them, Ellie?"

Her hand slipped right off the handle. She *must* have misheard him. That, or her eyes had gone, and it was John sitting on the couch with Tyler, and Logan was the one standing behind her. But no, Logan was in the process of draping himself over his boyfriend, his orange sweater bright and almost Halloweeny against Tyler's plum colored suit. He even reached up to adjust the knot of Tyler's tie. They were way too ensconced in each other to notice her and John in the kitchen.

Which meant John had actually just called her *Ellie.*

Slowly, she turned around, keeping her face carefully blank. She wanted to see if he'd caught his own verbal blunder, if he'd even realized he'd said it.

John winced, setting the bulging package of tin foil onto the stove. "Elle. Sorry."

Swallowing, Elle realized she didn't actually mind that he'd called her *Ellie.* To be perfectly honest, she kind of... liked it. It set off butterflies in her belly. The name, in his voice, didn't sound patronizing, or accusing, or disappointed. Nor did it sound placating or deliberately soothing. It just sounded like *home.*

Something warm bloomed in her chest.

"It's okay," she said, and smiled at him. "Really, it's alright. I'm amazed it's taken you so long to pick it up from Logan, honestly." She turned off the faucet and grabbed the dish towel to dry her arms off. "I mean, we've known each other for *years* . It was bound to happen." He still had that guilt-ridden grimace on his face, so she finished drying her arms and went to him, placing her hands on his chest. "John. Relax. I'm not upset." She patted his chest with one hand. "Now, go ahead and put that in the fridge for me, and then we can have some wine."

She must have startled him, because he looked down at her hands, then back up at her face, eyes wide. After a beat, he nodded and stepped away, and Elle went back to spoon the rest of the stuffing into the bird.

Once she'd finished the bird up, she poured turkey stock into the pan, and John put it into the oven for her. Humming, she washed her hands again, trying to convince them not to feel sticky anymore. When she finished drying them off, she turned around to find John holding a glass of wine out to her.

"You've earned this," he said as she took it. "Now go sit down before you give Logan an ulcer."

"Aye aye," she said with a wink, and strolled out to the living room to put up her feet.

Elle liked Tyler— and liked him for Logan. They looked completely at odds, short and tall, wiry and stocky. Tyler had rich olive skin, and Logan looked like a ghost in the wrong lighting. Except that, despite their fanfiction-trope appearance, Tyler treated Logan like he personally lit the stars every night.

A clutch in her heart drew her eyes back to John, sitting on the arm of her chair with a glass in his hand, staring at the door. Had he felt that way about Jackie? Had they been doomed to fail? He didn't seem inclined to date nowadays, even with Sarah basically throwing herself at him at every turn. Elle supposed it made him a gentleman, not putting any moves on her— his literal roommate— while she lived under his roof.

She must have stared at John for too long, because he noticed. He looked down at her, smiled, and tugged lightly on a lock of her hair that had come free of her hair tie. "They should be here soon."

"I'm excited to meet them." And nervous. John had been fretting, quietly, this entire week. Not in the distraught way Elle had back in September, but she'd caught him stress cleaning on multiple occasions and had talked him into doing more relaxing things, like handing her ass to her at MarioKart. His stress only made *her* stress, which left Logan as the only level-headed person in the house, and— no. That was a *terrible* idea.

"They're excited to meet you," John told her.

With a chuckle, Elle said, "Wow, no pressure."

John laughed, just as the doorbell rang again. His laughter cut short as he scrambled to his feet, all but jogging down the hallway to open the door, Elle and the other boys behind him.

The house was full of life, after that. Elle found herself wrapped up in so many hugs that she could barely keep track of whose arms were around her. John's mom was short, round, and enthusiastic about seeing "the kids." His father towered over her the same way John did, hair streaked with gray at the temples, his rugged good looks obviously the source of John's amazing genetic material. Moments later, John's sister, her husband, and their two and a half kids came in hot on their heels. The whole lot, save his brother-in-law, had the same honey blond hair.

"It's so nice to finally meet you!" Kellie, John's sister, clasped her hands over her baby bump as she spoke to Elle. "John speaks so highly of you."

"I'll pretend that doesn't make me nervous." Though she couldn't keep the laughter from her voice. Elle watched as Cliff, Kellie's husband, passed their toddler daughter off to her grandparents and shook John's hand.

"Oh, don't be!" All smiles, Kellie patted Elle's arm. "Mom and Dad are easy to impress, and I'm just happy you're not a psycho."

Elle smirked. "You shouldn't talk about Logan that way." Speaking of, she could see Logan and Tyler entertaining Kellie's little boy, Jeremy, who couldn't be more than six.

Kellie laughed. "Oh, Elle, you'll fit right in."

"Here," Elle said, remembering a little late that Kellie was, in fact, pregnant. "Come sit down, get off your feet."

"Oh, no, I'm— well, if you insist."

Just as Kellie settled down, her attention dropped to about hip-level on Elle. Elle felt a light tug on her sleeve, and looked down to find Jeremy. He stared up at her with big, bright green eyes, so similar to John's it actually startled her. "Miss Elle?"

"Yes, Sweetheart?" Elle put on an indulgent smile and squatted down to his level.

"Um— um—" Jeremy swayed back and forth nervously, wringing his hands. "Uncle John said I should ask you for a snack." His words were a little slurred, probably due to his missing front teeth.

Uncle John didn't notice Elle arching her eyebrow at him, too engrossed in his conversation with Cliff. "If Mommy says yes, you can have a snack. Dinner won't be for awhile yet." She looked to Kellie, who shrugged.

"He can have something now. I've also got carrots and apples for him, in case he doesn't like something at dinner."

"That's perfectly fine," Elle said, straightening up, "but I think I might have something he'll like better." She held out her hand to Jeremy, who slipped his tinier hand into it. "Do you like muffins?"

"Mommy gives me the blueberry kind for breakfast sometimes," he told her, following her to the kitchen.

"You'll probably like these, then." She opened the cookie tin, pulled out a scone. "It'll taste kind of like a gingerbread man. Have you ever had those?"

Jeremy nodded, eyes wide, as he took the scone. "Thank you, Miss Elle."

Elle couldn't stop the giggle that bubbled up in her throat. "You're very welcome."

She took advantage of being in the kitchen as Jeremy ran away, checking on the turkey through the oven window. Over her shoulder, she could hear Jeremy excitedly showing *Daddy* the treat he'd gotten. Moments later, she heard John's voice over the din of other voices.

"Look at you," He said, "you got a scone! You know, Miss Elle is the best cook in the *world*. And she gave you a scone! I would *love* to have one of her scones."

Grinning despite herself, Elle plucked another scone from the tin.

John seemed startled when she sidled up to him and put the scone into his hand. "You could have just asked," she scolded, "rather than charming me with a six-year-old."

"Hey, it worked," he said, and toasted her with the scone. "Have you held Daisy yet?"

Something bone deep in Elle thrummed at the thought of holding the baby, currently babbling nonsense on her grandmother's lap. "I... no, not yet."

"Here," he said, guiding her over to the couch, where his parents sat. "Sit, hold a baby. Let someone else do the work for a while."

"You and Logan," Elle started, but it was too late for protests. Anne Ebner shifted to the side to make room for Elle, John gently nudged her into sitting, and within moments, Elle held a cheerfully babbling and bubbling baby on her lap. Daisy made a point of batting her eyelashes at her uncle, who broke off a corner of his scone and handed it to her, winking at Elle as he walked away.

"He's sneaky like that." Anne clutched her husband's weathered hand in her own. The silver wedding set on her finger glimmered against the wrinkles of her hand, ageless against the wear and tear of time. "He gets it from his father."

"He's more of a mother hen than I am." Elle clasped her hands around Daisy, charmed by the baby's nonsense.

"Bold words from the resident theater mom," Logan interjected, picking up Tyler's wine glass from the coffee table and then wandering away again.

"John's told us plenty about your aptitude at the theater," Anne said.

"He thinks you'll own it someday," George Ebner said, with the same smirk John often used on Elle, obscured slightly by his greying beard.

"Not exactly a goal of mine," Elle admitted, "but I don't think anyone would let me say no. I think I want to direct first."

"Baby steps," Anne agreed, patting Elle's leg with her free hand.

"So you're an actress?" George pulled his wife against him in a hug, but his attention was firmly directed at Elle.

The easy affection melted something inside Elle. "I was. Now I usually stage manage, choreograph, or do audio, depending on the show." She adjusted Daisy on her lap, the baby deciding that laying against Elle was preferable to sitting up on her own. "Greg made me stage manage *Little Shop*, even though I wanted to cop out and run spotlight. Before this run, I *hated* this show, but now that we're almost done..." She glanced at John, who was still talking with Cliff, now with Jeremy on his hip. "I don't know if I'd want to be in it, but it's not as bad when I'm busy muttering into a headset like a lunatic."

"He was quite impressed with your performance in *Oklahoma*," Anne insisted. "He talked about it for nearly an hour. We were *so* disappointed that we missed it."

Elle felt her face go hot, watching Daisy put her tiny fist in her mouth. "I can't imagine why. People kept having to herd me through the blocking like a sheep, I'm pretty sure I paraphrased half the script, I forgot my blocking and walked right into his elbow—"

"Ah, yes, he mentioned that," Anne said wryly. "But he said you sang so beautifully. That's the most important part, isn't it?"

That wasn't how Elle had ever thought of it, no. "It's all important in the end, unless it's opera, I guess." She laughed, a little nervous, carefully shifting Daisy's head to a more comfortable spot on her shoulder. "We love a good park and bark. Though we do try not to talk about the local church's rendition of *The Magic Flute,* if we can avoid it."

"That bad?"

Elle tried not to grin at George's question, with mixed results. "Let's just say it was woefully miscast, painfully underfunded, and highly attended for its comedic interpretation."

"Oh, god."

"John wanted to be like Placido Domingo as a child," Anne recalled fondly, her eyes— almost the exact shade of green as John's— seeking out her son behind Elle's head. Elle resisted the urge to do the same. "Or was it Andrea Bocceli?" Anne shrugged. "He was obsessed with opera as a child. He loved Michael Crawford in *Phantom*."

"Oh, I love *Phantom*," Elle said. She glanced back at John, finding him crouched in front of the oven, basting the turkey, while Jeremy watched in awed rapture from a safe distance behind him. "I think it's my favorite, honestly."

"He ended up being a baritone," Anne continued, "but we got him lessons anyway. Singing, acting, a few dance classes. He's pretty good at waltzing." Maybe Elle imagined it, but that last comment sounded a bit suggestive.

"He basically carried me through *Oklahoma*," she admitted. "I wouldn't have made it through the first night without him." A soft snore drew Elle's attention downward. Daisy was out cold on her chest.

"She's so comfortable around you," Kellie observed, shifting in her chair. "*Oof.* This never gets any easier."

"I mean, there's a child on your bladder," Elle pointed out.

"Yeah, and it only gets worse from here." Kellie patted her belly, though, smiling fondly down at it. "I actually prefer to stand, usually. Which reminds me, if you don't mind me taking over your kitchen, I can finish dinner and you can relax."

Elle's knee jerk reaction was to panic. "Oh, that's okay—"

"No, no, I insist!" Kellie waved her hand behind her, to where John was listening raptly to Jeremy's tales from the first grade, clearly audible over every other conversation happening. "John can help me. I'm sure Jeremy would love to talk Logan's ear off."

That was probably true. Nonetheless, Elle opened her mouth to argue again.

"Oh, good," Logan said, hearing his name, "keep her off her feet for a bit." He took Elle's wine glass from the coffee table and forced it into her free hand. "Ellie, tell them about your knack for sewing. I think Sleeping Beauty here needs a princess dress."

"Oh, what a lovely idea!" Anne said.

"But—" she was outnumbered, she realized. "Oh, okay. Sure," she said in Kellie's general direction. "If you really want the kitchen, go wild."

"Lovely!" Instantly, Kellie turned around, her Mom Voice coming out full force. "Why don't you boys go out and play for a while? Work off some of that energy before dinner."

Jeremy cheered, and John rolled his eyes. "Come on, Logan," he said, following Cliff and Jeremy toward the back door.

"Take your boyfriend and his impeccable suit," Elle said, waving at Tyler. "Rough him up a bit."

"He's already rough enough, thanks." As Elle burst out laughing, Logan took Tyler's hand and obediently dragged him out the back door with the other boys.

"They're good boys," Anne sighed, watching them through the window. Elle watched, too, as John produced a ball out of seemingly nowhere and threw it across the yard. "We thought John might be gay, for a little while. Especially when he moved Logan in here."

"That's not saying much," Elle said. "In high school, everyone thought Logan and I were dating. He's just overly affectionate."

"Well, we wouldn't have minded." Anne reached over and pulled a lock of hair from Elle's face, gently tucking it behind Elle's ear. It was such an affectionate, mothering gesture, that it rendered Elle completely speechless. "But it turned out that John was just passionate about performing."

"He gets it from you." George kissed his wife's temple as she settled against his side again. Anne just laughed.

Elle felt her throat close. It was no wonder John was such an amazing man. His parents were everything she'd heard parents could be— kind, affectionate, understanding. They clearly adored their children as much as they adored each other. Stable, solid, obviously very much in love. Even after all the trials and tribulations of life.

Maybe Elle could find that, someday. Her eyes drifted back to the windows, where she could see John getting tackled to the ground by a six-year-old tornado. Having kids in the house felt so... so *right*. Having this close knit, happy family in their space, taking her into the fray and accepting her presence without question or critique.

She should feel guilty, she supposed, that Karen hadn't been included, but Karen had insisted she already had plans with Garth this year, so Elle had let it go. Besides, it was hard to feel guilty when she felt so at ease.

The hours ticked by at a relaxed, indulgent pace. Elle lost herself to her wine and the steady, even breathing of the child sleeping on her chest. Every now and then, peals of young laughter and amused shouts from the men drifted in from the back yard. The sun streamed in, warm and golden, while the house filled to bursting with the scents of dinner.

The sappy Lifetime movie they had on rolled its credits. Elle's eyes flicked to the timer on the oven and she sighed. "Would someone please call John back in?" She asked, hands still clasped around Daisy, holding her securely. "He'll need to get the turkey out in a couple minutes."

"I've got it," Kellie said, bracing her hands on the arms of her chair.

"Nonsense." Anne had sprung to her feet so quickly Elle hadn't even noticed her getting up. She crossed over to the back door, patting Kellie's shoulder as she passed. "You sit and relax, now. I can get the boys."

Delight spread across Kellie's face. "Watch this, Elle, it'll be great." Kellie herself turned awkwardly in her chair to follow her mother's movements. Elle craned her head to watch, fascinated.

Like an army general, Anne marched out onto the back stoop, hand firmly on her hip. "Boys!"

The motion and voices from outside came to a dead stop all at once. Several startled grunts followed as the men ran into each other, all of them scrambling not to step on anyone else. Even little Jeremy stopped short, craning his neck up at the men surrounding him curiously.

Anne nodded, once all (or at least, most) of the attention was on her. "I need to borrow John from you!"

John, Cliff, Logan, and Jeremy all reordered themselves, sweeping Tyler along whether he wanted to go or not. John sent the ball sailing through the air, and all the others charged after it, before he jogged back up to the house.

"What can I do, Mom?" He asked, ducking down to kiss her cheek.

"Retrieve the bird." Anne herded him into the kitchen just as Elle's timer went off. She silenced it with the press of a button, opened the oven for John, and then steered clear of him as he pulled out the turkey. "There you go, dear," she said to Elle, as she returned to her seat.

"Thank you," Elle said. "Someone take the baby so I can get the gravy on. Oh, and I need to put the sides back in to warm up—"

"Don't even try," Kellie said pointedly. "John," she called, using the same bossy sibling tone that Elle had used on Garth a million times. "Come help me up. I'm pregnant."

"You're not *that* far along," John said, but came over to haul her to her feet nonetheless. He caught sight of Elle's empty wine glass, still in her hand, and nodded toward it. "Want more wine?"

"I probably shouldn't," she said. "I'm too much of a lightweight."

"I know," John said, giving her a look. She remembered Halloween night and blushed.

"You're not going anywhere," Kellie insisted, taking the wine glass from Elle's hand. "You'll be fine with one more."

"You say that now," Elle said, laughing.

Dinner was nothing short of controlled chaos. Cliff rescued Elle from Baby Duty, and she added her hands to the kitchen, kicking everyone out besides John, who was carving the bird, and Kellie. Between the two of them, they reheated all the side dishes, pulled together the gravy, and got the pies in the oven. Platters crowded the dining table and the extra card table they'd set up beside it, plates and cutlery stuffed together around them.

Conversation criss-crossed the table as they dished everything up. Elle tried to keep track of anyone who said her name, but—

"Oh, Elle, this is *lovely!*"

"What do we say, Jer-bear?"

"Thank you, Miss Elle."

"Elle's cooking is fit for the *gods*."

"Well, if it keeps you two troublemakers occupied, it *must* be perfect." Laughter, across the table.

Elle learned several new things about first grade one minute, and an alarming amount about Armani the next. George and Anne drilled John and Logan about their lives in that polite, parental way. Kellie demurely asked Elle for prices for a princess dress for Daisy, either for Christmas or the toddler's second birthday in May. George asked her if she would audition for the next season of shows, and Elle answered truthfully that no, she hadn't planned on it, to which Logan immediately cut in, politely threatening to drag her into the auditions himself.

Logan and John cleared the table, and Elle followed them into the kitchen, intent on sending everyone home with leftovers. As she dished and divided, snapping shut tupperware lids, the men cleaned, keeping the mess around her to a bearable minimum.

"Miss Elle?"

A tug on the hem of her shirt distracted her from her sorting and dishing. Elle smiled down fondly at Jeremy. "Yes, Sweetheart?"

"Can I—" he stuttered, starting again. "Can I have another muffin?"

Elle took that to mean he wanted another scone and laughed. "Have you ever had pie?" He shook his head. "I think you'll like it. We're having some in a little while, when we're all done cleaning up." Once she'd closed the container in her hands, she reached down to brush the hair back from his face. "Why don't you go outside and play until then? I bet Logan will even go with you, if you ask him nicely."

She watched in awe as Jeremy followed her directions to a tee, using his most angelic smile. Her own smile threatened to show as Logan fell for it full stop.

"Will you be okay here?" He asked John, hand in Jeremy's.

"All that's left is the counters, I think." Elle heard the faucet turn off as she began stacking containers in the fridge. "Elle, you good?"

"Peachy keen," she sang.

She'd managed to tetris all of the tupperware in and, pleased with her results, straightened up out of the fridge.

"They like you."

If John had spoken any more softly, she wouldn't have heard him at all. As it was, it was a miracle she didn't jump at his voice in her ear.

"I hope so," she said, shutting the fridge door. "I like them."

"I know they're…" he winced as he heard his father's shout not too far behind him, cheering on the Turkey Bowl on the TV. "A lot," he finished. "You just rolled with it. You…" He hesitated, and Elle leaned against the fridge door, waiting for him to finish before she reminded him about her own family. John stared down at her, and then turned his eyes away with a shrug. "You fit."

Elle felt warmth spread through her chest again, and that same sense of belonging from earlier. "They're wonderful," she told him honestly. "They're so accepting. They're like—" *family.* They were almost as much of a family to her, in this short span of time, as her family at the theater. More, even, than Karen had ever been to her.

John nodded, as though he knew what she'd been about to say. As though he understood. He stepped closer— too close, maybe, close enough that all she'd have to do was straighten up to be pressed against him.

Elle felt her breath backup in her lungs, inexplicably. A tremor fluttered in her belly. Her heart stuttered in her chest.

His eyes were so intense, so *bright,* burning into her. "Listen, Elle—"

"Hey, John, do you have—"

John jumped back so fast he probably gave himself whiplash. Elle stepped to the side, away from the fridge and away from him, giving them room. Giving them *space.* Hoping some air would get back into her lungs.

Tyler held up his hands apologetically. "Sorry! I didn't—"

"It's fine."

"No, love, you're alright." Elle's eyes shot to John's as they spoke together, then away, back to Tyler.

"Um." Tyler, to his credit, did a great job of pretending not to notice them both being weird. "Okay. John, I've been sent to ask for either beer or scotch for your father."

John sighed. "Sounds about right."

"I'll just..." Elle skirted around Tyler to head back to the living room, deciding to just casually...*forget* about that almost-conversation with John. Either he'd bring it back up, or he wouldn't, but she wasn't about to do so. Besides, she had a party to host.

14

"I don't see why this is being so *difficult*," Elle whined, struggling to convince a pine garland not to slide right off of the curtain rod she wanted to hang it on. The ladder underneath her managed to stay steady, even with her movement.

Already, the house was a wonderland of garland and glitter, a wintery haven of green and silver and white. Like he had for autumn, Logan had arranged candles on every available surface, snowy white and silver and pine green. The room smelled like rich pine and more of Elle's spiced cider.

"Did you try tape, Doll?" Logan asked, busy with the family of caroler-themed nutcrackers he'd discovered in one of her Christmas bins, which were currently finding a home under the TV beside one of his decorative Menorahs.

"Contrary to popular belief, I don't actually carry gaff tape with me everywhere," Elle sighed, propping her hip on the top of the ladder for better leverage. "I know, I'm a disappointment to techs everywhere."

"It's because you should be performing," Logan teased.

"Right," she muttered. The garland slid down until the pretty drape she'd done was long enough to reach the window sill, the tail on the other end mere inches long. "Oh, come *on!* " She gave it a tug until it was the right length, then tried to twist it around the rod more securely. "There should be hooks for this. Something pretty and festive. And *easy.*"

While Logan laughed at her plight, the front door opened and shut. "Hey," came John's voice, just after.

"Hi my love," Elle called back, watching with dismay as the garland started to slide down again, the opposite way from before. "How was the club today?"

"Eh, you know." John's voice grew closer, raised slightly over the Christmas music playing softly on the TV. "Boring upper-middle class families with too much money and too much time."

"Suburban white soccer mom thinks her gingerbread men are unique because she added Fireball to the batter, more at eight."

John laughed, his voice right underneath her. Elle glanced down and gave him a smile, but her focus was mostly on this god-forsaken garland. "You look thrilled to be up there," John observed, a little wryly.

"I would be, if—" As she tried to tug it, the garland caught— either in itself, the hook holding up the curtain rod, or maybe one of the rings holding the curtains on. Whatever it was, it rendered the garland effectively frozen, the length completely wrong. "Oh, for *God's sake.*" It really was jammed in there, taunting her, *laughing* at her. Elle tilted further forward on the ladder, trying to reach the spot where it was tangled, but her arms were too short. With a growl of frustration, she grabbed the garland and gave it a firm tug.

The move overbalanced her. While the ladder— and the stupid *garland*— stayed immobile, Elle felt her center of gravity pitch backwards, and thought: *fuck.*

She expected to hit the ground. Maybe crack a rib or two— not like it would be the first time she'd fallen from a ladder and put herself in the ER for one broken bone or another.

The drop was short, her yelp of alarm cutting off as she landed— right into John's arms.

Elle's arms came up, automatically, to wrap around John's neck. The *oh* that came from her lips felt too small and insignificant to encompass the pounding of her heart, the shock of being caught, the relief that she hadn't landed on the floor.

John looked even more surprised than she was, eyes wide, lips parted. Her knight in cable knit, as it were, his golden hair dusted with melting snowflakes, his cheeks flushed. His arms tightened slightly around her, and she realized he was holding her bridal style.

Oh, she thought meekly. Heat spread up her chest, her neck, her face.

"You okay?" The words were merely a breath. He was breathing heavily, probably just as startled to have ended up in this position as she was.

Elle swallowed. "Yeah." Oh god, was that her voice? She sounded like a frightened child. "Yeah, I'm okay, thank you." John nodded. His eyes seemed a little unfocused. "You can— um, you can put me down if I'm too heavy."

John blinked, and then frowned. "Heavy?" With a snort, he flipped her, bringing her up over his shoulder while she squealed. "Please, Elle. You don't weigh anything."

"I have no idea how you're so uncoordinated," Logan said. "Aren't all techs supposed to be like cats, or something?"

"Just because it's called a catwalk doesn't make us cats," Elle laughed. "John, put me *down!*"

"No," he said defensively. "You still think you're too heavy for me."

"Fine, fine!" Elle wrapped her arms around his waist, because the ground looked too far away for comfort. "You're a regular Hercules, and I'm light as a feather, now *put me back on the ground—*" John grabbed her by the waist and lifted her again, setting her blessedly upright again on her feet. Elle still clung to his shoulders, just in case he decided to treat her like a ragdoll again.

"You two," Logan muttered. Elle glanced over her shoulder to watch him roll his eyes and sail down the hall toward the laundry room, an empty bin under his arm.

Weird reaction, Elle mused, looking back up at John. He just stared back down at her with an arched brow. "You good there?"

"What?" Oh, she was still holding onto him. Right. "Yeah," she said, stepping back, putting space between them. God, this was like Thanksgiving all over again. "Yeah, now that you're not tossing me like a salad."

John snorted. "That was awful. No more puns from you."

"Ha." Elle looked down and smoothed her shirt down, more for something to do with her hands than out of necessity. "Well, if you'd like to play tug of war with a garland for awhile, the ladder's all yours."

John peered up at the decoration with vague distaste. "What, you don't want to leave it uneven?" When Elle cringed, he laughed. "It gives it character."

"It's awful," Elle said. "I don't even want to look at it."

"Fine, alright," John appeased her, climbing two steps up the ladder and reaching the tangled garland with ease.

"Now that's just not fair." Elle watched him fumble with the garland for a moment. "Can we do the tree after this?"

"Sure," John said. "I don't usually do themes or anything."

"That's fine," Elle said, going around to hold the other side of the ladder, keeping it steady. "Gina and I had so many decorations between the two of us, we could have. I usually just work with whatever I've got."

"It's a lot of Disney in this house," John admitted. "People just keep getting me *Nightmare Before Christmas* stuff."

Elle laughed. "I've got a lot of Disney, too. My grandparents loved Goofy and Tigger, for some reason." The thought of them sent a bittersweet pang through her heart.

"Tall goofballs," John guessed, finally convincing the garland to slide.

"Probably." *They'd have loved you,* she thought.

John came back down the ladder, running his hand through his hair. The light from the window caught in it just so, glistening through it like strands of gold.

Yikes, Elle thought. First she fell on the guy, now she was falling *for—*

"No more ladders for you," John insisted, closing the one in question up.

"Then I guess you'll have to put the star on the tree," Elle replied.

"Good," John said, tucking the ladder underneath one arm like it weighed nothing. He really *was* strong. "That'll keep you from falling to your death."

"You'd catch me," she said, without thinking.

John was already past her, heading to put the ladder back in the garage. He paused and turned, pinning her with a look she could only describe as solemn. "Yes," he said, his tone certain. "I would."

It wasn't that Elle didn't like Christmas. She *loved* Christmas. The decorations, the tree, the smell of pine, the snow falling softly outside while she was warm and snug inside. She loved the music and the tacky movies. She loved baking Christmas cookies, naturally. She even liked wrapping presents.

What she couldn't stand about Christmas was the abhorrent tradition surrounding that god-forsaken plant: *mistletoe.*

They'd arrived at Nathan and Sylvie Whitmore's house while the party was in its early stages. The Whitmores lived in the same neighborhood, in a similarly enormous house with beautiful stonework outside and a slanted roof draped with lights, coppery window shutters that held draping garlands, and an emerald green front door with an enormous wreath. Unlike the open, airy design of John's house, their front door opened directly to a staircase, and several smaller rooms wrapped around the back, each festively decorated for the party.

It was, essentially, a two-for-one cast party for *Little Shop* and an early Christmas party. Venus flytraps and a few of the show posters had been mixed into various holiday decorations. Even the food was themed to fit both— and the look on Sylvie's face when Elle uncovered her red velvet Audrey II cookies was definitely worth the hours and effort of icing them.

Everyone dressed up for the occasion, too, just like at Halloween; even Logan, though he wore a blatantly Hanukkah themed sweater under his Christmas light necklace. Christmas music and songs from the show filled the house, accompanied by cheerful voices that only grew as more people arrived.

"Cute dress!" Elle was in the middle of pouring herself a cup of cocoa when she heard Haley's voice behind her, and she toasted the other girl with a grin.

"Thanks," she said, and out of habit added, "I made it."

"I love the giant snowflakes." Haley, dazzling in a red and white dress of her own, lifted the skirt of Elle's dress and held it up against hers. "Look at us, Christmas red and green!"

"A regular Rosencrantz and Guildenstern," Elle teased, passing Haley a plate of snacks— also out of habit, since Haley would end up stealing half of hers otherwise. "Here, eat cookies."

"You know me so well." Haley took the plate with a gleeful smile. "Oh, I brought mistletoe!"

Elle blanched, and couldn't keep the grimace off her face. "God, why?"

"Oh, it's fun!" Haley said. "I think I'll break it out in a little bit, after I've seen who's here."

"At least tell Nathan and Sylvie," Elle said, taking her mug and plate and making a note to avoid Haley at all costs.

"They asked me to bring it!"

Shoot, Elle thought. "How nice," she lied, and promptly disappeared into one of the sitting rooms, losing herself in the crowd.

Within an hour, Haley had announced the game at large, dangling the dreadful plant from a string on a stick like a cat toy. Elle managed to avoid it by the skin of her teeth, either by ducking out of whatever room she heard Haley's voice enter, or— as she was doing now— by holding someone's child, since kids were off-limits. Jack had kicked the game off by giving Haley a dramatic and romantic kiss, dipping her low as he had as Ali Hakim in *Oklahoma*, accompanied by a roar of laughter from everyone who saw them. Logan had been caught in less than ten minutes, and one of the techs had taken pity on him, giving him a gentle peck on the cheek. Sarah had gathered a group of girls somewhere, plotting their attacks on the innocent men around them, and then, inexplicably, sat down across from Elle.

"I think I'm going to do backstage stuff for the next show," Ben said, stretching out his legs beside Elle on the loveseat. "Once *Nutcracker* season is over."

"I can't wait for *Nutcracker* season to be over," Elle said. On her chest, Sylvie and Nathan's baby gave a tiny sigh.

"I'm just glad I don't have to watch John die every weekend," Sarah said, pouting at the man in question, who was talking with Jesse just through the door to the kitchen. "Poor John."

"You're gonna miss getting to crawl all over him during his song," Elle said dryly. Sarah's eyes went wide at the accusation. "The audience loved it, though. I don't think I've ever seen this show so blatantly sexual."

"Is *that* why you were stage managing?" Ben teased, poking her leg. "You got to be all up in the action—"

"If I wasn't holding a baby, I'd hit you." As it was, Elle shot him her most withering look, which he only grinned at. "I will miss swing dancing with Logan to the intro backstage, though. Maybe I'll talk Greg into doing *Grease* next year."

"Would you finally audition so he can stop nagging you?" Ben asked.

"For swing dancing?" Elle grinned. "Absolutely. John would be a great Kenickie."

Irritation colored Sarah's face. "I'm pretty sure it's Lindy-hop, not swing."

"They're sibling styles," Elle informed her coolly, and then turned back to Ben. "Bridget was so cute as Audrey. It was nice to see her as a lead instead of a swing."

Sarah scowled and stood up. "I'm getting more wine."

Elle managed to hold her laughter in until Sarah vanished in the crowd. She even managed to keep a straight face, barely. "Poor Sarah. I think she made a great hooker."

"Elle, that's *mean*," Ben scolded. Elle just laughed harder. "You're gonna wake Millie!"

"Millie's fine," Elle insisted, rubbing the baby's back and earning a soft huff on her neck. "How's your girlfriend, Ben?"

Ben's face lit up at the subject change. "She's great! Wanna hear about my present for her?"

Elle listened with half an ear, scanning the crowd for Haley. She wouldn't be able to escape forever; someone else would ask for the baby eventually. Most of the cast of *Oklahoma* had shown up along with the *Little Shop* cast and crew. A few kids still scampered about, though most of the ones she'd seen recently were sleeping on their parents' shoulders.

John crossed her field of vision, his cable-knit sweater the same dark green as her dress, by sheer coincidence. He towered over the crowd, which also meant that everyone saw him, stopping to talk to him.

Ah, the trials of being popular and charismatic.

She tuned back into Ben's monologue, nodding to show that she was listening, but something behind her caught Ben's attention. His beetle black eyes lifted behind his glasses, and the look of intense concentration faded into a smile. "Hey, Davy. What's up?"

Elle carefully turned her head, mindful of the baby, to smile up at Davy. "Hi, Hun. Good to see you."

"Hey," he said, with his pretty Southern Drawl. "Good to see you, too." He tilted his head to see which baby Elle had ended up with, but Millie's face was buried in Elle's shoulder. "Cute," he said, whether he figured it out or not.

"Yeah, Sylvie did a great job on this one. She's..." Elle frowned, turning her head, but she didn't see Sylvie in this room, or in the kitchen just through the door. "Somewhere?"

"Indulging in a well needed nap on her husband's shoulder," Haley announced, sweeping in— mysteriously without the mistletoe. Maybe she'd finally given up on her matchmaking crusade. She glided over to Elle and plucked the baby up, tucking her underneath her own chin.

"Thanks," Elle sighed, finally letting her arms rest. "God, Sylvie's going to have biceps like rocks."

"They'll match her dancer legs," Haley said, dropping down into the chair Sarah had vacated. "You've seen her calves."

"She's going to be one of those moms that looks like she was never pregnant." Elle laughed, and then looked up at Davy. "Here, I can move over now. Come sit." She scooted over, shoving Ben into the corner of the couch. "Move over, you couch hog, you can stretch out in the tech booth."

"No I can't!"

"Hush." Elle smiled at Davy as he reluctantly settled next to her. "Has John still been giving you trouble, Davy?"

"No," Davy said, sounding somewhat surprised about it. "He actually talked to me just a little while ago."

"I saw that," Elle said. "You should be safe from his big brother complex, now. I set him straight."

"That's a relief." Davy chuckled, draping his arm over the back of the couch, behind Elle. "Any luck on that front?"

"Absolutely not," Elle said. "Besides him being *way* over-invested in my love life, it's still the same old, same old."

Davy smirked at her. "He's jealous."

Now *that* made her snort. "Please. As if."

"Hi Jack," Ben said, having to raise his voice over Elle's and Davy's laughter.

Elle looked at him, frowning, and then made the horrible mistake of looking up. "Oh, *hell*."

Haley grinned like a lunatic from the chair while her boyfriend dangled mistletoe over Elle's head.

"I thought I'd gotten out of this," Elle said, glaring at Haley. "You're really underhanded, you know that?"

Haley responded with kissy noises.

"Too bad John's not around," Davy muttered beside her.

"What?" Elle started to turn her head, but Davy stopped her by leaning down and kissing her cheek. "Oh—!"

"There, she got her kiss," he said, giving Haley the same glare Elle had. "Let the lady live her life."

"My hero," Elle said, though she was also back to glaring at Haley. The other woman merely laughed.

"I don't know if that counts," she said, but settled further into her chair with Millie.

"Was that better or worse than being mauled by a nineteen-year-old?" Ben asked Davy, while Elle settled back into the couch, her hand on her brow.

Davy grimaced. "I think you already know."

The crowd thinned, most of the families with kids disappearing as the party wore on. Elle herself was starting to get tired, too. Somewhere along the line, Elle laid her head on Davy's shoulder, just listening to people talk around her. Neither of her roommates had made an appearance in so long, she started to get a little antsy. She had no idea how long she'd been sitting there.

"I'm gonna go find the boys," she said. "Otherwise I'm going to fall asleep on you," she continued, patting Davy's leg.

"I wouldn't mind it," Davy said, "but you only just got John to stop glaring."

Elle laughed and got to her feet, stretching. "Consider that bullet dodged, then." With a wave, she headed into the kitchen, humming along with the Christmas music.

There weren't many people left in here, with most of the snacks and drinks gone, including all of Elle's cookies. Bridget, Miriam, and Nathan all stood around the counter holding drinks, gossiping about one thing or another, but there was no sign of her roommates.

"Anyone seen Logan or John?" Elle asked, stepping up to their group as the conversation lulled.

"That-a way," Miriam said, her watered down Southern accent coming through with a slight slur. Her weathered hand almost collided with Elle's nose as she gestured toward the living room.

"Oh!" Elle ducked, and began to laugh. "Well, thanks. You okay?"

"Happy as a clam," Miriam crowed, flinging her arm around Elle's shoulders. "You tell that roommate of yours to get kissin' on you, or I'll do it myself."

Startled, Elle glanced at Nathan and Bridget. Both were sputtering behind their drinks, clearly trying not to laugh. She didn't even know where to start with Miriam's announcement. Which roommate? And Miriam was married— and straight, as far as Elle knew— so what did she want to kiss Elle for? "Um—"

"He *should* have given you a proper kiss during *Oklahoma*," Miriam insisted, leaning away. Elle scrambled to wrap her arm around Miriam's waist, if only to keep her upright. "Instead, he gave you a proper *bruise,* the brute." With a crack of laughter, she added, "He could have kissed it better! Now, *that* I'd pay to see!"

Oh, god, Miriam was *wasted*, Elle realized. She steadied Miriam again as the older woman swayed dangerously. "Please tell me someone's driving you home."

"I'm just happy," Miriam insisted, patting Elle's cheek.

"Uh-huh."

"I've got her," Bridget said. "We carpooled here, and I have the car keys."

"Oh, good." Elle casually snagged Miriam's drink and passed it off to Nathan, who had come to stand beside her. "Speaking of going home, I need to find the boys."

"Here, Elle," Nathan said, and carefully managed to switch places with Elle, freeing her from Miriam's embrace. Miriam promptly kissed Nathan— very noisily— on the cheek.

Laughing, Elle sashayed away, leaving Nathan and Bridget to handle Miriam's enthusiastic affection. She made her way into the living room and caught sight of John— not hard, with his height— with Logan beside him, deep in conversation.

And Jack, sneaking up on them, with the mistletoe stick in hand.

"Oh, no," she said to no one in particular. She thought they'd finished with that nonsense. Logan had already *had* his turn, which meant—

"*Please* pick John," Someone said. Elle's head whipped around to find Sarah back in the kitchen, making a beeline toward the men.

Elle connected the dots and felt panic shoot through her. With absolutely no plan, she surged forward, almost jogging through people to reach John before Sarah did. It felt like *eons* passed by the time she reached them, but somehow, she managed to beat Sarah.

"Hey," John said when he saw her, lighting up as she stepped up beside him. "There you are. I figured you'd fallen asleep somewhere."

"Sarah's gunning for you like a hunter in duck season," Elle said, watching Jack get distracted by Jesse— who was *definitely* doing that on purpose. Bless him.

John groaned. "Who's got mistletoe *now?* I haven't seen Haley in an hour."

"Jack." At the sound of his name, Jack's head turned, but Elle grabbed Logan and dragged him over in between them. "Run while you can."

"God—" John turned around, Elle right behind him, only to find Haley standing behind them with a mischievous grin— and the goddamn mistletoe, dangling over John's head.

"Your turn, John!" she crowed, cackling. Right behind her, Sarah had a look of pure murder on her face, mysteriously stuck in the kitchen with Miriam draped boisterously against her side.

John grabbed Elle's waist. Startled, she put her arms on his chest, losing her balance so badly that she ended up plastered against the front of him. When she looked up, it was clear he was aiming for her cheek, having to bend down, down, *down,* because he was just so damn tall compared to her.

Like a lightbulb flashing on in her mind, Elle remembered her deal with Logan.

She turned her head.

It was like it had been during *Oklahoma.* John froze the moment their lips met, as though he wasn't sure whether or not it had happened on purpose. His hands, however, tightened on her waist. For a moment, she wondered if he'd push her away.

He didn't.

Ever so slightly, John pulled her closer. Elle flexed her hands on his chest and rose just a bit higher on her toes, pressing her lips more firmly against his.

This was… god. There weren't words for this. Something sweet and liquid coiled in her belly, warmth spreading through her. This was *right.* This was *wonderful.* This was—

This was her roommate. The one she lived with. The one who treated her like a kid sister.

Elle jerked back so fast she almost fell backwards, and then just… stared at John, lips parted. He blinked at her for a second, and then, as though remembering who he was looking at, his face went blank. He turned away from her only seconds before her eyes shot to the ground.

"Alright, you had your fun," Logan said to Haley. "Go torment somebody else."

Haley laughed merrily, saying something Elle didn't catch, because Logan had seized her arm and started to drag her away from the whole scene. On the one hand, she was grateful, because— god, she wasn't even sure she could talk to John right now. On the other hand, she knew Logan, and he was dragging her *away* from the crowd, which no doubt meant—

"How was it?" Logan asked, stopping in front of the staircase at the front of the house.

"I don't know," Elle said honestly. Panic started to rise in her chest.

"What do you mean, you don't know?" Logan scowled. "Was it good?"

She didn't know. She wasn't even entirely sure what had just happened, it had gone so quickly. "I don't—"

"Elle, are you okay?" Saved by the drawl, Elle thought as Davy appeared. He looked between her and Logan, eyes narrowing with concern. "What happened?"

"John kissed Elle," Logan said, at the exact same time Elle said, "I kissed John."

Logan's head whipped around, eyes wide. "Wait, what?"

"I turned my head," Elle explained. Her hands were shaking when she brought them up to her cheeks. "He was going for my cheek, but I remembered my deal with you, so I—" She sucked in a breath as she realized what she'd done. God, this could *ruin* her friendship with John. What the *fuck* had she been thinking? That he'd— what, suddenly decide he didn't see her as a kid sister? Or forget everything Karen had said about her? Or—

"God, *finally*," Davy said, oblivious to Elle's thoughts. "John's an idiot if he doesn't realize how you feel about him." Then, inexplicably, he turned to Logan. "And you owe me ten dollars."

"*Shit.*"

Elle— she really wanted to chime in on that, to say *anything*, but she was starting to hyperventilate, air rushing into her lungs and staying there. God, she'd just kissed John. Or forced him to kiss her. Tricked him into it. Her hands cupped over her mouth and nose, trying to slow her breathing. He would think she was playing him. Or that she'd only moved in with him to make a move. Or that she thought he might actually *like* her, like that, despite him never indicating it.

She was getting lightheaded. She—

"There you two went," John's voice said behind them. "I thought—Elle, are you okay?"

"I ran into the wall," Elle lied. Her voice was high pitched and strained, but she turned to John and made a show of smiling at him. Davy and Logan, wisely, didn't contradict her lie. "Good thing you're driving. I'm too tired to be trusted with a car right now."

John frowned and looked her over. "Let's get you home to bed, then."

It took nearly ten minutes for them to track down their hosts, say a million goodbyes, grab Elle's cookie tin, and get their coats on. Elle felt like she'd aged ten years trying to keep herself together enough to be convincingly okay, all while trying to stay out of John's reach.

"Get home safe, guys," Davy said with a wave, also heading out. "Logan, I'm coming for that ten dollars this weekend. Don't forget."

"Ten dollars?" John asked, holding the car door open for Elle. The frigid winter air helped to ground her, biting into her lungs as she breathed it in.

"I lost a bet," Logan said with a brief glance at Elle as they all got into the car, but he left it at that.

"Figures," John said. Whether he understood the meaning of Logan's words was a mystery.

Elle just sank down in the back seat of John's Lexus and wished for the night to end.

15

He should have kissed her. Really kissed her.

It felt like ages since John had lain awake in his bed, overthinking about Elle. He was *sure* he'd gotten past that part of his life. And yet. Here he was, once again.

This was the *fourth time* he had chickened out. In *Oklahoma*, he hadn't really had a choice. That day in the tech booth, he'd been cutting it too close to show— and not like he should really kiss her at work, anyway, unless it was on stage, in show. Thanksgiving had almost dissolved into chaos with him getting too caught up in his feelings. Imagine, him kissing her in front of his family— not that they hadn't figured out his feelings for her anyway, at least two years ago, if not before that. And now this.

John hadn't been planning to kiss her at all. He'd already heard someone mention that Davy had kissed her, and it had taken three people telling him he'd only kissed her cheek for John to stop seeing red and planning the other man's murder in alarming detail. After that, he hadn't seen Haley with the mistletoe stick for nearly an hour. He'd figured she'd finally gotten bored of playing matchmaker. *Wrong.*

With a sigh, John turned his head, watching as the snow fell softly outside. No, he hadn't planned on actually *kissing* Elle. Just a peck on the cheek, and then he fully intended to take that mistletoe monstrosity out of Haley's hands and chuck it into Nathan and Sylvie's fireplace. But then Elle had turned her head.

God, she'd turned her head. *She* had. Which meant... maybe, just *maybe*, she might actually...*want* to kiss him.

He had to try again. He *had* to. At some point, he'd find a moment alone with her, and he'd find out what it was *really* like to kiss her. Even if he had to orchestrate the whole scene himself, he'd find a way. Then, at least, he could say he'd kissed her, *really* kissed her, once. Even if he found out she didn't want him. *Especially* then.

And then maybe, just *maybe*, he could convince himself to let his obsession with Elle go.

"If I hear the word *Nutcracker* one more time, I'm gonna puke," Elle said, flopping down on the couch at midnight the day before Christmas Eve. Every cell in her body ached from closing up the Theatre for their two-week winter interval. "I'm not moving from this spot for the next three days."

"You'll get up to take one of those molten showers you like," Logan teased, spread out on the other side of the couch.

"And then sleep all day tomorrow." And, with John still down at his parents' place in Florida, where he'd been for the past three days, she didn't have to worry about bothering him.

"I still can't figure out how you like that show," Logan said, queuing up *Muppet's Christmas Carol* on the TV.

"I mostly like the music." Elle stretched out her legs and groaned at the tightness that settled into her muscles. "The dancers are sweet, too. I never did *pointe*, so I love watching other people who do. They're so graceful."

Logan hummed noncommittally. "That kid you recruited seemed nice."

"Oh, Owen?" Elle huffed a stray hair out of her face. "Yeah, he seems really sweet. I loved his idea for the *Beauty and the Beast* set. I just hope he stays on afterward."

"Oh, I'm sure he will," Logan said. "You have a way with these kids. And if you don't convince him, Greg will."

Elle laughed, but even *that* made her sore muscles throb. It became a groan. "I'm gonna have Christmas on the floor. Just drag me to the tree."

Logan burst out laughing. "Not a chance; I'll just bring you your presents in bed. That can be how I thank you for celebrating Hanukkah with me this year."

"No need to thank me for that. It was nice." She rolled her shoulders and then, forfeiting any hope of stretching away the tension, just pitched herself sideways to lay on Logan's lap. "I'm not really a religious person anyway, so why not celebrate your holiday?"

"You just wanted to learn what to cook for me." As Elle laughed, Logan reached over to turn the end table light off, plunging them into a cozy darkness, lit only by the flickering of the TV. They sang through the first song of the movie together, an age old tradition between them, before he spoke again. "It was sweet of John's parents to invite us for Christmas."

"Yeah," Elle sighed. "Too bad we had to work." She rolled her eyes, her words dry.

"They really liked you over Thanksgiving."

"I liked them," Elle admitted. "They're so…"

"Accepting," Logan supplied, and Elle nodded against his thigh. "They take people in— not like your mom, though."

"No," Elle agreed. "She collects strays to fill the emptiness of her life."

"John's parents just accept everyone like their own." Logan started to comb his fingers through her hair. "Is your mom coming for Christmas?"

"No." And, truth be told, Elle was relieved. "She's with Garth again. I thought about going, too, but…" Maybe she still should. Tomorrow was Christmas Eve. She'd have time to drive up to Garth's place before nightfall, if the weather and the traffic weren't—

"No," Logan said firmly, as though he knew the direction Elle's thoughts had taken. "I promised you a cozy, us-only Christmas, since you spent Hanukkah putting up with me and Tyler being all couply for eight nights in a row."

Elle just laughed, and then they were singing again.

"Speaking of couples." Elle tilted her head up to look at Logan, waiting for him to continue. "You've been mysteriously normal around John after kissing him two weeks ago. What gives?"

"I don't know what you're talking about." Except she did. She'd been trying with everything she had to keep up appearances, to keep things normal between everyone. John had been acting the same— or maybe he actually didn't care that she'd kissed him. She kissed Logan all the time, the same way she kissed Garth and her mom, with absolutely no romantic inclination at all. Just familial affection. Maybe he felt the same way about her.

"You're fretting," Logan pointed out dryly. "I can see it in your face— and you're not singing. So," he said, pausing the movie, "I repeat: what gives?"

Elle chewed on her lip. She never kept secrets from Logan— but Logan never backed down from a chance to play matchmaker, even if he was less blatant about it than Haley was. "I... it's nothing. It wasn't a big deal."

"You had a panic attack!"

"Yes, and then I got over it!" That was a blatant lie. Elle had never gotten over anything in her life. That kiss alone would keep her up for years, even after she eventually found a place of her own and moved out to be a responsible adult.

"Well, what went through your head *during* the kiss?" Logan demanded. "You had to have had *some* reaction to work yourself into a panic."

"I didn't—" *let that one go, Elle.* She huffed. "I... I don't know. I thought about my deal with you, and so I turned my head, and then..." Elle sighed. How was she supposed to describe it? Like a fleeting breath. Something good and right that blinked into her life and then right back out before it could take shape.

"You caught feelings."

"Oh my god," Elle said, jerking up off of his lap. He was right. He was absolutely right. Whipping her head around, she gave him a pleading, desperate look. "Don't tell him."

"Elle!" Logan burst out laughing, covering his face with his skinny hands. "Elle, my love, my darling."

"Please, Logan," she begged, grabbing one of his arms and shaking it. She could feel tears prickling behind her eyes. "Please don't tell. I don't want to freak him out. He's been so generous. He's letting me live here."

The laughter started to fade from Logan's face. "Oh— Elle, honey, are you still on that?" When Elle didn't respond, his smile dropped away completely. "Oh, honey, no. No." He leaned forward to fold her into his gangly arms, squeezing her tightly. "We agreed back in— god, September, now? You live *here*. With us. You're not just passing through—"

"I can't live here with you two forever," Elle wailed. "This is John's *home*. He'll want to— I don't know, date. Have kids. Actually have his own space in this house, since it's his."

"Elle."

"And it's not like *I* can date anyone, with his brother complex. God, he's worse than you! He's worse than *Garth!*"

"So date John."

Logan said it so calmly, so matter-of-factly, as though that was the obvious solution to her problem. Elle almost fell for it, for about two seconds, while her brain turned the words over a few times to process them. Then she pulled away from the hug to gape at Logan. "What? No. I couldn't do that."

"Why not?" Logan asked.

"He— I'm not—"*good enough.* But telling Logan that only made it bigger and scarier.

"You're not what?" Logan scoffed. "Don't tell me you're not interested. We passed that ages ago, whether you want to admit it or not."

"Alright, Doctor Logan," Elle snapped, scowling. "What do *you* think?"

"I think you should ask John how he feels. I'm serious!" He insisted, when Elle snorted. "Ask him, or better yet, kiss him again without Haley pressuring you—"

"*You're* pressuring me," Elle muttered.

"Or an audience," Logan continued, ignoring her. "Give him all you've got, and see what happens."

It seemed like a perfectly rational idea, except—"Logan. I... I *can't.*"

"What do I have to do?" Logan demanded. "Lock you two in a closet?"

"No, it's just—"

"Do you think you can just avoid this forever? That it'll magically go away if you don't acknowledge it?"

"*No, I—*"

"Then *what* , Ellie?"

"*What if I'm not good enough?*"

Her words rang through the room like a gunshot.

"Oh," Logan breathed. Elle shut her eyes, desperate not to see the pity in his voice reflected on his face. "Oh. You're scared he'll feel about you the way your mom does." Elle flinched. "Your mom's got you so fucked in the head that you can't imagine anyone loving you just for you, and you can't even see it when someone does."

Elle recoiled, curling in on herself in the corner of the couch. "That's not—"

"It's okay," Logan interrupted. "It's okay, Ellie. I understand."

He didn't. He *couldn't.* How could he, when he'd never had to tread that wire between *too much* and *not enough*?

Elle didn't realize she'd started crying until Logan pulled her against his side. Unable to stop herself, she twisted around, pressing her face against his chest while tears poured from her eyes. It took ages for her to calm down again, her chest and face sore.

"I don't want to ruin my friendship with John," she said at length. "He's too important to me for that."

Logan kissed her temple. "If you didn't feel anything, you wouldn't be so torn up about this."

Elle sighed. "I know."

He kissed her temple again, then nudged her until she was laying in his lap again, his hand back in her hair. "It'll work out, Ellie. I promise."

Silently, Elle nodded. She hoped it would. One way or another.

16

Ten minutes to go.

John's eyes flicked away from the clock, and back to the TV, where some pop singer he didn't recognize wailed like a cat in heat. Scowling, he stole a handful of popcorn from the bowl in Elle's lap beside him. "Who even is this?"

"I haven't the faintest clue," Elle replied. "Do you just want the bowl?"

"Give it to Logan," he said. "He's the one eating most of it."

"No, that'd be you." Elle sent him a mischievous little grin, which he responded to by tugging on her ponytail. From the armchair, Tyler glanced back and forth between them, and then pointedly gave his attention back to the TV.

Nine more minutes.

"What's everyone's New Year's resolution?" Logan asked, turning the wailing on the TV down to an almost bearable level. "Mine is to start working out."

John tried not to snort, with little success. Elle elbowed him.

"Come on, Logan," Elle said, throwing a piece of popcorn at him. "*Nobody* keeps up with their resolutions. Most people just subscribe to Planet Fitness and then never leave their house."

"What if my resolution was to make Logan dress less like he's homeless?" Tyler asked, with a teasing smile at his boyfriend.

Now Elle snorted. "Good luck. Do you own a pair of jeans that's not ripped?" The question was directed at Logan, who scowled.

"Yes!" He crossed his arms over, his glare going back and forth between Elle and John— who was trying his best not to burst out laughing. "Do *you?* Nevermind—"

"You literally organized my closet, Logan." Elle turned to John and poked his leg. "Back me up, here."

"Resolutions are for people who like change," he said diplomatically, and then had to shield himself when Elle threw popcorn at him. "Hey! Popcorn is for eating, not throwing!"

"Not for you, it's not," Elle said, thrusting the bowl into Logan's lap. John gave her a flat look, and promptly laid down across her to reach the bowl. "Hey! Get off me, you big lug!"

"But you're so comfy." Elle gave him a shove, which he pretended to be affected by. "Hey, you're getting stronger! I could actually feel—"

"I will pour my Dr. Pepper on you. This dress is black. No one will know."

Laughing, John sat back up. "Just to keep your dress clean," he clarified. Elle rolled her eyes.

Seven minutes.

Ugh. He had a goddamn *plan*, this time. Developed from all those nights he spent staring into the ceiling, thinking about the *maybes* and the *almosts* and the *what ifs.* He'd remembered his conversation with Elle from their night in *Oklahoma* together, the memory bringing him out of a dead sleep the night before. If this clock didn't get a move on, he was going to go *insane.*

"This is better than being drunk with Gina, isn't it?" Logan asked, patting Elle's thigh. Elle's lip curled.

"Do *not* get me started." She took a sip of her soda, glaring at the TV. "That was the worst New Years of my *life.*"

"Worse than the one with Kacey?" As Logan led Elle down memory lane, John picked up his beer and glanced at the time. Six more minutes.

"Definitely," Elle said, the word distorted by her wry laugh. "It was worse than the threesome I had sophomore year of college."

John choked on his beer. "The *what?*" he sputtered, almost spitting beer down himself.

"Five til," Elle chirped, getting to her feet. "I'm opening the champagne."

"She was kidding, right?" John asked Logan, while Elle danced her way to the kitchen. The short black dress she wore swished around her legs, baring a whole lot of creamy, smooth skin. "Logan. Come on. She was joking, right?"

"I'll never tell."

"I don't think she was joking," Tyler said.

"Someone come help," Elle called. Her brow was furrowed as she fidgeted with the champagne bottle in her hands. "I can't get the damn bottle open."

Logan and Tyler both looked at John. "What?" He said.

"Go, dumbass," Logan hissed.

John rolled his eyes, but stood up. As he passed Tyler, he heard a distinctly muttered "Get her, tiger."

God. They were worse than Haley and her mistletoe.

"Hand it over," he said to Elle, reaching the kitchen. With a huff, she handed over the bottle, and continued to scowl at it while he opened it with a loud *pop*. "Here you go."

"Thanks," she said, already pouring.

"Is this the first year you won't kiss a girl, Elle?" Logan asked suddenly, sounding nearly ecstatic about it.

"Yeah, actually," Elle said, "unless you count the threesome." God, she hadn't been joking. "It's okay, though. I'll just kiss John."

"At least he's taller than you," Tyler chimed in, craning his head around to look at them. "Aren't all of your friends your height?"

"Kacey isn't even five-foot."

"Hang on," John said, as Elle shoved two champagne flutes into his hands.

"Go, give those to the lovebirds."

John had half a mind to stay right where he was, just for that comment, but thought better of it. There were only two minutes left until midnight, and—

Well. He'd been planning to kiss her anyway. May as well have her on board with it, right?

"Here," he said to Logan, handing over one of the flutes. Logan pinned him with a glare, eyes narrowed over his slightly hooked nose. "What?"

Kiss her, Logan mouthed, then shot his gaze toward Elle and back.

John rolled his eyes, rubbed his hand over them.

"One minute!" Tyler said as he took his own glass.

"John, do you want champagne?"

"Yeah," John said, ignoring both Logan and Tyler's pointed looks as he went back to the kitchen.

She poured the glass, obviously preoccupied with humming one of the endless streams of pop songs that had led up to this, because when she turned around, she jumped.

"Sorry," he said, taking one of the glasses from her hand. "Did you mean it?"

"Hmm? Oh." Elle laughed, a little nervously, and ran her free hand through her long, lovely hair. "That I'd kiss you? Sure." She shrugged. "I mean, we've already kissed, haven't we?"

Not really. "Yeah."

"So what's wrong with two friends sharing a New Year's kiss?" She batted her eyelashes, and John's vision went a little fuzzy.

That's not what it is, he wanted to say. *This is so much more than that.*

"Thirty seconds!" Logan shouted. Elle whipped around, her champagne in hand, her smile radiant, bouncing slightly on her toes with excitement.

John set his glass down on the counter. Elle's, too, pulling it from her hand while she was distracted. She turned to frown up at him with a startled *hey*, but he ignored her, cornering her. His arms caged her in, landing on the counter on either side of her.

Elle gasped.

"You said you wanted it long," he reminded her. "With tongue."

Elle's eyes widened, her mouth dropping open. He saw the glimmer of realization in her eyes as she remembered the same thing John had. In the other room, the guys started to count down.

"You surprised me at the Christmas party," John murmured. Before Elle could respond to that, he grabbed her waist, delighting in the catch in her breath. His hand cupped her neck. "My turn."

As the others shouted their excitement, he closed the distance between his lips and Elle's.

She melted against him. He couldn't have described it any other way. From the second their lips met, hers opened to him, allowing him entrance, and—*god*. The *taste* of her. He knew she'd be sweet, but he couldn't have imagined this.

Elle sagged, her hands fisting in his shirt, until he was holding her up with one arm. The noise she made, the tiny little mewl, went straight to his core. He felt like he was floating as he finally fulfilled his fantasy of sliding his hand into her hair while he kissed her.

John held onto her, even when she pulled away. He couldn't stop staring down into her eyes, sparkling like turquoise gems. If she couldn't feel his heart, slamming against his ribs between them, he'd be shocked. He swallowed as he waited for her to say something, desperate to catch his breath.

The moment stretched on between them, endless and soft. She stared right back at him, searching, as though she could see the adoration pouring from him. Then her eyes dropped to his lips.

John tensed, ready to release her, in case she—

Elle yanked him back against her so hard he almost fell over. Her lips met his, hungry, seeking— and he gave what he was given, tenfold. He slid his hands up her ribs, clutching her just where he wanted her, while her hands threaded through his hair and tugged. He gasped, only for her to suck his bottom lip between her teeth.

God, he was going lightheaded. This was better than he could ever have imagined. This was the best thing that had happened to him. *Ever.* Hands down.

John was so caught up in her, in how much he wanted her, he didn't notice himself picking her up until she gasped. He settled her onto the counter, barely clear of the champagne glasses he'd set there minutes before. The moment he had her where he wanted her, his hands came up to cup her face. Inexplicably, *amazingly*, her legs wrapped around his waist.

This was a dream. An absolute *dream.*

At least until Elle gasped again, putting her hands firmly onto his chest and pushing. John jerked away from her instantly.

Wide-eyed and panting, Elle's entire upper body whipped around. John followed her gaze to the living room, only to find Logan and Tyler gone. Music from the TV still played softly in the background.

With a shuddering breath, Elle turned back to him. Her eyes went directly to the ground between her dangling legs. "Um."

Yeah, John thought, shifting further away from her. *Um.* She probably wouldn't enjoy finding out how hard he was, right now.

He swallowed. "Are you…?"

Her fingers came up to touch her lips. Such a small gesture, and it could have brought him to his knees. He ground his teeth, desperate to keep it together.

"Who needs brain cells anyway?" She said to the floor. When he didn't respond— because what the hell did that mean, anyway? — she looked up. "That was a compliment."

"Oh."

She nodded, her gaze lowering again. Her hands were gripping the edge of the counter so hard, they'd gone white. Her breathing still hadn't evened out.

For a split second, he wondered if she was having a panic attack.

"Elle?" He reached out, to— god, he didn't know. Comfort her. Ground her. Pull her close and start kissing her again. "Are you…?"

"Can we…" She shook her head. Her voice was tight and strained, almost— almost like it had been the night of the Whitmore's party. "Can we please just— not talk about this right now?"

John dropped his hand before it ever made contact. He took a steadying breath. Then another. Then—

"Yeah." He nodded, staring at a spot on the wall above her head. He couldn't bring himself to look at her. "Yeah, we can…" Probably never talk about it at all.

John shut his eyes. There was nothing left for him to do, here, unless he wanted to make himself— and Elle— miserable.

"Goodnight," he said abruptly and turned to go.

He heard her mumbled response as he went, followed by the sound of her getting off the counter. He'd never be able to look at that counter the same way again. All because he was an *idiot* who'd lost control.

Happy New Year, indeed.

Elle jerked awake at the bright, cheerful music from her alarm, and groaned. Everything was fuzzy to look at. The sunlight was trying to personally gouge her eyes out. Her head *throbbed*, her neck and shoulders stiff and sore.

Hangovers. *Ugh.*

She definitely shouldn't have nicked the champagne.

God. That *kiss.* She'd be dreaming about that for the rest of her life. A split second of perfection, of *knowing* what John would be like, if he—

God. He'd remembered what she'd said after *Oklahoma*, and he'd delivered. And then she'd tried to climb him like a tree.

Elle winced as she rolled onto her side to turn off her alarm. It took her a moment to realize why she felt so weird— opening her eyes, despite the hellish sunlight streaking through her window, she realized she still had her dress on from last night.

Her head pounded as she started to sit up. With a groan, she pressed a hand over her eyes and dragged her legs off the bed. The dress was wound uncomfortably over her chest, squishing everything down almost painfully. Once she'd dragged herself from the bed, she wrestled it off, flinging it into the hamper. She almost fell over trying to dress herself in the blissful darkness of her closet, but emerged in sweatpants and a tee shirt several minutes later, feeling vaguely more human. All she wanted was to down a pot of coffee and the greasiest food she could get her hands on, and then maybe take another six hour nap.

She smelled bacon halfway down the stairs, and groaned again. "Whoever's making bacon, *please* share."

Logan's laugh reached her first, then Tyler's. Then, more softly, John's.

Great. She had an audience for her post-stupidity hangover.

At the foot of the stairs, she sneered at the sunlight filling the first floor, then made her way to the bar top.

"Good morning, sleepyhead," Logan said. "I see you enjoyed the champagne."

"I will end you," Elle replied, shutting her eyes. "*After* I eat the greasiest thing in the house."

"Too bad Jim's not here, huh?"

Elle groaned.

A plate of bacon landed in front of her. Elle followed the length of John's arm with her eyes, until—

They both jerked their gazes away from each other at the same time.

"How did you get so hungover?" Logan asked.

"Don't talk to me until I finish this." Despite her vague nausea, Elle attacked her bacon. The noise that came out of her mouth was just this side of obscene. It only worsened when a mug of coffee appeared beside her plate, also courtesy of John. "Light of my life," Elle said without thinking, taking a deep gulp of liquid caffeine. "Logan, I'm throwing you over for John."

"That's perfectly fine," Logan said, taking Tyler's hand in his own. "I have this guy."

"We can get Five Guys later if you're still hungover," John suggested, putting a plate down in front of Tyler next. Elle made another vaguely sexual noise.

"Not unless you plan on shoveling us out," Logan said, eyeing the windows past Elle. "We got a good six inches last night."

"God, it's like Snowmageddon all over again," Elle said, and then patted Logan's leg. "Remember Junior year of high school?"

"*Ugh.*" Yep, he remembered. "Pennsylvania is the *worst*. It'll still be like this in April, up there."

"Yeah, at least we actually have spring here," Elle agreed. She was already starting to feel better, the bacon grease working wonders for her headache. All she needed now was—

As though reading her mind, John topped off her coffee, simultaneously setting a plate of mangled eggs in front of Logan. He didn't look at her as he did it, even when she murmured her thanks.

God. He was probably disgusted with her. She sure was.

"Hey, remember when classes were cancelled at MU?" Logan asked, referring to their college. "When Mr. O'Beirne and Ms. Morris started that snowball fight?"

"Oh my god, *yes!*" Elle perked up, remembering that day vividly. "Man, that was so *fun —*"

"It was a *war,*" Logan cried. "We would have won, if you cheaters hadn't dumped snow down Ms. Morris's back!"

Elle held up her hands innocently. "Hey, I had nothing to do with that brilliant and battle-winning idea." But her grin definitely gave her away.

Logan rolled his eyes. "Sure you didn't."

John frowned, staring into space, his own breakfast in his hand. "...I remember that."

Elle felt her stomach swoop. She couldn't even remember what year that had happened. "You do?"

"Yeah," he said, setting the plate down and then just staring at it. Reminiscing, maybe. "I was on O'Beirne's side, when it started. I helped build the snow wall by the science and tech building."

Elle remembered it, like a developing Polaroid photo. "We had a tree," she recalled. "By the art building. Jake Roberts climbed up it and shook snow onto Morris's team when they got too close."

"I saw that!" John's head came up, the grin on his face brighter than the sunlight outside. It made Elle's heart jump. "We tried to help keep them back. I completely wasted someone with a giant snowball."

"That was *you!*" Elle shrieked. John's eyes went wide while hers narrowed, seething. "If I didn't need this coffee, I'd pour it on you." Just to keep herself from changing her mind, she brought the mug to her lips. John actually started to *laugh.* "You monster," she said, indignant. "I couldn't feel my face for an *hour.*"

"Run while you can, John," Tyler warned. "Elle knows where you sleep."

"I'll get you back eventually," Elle agreed, grinning— and then she remembered the night before.

Her smile vanished.

"You two are *both* heathens," Logan griped. "We would have crushed you, if the dean hadn't come."

John snorted at him. "You screamed like a girl when I dumped snow over you." Logan scowled, but didn't bother denying it. "Didn't O'Beirne and Morris end up married?"

"Brought together by frostbite," Logan said, rolling his eyes. "How romantic."

"Marriage looked good on both of them," Elle said. "And you looked good with snow in the hood of your coat." Ignoring Logan's glare, she poked his nose. Out of the corner of her eye, she caught John's faint smile, before his face went oddly blank.

It's me, right? She thought bitterly. *You're upset with me.*

"Yeah, yeah," Logan said, clearly missing Elle's shift in mood. "Hey, what show are they doing this spring? We should go see it."

"I don't know," Elle said, staring at her plate. "They did *Legally Blonde* last year. It was…" She cringed. "Not their best work."

"We should go!" Logan said. "Maybe we could get new recruits for Greg!"

"We could make a day of it," John suggested, looking at Logan. Avoiding Elle's eyes.

"Yeah," Logan said, latching onto the idea with delight. He turned to Tyler, grasping his boyfriend's hand and squeezing. Elle's eyes dropped into her mostly empty coffee cup. "We could go to MU, get lunch, see the show—"

"Talk to the professors, see what's doing." John nodded.

"I still have some friends in the theater program," Elle said, forcing herself to at least *act* excited. "Maybe they'd like to come work with us." The more her head cleared, the more she wanted to cloud it up again. All she could think about was John's face, just before he'd left this very kitchen. The hurt there, and then that awful blankness, which he still had, even now—

"We'll talk more about it later," Logan said, cutting off her train of thought. "Tyler and I are going upstairs to Skype his parents."

"Is that code for—" Elle cut off as Logan reached over to tickle her. "Hey!"

"Mind out of the gutter, Doll," Logan said dryly, standing up. "Thanks for cooking, John."

"Sure thing."

Logan stacked his plate onto Tyler's, then turned to Elle.

"I've got it," she said, putting her empty plate on top of the stack and then taking it.

Logan's eyes widened. Behind him, Tyler frowned at her. "Are you—"

"Yeah," Elle said, rising up on her toes to peck Logan's cheek. "It's fine. Go talk to your family."

Logan looked her over. Whether he was suspicious, or just concerned, she didn't know— or, really, care. She just forced herself to smile and rounded the counter, watching John put his own plate in the dishwasher, and continue to avoid looking at her.

"We'll be back," Tyler said, filling the uncomfortable silence. "Maybe we can recreate that epic snow battle."

"And win this time." Linking arms, the lovebirds headed toward the stairs. Logan shot one more concerned look Elle's way before they disappeared.

"Good luck with that," Elle called after them, smirking. The amusement died when she saw John inching his way out of the kitchen behind her, like he was trying to escape unnoticed.

Her eyes landed on the counter. The same one where he'd set her last night. Where she'd realized, without a shadow of a doubt, that she was in too deep. And then remembered who she was kissing.

God, she thought miserably, looking at the dishes she'd set in the sink. He'd never once shown romantic interest in her, and she'd taken it way too far, reaching for more and more. More than she deserved. More than he wanted to give her.

"I'm gonna..." John started, and then paused, as though searching for the right excuse to give her. Elle nodded, focusing on rinsing the dishes and getting them into the dishwasher as fast as she could. She didn't even look at him, too busy trying not to sink into herself, not to let her mind go where it always went, not to—

"Wait."

John was— Elle looked up as the word left her mouth, and realized he wasn't even there anymore. She had to actually look around before she found him, two steps up the stairs already. He looked startled, and— yeah, Elle felt kind of startled, too. She squeezed her hands in front of herself, clasping them together until they almost hurt. "John, are we…"

John's eyes shut. He wasn't even facing her the whole way, but she could see the irritation and resignation that crossed his face as he turned to grip the banister, all the way from the kitchen. It struck her like a slap in the face, and—

You fucked it up before it could even start.

If she hadn't remembered Logan and Tyler, she'd have probably let John go a lot farther than he had. Once the kissing— the incredible, amazing, *life altering* kissing— had stopped, she'd realized what she'd done.

"Can we just…" John sounded tired. Annoyed. "Can we not talk about it?"

Elle's breath caught. They were basically the same words she'd used on him last night. She swallowed, desperate for her voice to remain even. "You mean… pretend it didn't happen?"

John was silent for a moment. Then he nodded. "Yeah."

Again, she swallowed. Somewhere in her chest, a hole where her heart should have been was growing, eating up everything inside her. "Yeah," she said weakly. "Yeah, we can—" God. *God.* She nodded as her throat began to close. "Yeah."

She couldn't take her eyes off of him. She saw him grip the banister so tightly, the muscles in his arms bulged. He looked like he was struggling not to shout at her.

Not like she didn't deserve it.

Elle looked down at her feet. This was… harrowing. The silence. The tension. And it was all her own damn fault.

She listened to John leave, unable to bring herself to look back up. By the time she convinced herself to move, his door had long since clicked shut above her.

She'd upheld her deal with Logan. That was the best she could ask for. He would leave her alone about it, now. John clearly didn't want her.

He was obviously hurt by what she'd done, by how far she'd tried to take it.

God. She was a *monster.*

When she reached her bedroom, she grabbed one end of her comforter. It was heavy, sliding slowly from her bed like a thick cloud as she dragged it over toward her closet. At least in there, John wouldn't have to see her, to be reminded of everything she'd done to him.

Besides, she thought, shutting herself into the darkness. Monsters belonged in cages.

17

There was something distinctly depressing about John spending his birthday alone. Especially with this whole situation with Elle. Though what a nice birthday present it would be, if she waltzed in and decided she'd changed her mind about wanting him, or maybe returned his feelings.

Hey, I don't see you as a brother anymore!

Yeah. Right. In his dreams.

She'd done exactly as he asked. They did not discuss *The Kiss*. In fact, after New Year's Day— when she'd slept off that hangover of hers for almost twenty-four hours— she acted like it hadn't happened at all. Nothing out of the ordinary on Elle's side. No drama, no unrequited feelings. No, sir.

John was doing the same. Absolutely. He certainly hadn't spent the past several nights wanting to trash his bedroom, or his mornings glaring at his mirror and wondering if that *seven years of bad luck* superstition had any merit.

Just. You know. The usual.

The theater's two-week interval would end after this weekend. Auditions for Disney's *Beauty and the Beast* happened, callbacks were this morning— which, naturally, was where Elle was spending the day, on the casting panel. She'd taken costumes and choreo, this time, to Greg's immense disappointment.

It was a relief, in a way. He didn't blame Logan for making plans on his birthday— Tyler would be out of town starting tomorrow, so it was only right that they spend the night together. Unless, of course, this was Logan's way of getting John and Elle alone together, in which case—*yeah*. He blamed Logan. A Lot.

John stared at the snow covered backyard from the kitchen, an untouched beer on the counter beside him. He just wanted things to get *better*. Or at least, to not still be completely *gone* for Elle, even now. He'd give anything for them to go back to how they'd been before...

Before he'd manhandled Elle like a caveman.

Ugh.

Speak of the devil, he thought, as he heard the front door open. Elle was humming, probably one of the songs she'd heard at auditions yesterday.

"Hey," he said, hoping he didn't look as out of it as he felt.

"Hi," she said cheerfully, hanging her hat and scarf in the coat closet.

One of these days, he'd stop staring at her like some sort of creep. John picked up his beer instead and pretended it was remotely interesting. "How were the rest of the callbacks?"

"Greg's sure got his work cut out for him," Elle said, smiling at him as she came down the hall. "I think you've got Gaston in the bag. Don't tell anyone I said that." She held her hand behind her back as she walked, her smile angelic in an almost distressed way.

John narrowed his eyes. "What have you got there?"

"Nothing," she said, side-stepping him. "Just like I'm not about to bake anything, because it's obviously not anyone's birthday." John felt his stomach swoop as she skirted around him, dropping the grocery bag she'd been hiding onto the counter. "I *definitely* didn't have to find that out halfway through the day from our roommate, either, since the not-birthday-boy managed not to tell me his birthday for our entire friendship." John ducked his head at her accusatory tone. *Logan.* Of course. "Since only people with birthdays get chicken fried steak and cake, this obviously isn't for you."

She still had something she was holding, keeping it carefully out of his view using her body as a shield. John rolled his eyes and caught her easily around the waist, ignoring her squeal. "Nice roommates don't hide people's birthday gifts," he told her, trying to reach around her to get at whatever was in her hand.

"Who said it was a gift?" Elle said, but her words turned to giggles as he wrapped both arms around her middle, picking her up. "Put me down! *John!*"

John set her onto one of the barstools, putting on his best pout. "Come on, Elle, it's my birthday."

She glared at him, though the effect was lost since she was too busy laughing to give it any heat. "Your puppy dog eyes won't work on me, mister."

"No?" His pout deepened. "But Elle."

"Don't you *but Elle* me," she snapped. She set the gift— a small, thick box wrapped in bright blue— onto the bar top and slid it out of his reach. "Nothing for you, just because I had to find out from Logan. *After* the day was half over."

"But you already got the stuff for cake," he said, arms still encircling her waist. Elle just scowled half-heartedly up at him. "You're the best cook in the *world*."

"Flattery will get you nowhere."

Right, John thought. Time to fight dirty. He squeezed Elle in a hug, chanting *please* into her hair over and over while she struggled and laughed.

"Fine!" Elle shouted, shoving at his chest. "Get off me, you lug!"

He pulled back, laughing for— the first time all year, it seemed. God, he— he was still so, *so* in love with her. He couldn't imagine not loving her, in moments like these. Even if she didn't return his feelings.

He didn't have time to overthink it before Elle put the gift in his hands. The paper was wrapped with the same precision she used in everything else, yellow ribbon tied around it in a neat bow. "God, Elle," he said, gently tugging the ribbon off. "Is there anything you can't do?"

"You'd be surprised." Her tone was… strange. A little distant. He'd heard it before, but he couldn't place when. Of course, the thought fled from his mind when he managed to get the paper off of—

"Oh my god." John couldn't stop staring at it. *Resident Evil*, the collector's set. On blu-ray. "Elle."

"You said the games were your favorite," she said, "but I didn't see the movies in your collection."

John stared at her.

She bit her nail, her smile gone, looking between his face and the movies in his hands. "I thought maybe you'd like watching them as much as you like playing them." For a second the smile came back, just faintly. "Even if you do keep dying."

He cracked then, chuckling. "It's you, I swear. I used to be an expert gamer."

"Hey, you don't have to defend yourself to me," Elle said, holding her hands up. "I'd probably cry if I tried to play. I can't stand zombies."

"I know," he said. And, like an idiot, he leaned forward, placing a gentle kiss on her cheek. "I love it. Thank you, Elle."

Elle blinked at him, and he realized— oh, god, had he crossed another line?

But then her face broke into another smile. "You go set that up while I start dinner," she told him, giving him a gentle push. "We can probably get through the first one while stuff is cooking."

Yeah, John thought, listening to her set herself up in the kitchen while he turned on his PlayStation. He was still *very* much in love with her.

The front door banged open so hard, Elle almost dropped the spoon into her soup pot. As she turned away from the stove, Logan swept into the room like a windfall, waving his phone frantically at her. "The cast list is up!"

"What— already?" She put the lid on the soup pot and rushed around the counter to peer over his shoulder. "Callbacks were *yesterday*."

"Oh, please, you already know who's who." Logan spun, keeping his phone up over Elle's head, way out of her reach.

"I do not!" She insisted. "Greg kicked me out because he thinks I'm biased!"

"You mean you're not?" John strolled down the stairs— summoned by the commotion, she figured— to watch them from the landing.

"Very funny," Elle said. She launched up onto her toes, trying to reach Logan's phone. "Come on, Logan, I wanna see who's who!"

"Well, *you* didn't audition." Logan stepped back and caught Elle around the waist when she began to topple over. "Sarah's Belle, naturally."

"*Ugh*," Elle said, rolling her eyes. "Whoops, did I say that out loud?" Since Logan didn't seem to be forfeiting his game anytime soon, Elle gave up, heading back to her soup pot— but not without jabbing Logan in the side first.

"No bias at all."

Elle shot John a withering look, but he just smirked at her from over his folded arms. Honestly, it was so *nice* to have things somewhat back to normal. So long as she didn't think about New Year's too hard—

Cut it out, Elle told herself. Better to stop her brain before it could start that shit up.

"We're going to have a southern Beast," Logan sighed. Elle heard him settling down onto a bar stool behind her.

"Oh, Davy got it?" Elle lifted the lid again and went back to sprinkling spices into the soup. "I was actually thinking Greg would go with Paul."

"Paul's too short to pull off the beast," Logan said. "Especially since John's Gaston."

"I'm shocked!"

"Don't oversell it, Elle," Logan said dryly, while John laughed. "Lucky for you, big guy, I got Lefou. So we can practice our scenes at home."

"Workaholics," Elle said, waving between the two of them with her wooden spoon. "Both of you."

"Pot, this is Kettle," Logan said. "You're black." Elle stuck her tongue out at him.

"You said Sarah's Belle?" John said, finally coming down to the first floor.

"Yeah," Logan said.

"I didn't like her audition," Elle said, "but hey, I'm just the costumer, choreographer, audio tech, and personal assistant to Greg." With each title, she gestured with her spoon. "What do I know?"

"Your lack of bias is showing again," John drawled, propping his arms against the bar behind Logan. "Is it too early to quit?"

"Now who's biased?" Elle smirked over her shoulder, and John rolled his eyes.

Yep. Almost completely normal. Maybe they'd both forget that New Year's kiss ever happened. Or it could become a joke between them. Besides, just last night, John kissed her on the cheek. That must have counted for something, right? Some tiny sign of forgiveness?

"John has a point," Logan said, pulling Elle from her thoughts. "Sarah's been following him around like a puppy since *Oklahoma* rehearsals started. She might try to accept his proposal."

"Hell, John, if you sell it right, half the girls in the cast would accept it." Narrowing her eyes, Elle pointed the spoon at him again. "That's my favorite song in the show, for your information. Don't screw it up."

John rolled his eyes at her. "Maybe I'll practice on you."

"Careful," Elle said, giving him her back. She couldn't face him with that image in her mind. "I might swoon."

"I think that's the point."

"*Anyway*," Logan said tersely. "What are you going to do for the Beast costume, Elle?"

Elle chewed on her lower lip. "Actually, I may borrow pieces from a cosplayer friend of mine," she decided. "He's done both the Beast and Gaston, and he has a partial fur and a full fursuit I could pick pieces from."

"Convenient." It was John who replied. Elle just shrugged. "Am I getting leather?"

"Absolutely." Which she didn't want to think about, because— John. In *leather*. She'd probably drool. "Suede, leather, a really nice wig." Pursing her lips, she looked him over. "You probably won't need a muscle pad, unless you want to make this *really* ridiculous."

"*Please* wear the muscle pad," Logan begged, reaching out to grab John's arm across the counter. John laughed, tugging his arm away. "No, really. You'll look *hilarious*. Buff, but in a cartoonish way."

"I'll try it on and have Elle take pictures for you," John said. "Happy?"

"You should put on one of Elle's Belle dresses over it," Logan said. There was a mischievous gleam in his eyes that Elle had seen there before, whenever he got a truly wild idea. "There's a meme of that on the internet somewhere. We could use it for promo pictures on Instagram."

"Absolutely not," John said, but at least he was laughing.

"I might have to make something for you," Elle said, turning away from them both. "Blaine is bulkier than you, but he's shorter." She put the lid on the pot again, and started putting spices back into their cabinet. "It's too bad he was such a player. He was *so* pretty in college."

"Pretty *stupid*," Logan said, over what sounded like John choking. "That man *still* calls you Emma."

"How did he even get *Emma* from *Elle* ?" John demanded.

Elle waved off that question. "It's fine," she insisted. "We weren't that close."

"When you've had a man's dick in your mouth, he should know your name!" Logan's indignant opinion was met with Elle's rolled eyes, and— yep, John was choking, trying to hide his coughs behind one fist.

"When *what?*" He asked, once his coughing had died down some.

Elle just grinned. "Remember that New Year's threesome?"

"Oh my god." John covered his eyes with his hands. "I didn't need to know. I don't want to know. I want to forget that image."

Elle laughed, but— yeah. He probably *didn't* want to think of her in a sexual way. Definitely brotherly feelings there. Cheek kisses? Definitely. Talking about her sex life? No go.

Kissing her senseless on the kitchen counter?

Yikes.

She sucked in a breath, biting back the sudden wave of emotions that reared its ugly head. "Look at it this way," she said, her smile almost painful from the effort it took to keep it up. "If I'm making you a brand new costume, it means I'll need to actually get my sewing stuff from storage like you told me to." There, something nice and safe to talk about.

John's head came up, his smile fading. "We never got to that, did we?"

Elle shook her head. "I hand tacked the patch back onto your jacket for Halloween, remember?"

He nodded slowly. "Yeah. Yeah, we should definitely get your stuff." His eyes wandered off, and his brow furrowed. "I can't believe we haven't done that yet. We should have had you all moved in *months* ago."

She felt like all she did was shrug, today. "It's fine. I'll be all moved in soon enough, right?"

John's eyes met hers. She wondered, briefly, if he could tell how she was feeling, just from looking at her. Hopefully not.

"Yeah," he said at length, "you will."

18

Elle came in giggling, and—*oh, no*, John thought— stumbling. Was she drunk?

He leaned sideways over the arm of the couch to watch her as she swung on the door, blowing a noisy kiss out to a car that honked twice in response— Haley's usual signal, he'd recently learned (after mistaking it for Davy's for two months). After closing the door, a little harder than necessary, she leaned against it to kick off her heels, then swerved and stumbled her way toward the living room, still giggling the entire time.

Yep. She was drunk.

They'd gone to dinner hours ago, her and Haley. To celebrate something— maybe it was the first week of rehearsals being over, or coming back to work after their winter break. Maybe it was Haley's birthday. Who knew? Not John, that was for sure.

Even drunk, Elle was precious. She peeled off her sweater and tossed it on the banister, then caught sight of him. Her grin widened.

"Hi!" She caught the edge of the bartop to steady herself and leaned, peering over at the TV. John's stomach dropped as she tilted dangerously low, squealing delightedly. "It's my boy!"

He was gripping the arm of the couch so tightly his knuckles hurt. His eyes flicked to the screen, where Harry was trying to escape a dragon. "Harry Potter?"

"Yes!" John felt his blood pressure spike as she snapped back up, dancing her way over to him. "You're almost on my favorite one."

"Five?" She'd mentioned it at least once before, he thought.

"Yes. Oh, boy." She almost made it past him before she stumbled, yelping. John grabbed her by the waist, steadying her, his heart pounding in his chest. Elle's hands landed on his upper arms.

His eyes roamed over her face. She was flushed, her eyes a little glassy, but she was smiling, still stifling giggles. "Are you okay?"

"You're so much bigger than me," she said. Her hands began a clumsy trail up to his shoulders. "Look at my waist. There's no waist left. Just your hands."

John swallowed, trying not to focus on her hands. They stroked, feather light, over his collarbone. His heart lodged in his throat, and all he could do was gasp. "Sorry."

"I like it."

He was going to *die*. He knew it. Just from her touching him.

"Where's Logan?" she asked, eyes sliding toward the empty side of the couch.

"Tyler's." Where he'd been spending more and more time since New Year's day. John was actually starting to think he might just move.

Elle's hands slid up the side of his neck, across the edge of his jaw. "You're unfairly pretty."

"Elle." He squeezed her waist, bringing her back from whatever headspace she'd gone to. Her gaze lifted to his, still a little glassy. One of her thumbs grazed over his cheekbone. "You're drunk."

"Yeah." She giggled as she said it, swaying slightly in his grip. "You're not."

"No."

"But you're still holding my waist."

Yes. He was. "I don't want you to fall."

She stroked the length of his nose with one finger. "You'd catch me."

John's breath caught. Elle slipped one finger over his bottom lip, then went back to stroking his jawline. His skin was on fire, everywhere she touched. "How did you even get this drunk, Elle?"

Elle hummed, then— god, she bit her lip, and everything in John zeroed in on that one spot. Like tunnel vision. "I think I had... three peach sangrias?" She shrugged. "It was *ages* ago. They messed up our orders, so they brought us a free round." She giggled again, her hand leaving his face to cover her mouth. "Haley wasn't even tipsy. She got a version margo— a *virgin margarita*." Pleased with having said the words without slurring, Elle nodded, and draped her hands around John's neck, leaning forward. "How come *you're* not drunk?"

John shrugged, acutely aware of her arms. If he hadn't been holding her so far away from him, she'd be in his lap by now. "I haven't had anything to drink."

Elle huffed, sending a stray lock of hair off of her forehead. "Well, get on my level," she snapped, with absolutely no heat whatsoever. "Then we can share secrets we won't remember tomorrow morning. Confess things we've never told anyone. Make really shitty decisions."

She was rambling, he realized. "Elle. You're completely wasted."

"Not yet, I'm not," she insisted, and made to stand fully, bracing her hands on his pecs. John tightened his grip around her waist, even as she let him go and tried to walk. "Hey!"

"No more alcohol for you," he insisted.

Elle's pout was almost childish, but her hands came down to cover his on her waist. "No fair. You trapped me."

"I don't want you to fall," John said again. Elle was already swaying back and forth like a rocking chair.

Her eyes narrowed. For a second, her expression was almost sober—but that couldn't be. She was too obliterated to have sobered up already. Maybe in an hour or two, but not yet.

Elle leaned forward again, one hand bracing her up on his chest. The other hand came up to hold his chin, forcing him to look at her lovely face, into her pretty eyes. "That's not it, is it?" she murmured.

No, he wanted to say. He held on tight as her thumb made its way over his lips again, his eyes falling closed of their own accord.

You could ruin me, he thought, lips parting slightly. Then again, maybe she already had.

"I love you."

John's eyes flew open.

She looked serious. She *sounded* serious. But she'd just said—

"Elle," he whispered. "Elle, you're just drunk."

She shook her head. "No. I love you when I'm sober, too. I'm just *saying* it because I'm drunk."

"Why?" Why? *Why?*

Elle's breath hitched. She stared at his lips, her eyes starting to water. John's heart squeezed in his chest. "Because I know you don't feel that way about me."

What?

What?

She— she—

Oh my god. How could she think...?

John gaped up at her. "Elle—"

"It's okay." Her words were so quiet he almost didn't hear them. "I just thought you deserved to know."

"Elle." God, he'd never let her go. Not now. Not ever.

"I'm sorry about Christmas," she said suddenly. Her hand dropped away, joining its counterpart on his chest.

"What?" He hadn't even been here for Christmas. "What are you talking about?"

Elle frowned, her eyes screwing shut. "Wait— no. The party. Nathan and Sylvie's party."

Oh. That. "The mistletoe thing? That was Haley's—"

"No, when I—" she shook her head. "I turned my head."

John just stared at her. She *had* turned her head. For a fleeting, *wonderful* moment, he'd thought they actually had a chance. Until she'd jerked away from him.

"I crossed a line," Elle continued, completely unaware of where John's thoughts were headed. "And then again at New Year's."

"At New Year's?" John had kissed *her* on New Year's. And almost gone a lot further, if she hadn't pushed him away. *Again.*

Elle just nodded, though, and sniffled. A tear escaped the corner of her eye, rolling slowly down her cheek. "I know you don't— I mean, you're not into me like that. I'm sorry I took things too far."

"You—" What the hell was she *saying?*

"I know you see me as, like, a— a kid sister," she continued, voice shaking. Another tear slid down her cheek, and John reached up to brush it away.

It was a mistake on his part, apparently. Elle stepped out of his reach the moment she was free, her hands flying up to her face, trying to stop her tears as they began to free-fall.

"I'm— I'm *so* sorry," she choked out, fully crying at this point. "I—" She sucked in a sharp breath, backing up as John scrambled to his feet.

"Elle—" but she was gone, turning on her heel and fleeing up the stairs.

Shit. *Shit.* She loved him. She thought *he* didn't love *her.* And his distance was only adding to her misconception.

John dropped heavily back onto the couch, cradling his head in his hands. How in the world was he going to fix this?

God, her head hurt.

Elle surfaced from sleep in the dead of night, momentarily confused— her room was dark, and she was fairly certain her sleep shirt was on backwards, she was still wearing her bra for some reason, and the throbbing in her head felt less like *I've had too much to drink* and more like *I've been crying for hours.* Even her throat was sore.

Except why would she have been crying? Dinner with Haley had been perfectly enjoyable. They'd both had a wonderful time, good food, good drinks. Sure, Elle had been significantly past tipsy by the time she'd gotten home, but John hadn't seemed to—

John.

Gasping, Elle sat bolt upright. *John.* John, who she'd practically draped herself over when she'd come home. John, who had caught her, as he always did, when she'd fallen. John, who she'd just admitted to being in love with.

Good lord. What had she been *thinking?*

She hadn't been. That was the problem. She never thought through things around John, anymore. She just— she'd gotten so *comfortable* around him, she'd forgotten that, really, she was just an extended guest in his—

No.

No. Absolutely not. Not this shit again.

Fury welled up into Elle's chest. That horrible, snide little voice in her head wasn't her own common sense— it was just a reproduction of her mother. Logan had been absolutely right at Christmas. The second she imagined any kind of hesitancy from someone, or got any kind of potentially-negative reaction, some part of her just *became* her mother.

And Elle was *tired* of it.

She'd run away from John like a coward, but it had given her time to sober up. Now her head was clear, and she could think straight.

She and John had unfinished business.

Elle found him on a bar stool, a barely touched bottle of beer in front of him, just staring into space. The clock on the oven told her it was just shy of midnight— he'd probably been here awhile.

He frowned when she came around the counter. "I thought you'd gone to bed."

"I did," Elle said, "and now I'm awake." With that, she swiped his beer off the bar and headed for the fridge.

"Hey!"

"Sorry love," she said, "but I want you sober while I talk to you."

John just looked vaguely disappointed by the ring of condensation left by his beer. "Talk about what?"

She could do this, she reminded herself, and sucked in a breath. "I know you said you don't want to talk about the New Year's kiss—" the very words made his head snap up, his eyes going wide—"but I *do.*"

"Alright," John said, eyeing her warily. "Do you want to, maybe…" He gestured to the stool beside him. "Come sit down?"

"Nope." If Elle went around that bar, it was game over. She'd either kiss John, or she'd flee like a coward again. Neither of those were options. Instead, she hopped up onto the opposite counter to face him, clutching the edge of it to keep her balance.

"Right," John muttered. His gaze slid down for a split second, landing on her bare legs, where her sleep shorts had ridden up considerably. He snapped it back up to her face, clearing his throat. "So, what about—"

"Were you jealous of Davy?"

Of all the questions she could have asked, that one clearly hadn't been on his radar. "Was I—*What?* "

"Were you jealous of Davy?" Elle repeated patiently.

"I…" The sheer guilt on his face was telling enough. "Why would you ask that?"

"Well, when we went on that date, and I spent the whole time trying to find ways to let him down gently—" At this, John's jaw dropped— "he ended up letting *me* down, and then told me you'd been glaring at him all weekend."

John recovered just enough to give an eloquent, "Um."

"And then," Elle continued calmly, "at the Halloween party, he said you were *still* glaring at him, and asked me if I'd told you he and I weren't seeing each other." She chuckled. "I was actually coming to tell you that when you found me, but I was too drunk by that point to remember what I was saying."

At this point, John was just staring at her, lips parted.

"Did you know he and Logan were betting on us kissing?" She asked. "That was the bet Logan lost at the Christmas party. Fun facts."

"That doesn't surprise me, but can we go back to your date with Davy real quick—"

"Which part?"

"The part where you were trying to let him down."

"Ah! Yes." Elle nodded. "Well, it wouldn't have been fair to him for me to date him, since I was rapidly developing feelings for you."

Several seconds ticked by. It was as though Elle's words had done a factory reset on John's brain. He just *stared* at her, blinking occasionally, while he processed what she'd said.

"…I think maybe *I* should sit down," John said distantly.

Elle felt her lips quirk up. "You're already sitting, John."

"I need to sit *further* down." Elle chuckled. John rubbed his hand over his face, his eyes flicking his gaze toward the fridge. "Can I have my beer back now?"

"Nope. I'm not done with you." Something passed over John's face as she said it, too fleeting for her to identify. "Anyway, seeing as you *obviously* couldn't have been *jealous* of Davy—"

"No, I was."

Busted, Elle thought smugly. At the same time, a hopeful little flutter started up in her chest. "Were you?"

John nodded. "Yeah. I… might have fantasized about putting my fist in his face a few times… and used zombie games as catharsis."

"John."

"What?" He started to raise his arms defensively, but Elle just gave him a fond smile. "It wasn't like I was going to just *stroll* up to you and say, 'Hey, you can't go on that date with Davy because I'm in love with you.' Who does that?"

Elle gasped, at about the same time John seemed to realize what he'd said.

His eyes went wide. "Wait—"

"God," Elle cut him off, "why didn't you?"

"I mean— huh?" For the second time, John seemed to need a second to work through her words, like she'd just chucked a Rubik's cube at him and said *solve it.* "Why would I have?"

"Well, hell, John," Elle said. She was feeling lighter and lighter by the second. "You'd have saved us a whole lot of time if you had."

There was a beat. "So let me get this straight," John said. "If I had intercepted you before you went on that date with Davy, you'd have gone out with me instead."

"That was the weakest way you could possibly have asked me out," Elle said flatly. "You can do better than that."

"Wait, hold on— what about New Years?" John asked. "You pushed me away. You said you didn't want to talk about it."

"Well, yeah," Elle said. "For one thing, I was still under the impression that you just had an enormous and impossible brother complex."

"I do not—"

"Or would you rather me call it your hero complex?" John just grumbled at that one. "Anyway, I also thought Logan and Tyler were still in the room. And seeing as I was fully ready to get naked on the kitchen counter—"

John sucked in a breath, his eyes shutting tight. "You... probably shouldn't say that, Elle."

Elle smirked. "What, you mean you *weren't* planning on putting your hand up my dress?"

John's expression darkened. "I didn't say—"

"First that lousy attempt to ask me out, now this." Elle sighed dramatically, looking up at the ceiling. "It's like you're not even try—*mmph!*"

She might have finished her sentence, really; except that out of nowhere, she was being yanked up against John's firm chest, his lips crashing down against hers.

Elle grabbed his arms, leaning up into the kiss. Before she could let herself overthink it, she widened her legs, giving him more space, pulling him closer to her. He kissed her as though his very existence depended on it, his hands cradling her face. Elle tried to keep up, to hold on, but it was too much— this whole thing had already spun out of her control, and she was hopelessly lost to it.

As he deepened the kiss, her brain screeched to a halt. Everything around her receded, blurred away until all she could focus on was his lips against hers. Gentle, but firm, almost desperate. As though he'd been holding himself back from her.

The thought rocked her to her core. And to think, she'd been missing out on this for *months*.

When he pulled back, she was practically hanging off of him, fingers clenched in his tee shirt, her front pressed fully against him. She could barely breathe. And the look on his face—

"Elle," John murmured against her lips. Elle, who had no intention of letting him get away this time, merely hummed. "Elle, are you sure?"

"Sure about what?" she asked.

"Shouldn't we—" he cut off as she tugged at his bottom lip with her teeth. "*Elle.* "

"Hmm?"

"Shouldn't we finish talking about this first?"

That was probably the *smart* thing to do, but Elle was tired of doing the smart thing— tired of the pining and the miscommunication and the goddamn *waiting*. Especially with both of them on the edge of something they both so clearly wanted. "John," She murmured, pulling back just enough to smile up at him. "Can I ask you for something?"

His hands slid down her arms, then dropped to her waist. His expression was almost reverent. "Anything."

Elle slid her hands up around his neck and batted her eyelashes. "Can we talk after?"

"After wh—" John's eyes widened. Clearly, her meaning got through. "*Oh.*"

"I mean, not that we have to," Elle assured him. "If you didn't want—"

John yanked her against him so hard she actually slid forward on the counter, the very center of her pressed against—

Oh.

Elle sucked in the breath that had somehow escaped her lungs. "Oh."

"I want to," he assured her, pressing his lips against her temple. "I've thought about it—" he winced—"probably way more than I should have, considering, but—"

Elle stretched up to press her lips against the edge of his jaw. Her legs came up slightly, closing around his waist, holding him against her. She could feel how much he wanted this.

"*Elle.*"

"Yes?" She trailed kisses along his jaw.

"You're killing me."

"No, I'm kissing you." To emphasize her point, she kissed the spot just behind his ear, her tongue darting out to taste his skin. His breath caught, and his hands tightened around her waist. "I'm perfectly sure, John," she added.

"Right," he muttered, voice strained. "In that case."

The way he kissed her stole her breath away. It only lasted a few seconds before he pulled away again.

Come on, Elle thought, opening her mouth to protest.

"Can I take you to bed?"

Ah. "Yes," she breathed. When John lifted her into his arms, she giggled, clinging to him.

"Still think you're too heavy for me to carry?" John teased, lips against her hair.

Elle laughed. "As I said, you're a regular Hercules." She tilted her head to kiss his cheek. "My hero."

At the top of the stairs, John turned away from her room.

Elle huffed another laugh. "There's a perfectly good bed in my room, Sir."

"I'd like you in *my* bed," John growled, and it was probably the hottest thing anyone had ever said to her. Bar none.

She'd never been in his room— why would she have— but it was so incredibly *him* that ending up in it felt like coming home. The art on the walls, the figurines on the dresser, the muted colors— they were all so inherently *him*. That was all she registered before she landed on his bed with another startled yelp.

He climbed on top of her like an *animal*, cupping her face and kissing her until she got dizzy from it. Elle dragged his shirt up, spreading her hands over his bare skin as she did so. She wanted to feel every inch of him, to memorize his body with her hands. John barely broke contact with her long enough to yank his shirt over his head and toss it aside before he was back on her, his lips going for her neck. She let her head fall back to give him access to all of her, and let herself get lost in the heat coiling in her belly.

"God," he rasped. His hands seemed to be everywhere, all at once. One of them brushed underneath the hem of her shirt, over her bare waist, and she sighed, arching into his touch.

"Off," he murmured, tugging at the fabric. Elle sat up just enough to help him get it off of her, and he flung it across the room like it had offended him— then froze.

"You are..." His hands found her waist again, and just stayed there as he looked his fill. He didn't have to finish the sentence. His expression alone told her all she needed to know.

He'd done so much touching, kissing, nibbling. Driving her insane, making her *want*. Elle had barely had the chance to return the favor.

Something to remedy.

Grabbing his shoulders, she leaned up and licked a stripe up his neck. He tasted like salt, like sweat. Like *him*.

Perfect.

John made a noise, deep in his throat, of either surprise or pleasure. Maybe both. Then his hand was in her hair again, his lips crushed against hers—*oh*. Oh. This— this was just like New Years; the heat, the intensity, the burning need to *consume*.

One of his hands fumbled with the clasp of her bra. Elle bit his lower lip, delighting in the groan it earned her, in the way his fingers slipped away from the clasp and danced down her spine. It took him two tries— and she giggled the second time, when he gave her a suffering look. "Tease." John leaned back and sent her bra wherever her shirt had gone, and then filled his hands with her breasts. "Let me…"

Elle nodded, and—*oh*.

He guided her back, laying her down like something precious, while his mouth did wicked things to her, things that had her gasping for air.

"Is this okay?" He asked. Elle had been so focused on what his mouth was doing, she hadn't really noticed that she was fully naked underneath him, or that his hand was sliding up her thigh, pushing her legs open. Baring her to him. Just the nearness of it to where she was already aching made her breath shorten.

"Yes." The word didn't even sound like her own voice, breathless and delirious and *wonderful*. "Yes."

His hand slid up, just a little further, and—

The air left Elle's lungs in a rush.

There was no way she could already be ready for what his fingers were doing. They'd barely done anything, barely begun, and yet— well, here they were, and here she was, making noises she hadn't known she was capable of. His lips kept switching between her own lips, her neck, her breasts, cranking her up further and further. She shivered as her nerve endings all seemed to reroute to where he was working a third finger—*a third finger* — into the mix.

This was impossible. Unsustainable. There was nothing like this, had never *been* anything like this. Not for Elle.

John pulled away too soon, dragging her back to reality as he did so. She sat up to watch, dazed, as he shoved his jeans off and threw them out of his way. The moment he did, she reached for him again, and—

Oh. Oh, *god*. Would he even fit?

John stilled as her hand landed on his thigh. He seemed tense as a bowstring as she slid it closer, closer, finally wrapping her hand around him. Her fingers didn't even close.

His hand closed around her wrist, gently tugging it away. "I'm not going to last if you do that."

Elle laughed, husky and breathless. "I don't know, that sounds like quite the compliment."

John laughed, too, kissing her temple. "Minx." Then he reached for his nightstand.

Oh. Right. At least one of them was thinking clearly enough to remember protection.

The box, Elle noted, was unopened, when he pulled it from the nightstand. She leaned forward as he took care of it, trailing kisses across his collarbone, leaving quick little love bites on his skin and kissing them away again.

"You drive me crazy," John said, though the words were nothing short of reverent. He turned to her, cradling her face in his hands as he kissed her, as he laid her back onto his bed and made room for himself between her legs, as he opened her up to him, and pressed his way into her, inch by glorious inch.

He bottomed out. Which—*impossible*. It couldn't be. There was *no* way her body could be ready for him, for *all* of him, already. And yet.

"*Elle .*" His hands— she'd have bruises tomorrow, from how tightly he was grasping her hips. She couldn't bring herself to care. Whatever fragile control he still had wavered as he rocked forward, one slow motion that sent Elle's mind spiraling. "Are you okay, Sweetheart?"

"I'm okay." She was better than okay. She was magnificent. Her hands slid around his neck, and she tilted her hips just *so*, giving him more room. "I'm okay. You can—"

John rolled his hips again, and whatever she'd been about to say dissolved in her mind like sugar into hot water. She groaned instead.

"Elle?" He leaned down to kiss her. "Can I...?"

"*Yes.*" *Yes.* He could.

John kissed her again, and then began to move.

There was an impossible stillness, after. Silence, like a warm blanket, laid over them. Elle tried to slow her breathing, laying on top of John, his heartbeat pounding against her cheek the same way hers pounded against her ribs.

She must have fallen asleep at some point, because she woke, slowly rising from the cottony stillness of a dream, to John stroking her hair. She felt deliciously drained.

"Are you okay?"

Elle smiled against his chest and nodded. "Are you?"

"I'm perfect."

"I know, but are you okay?" He laughed, and Elle sighed, completely content. "Are we gonna talk?" He may very well have taken her question seriously if she hadn't yawned a second after asking it.

"In the morning," he told her, stroking her back.

"I love you."

"God, Elle," John whispered, squeezing her more tightly against him. "I love you, too."

John made her breakfast.

It was nothing new. He'd been making her breakfast for months. Only today, she was wearing his tee shirt from yesterday, which she'd scooped up off of his bedroom floor after finding it amidst the pile of her own clothing. It went halfway down her thighs.

He would look back at her from time to time, to where she leaned against the counter and watched him cook, coffee in hand. His eyes would go straight to the hem of her—*his* — shirt, and then he'd smirk.

After the third time, Elle just sipped at her coffee and deliberately bent one knee, letting the shirt ride up nice and high on her thigh, baring most of her leg.

"Don't think I won't put you over my shoulder and carry you back upstairs," he warned, handing her a plate of waffles and bacon.

"You wouldn't." She rose up to give him a quick peck on the lips, and then made her way around the breakfast bar to a stool. "You'd feel too guilty about getting between me and food."

"Nah," he said, with a roguish grin. "We could both eat."

Elle sputtered her coffee, giggles erupting from her throat.

This whole thing was amazingly *easy*. Effortless. She had woken up in his arms, and that rightness that crept into her whenever he held her had soaked through her entire body. Even now, it lingered, just under her skin— a stillness that she was unaccustomed to. It was as if some frantic, grasping part of herself had finally been soothed.

They still hadn't talked. At this point, she wasn't sure they needed to. Everything she needed to know was in his eyes, in his smile. In the way he touched her, gentle and reverent. The way he made her breakfast, and let her wear his shirt.

The front door swung open. Elle met John's eyes and arched a brow up in silent question. John winked in response, then turned back to his own waffles.

"I'm home," Logan sang, floating into the room with a dreamy expression, absolutely glowing.

"Hi, Logan," Elle said, casually biting into her bacon.

Logan drew up short, his smile dropping away. His eyes went to Elle's bare legs, narrowed on her shirt, then flicked over to John, who was only wearing jeans, his back to them.

Eyes widening, Logan gasped. "Did you two...?"

"Make enough for you?" Elle guessed, pushing her plate toward him. "Probably not, but I don't mind sharing. I'll just mooch another waffle off of John when he's done with his." She said it while gesturing toward the man in question with her bacon, before taking another bite.

"That's not what I'm talking about and you know it." Though Logan did take a piece of bacon from her plate. "Did you two finally sit down and talk?"

"I wouldn't call it sitting," Elle said, frowning at John. "Would you?"

"Not exactly." He set a plate of waffles on the bar top in front of Logan, who just scowled.

"You're wearing his shirt," Logan accused gleefully, reaching for the hem. "Is there anything underneath?" Elle swatted his hand away.

"Hey, that's my job!" John said.

"Yeah, that's his job!" Elle parroted, pointing at John. They looked at each other for a moment. Elle's face twitched as she struggled to hold back her smile. John's eyes were bright, but his face was blank— for about three seconds.

"*I knew it!*" Logan cried, triumph burning in his eyes. Elle just grinned and finished her slice of bacon. "Fucking *finally!*"

"Well, that's a bit on the nose," John said.

Elle snorted, almost sending her bacon up her nose. She barely managed to swallow it down, gasping. "God, John, I almost choked."

"Well, I bet," Logan said dryly. "John's huge."

This time, Elle *did* choke, trying to swallow coffee to dislodge the bacon that had stuck in her throat. John just dropped his head into his hand, snickering.

"*Jesus,*" she sputtered, once her coughing had died down. She swatted Logan affectionately on the leg, but all he did was laugh at her. "You are *terrible.* No more bacon for you." She batted his wandering hand away and dragged her plate out of his reach, turning it so that her remaining pieces of bacon were facing away from him.

"How are you even interested in our love life?" John asked, finishing off the last waffle and putting it onto a plate for himself. "Didn't you just get back from being bent over every flat surface you and Tyler could find?"

"And a few less than flat surfaces," Logan confirmed with a smirk. "Come on, Ellie, this is big news. You two finally got your acts together." When both of them merely glared at him, he shrugged.

"What? I've known you two were hopeless idiots for *months*. You just had to figure it out yourselves."

"Your support and assistance is greatly appreciated," Elle said dryly, cutting into her waffles. Though the confirmation that John was just as much of a pining, angst-ridden *disaster* as Logan had insinuated was nice.

John met her eyes, a put-upon expression on his face. Elle closed her teeth around her fork and, feeling bold, winked at him. His eyes darkened immediately, and—

God, how had she missed this? For *months?*

"Hmph." Logan began to plow through his waffles, still looking between Elle and John as though they were keeping some big secret from him, even though he knew full well what had happened. "Oh, *hell,* this means I've lost the bet."

"What bet?" John said darkly, while Elle just sighed, "Another one?"

"*Another one?*" John parroted, this time looking at Elle.

Elle chuckled. "I told you last night, I made him lose the last one to Davy at the Christmas party."

"Dammit, I lost this one, too," Logan said. "I said you'd hold out until Valentine's day, and he said around New Year's."

"New Year's was almost three weeks ago!" Elle said.

Logan rolled his eyes. "I'm aware." He patted her bare thigh. "Try to find some pants before this afternoon, Ellie. We're getting your stuff from storage today, in case you forgot."

"Oh, shoot," Elle sighed. "I need to get stuff from Blaine today, too."

"You *did* forget." Logan shoved her leg playfully, and she returned the gesture. "That's alright. At least we don't have fittings until tomorrow."

"God bless." Though the idea of getting John into some leather had its appeal. Getting him *out* of it had even more appeal. Except— she groaned. "I don't wanna deal with Sarah."

"Why not?" John asked. "Not that I want to, but she's been gunning for me since July." His eyes narrowed, jade gaze piercing Elle. "Are you jealous?"

"Me?" Elle snorted. "No. But she will be." And Elle had to spend a good half hour tomorrow putting clothing on her. "Our last encounter was... not great," she added, remembering the Christmas party with a wince.

John grimaced. "You're right. I hadn't thought about that."

"She wasn't too thrilled about me kissing you at the Christmas party." Elle sighed and pushed the last few pieces of waffle around her plate. "It's fine. I'll deal with whatever she throws at me."

John came around the counter and smoothed his hand down her hair. The gesture was somehow more comforting than it had ever been. "We can handle it together."

Elle smiled up at him, and he smiled back.

"So," Logan said at length. "When are you going to give me a play-by-play?"

"Never," Elle and John chorused.

19

The costume room had been reorganized— by Elle— and cheerfully arranged— also by Elle— to display the costumes she'd borrowed from Blaine, and brought from her own cosplay collection. It looked like a completely different room, a wide folding table set up for accessories, a tall mirror propped against the only wall with a window. All the racks and boxes she had neatly arranged on the far side of the room, in garment bags— a concept— and sorted by both gender and clothing article.

Deceptive, she mused, arranging golden gloves on the table for Sarah. She really wasn't looking forward to whatever conversation ended up happening between them. Though there was always a chance they'd just, casually, never talk about it. Elle hoped.

"Elle?"

At Sarah's voice, Elle looked up and smiled faintly. "Hi! Ready to play dress up?"

Sarah stood by the door in just her yoga pants and tank top, her sunny hair up in its usual top knot, a dance bag over her shoulder. She rubbed a hand over her arm, eyes flicking away from Elle's in blatant discomfort. "Actually… can we talk, before we do costume stuff?"

Here we go, Elle thought, suppressing a sigh. "Sure we can. What's up?"

Sarah approached like a timid pet, tracing one finger across the edge of the folding table. "So… you and John, huh?"

It was a nice enough way to ask, Elle supposed. No sense of accusation, no scowl, not even a hint of anger or jealousy. "Yeah," she said at length. "Me and John."

Sarah hummed, a little thoughtful, a little distant. "I guess that's why he barely gave me the time of day during *Oklahoma* and *Little Shop.*"

"Oh, we weren't—"

"I know," Sarah said, holding up a hand to stop Elle. "But he was already set on you, even if nothing was going on between you two yet." She shrugged. "I thought you and Davy were together, so I thought I had a shot, but he only had eyes for you. Everyone knew it."

Elle winced. "I didn't."

With a snort, Sarah said, "Yeah, no. You're too oblivious for that." Before Elle could reply to that, she continued. "I'm sorry I held that against you."

"Don't be." Elle ran a hand through her hair, scooping it back off her face. "I'm sorry I was a bitch at the Christmas party."

Sarah actually laughed at that. "Just two girls pretending not to argue over a man. Nothing new there."

Elle smiled, too. "Yeah, but still."

"Don't worry about it," Sarah insisted. "No hard feelings."

"You sure?"

A nod. "Besides," Sarah added, "I'd rather us bitch *about* men than *over* a man."

It was like a weight lifted from her shoulders. Elle reached out a hand, and Sarah took it. "Me, too." She gave Sarah's hand a squeeze. "Now, let's try on dresses."

It went well, from there, Elle realized. Things were surprisingly easy, and better still, *friendly.*

She put Sarah into a wavy brown wig, one they planned to use for most of act two, and then had her try on a few blue dresses. Sarah listened patiently while Elle described the quick changes and how each dress would work for them.

"I like this one," Sarah said, holding out the skirt of the dress she was in and turning to each side. It was, by far, the closest to the animated movie that Elle had.

"It's pretty," Elle said. "And it has pockets."

Sarah laughed, her hands instantly sinking into the sides of the skirt. "Every girl's dream."

While Sarah stripped back down to her camisole and leggings, Elle crossed *village dress* off in her costume notebook and tossed it aside onto the cluttered vanity stuffed into one corner of the room. "Alright, ballgown time."

Belle had always been Elle's favorite princess. She had no fewer than five versions of the ballgown, ranging from simple to gaudy, from professionally finished to barely-cosplay-ready. She dragged the first, and simplest, from the rack, and held it out for Sarah to look at. "This is the lightest, and the closest to the animated movie, but it's also the plainest I have."

Sarah nixed it, on account of it being *too plain*. They inspected two more dresses, a frilly and over the top monstrosity, and one that looked like the Disney Parks, but with more gold and sparkle.

"I like that this is two pieces," Sarah said of the latter, inspecting the bodice with a thoughtful frown. "It could be useful."

"I'll set that one aside for now." Elle hung it off the edge of the rack, and then reached for the next dress. "This one is my favorite. I'd wear it as a wedding dress if I could."

The gown was something else, in Elle's eyes. As though, despite it being her pattern, her fabric, her hours and hours of effort, it hadn't really been *her* that had made the dress, but something otherworldly that had used her body. *Ethereal*, Logan called it. The bodice was sleek and smooth, the sleeves gently draped, the skirt voluminous and soft as a cloud. It was, by far, Elle's favorite possession and creation.

"Oh, I couldn't wear your favorite," Sarah said instantly. "It's stunning, don't get me wrong, but I'd be too nervous to mess it up onstage."

Elle tried not to feel the wave of relief that swept through her, but nodded. "I appreciate that."

"Why not use it as a wedding dress?"

The question caught Elle so off guard, she dropped the last dress. "What?"

Sarah pointed at Elle's favorite again. "Why *not* use it as a wedding dress?"

Elle frowned. "Wouldn't that be kind of… tacky?"

Sarah shrugged. "Who cares? It's *your* wedding. You should be happy."

For a long moment, Elle stared at the dress. She felt like a princess every time she wore it, but it was really made for conventions, *maybe* the stage. "I... no," she said finally, shaking her head. "I would want to make something new. Something special, just for J—" John's name was on the tip of her tongue, but she stopped short, choking on it before it even left her mouth.

God, *marriage*. That was... awfully fast, for her to be thinking about that... wasn't it?

"For John," Sarah finished for her. "That's... actually really sweet." She huffed a laugh. "I wish someone would look at me the way he looks at you."

A pang went through Elle's chest, and she turned back to Sarah. "It'll happen," she assured the other woman. "Don't give up. John's apparently been stuck on me forever." She reached out and put a comforting hand on Sarah's arm. "Maybe there's someone you haven't noticed."

Sarah hummed thoughtfully. "Yeah. Maybe."

Dresses, Elle thought, and held up the last one. "Last, but definitely not least."

Sarah's eyes widened. Then misted.

Really? Elle thought, keeping her expression completely blank. *This one?*

It was, by far, Elle's least favorite. Her first attempt at using multiple fabrics, trims, and other decorations. Clusters of tiny red roses marked the end of each gathering on the overskirt, and the center of the neckline, where the stiff sleeves came together. The skirt of the gown was layered, delicate lace over printed silk. The bodice was straight brocade, a little too close to orange for Elle's taste. It had all the gaudiness of the fanciest dress, with none of the coherence.

"This one," Sarah said, mimicking Elle's thoughts. Awed— that was the only word that came to Elle's mind. Sarah was *awed* by this lacy, flowery horror.

"This one?" For the life of her, Elle couldn't explain what possessed her to ask, *"Why?"*

"It's perfect," Sarah said simply. One hand came out to ghost over the skirt. "Can I put it on?"

Stumped, Elle huffed a laugh. "Absolutely. Do you want to put the wig on, too? For the full effect?"

Sarah smiled. "The gloves too, right?"

"Hell, you can wear the bloomers for all I care."

It took them ten minutes of searching for bits and pieces, peppered with Elle explaining that she'd personally train a few techs and dancers to help with the quick change. Elle even put her into her favorite of the wig options. "It's the happy medium between fancy and simple," she explained, fastening the last pin into it. "Alright, you're all set."

Sarah took a deep breath, and then turned to face the mirror on the back of the door.

Ah. That was why. Elle knew the look on Sarah's face intimately. She'd worn it herself, multiple times. Awestruck, dazed. Like her own reflection wasn't even her, but some goddess's attempt to look like her.

A tear slid down Sarah's cheek.

"Keep it," Elle said. "It's yours."

Stunned, Sarah met Elle's gaze in the mirror. "I... what?"

"I never wear it," Elle continued. "I can't stand it, actually. It's been stored away since high school, when I wore it for our show." She nodded at Sarah, who continued to gape at her, another tear escaping her eye. "That's *your* dress, Sarah. You should have it."

Sarah looked at herself in the mirror again. "Are you sure?"

"Positive."

The grin that spread across Sarah's face was radiant. "I'll take it." She smoothed her gloved hands over her waist. "Elle?"

Elle had already made her way to her notebook to jot down ideas for the quick change, and cross out *ballgown* on her list. She didn't even bother to look up, expecting more commentary about costumes, or the dress in general. "Yeah?"

"John's really lucky to have you."

Elle's head snapped up. Sarah wasn't looking at her, but she sounded sincere all the same.

"No," Elle said softly, thinking of everything John had done for her, in the past few months alone. "I'm the lucky one."

John opened the costume room door to find Elle and Sarah... laughing. Together. Sarah was clutching a horrifying pink monstrosity to her chest, and Elle was saying something about visual comedy, and...

God, how weird was *this?*

"Thanks, Elle," Sarah said, hanging the dress beside the classic blue village gown and a truly impressive golden ballgown. "I'll send the boys— oh!" She caught sight of John just as she reached down to pick up her dance bag. "Speak of the devil. Hi, John!"

"...Hey," he said carefully, trying to find any glimpses of jealousy or contempt in her face. There weren't any. "How'd the fitting go?"

"Wonderful!" Sarah positively beamed at him. "Your girlfriend is a saint. She's giving me the ballgown when this is over."

"That's great." He tried to sound excited, but mostly, he was just *confused.* Elle was humming to herself, which she wouldn't be doing if she wasn't cheerful. Clearly, she and Sarah had—

Wait. *Girlfriend?*

So she knew. They'd obviously talked, and come to some sort of agreement. Sarah didn't appear to be upset, and Elle was as high-spirited as ever.

Really, that was all he could hope for, wasn't it?

"I can't wait to see it on you," he added, with a genuine smile. "Elle's got a real talent for costumes."

"Elle's pretty talented in general," Sarah said. "At least I know who can understudy for me if I get the plague again." With a chipper laugh, Sarah breezed past John, headed back to rehearsal. "Have fun getting fitted!"

"Will do." John didn't even bother looking at Sarah, arching a brow at Elle instead. "She's in a good mood."

"Me, too," Elle confirmed. "We talked it out. She was a really good sport about it."

"That's good... I think?" Enough chatting, John decided, walking up to Elle. She was scribbling something in her old, tattered costume notebook, but that didn't even deter him. He just put his hands on her waist, and instantly, he had her attention, her head tilting up so she could look at him with those gorgeous eyes of hers, her hair falling out of its bun to frame her face. With her hands on his chest, she rose up on her toes to kiss him.

Please, god, may he never tire of kissing her. Even short, sweet kisses like this.

"Thank god," said a voice behind John, which made his back go rigid. "I thought y'all would never sort yourselves out."

John turned to face Davy with a carefully blank expression, keeping one hand around Elle's waist. Davy just smirked back at him, eyes going to John's hand and then back to his face.

"Yeah, yeah," Elle said. "You were right all along."

"I know." Davy met John's gaze, and his smirk deepened. "At least you stopped glaring at me like a starved wolf."

"I didn't—" he *did*, John realized, and stopped talking.

"You did," Davy confirmed with a chuckle, "but it's fine. I get it. Elle's a special lady."

"And you two are old fashioned," Elle said. She gave John a pointed look, and— god, he'd move worlds for her, if she asked him to. "Here, start putting pieces on." With that, she sashayed out of his arms and over to the costume rack, chucking a piece of black colored leather at him.

John gave Davy a long-suffering look, then rolled his eyes.

"No onesies," Elle said to Davy, while John unzipped his jeans. "I've got my friend Blaine's cosplay pieces here, and we'll rig up something that will work for the quick change at the end. Okay?"

"Sounds good, Miss Elle."

John listened with half an ear as Elle described the body and leg pieces to Davy, and started to work his way into the leather pants. He'd seen them himself when they'd picked them up from Elle's friend's place. The guy was now happily married, apparently, though Elle had been right— he still called her *Emma*. He really was dumb as a brick. Somehow, John hadn't even felt jealous, meeting him.

John had won out on that front, anyway.

He managed to get the pants fastened in the front, a zipper with a clever fake-lace-up panel snapped over top, and turned to watch Elle work. She truly was a costuming genius, he realized, listening to her describe the quick change in full detail. He should have known she'd block out the scene for Greg— she basically ran this theater by herself, and everyone knew it— but there was an irresistible light in her eyes as she showed Davy the clasps on the Beast chest piece, the way his prince costume would fit underneath for the fight scene and transformation, and how he would have to rehearse in the boots to get used to them.

"Here," she said, handing Davy blue and gold fabric. "Try the suit on with the chest piece." With that, she turned to face John— and her jaw dropped.

Hell yeah, he thought smugly, as she arched a brow and blew out a breath. "Are they okay?"

"Take those home with you," she told him, and then reached for another costume piece. John burst out laughing, only stifling it when she threw another bundle of leather and cotton at him. His grin went nowhere, however. "Put that on so we can see if I need to make something else for you later."

John continued to laugh while he changed, once again listening to Elle talk to Davy. This wasn't so bad, he decided. Davy was being a good sport— the same way Sarah, apparently, had been. It was a relief, in a way.

The door opened yet again, and Logan's head came around the door. "Ooh! *Yes*, John!" he said, giving John a sly grin. "The leather works. Elle, darling, we need him as soon as you can let him go."

"Sure thing," she said, waving Logan off. She glanced at John, then, and—

Oh, he was *definitely* taking this costume home.

Her eyes slowly slid up to his, her smile feline and feminine. "You definitely don't need the muscle pads." She winked at him, and John—

his *heart*. He couldn't take this. "Go ahead and change, my love. I still need to get Davy into a few more costumes."

"Sure thing." John met Davy's eyes, and caught the smugness in them, before Davy politely gave his attention to Elle. Honestly, the man was as bad as Logan.

Once changed, he put his name into his costume on a piece of masking tape and hung it up on the rack, behind Sarah's divider. One of the gowns caught his eye, a gentle sweep of soft fabric that melted into silk. In all honesty, it looked more like a wedding dress than Belle's ballgown, a creamy, hazy fabric embroidered with delicate golden flowers, draped delicately over the palest gold silk he'd ever seen. John reached out to touch it, admiring Elle's work— it was, truly, a stunning gown.

Out of nowhere, the image of Elle wearing this dress, walking down an aisle, sprung fully formed into his head.

John snatched his hand back as though stung, eyes going wide. It wasn't that he'd never thought of marrying Elle, it was just— those ideas had always been hypothetical, imaginary. Impossible dreams and fantasies for him to toy with when he felt like torturing himself. Only now...

His eyes slid to Elle, contentedly writing notes in her notebook.

"So," Davy said, startling John out of his own head. "Does this mean you'll stop sulking all the time?"

John opened his mouth, fully prepared to argue that, no, he didn't *sulk*, except... yeah, he *had* been sulking. Everyone in this damn theater knew he'd been stuck on Elle. It was a wonder they hadn't thrown a party for them yet.

Maybe they were waiting until the *Beauty and the Beast* cast party, he thought wryly. Two birds, one stone, and all of that.

"Yeah," John finally said, cracking a smile. His eyes went to Elle, who gave him a small, witchy look that melted his brain into his spine. "Yeah, I think I can stop sulking now."

"Good," Davy said, snapping the shiny blue prince jacket closed. "You're a pain when you sulk."

John couldn't help but laugh.

The three housemates arrived home from rehearsal later that week in high spirits. The show was really coming together, and Elle had gotten to work with a few college kids she'd met her senior year, now seniors themselves. They were taking to the Theatre like ducks to water.

"I'm so proud of the kids," she said, setting her backpack on the stairs to take up later. "I think Greg's gonna have a great new crew to work with. Maybe he can finally fire Jimbelina." She looked wistfully into the distance. "At long last."

"They're really enamored of you," John said, kissing her head. "Maybe the girls will take notes. Greg needs more tiny, sarcastic women telling him what to do."

"He does not," Logan said. "That's Elle's job."

Elle made a beeline for the kitchen with a laugh. "That's okay, I can concentrate my evil powers on John, now." To prove it, she pinned John with a seductive stare and shimmied her shoulders. He rolled his eyes, but they grew noticeably darker. *Ha.*

"You just love to be dramatic," Logan continued. "You always get over things, but the drama comes first."

"Too true." Elle started pulling ingredients out of the fridge for dinner.

"Here, Ellie," Logan said, trying to take food from her hands as she picked it up. "I can cook, for once. You two can go shower."

"Subtle," Elle said wryly, "but I can't. For one thing, this is a family recipe, and if you mess it up, I'm making you eat the whole thing by yourself." Logan grimaced, and from the other room, John laughed. "For another, I promised to call Mom and catch up, and I need to catch her between work and her pottery class."

"Your mom makes pottery?" John propped his elbows on the counter to watch her, in that sweet, semi-possessive way that Elle loved.

"It's her one and only hobby outside of work," Elle said. "I won't tell you about her botched Samba class when I was fourteen. I'd like to forget it ever happened, honestly." She swatted Logan away again, stealing the cream of mushroom soup he'd pulled from the pantry. "Thank you. Now go shower. You already smell like Lefou."

"Bossy," Logan said, but kissed her cheek. "You're right, though. This show is going to run me out of spray deodorant."

Elle groaned. "I didn't need to know."

As Logan left, his laughter floating down in his wake, John came to wrap his hands around Elle's middle, tucking her safely against his chest while she popped open a pack of chicken. "Do you want me to stay?"

She wanted to say *yes*. Always. The low-level hum that existed just under her skin seemed to swell at the thought of calling Karen. Anything to *do* with Karen made her tense.

"No," she assured John, turning her head awkwardly so she could kiss his jaw. "It's just a phone call, a little bit of catching up. Besides, we're gonna talk about girly things."

"So, me?" He grinned, and Elle laughed.

"Exactly. Go ahead up and set up the shower." Though she was perfectly content here, preparing dinner with his arms around her, present but out of her way. "Or you can give me a few minutes to get this ready, and run a bath. I'll come up and join you when I'm done here."

John's voice dropped lower than usual, his lips ghosting over the shell of her ear. "I like the sound of that," he husked, and Elle almost dropped the can opener she'd just picked up. With a fleeting kiss to her temple, John stepped away. "Don't let her ramble too long, Ellie."

"I won't." She *wouldn't*. She'd be perfectly clear that this was a short *hey how's it going* conversation, make her excuses with dinner or the bath or anything else she could think of, and then escape unscathed.

The sound of her mom's phone ringing on the other end of the line just amped her anxiety up an extra notch. Elle swallowed it down and put her phone on speaker on the counter, and set about pulling her chicken together.

"Hi, Cupcake!"

Timeless and strange, that same sense of ease Elle always got washed over her. "Hi, Momma. How are you?"

Karen talked her ear off for a full five minutes, while Elle wrapped her chicken in bacon. She actually found herself smiling, imagining Karen's regular patrons and their new hairstyles, or the pottery Karen was making. Karen even asked about the theater and how the show was going, and didn't once say anything condescending about Elle's job. A true miracle.

"So, how's John?"

Elle smiled to herself, trying to figure out the right words. "We're giving each other a try."

"Dating?" Karen sounded excited, which— after their last time seeing each other— was an honest to god relief.

"Yeah, I suppose. I mean, we already live together." And Elle hadn't slept in her own bedroom for several days, at this point. "We haven't really put a label on it, but yeah. We're dating."

"The honeymoon period." There was an understanding wistfulness to her voice, but something lurked underneath it— or maybe Elle just *expected* it to. She decided to let it go, pouring cream of mushroom over her chicken and bacon.

"I'm glad things are going well," Karen said, again sounding sincere. "I suppose you won't be needing your furniture after all."

Once again, Elle found herself expecting that underlying *something* in her mother's tone. Was it really there, or had Elle just reached a point where she couldn't even trust her own *mom?* "No, probably not."

"Well, when he gets tired of you, I'll help you move into a new place."

"What?" Elle felt her brain slam back into the moment, almost dropping the empty soup can into her casserole dish. "When he *what?*"

"Cupcake, you've got so much more learning to do in life!" *There it is* , Elle realized. The thing that her brain had warned her about, even before it was actually there. "You'll need a real job eventually, something steady that pays real money!"

"My job *is* steady," Elle insisted. Her face was getting hot.

"Ellie, you've never lived on your own. You don't really know what it's like to be an adult!"

"I *am* an adult!" Was her voice rising? God, no. *No.*

"You barely even know who you are, Ellie. What do you expect from this relationship?"

Elle didn't know. She couldn't even think about that right now. She was too busy shaking, staring at the preheat light on the oven, wishing she had the guts to scream and rage and tell her mother *exactly what she thought*—

"I just want you to be prepared in case the worst happens," Karen continued, oblivious. "If he hasn't even given you a label, what makes you think this will be a lasting thing?"

"He—" *He loves me,* Elle told herself firmly. *He said he loves me.*

"You can't pretend your way into happily-ever-after, Ellie."

Right, Elle decided, her anger turning to stone in her chest. *This is over.* "I have to go, Mom," she said, sliding the casserole dish into the oven as if on autopilot. "Dinner's about ready."

"Alright, Cupcake," Karen said, bizarrely cheerful. "Keep me posted. I love you!"

"Love you too."

Elle hung up the phone, and then stared at it, anger churning inside her like a stormy ocean, welling up into her throat, her face. Her eyes.

Before she could think it through, Elle turned around, rearing her arm back, fully planning on chucking her phone at the wall.

John stood on the stair landing, eyes wide. With a yelp, Elle grasped her phone tightly against her chest.

"What happened?"

"John." She closed her eyes and let out a slow, steadying breath. "How long have you been there?" *How much did you hear?*

"I heard you raise your voice," he said, "but I only heard you say goodbye, if that's what you mean." He narrowed his eyes, looking her over, and she saw his gaze linger on the phone in her hands. "Are you okay?"

No, Elle thought, *but it doesn't matter.* "Just... Mom." She shrugged. "Saying things that she thinks are helpful, and are actually..."

"Bitchy?" John finished. Elle chuckled, but the sound was nearly humorless.

"I don't..." Elle scrubbed her eyes with one hand and sighed. "I don't want to talk about it."

"Okay." And that, there, the easy acceptance of Elle's boundaries, was what made John so... so *him*. Elle felt a smile slowly return to her face. "If you change your mind, I want to listen," he told her. "Anytime, anywhere. For any reason."

Of *course* he did.

Elle's anger melted into something less sharp, less hot. Less consuming. Fully smiling, now, she made her way up the stairs to John, taking his outstretched hand. "Come on," she said, pausing one stair above him to kiss his cheek. "Let's go take our bath."

20

It seemed like they turned around, and Hell Week for Disney's *Beauty and the Beast* was upon them. The road to it had been chaotic, at best. It was more than the complex choreography Elle had created for John's solo and the Tavern Scene, or seeing her try to train techs and dancers for both Davy's and Sarah's quick changes. It even went beyond the publicity filming Greg had arranged and the fact that their first two weekends were already sold out.

Somewhere in the last week, Sarah had gotten distant out of nowhere. It seemed she was always distracted by something that had to do with her phone, having to excuse herself every so often to answer calls. She had her lines and blocking down, and she seemed to be in character when she was on the stage, but it didn't sit well with John. He couldn't really place why.

They got to the theater early on the first night of Tech, so that Elle could help Ben with lighting things. John had dragged Logan along so that they'd have extra hands, and sat at one of the tables in the audience running lines with him while Elle stood on the stage in various positions throughout an *extremely* abbreviated run of the script, shouting wryly to Ben about spotlight colors.

"How's it look, Ben?" She asked, shielding her eyes at center stage.

"Yellow," Ben replied dryly, and he was right. The entire stage looked like it had a particularly bad Instagram filter on it.

"Try the pink," Elle suggested. The spotlight went glaringly white for a split second, causing her to wince, and then turned glaringly *red* instead. "*Pink*, Ben," she said again, rolling her eyes hard enough for John to see from the front table. He snorted. The light turned a soft, rose-tinted white that lit Elle up in an almost romantic way. "Thank you."

God, she was gorgeous, John mused.

"Will it work with Sarah's ballgown?" Ben shouted.

Elle shrugged. "It should. She's not here, or I'd put her in it to run the scene."

"Can't you wear it?" Ben asked.

"I'm pretty sure that's bad luck," Elle said. "I can at least go get it, so that we can see what it looks like in—" Behind John the door to the theater slammed open, followed by a commotion that turned his head. "Greg?"

In his usual three-piece suit, Greg bustled through the tables of the audience, huffing the entire way, until he reached the front of the stage. "Sarah quit."

"Sarah *what?*" John, Logan, and Elle all spoke at the same time, and from the booth, Ben echoed them.

Greg panted, pulling a handkerchief from his breast pocket to wipe his dewy brow. "Her father's in the hospital. Looks like a heart attack."

"Oh my god," Elle gasped, her hand flying to her heart.

Oh, thought John. Oh, *shit.*

"He's been having troubles for quite some time," Greg continued. "She warned me that she may miss a rehearsal or two, but since she has to fly out to Oregon now—"

When it clicked, John's jaw dropped. *That* was what had been bothering Sarah this past week.

"What are we going to—" Elle began to ask, and then her face shifted. "Greg."

He was already grimacing, and John—

Oh, John thought again. Oh, *yes.* This was *perfect.*

"I'm sorry, Elle, but Sarah specifically asked you to take over for her." Elle just gaped at him, her face going through at least three of the five stages of grief in rapid succession. "I've called Jim in to take over spot, and Hank can do audio—"

"No," Elle said, cutting him off. "Get one of the kids I trained last week. Send the Country Bear Jimboree back to Hell where he belongs."

Beside John, Logan snorted. John himself had to press his palm to his mouth to hold in his laugh. "Don't disgrace that show by linking it to Jim," Logan yelled.

"Point," Elle said. "Greg, if you hire one of the new kids and fire Jim, I'll take over for Sarah."

"*Done.*"

John blew out a breath, and then grinned up at Elle. "Super Elle saves the day, once again."

"Try not to elbow me this time," she said, grinning down at him. John put a hand to his chest, feigning offense, but she just turned her attention back to Greg. "I'm using my own costumes, not the ones she chose."

"Elle, you could sew a brand new outfit every night for all I care," Greg told her, already making his way back toward the tech booth. "And you're getting a raise."

Elle snorted. "Thanks." She looked at John and Logan again, shielding her eyes from the spot that still shone on her. "Do you two want to come back and help me pull my costume pieces together?"

"I've got it," Logan said, rising. "John, you stay here and try not to gawk at how pretty your girlfriend is."

"I do *not* gawk," John argued. Both of them rolled their eyes at him.

"That's alright," Greg said. "I'd like to discuss something with John." He gave John a pointed look, beckoning for John to follow him to the tech booth.

With a wary glance at Elle and Logan's retreating forms, John followed.

Greg was already in the rolling chair with his hands steepled when John reached the tech booth. Before John could ask what was wrong, he said, "I hear you're besotted with my Elle."

What— *this* was what Greg wanted to talk about?

John shifted uncomfortably on his feet. "Uh…"

"Now, I know you've been stuck on her since the dawn of time," Greg said, with a level expression that somehow made John feel much smaller. "I'm honestly surprised I never had to break up a fight between you and Davy. Your loyalty is mighty admirable."

Was this... was this Greg's way of giving John his approval? "Um, thank—"

"But you listen to me, young man."

John snapped his mouth shut as Greg leaned toward him. His dark eyes were sharp, and hard as steel. Greg very rarely spoke in that tone, and when he did, it was often followed by—

"If you do *anything* to hurt my Elle, Logan won't be the only person you'll answer to."

— A threat.

Speechless, John swallowed. He'd never been on the receiving end of one of Greg's threats before. It was, honestly, a little terrifying. Though, he supposed, with how close Elle was to him— practically running things in his stead, following in his footsteps— it made sense.

Like he had any intention of *hurting* Elle, though. The thought was laughable.

"Do you understand me, John?" The look in Greg's eyes made John feel exactly like a child being chastised by a parent. The feeling was unsettling, at *best*, and his response came tumbling out of his mouth automatically.

"Yes, Sir."

Greg leaned back, satisfied. "Good man."

"Hey!" John practically leapt from his skin at Elle's waspish tone behind him. He turned to find her leaning in the doorway, glaring at Greg. "Can you be done threatening my boyfriend to defend my honor?" She snapped. "I want to run a few scenes before we have to deal with the whole cast."

"He's all yours, Elle," Greg said, indulgent as ever with her. John tried to hide his sigh of relief.

Elle just rolled her eyes at Greg, then smiled fondly up at John. "Come on, big guy. You can practice wooing me."

"I think I've got that down," John teased.

After the initial emergency rehearsal, things fell pretty well into place—at least, in John's opinion. Watching Elle learn the four different kick sections of *Be Our Guest* that she'd choreographed had been a delight, seeing the elated grin on her face throughout the song during the first run through. Getting to manhandle her himself had been just as fun, making her giggle and break character through the first two tries, with Greg sighing exasperatedly from the front of the stage.

Even Davy was handling it well. The stop-and-start run-throughs of each act gave Elle time to solidify her blocking, and gave John time to watch them sort out the romantic stuff. Though, when Elle caught him staring from the wings, she made a point to pull him into a dark corner once the scene was over and—

"You get more than one kiss a night," she reminded him, splaying her body against his. John's eyes widened, especially as her hand stroked across one of his hips. Then she was gone, taking a tech's hand and talking the younger girl through the quick change at lightning speed.

God, John thought. *God.* That... that would never get old.

Dress rehearsal was his chance to get her back, and he did from the moment he walked out of the dressing room. In her pretty blue ensemble, with her sleek brown wig on, Elle sat on the couch, reading over her script as she waited for places to be called. Her eyes flicked up, and then *came* up, dragging up the length of John's body, and all the leather he was wearing.

He smirked down at her. "See something you like?"

Elle hummed noncommittally. "You're taking that home after the show closes, you know."

"Isn't this your friend Blaine's?"

Elle's grin went wicked. "He doesn't have to know." The thought had John squeezing his fist until his nails bit into his palms, just to keep him from getting too excited. "I'll get you back for that later, by the way."

"Get me back for what?" John said innocently. Elle just gave him a droll look.

They made it through the first act in a vaguely decent amount of time, as it turned out. Ben only had to stop them a handful of times to shift light colors, or correct Hank on spot. The new girl was doing phenomenally with audio, the music loud enough to hear but not overpowering, and their mics at a manageable level— and, like magic, never on at weird times, like when people weren't on stage.

"You trained her well," John told Elle between scenes. Elle positively preened before slipping back into character for her next entrance.

This was the one rehearsal where people were allowed to sit in the audience when they weren't on stage, to see everyone else's costumes. John had seen most of the show from the table at the middle of the house, the best seat by far, and that's right where he ran when his last song finished. Greg merely scooted his chair over and let John take the seat next to him without a word.

"You're gonna do the thing again," Logan whispered when he sat down next to John, a few moments later.

John wasn't actually listening. Elle had been on the other side of the stage changing when he'd left after his scene, and he wanted the full effect when she came onstage. "What thing?"

"You're gonna make the face."

"What face?" But it was too late.

The spotlight bloomed to life, tinted with rose, and there stood Elle in the heart of it, at the top of the staircase, in the pale golden gown John had seen during his fitting.

His heart stopped in his chest.

She was *ethereal.* The gentle curls framing her face, the silky opera gloves, and that gorgeous gown. The light seemed to shimmer off of it, like sunlight on water, like the dawn on a hazy morning.

He registered the soft, lilting music as though from afar, the band playing so sweetly he could barely breathe. The dress trailed gently behind Elle as she descended in time to the music, and—

"I'm going to marry her," John breathed. It should scare him, or shock him, or affect him in some way— they were barely dating, they'd been official for less than a month— but it didn't. There was only a bone-deep sense of certainty, and underneath it, down to his very soul, was the love John had felt for Elle for as long as he could remember.

He couldn't do it yet. It was too soon. But John knew, without a shadow of a doubt, that the woman on that stage was going to be his wife. Someday.

Beside John, Logan reached out to pat his arm. "I know, big guy."

John awoke on a particularly warm, bright morning to Elle pressing kisses to his collarbone. It was less like waking up, really; more like drifting out of one pleasant dream, and into an even better one. Elle's body was flush against his side, in only the tee shirt she'd stolen from him the night before. Her hand trailed down his chest, slow, gentle, searching for—

Ah.

John pried his eyes open to look at her. Her hair was tangled and frizzy, her face red where it had been pressed against him all night, her eyes still heavy-lidded from sleep. She'd never looked more beautiful. It shook him to the core.

"Good morning," she purred, when his hand came up to stroke the length of her back. His train of thought dissolved before he could corral it into a coherent greeting when her fist wrapped around him. The air rushed from his lungs all at once.

God, this was—*god.* His spine went liquid, his mind not far behind.

Her hand did wicked things that made John close his eyes and gasp. Her throaty, *smug* laugh brushed against the skin of his neck, melting him even further underneath her. Somehow, his hand found its way into her hair; he didn't even realize until it closed into a fist, and she made one of those little noises that cranked him right up. Her response was to bite down his neck, a little harder than the nibbling she'd been driving him insane with, and—

It was so easy, with how much bigger than her he was. One fluid movement, and Elle was situated right on top of him, her legs on either side of his hips.

"What—*oh...* " Her eyes fell shut while he arranged her the way he wanted her, his hands gripping her hips, guiding them down. His shirt swamped her, pooling across his lower belly, but her hands held his shoulders with surprising strength.

"Elle." The first word he'd spoken this morning— the first word he thought *every* morning, and the last word he thought every night. She was like his own personal sun, his true north, brightening everything he did. Even when she wasn't around. He hadn't realized how grey his life had been until she'd come to fill it with color and light.

She grinned down at him, sleepy and breathless. John slid his hands up underneath the hem of the tee shirt, seeking the smooth skin of her waist. He wanted to feel her in his hands without barriers.

Elle's hand traveled up to his cheek, her thumb swiping over his bottom lip. "We should get flowers for the house."

"What?" The shirt was in his *way*. He wanted more— he wanted the damn thing off of her— but she seemed perfectly content to stay like this, and he was *loath* to interrupt her flow of experience.

"Flowers," she repeated sweetly, tracing down his neck and chest with one slim finger. His heart hammered, as though it was trying to escape his rib cage, so she could hold it in her hand. As if she didn't already. "It's almost spring. We should have some flowers in the house."

It was— she had to be doing this on purpose. Seducing him into saying *yes*. He couldn't imagine why; it wasn't like he could refuse her anything, anyway.

"It's February," John said. He pushed the shirt up, until she relented and pulled it off, throwing it out of the way. *Better.* "Can I...?" He traced the line of one of her hips, and she nodded, lifting herself up for him. He angled himself against her, and she parted on him like water.

Elle's hands tightened on his shoulders. "John."

John couldn't respond. His entire focus was on not moving yet, until she'd had a chance to adjust to him. She needed *time*, to prepare herself, to relax a little—

"*John.*" She rocked her hips, and he felt his control begin to erode around the edges. His hands on her waist were the only things grounding him, keeping him from losing it completely. She felt better than anything he could ever have imagined.

"Can I?" He begged again, because she *felt* ready, fidgeting on top of him, and he wasn't sure his control would last much longer.

Elle moaned, and did what she did best— shattered whatever restraint he'd thought he had. John threaded his fingers through her hair and pulled her tightly against him, letting his control snap away.

He felt her hit her peak first, her breath hot against his neck in a series of whimpers that undid him entirely. His vision whited out before she even finished coming. When he finally came back to himself, Elle had resumed her task of kissing his neck and jaw.

There was *nothing* like this. Nothing compared to the blissful, quiet aftermath of *Elle.*

They stayed like that for awhile, the morning sun spread golden and warm across them, like a spotlight on the love of his life. She was a vision like this, her back bare on top of him, her hair sprawled across her shoulders, across his arm.

"So," Elle said at length, sounding significantly more awake than John felt. He looked up to see her, clear eyed and smiling, her face still flushed. "Flowers?"

John laughed. "You can have flowers if you let me take you out next Wednesday night."

"You can always take me out," Elle said, stroking his collarbone with the tip of her finger. It seemed to be one of her favorite spots on him. "Why Wednesday?"

"It's the day before Valentine's day," John explained.

"Why not— oh, shoot, Valentine's is Thursday. We work."

"Yep." Though, speaking of flowers, John mused. His eyes went to the clock on his nightstand. "Come on, gorgeous, let me feed you."

"I never wake up before you," Elle said, sitting up and— *oh*— dismounting herself from him with the swing of one of her lean, toned legs. "This was fun."

"You can wake me up whenever you like," John said, standing. He had about ten minutes to get her downstairs. "What about Wednesday?"

"It's a date," Elle said, already pulling his tee shirt back on.

"Don't forget pants," John reminded her, pulling his own on. "Logan's home."

Elle just hummed at him, but when he came out of his closet, she had leggings on, and was pulling her mile-long hair into a ponytail. "We wouldn't want to shock him, would we? What would he think?" John rolled his eyes as he followed her out of their bedroom—*their* bedroom, where she'd been sleeping for weeks, even though she still went back to her old room to get her clothing and do her makeup. "We'd better not tell him we're together. He'd have a stroke."

"Hardy har," John said flatly. Just as they reached the first floor, the doorbell rang. "Hey, speaking of flowers." Elle frowned at him, but he ignored her in favor of getting the door, and thanking the delivery guy, who handed John's surprise over with a knowing grin. The moment he turned, roses in hand, he found her behind him. She gasped. "Happy opening ni—*oof!*"

He didn't even manage to get the words out before she was on him, yanking him down for kiss after kiss, until he got dizzy from it.

"I love them," she said, when she finally relented. "I love these, and I love you. God, I love you." She grabbed him before he could straighten and gave him one more kiss, then practically sprinted back toward the kitchen, John strolling along behind her.

"I take it she liked the flowers," Logan said, still rumpled from sleep and propped against the upper banister.

"She liked them," John confirmed, grinning.

21

Beauty and the Beast opened to a packed house. Opening weekend was so laden with compliments, excitement, and relief, Elle found herself wondering why she'd been off the stage for so long. She even considered auditioning for *Peter Pan* in March. The moment she told Greg as much, the man literally *wept* with joy. Figured.

Things with John were still going smoothly, too. She slept in his bed every night, and found that she didn't even miss her old bedroom whenever she walked into it to get clothing or do her makeup. Logan was spending more and more time with Tyler, so much so that Elle would be surprised if they didn't move in together in the near future. She and John basically had the house to themselves.

It was nice. Domestic. *Wonderful.*

He'd insisted— in his patient, understanding way— that she meet some of the country club members, since she'd lived in the neighborhood for so long at this point. The community had a Valentine's party every year, and he'd wanted her to go; of course, as he'd asked her in the middle of the night (*after*, of course), she'd just contentedly agreed, without thinking about what that really meant.

So here she stood, in a vintage-style pink dress of her own creation, surrounded by adults in dress-casual, waiting for John to bring her another drink. She'd managed to find an unoccupied high-top table, slightly apart from the groups of gossiping socialites. Even dolled up, she felt out of place here. These people had *real* jobs, jobs in business and accounting, doctors and lawyers. Important people who made real money.

Your Karen is showing, Elle chastised herself.

Elle and her mother had never belonged to their own neighborhood community— committee—*whatever.* It was the one facet of social skills that Elle had never managed to pick up from her grandmother, and the closest she'd come was her involvement in theater, thanks to her Aunt Roxy. Anything more *community* than the Theatre on Main or the Middleton U theater program, and she was sunk.

At any rate, she had to admit that the club was lovely. Whoever had decorated had managed to make the Valentine's theme both festive and sophisticated, without being tacky. Elle couldn't say the same for their home, where she'd put those obnoxious stickers on the front window, and hung a string of heart-shaped lights off the front of the breakfast bar. John found it adorable— his word— so she didn't really care how tacky it was; she enjoyed it.

"Hiding, I see."

A truly stunning blonde sidled up beside Elle, a faint sneer on her overly made-up face. "Do I know you?" Elle asked, hoping for a polite tone.

The woman stuck out a flawlessly manicured hand. "Jackie Hart."

Jackie.

Elle's smile stayed in place by sheer force of will. She shook Jackie's hand and then snatched her own back as quickly as possible, giving her as discreet a once-over as she could manage. Her silver sheath dress fit expertly, but had a slit up one side that might have been a few inches too high for the setting. Her hair was in a sleek ponytail, diamonds sparkling at her ears and throat, as well as a massive one on her left hand.

"Nice to meet you," Elle lied. "I'm Elle Williams."

Jackie hummed. When she looked Elle over, it was significantly less discreet. Her sneer only deepened. "I believe I've heard of you. You're John's newest fling, right?"

Wow, Elle thought mildly. "Seeing as I live with him, I'd say it's more than a fling, but yes. He and I are together."

Again, Jackie hummed. Elle could see the disbelief there, in her eyes, as she flipped her ponytail over her shoulder. "How's that going for you?"

She's got a tree up her ass, Elle remembered, as though Logan had said the words right into her ear. Her smile came back full force, deliberately sweet. "It's going wonderfully, thank you." She gestured at Jackie's hand, the one with the very expensive-looking engagement ring. "Your ring is beautiful. Who's the lucky guy?"

Jackie's haughty expression faltered. She looked at her ring as though she'd momentarily forgotten about it before she responded. "Thank you. His name is Parker."

"He's a lucky man," Elle said. Not that she meant it. "I hope John and I can be as happy as you two are."

Jackie's sneer returned. "John could have had me back, if he wanted." Her eyes roamed over Elle again; Elle refused to feel self conscious about it. "He was too proud to admit he made a mistake in letting me get away."

Do not laugh, Elle told herself firmly. "Right," she said instead, eyes scanning the room. No sign of John yet. God, where *was* he?

"I feel like I should warn you, though," Jackie continued, "he's got a wandering eye."

The snort that escaped Elle was completely involuntary. "I *highly* doubt that."

Jackie's eyebrow hitched up high over her cool gaze. "Oh, darling, you don't think he'll stick around with *you*, do you?" She gave a light, cruel laugh. "Oh, love, no. Didn't he tell you why he left me? He's been stuck on this girl from his college for *years*."

Elle grinned, feeling surprisingly warm inside, given how cold her next words were. "Yes, I know."

"And you don't mind?"

"Well, seeing as how he got me in the end, I'd say it worked out for both of us." Jackie's jaw dropped. "Too bad it took him so long to tell me; we'd probably be married by now if he'd realized I was single and asked me out back in college. Though I suppose he wanted to take some time to recover over the way you dropped him like a dog in the pound and then expected him to wait around for you."

Jackie's face blanched, and then began to turn red. "You'll end up leaving him, too," she spat. "He's not worth your time. He's not worth *anyone's* time."

Like whiplash, Elle felt her entire body go cold. "You be *very* careful what you say to me about him," she warned. "And you must have a very poor opinion of me to think that I'd just *leave* the love of my life."

"That's not—" Jackie began, but Elle cut her off.

"You don't know anything about me," Elle said coldly, "and you've got a lot of nerve for someone who hasn't dated John in five years." While Jackie opened and shut her mouth like a fish, Elle's eyes dropped pointedly to the ring on her left hand. "You should probably reevaluate your commitment to your fiancé, seeing as you're so hung up about *my* boyfriend. I might suggest therapy."

"How *dare* you—"

Jackie might very well have continued, but a tall, dark skinned man in a dove grey suit stepped up behind her, looking like he'd rather be anywhere else and *with* anyone else. "My love," he said, completely devoid of affection. One of his hands went to Jackie's back. "I think it's time for us to leave."

Jackie glared up at him, but remained silent.

Neat trick. Elle tacked on a smile and held out her hand to the newcomer— Parker, the fiancé, she deduced. "I don't believe we've met."

"Parker Jackson," Parker said, shaking her hand with a firm grip. "I'm sorry if my fiancée has been rude."

Although Jackie gaped up at him, clearly offended, Elle felt herself relax into her own real grin. "Not at all," she admitted— because this, by far, was probably the most polite argument she'd ever been part of, and she had *plenty* of practice. "It was a pleasure to meet you."

"Likewise," said Parker.

With a nod to excuse herself, Elle sidestepped the happy couple, heading for literally *anywhere* else. Maybe she'd actually manage to find John amongst all the *people*.

She found him two rooms over, after bumping into Nathan and Sylvie and ending up playing catch-up. He stood by one of the club's enormous arch windows, looking every bit as pained as Parker had only minutes ago. Across from him, chattering animatedly, was a middle aged woman in a shockingly red dress and jacket combo, with a fancy matching hat perched on her greying black hair. The moment he caught sight of Elle, his entire face lit up.

"Elle!" She got the distinct impression he would have waved her over, had it not been for the glasses of wine occupying his hands.

The woman in scarlet turned, delighted, and reached for Elle the second she was within grabbing distance. "Oh, you're so *pretty!* "

Elle found herself abruptly folded into a very matronly, overly-familiar hug. "Uh— thank you?"

"Oh, John, I'm so proud!" The woman barely released Elle, who shuffled toward John to avoid any more physical affection. "You've finally got yourself a trophy wife!"

Elle clapped a hand over her mouth, in a desperate attempt not to release her howl of laughter. John, to his credit, looked very much like he wanted to sink down into the ground and never come back up.

"Elle," he said, voice strained, "this is Mrs. Henderson."

It took a long, deep breath, and inching closer to John's side, for Elle to convince her face to even out into a pleasant, *definitely not laughing* sort of smile. She took one of the wine glasses from John— though he looked like he might need both to keep talking to Mrs. Henderson— before inclining her head toward the older woman. "It's wonderful to meet you. John speaks very highly of you."

Mrs. Henderson tittered into her manicured hand, her nails the same scarlet as the rest of her. "Oh, he's such a sweetheart. And quite the catch, I might add." She said it with a suggestive wiggle of her eyebrows, and Elle practically choked on her own laughter.

"I'm well aware," she managed tightly, and then took a deliberate sip of wine to stop herself from saying anything further.

"I was just telling John the idea I had for an Easter Banquet," Mrs. Henderson began.

"What about Yom Kippur?" Elle asked, frowning. "Doesn't that come first this year?" Logan would know, Elle mused.

"Oh, heavens—" Elle almost dropped her drink when Mrs. Henderson's hand flew to her heart. She was almost expecting something deliberately prejudiced, from the look of near-terror on Mrs. Henderson's weathered face. What she got instead was, "I've been trying to convince the committee to celebrate non-Christian holidays for *years!*"

Elle looked up at John for an explanation, arching her brow.

"They say it's *not in the budget,*" He said, rolling his eyes. "We keep getting out voted."

Elle's lip curled. "So, scrap a couple of the summer cookouts and use the money for a few Jewish holidays."

"I *like* her, John," Mrs. Henderson said. "You got yourself a *smart* trophy wife."

Elle dropped her head into her hand and started to giggle silently into it. John's free hand came up to pat her back consolingly.

The sound of raised voices brought Elle's head back up, just in time to see Jackie and Parker arguing in the next room over. Jackie's face was horribly red, tears clearly visible in her eyes even from a distance. Parker fumbled in an attempt to reach for her, and after a few choice curses, Jackie stormed out of the building, leaving a harried looking Parker in her wake.

"Ah," Elle said evenly. "I see Jackie has left the building." Then as she brought her wine to her lips, "Good riddance."

When Elle looked at John, his face was blank, his jaw set. His eyes hadn't left the spot where Jackie and Parker had just been fighting.

Oh dear, Elle thought, turning to Mrs. Henderson. "It was lovely to meet you," she said, putting a friendly hand on the other woman's arm. "I think John and I are going to bow out."

"Oh, likewise," Mrs. Henderson cooed, either oblivious to the commotion from earlier or pointedly ignoring it. "You two get home safe now. And Elle, I'd love to have you come to committee meetings and do a pitch."

"I'll talk with John about it," Elle said diplomatically, looping her arm through his and, with another polite nod, dragging him away.

He remained silent all the way to the foyer, where Elle passed their glasses off to a server. "So I met Jackie," she said, conversationally, when his silence became disconcerting. "I can see why she wasn't on your Christmas Card list."

John's mouth quirked up, but he didn't respond. Nor did he look at her.

A pang of alarm shot through Elle's chest. She ignored it, keeping her country-club-approved smile in place as she asked the doorman for their coats. "She said some really interesting stuff, too. First she tried to tell me you were in love with someone else— that someone else, obviously, being me. Then she talked about how you left her for me, which if I remember correctly, is the exact opposite of how that went down, and then she tried to insinuate that I'd... I don't know, get bored of you?" Elle shook her head. "I didn't really follow her logic, to be perfectly honest, but it's not like I have any intention of leaving you—"

"You don't?"

Being the first time he'd spoken in several minutes, the words startled Elle, but once she'd registered what he'd said, she only got more worried. "What part of our relationship makes you think I would?"

John did the same fish thing Jackie did. "I— I don't," he stuttered. "I just..."

Elle put a soothing hand on his arm. "I meant it, John. I'm not going anywhere. I don't plan to. I don't *want* to."

They took their coats and pulled them on, stepping out into the chilly winter air. Elle shivered, watching her breath puff out, and leaned against John, her hand searching for his. Something was clearly bothering him, but still, he didn't talk to her.

Elle lifted her chin to look up at him. "Hey." John glanced at her, but said nothing. "*Hey*," she repeated, tugging on his hand. "Look at me."

"We're in the middle of the street," he grumbled. The moment they reached the grassy bank surrounding the parking lot, he stopped, and looked down at her.

Elle put her hands on his chest. "Do you think you're disappointing me? In any way?"

John turned his face away.

"Stop that," Elle snapped, reaching up to cup his cheek. "Come on, John, I need you to talk to me. I can't fix things if I don't know what's wrong."

"Like you talk to me about your mom?"

Elle drew back, stunned. John seemed to realize the moment he said it that he'd made a critical error, and opened his mouth to say something else.

"No—" Elle sighed, putting her hand back onto his chest. "No, don't apologize. That was fair." She shrugged. "I feel like if I don't talk about what Mom says to me, it's not real. Just more of her brainless chatter."

"It gets to you, though," John said.

"Yeah," Elle said, "but you know what makes it easier to deal with?" He shook his head, and she smiled faintly up at him. "You do."

John's head ducked. "Whatever she said was probably true."

"Jackie?" A nod. "Well, hell. Which one of her outlandish claims wasn't complete bullshit?"

"The part where I left her for you."

Elle frowned. "Logan always said she left you."

"She did," he said, nodding. "And then she came back and asked if I wanted her back— I think her question was if I'd learned my lesson yet." Elle rolled her eyes, and he nodded again. "Yeah, not her greatest moment."

"Does she have any good ones?"

John snorted. "I'm not answering that. No," he continued, taking Elle's waist in his hands. "I told her I wasn't going to date her again because there was someone else. That was you."

Elle traced one of the buttons on his coat, her breath misting in front of her from the cold. "You barely knew me. We'd been friends for barely—"

"Seven months," he said. "We met in October, and she dumped me in April." His lips quirked into a faint smile, the way they had in the foyer, but there was still some sort of pain lingering in his eyes that broke Elle's heart. "It's probably weird that I remember."

"It's not weird." It was a *little* weird, but then again, Elle could probably name all of the dates she'd kissed him off the top of her head, right this second, so they were pretty even.

"Sure it's not," John said, seeing right through her. "I was already in love with you, I think."

"When did you know?" Elle asked. "That you were in love with me?"

He shrugged. "I see you, and the world gets brighter. It's been happening for *years.*"

"Years?" She glanced up at him, and he kissed her forehead.

"Remember when we met?"

"Costuming for *Seven Brides,* yeah." Elle had been a freshman, in a costuming class, learning to design. The show was the school's biggest production of the year— they knew they were designing for it months before they actually bought the rights.

"I saw you drawing in your notebook, sitting next to Logan."

"I remember," Elle said softly. She still had the notebook somewhere, more than likely.

"You were so quiet," he recalled, "I wasn't sure if you were even old enough to be in the class. You just kept catching my eye, anytime you were around."

"Logan kept introducing us," Elle reminded him, smiling. "He couldn't remember if we'd met."

"Yeah. Then I ran into you two at that awful Christmas Party at the Wilson building, in that white dress."

"The snowflake one." She still had that, too. She'd almost worn it to the Christmas Cast party, but had gone for green instead, in favor of the *Little Shop* plant aesthetic.

"*Yes.*" John's hands tightened on her waist. "You looked so beautiful, and you were so bubbly. I couldn't keep my eyes off of you. Whenever you noticed me, though, you got all quiet." He ducked his head. "I thought you didn't like me."

"No!" Elle wrapped her arms around him, her gaze pleading. "No, I was just shy."

"I know. I'm big and intimidating." Elle opened her mouth to counter that, but he rolled right over her. "You'd only talk to me around Logan, really, so I started hanging out with him more, hoping you'd be around, too." It was sweet, Elle thought, smiling. She rested her cheek against his chest. "You always seemed so happy to fix my costumes at school. I started pulling buttons off, just as an excuse to come talk to you."

"Those poor costumes," Elle said, then frowned. "Is that why you came to the tech booth during *Oklahoma?*" When John didn't respond, she gasped, turning her face up to his. "It is!"

"I wanted to talk to you about Davy," he grumbled. "Then Chef Rossi came, and then Jesse, and—"

"Yeah, yeah," Elle said, scowling. "No more damaging your costumes on purpose."

John laughed. "Deal." He started to stroke her hair, pulled into an almost-vintage style off her face. "I wanted to ask you out, but you seemed so unsettled whenever I was around. I kept balking, because I didn't want to scare you away."

"So you *pined* for me," Elle simpered, arching back dramatically.

"I was *pitiful*," John confirmed. "I came back to Main from the Opera House because Logan mentioned you worked there. Then he moved in, and I got to see you on a regular basis. When Logan told me you might need a place to stay, I think I had an out of body experience."

"And now, here we are," Elle finished. She smiled up at him, and John smiled down at her, and even in the frosty February air, she felt warmth spread through her. "I love you."

"I love you too, Elle."

"And I'm not going anywhere," she added. "Unless I die of frostbite out here."

John laughed, letting her go, only to take her hand in his to lead her to his car. "Let's go home."

Elle hadn't been so excited to go on a date in *years*.

The thing was, she didn't feel pressured. She could wear jeans if she wanted to, and John wouldn't mind. She could dress up a little, and he'd probably try to match her. She could brave the cold in a dress and the snow in heels, and John would— actually, he'd probably tease her about having a death wish, and coerce her into something more sensible.

No Logan, this go round. He was, naturally, off with Tyler for their own pre-Valentine's evening. Though he'd been spending so much time there, nowadays. She wondered if he *was* actually planning on moving out soon. Maybe she would talk to him about it tomorrow when she saw him.

Honestly, good for him. Even if it *did* mean she had to brave her own closet.

In the end, she settled for a pretty red skirt with leggings, a white turtleneck, and a black button up cardigan— which John would no doubt make fun of her for, but still. It was cold out. Though she wasn't going to attempt heels; she decided on her cowboy boots instead. A little nod to the show that brought them together.

Hair curled, makeup on, and dressed to impress, Elle twirled in front of her mirror. Things couldn't possibly be working out better, she thought with a smile. Especially after their trip down memory lane the other night, it felt like everything was going just right, for once.

Though maybe she should talk about moving her clothing into his room. If he was okay with it, that was. She slept in his room, showered in his room— often with him, and not even in the kinky way— but all of her belongings stayed in this room. Was she moving things too quickly, though? It hadn't even been a month yet. Things had just gone from one thing to the next so quickly, she hadn't really had time to stop and think.

Shoot, now she was anxious. She'd been doing so well on that front, even after her call with her mom a couple of weeks ago. Things had been so easy, so effortless, she hadn't even bothered to worry. He was already in love with her, they already *lived* together. What more could she really ask for?

What do you expect from this relationship?

Karen's words shot through her mind, as loudly and clearly as though they'd been said aloud. Elle realized she was staring blankly at her own reflection, and frowned. No, that was ridiculous. He'd known her forever— he'd been in love with her just as long, if what he said on Monday night was anything to go by. If he wasn't tired of her yet, then he wouldn't get tired of her at all.

He *wouldn't*.

Clutching the small black purse she'd thrown her phone, wallet, and lipstick into, Elle turned her back on her reflection and swept out of her bedroom. Her mother's bullshit wasn't going to get in her way tonight. This night was about her and John, and the love they shared.

The man had bought her roses for opening night, for god's sake. She clearly had nothing to worry about.

She flounced down the stairs and into the living room, and found herself grinning. John had actually taken her flower shopping, so that she could decorate the house. Pale pink and blue hydrangeas bloomed in the living room, while purple and white hyacinth and white carnations brightened the kitchen. They were all fake— Elle was a firm believer in getting things that would last, things that she could reuse— except, of course, for her roses, which stood proudly in the center of the dining room table.

As she reached the living room, she paused by the entertainment center, carefully adjusting one of the hydrangea arrangements. Strong arms came around her middle, and gentle lips pressed a kiss into the crown of her head.

"Stop fussing," John told her, guiding her hand away from the flowers and around her waist with his, their fingers entwined. "They're perfect."

"They're happy flowers," Elle agreed. She tilted her head back to look up at John, grinning. "Do they make you happy?"

"*You* make me happy," he clarified. "So if flowers make you happy, by all means, we can get more flowers."

"We'll have a garden in here, if you keep spoiling me."

"For your smile?" John pulled away, tugging on her to make her turn around and face him. "Worth it." It was hard not to blush, when his eyes slid down her body and back up. "Pretty. Even the cardigan." Elle snorted. "Did you get dressed up for me?"

"No," Elle said, spinning. "I got dressed up for Logan. He's taking me out for Valentine's day, you see, and—" Elle cut off with a shriek as John scooped her up into his arms, tossing her over one shoulder like it was nothing. "Hey! Put me down!"

"Nice boots," he replied, making absolutely no move to release her.

"We're going to be late for our reservations!"

"We won't," John said. "I'm not missing a chance to show my beautiful girlfriend off."

Girlfriend. Elle's heart stuttered, and she stopped struggling. Then the rest of his sentence registered. "You want to show me off?"

"Hell yeah." Apparently deciding that he'd tortured her enough, John set her back on her feet. "I feel under dressed. Maybe I should get a blazer."

Elle took in his light blue button down, his dark slacks. "Absolutely not. I'll never get the ladies off of you."

"We'd both be fending people off."

He leaned down to kiss her, and— it was like the first time, every time. Butterflies set off in her belly, even though the kiss was fleeting.

"Come on, Beautiful" John said, straightening up. "I can't wait to be the envy of every man. After I fight off Logan."

Elle let John lead the way, her laughter echoing through the house.

22

The thing between them— it worked.

John didn't think it was possible to fall more in love with Elle, but here he was, seeing intimate little things about her that he'd never noticed before, and loving her all the more every day. He realized one morning that he could touch her whenever he wanted now; brushing a hand over the small of her back as he walked past her, sweeping his hand over her hair while she read beside him on the couch. She touched him, too, in bigger ways; hugging him at any opportunity, sitting in his lap whenever possible. He found himself kissing her constantly. Light, fleeting kisses, usually because she wanted them (and he couldn't refuse her anything).

Everything was going so smoothly. He still hadn't managed to convince her to bring her things into their room, though he wasn't sure if she was ready for that yet. He'd been dropping hints, making sure their laundry was together, hanging things for her in his closet when she wasn't looking, but she had yet to actually make the full shift. John didn't want to press, but at this rate, he was just going to swipe all the stuff from her room a little at a time until it was done, right under her nose. Hey, if it worked, it worked.

The phone call came around dinner time, which usually wouldn't have mattered to him, but since John was in the midst of kissing Elle's neck, he found it incredibly annoying.

"John," she moaned, trying to escape. He tightened his arms around her waist, nipping her shoulder, bare under the thin strap of her shirt. Her back was pressed deliciously against his front while she cooked, holding the pot and spoon in her hands while he held her waist in his. "John, it's my mom," Elle insisted, but he could hear the amusement in her voice.

"All the more reason to ignore it." With that, he reached in front of her to turn off the stove, distracting her with another kiss to the crook of her neck.

"*John.*"

He sighed, stepping back. She gave him a reproachful look as she turned the burner back on, already tucking her phone against her cheek. "Hi, Momma. I'm cooking, can I put you on speaker?"

A moment later, Elle's phone lay on the kitchen counter as her mother's shrill voice filled the room, chattering incessantly about her patrons, her pottery class. Elle just went about stirring her risotto, giving the appropriate responses whenever Karen paused to breathe. John kissed her temple, then took to setting the table for them. Only two settings tonight; they hadn't seen Logan outside of the show in ages, at this point.

"I'd love to come down and see the show," Karen said, instantly catching John's attention. He paused in the act of setting down a fork and glanced at Elle, who kept stirring, steadfast and true.

"Then come down," Elle said.

"Well, are you still in the same place?"

John dropped the silverware onto the table.

"Have I mentioned moving recently?" Elle snapped.

Not this bullshit again. John abandoned his task completely and strode toward the kitchen instead.

"Well, Cupcake, I figured if John had moved on already, you'd need to process it before you told me."

"I'm right here, you know," John informed her, at the exact same time Elle said, "He can hear you." Her icy tone startled him, even more than Karen's misguided notion that he'd ever willingly leave Elle.

"Hi, John!" The greeting was far too bright, as though this sort of exchange was *normal*. "Glad to hear you're not tired of Ellie yet!"

"Not gonna happen," he told her, catching the edge to his own voice. Elle had gone completely still at the stove. She didn't even acknowledge him when his arms went around her waist. "My life is too empty without her in it."

"Aww."

She was too tense. John carefully wrapped his hands around hers, guiding them back into stirring, while pressing kisses into her hair. *"Let me,"* he whispered, and she nodded. While he took over the stirring, she turned to face him, wrapping her arms around his waist.

"So anyhow," Karen continued merrily, "I'll try to come down the week before closing. I know how you theater kids are on closing night!" She tittered like a bird. "Wild party animals, all of you! I wouldn't want to interrupt that."

"Mhmm." Elle laid her cheek against John's chest and squeezed her arms. He kissed the crown of her head.

"Maybe we can all go get breakfast before the show!"

"Sounds good." It didn't, John mused, but Elle's voice was too weary to bother arguing with her. "Dinner's ready, Momma. I've got to go."

"Alright, Cupcake. I love you!"

"Love you too."

"Bye, John!"

John grumbled a goodbye and then waited, watching Elle's phone go dark and silent. Careful not to jostle Elle too much, he turned off the burners and dished the food up— the benefit of long arms— until he noticed his shirt had grown damp.

Elle had buried her face in his chest, arms weakly around his hips. Her shoulders trembled, and he could hear her muffled, disjointed breathing, could feel it in hot bursts against him.

"She's wrong, you know," he murmured, closing his arms around Elle. She didn't respond, except for a soft, muted sob. "I could never get bored of you. Hell, I can't get enough of you." With a snort, he added, "Sometimes I wonder if I have a problem."

He heard her sniff, but then she gave a soft, watery laugh. When she pulled her head back to look at him, her eyes were rimmed with red, but clear. "Thank you for finishing dinner."

Of course, he thought, but merely nodded. "Are you okay?" She nodded. "You sure?"

"Yeah." She puckered her lips, and he bent down to kiss her. Anything, if it would ease her pain. "It's nothing new. Maybe she'll even back off a little, now that you've called her out."

"Here's hoping." *For your sake.*

Elle clung to him through the rest of the night. She curled against his side on the couch after dinner, practically wrapped around his arm. Later, when he made love to her, she tucked her face into his neck and stayed there, burrowing against him. Her hands never left him, pulling him closer at every turn, until she eventually fell asleep in his arms.

John cradled her against him with a hand threaded in her hair, still awake long after her breathing had evened out. He would do *anything* to make her happy. To keep her that way. Karen really had a screw loose— probably more than one— if she thought he'd ever get tired of her. Hell, just a couple of weeks ago, he told Logan he'd *marry* her.

The idea sprang fully formed into John's head, so suddenly he gasped aloud. Beside him, Elle stirred— but all she did was sigh, roll onto her other side, and slip back into the stillness of slumber.

The opportunity was too perfectly timed to pass up. Moving carefully, so as not to disturb her, he slipped out of bed, wandering over to his dresser and opening the top drawer. It took some digging (god, *why* did he own so many socks?), but he finally found what he was looking for, pulling it out with a quick glance over his shoulder. Elle slept on, completely unaware.

John regarded the black velvet box, strangely small in his hand. His grandparents had left it to him after their deaths, and he had hidden it away, too emotional to look at it, but too sentimental to get rid of it.

With a slight frown, he lifted the lid. Inside, in a bed of white silk, sat the glimmering gold bands of his grandparents' wedding set, and the simple engagement ring that had rested on his grandmother's hand for over fifty years. Just looking at it made John's eyes itch.

It was nothing fancy. Just a plain marquis diamond with two tiny diamonds on either side, set in a gold band. Small and dainty, like Elle, but strong enough to withstand the trials of time— also, John thought fondly, like Elle.

John looked at her again. He could see his whole future with her. Waking up each morning in her arms, and falling asleep beside her each night. Handing her coffee at breakfast, and helping her cook dinner. Elle arranging flowers throughout the house and begging him to carve pumpkins with her. He wanted that— all the big moments, yes, like a wedding and children, but all the small moments, too. *Especially* those.

Maybe it was too soon. They had barely been together for a month, but at this point, it could possibly be the one way he could convince her— and her *idiot* mother— that he wasn't going anywhere. Period.

Of *course* her mom didn't back down. Elle had been a fool to even consider the possibility. In fact, Karen was, in Elle's honest opinion, worse than ever.

If nothing else, Karen had loved the show. She'd spent most of the evening waxing enthusiastic about the show, from Elle and Davy's "lovely performance" to John's "roguish" Gaston. She'd even—*gasp* — complimented Elle's choreography and costuming.

At this point, Elle couldn't sit still. She kept waiting for Karen to say something rude or ask something wildly inappropriate. So far, the most she'd done was politely— or as politely as she was capable of— interrogate John about his childhood, his family, and the house. After half an hour of playing twenty questions, Elle was so stressed she was basically vibrating in her seat. She needed to do something to distract herself. *Anything.* Hell, she'd do *dishes* if it meant not having to listen to Karen.

"So you grew up in Florida?" Karen asked John. He nodded. His hand hadn't left Elle's since they'd taken up residence on the couch, long after the show and dinner had ended. "Did you go to Disney a lot?"

"We were pass holders, so yeah."

"That's so nice! Did you ever think of performing there?"

Ugh. Time to move. Elle patted John's leg twice and stood up. They'd come up with the signal right before Karen's visit; Elle's way of signaling that she needed to decompress, to have a little space from Karen. His eyes followed her evenly for a few seconds as she made her way toward the kitchen, listening with half an ear.

"I thought about it, but it wasn't really my style. I have a friend who's equity there, though."

"What made you move up here?"

Elle opened the cabinet door for a glass and found it empty, and huffed to herself. Dishwasher, then.

"When my grandparents got older, my family moved up here for a while to help them out," John told Karen. "Kellie and I stayed through college, but my parents moved back to Florida when they retired."

"And you've never thought of moving back south?"

Elle rolled her eyes as she emptied the top rack of the dishwasher, setting aside a glass for her water. Leave it to Karen to try to find any shred of a chance of John leaving her.

"We like it here," John said easily. Elle looked up to find him smiling at her, and she returned it, adding a wink so he'd know she was okay. "Elle's performing again, and I think Greg might make her an offer for a directing position soon."

Greg *had* been hinting at that, Elle mused, moving onto the bottom rack of the dishwasher. "I think he'll spend a little while longer throwing me in the shows against my will," she joked dryly.

"Well, if you don't like it, why do you do it?" Karen snapped.

"I never said I didn't like it," Elle responded coolly, turning her back to her mom to put plates in the cupboard. "I just don't want to be pigeon-holed as a performer. I want to do a little of everything." Dishwasher empty, Elle closed it up and smiled across the counter at them, even though Karen was scowling. "Anyone want dessert? We've got brownies!"

"How *do* you put up with her?" Karen demanded, turning her scowl toward John.

"I beg your pardon?" John's voice had such an edge to it that Elle found herself clutching her empty glass to her chest. It was the voice of someone who wanted to politely hint that they were offended without being rude themselves.

No, no, no—

"She's got such an overwhelming energy," Karen said, as though Elle couldn't hear her. "And she's so high maintenance! She always *needs* something."

"Good thing I would do anything to make her happy." The easy certainty in his voice had Elle's shoulders relaxing, albeit marginally.

"But she's so *negative*," Karen griped.

"Not really."

"Give it time."

John snorted. "She's been living here for over over six months. I've known her for *years*. When exactly is that gonna hit?"

Stop. Elle carefully set her glass down, horrified to find herself shaking again. She didn't want them to fight. She didn't want *any* of this. Her mom was right and always had been, but to drag John into this—

"I've known her for her whole life," Karen snapped. "I think I know her better than you."

"Why are you like this?"

It took several seconds of confused staring between the three of them for Elle to realize that she'd been the one to speak. John's face shifted first, a hint of pride overtaking the shock on his face.

Karen, on the other hand, gaped openly. "What?"

"Why are you like this?" Elle asked again. Inside her, anger churned, hot and molten, rising above any other emotion she might have. "Why do you say things like that? Like you're giving him reasons to want to end our relationship?"

Karen snorted. *"You're* the one giving him reasons. I'm just shedding light on them."

"Bullshit." Oh, god; Elle had *never* spoken to her mother this way. Not even during her teens.

Karen's face turned mutinous. She curled a scarlet clawed hand against the arm of her chair and narrowed her beady eyes behind her glasses. Then, haughtiness radiating from her very skin, she turned back to John. "This is exactly what I was talking about."

John gave one single, firm nod. Elle's heart sank. Then, evenly, he said, "I'd appreciate it if you'd refrain from projecting your fear of commitment onto Elle while in our home. Just because you had three failed marriages, doesn't mean Elle is destined to follow in your footsteps."

Elle's jaw hit the floor. While Karen sputtered, her fury spiking visibly, Elle managed to recover quickly enough to say, "Actually, it was *four* marriages."

Karen leapt to her feet. Elle flinched instantly, every part of her body screaming at her to run, to flee, to escape. She held her ground as Karen whirled on her, pointing a claw at her. "Elodie Marie, you keep your mouth *shut*. That is *none* of his business."

"That's a matter of opinion." Hands balled into a fist, Elle watched Karen advance, still pointing an accusatory finger at her chest. Behind her, John also stood, in one fluid, powerful motion.

"You have *never* taken responsibility for your actions," Karen said. "I tried to give you everything you wanted and needed as a child, and you grew up to be an ungrateful, manipulative *bitch*. You're lucky John's willing to overlook that for whatever you're giving him in bed."

The room froze.

Cold, like nothing Elle had ever felt before, soaked through Elle's body. It felt like having quick-dry cement poured over her. She could barely move through the rage that had replaced the blood in her veins.

"How *dare* you?" While John seemed too horrified to even form a coherent sentence, Elle felt like she'd never been able to think more clearly. Karen glared at her, but she glared right back, tenfold. This woman— this *monster* — dared to stand in front of her and talk to Elle about responsibility? About manipulation?

No.

No.

"Get out." The second Elle spoke, John moved, striding past an apoplectic Karen without a second glance, coming to stand beside Elle. To stand *with* Elle. One unmovable wall of support, right at her side. Elle was quaking with rage as she continued. "Go. Get out." When Karen made no movement to follow directions, Elle did the most horrific thing of all— she raised her voice. *"Get out of my house."*

Karen's face hardened. She clenched her fists at her sides, looking over Elle and John with blatant disgust. "Isn't that just typical," she sneered. "After everything I've done for you." She shook her head, then walked around the chair and headed down the hallway. Elle grabbed John's hand and dragged him along as she followed, intent on seeing Karen all the way *out*. "You can't spend your life cowering behind John, Ellie," Karen told her. "Eventually you'll have to grow up, and then you'll see."

Elle watched Karen pull on her coat and grab her purse, too angry to chance speaking. She wasn't certain if what would come out would even be words, or just an inhuman screech.

With one hand gripping the doorknob, Karen turned back to face them. "You're using him, Ellie. How can you be so selfish?" With that, Karen sailed out of the house, slamming the door behind her.

The seconds ticked by as they both listened to Karen's car wheeze it's way to a start, and then drive off. Seconds that left Elle retreating into her head, processing her mother's words as though from a long distance away.

Using him.

Manipulative.

Needy.

Ungrateful.

Elle's vision dimmed. And then she realized what she'd done.

"Wait!" Panic searing through her, Elle lunged forward, reaching for the door. God, she'd just kicked her own *mother* out of the house. Without even saying goodbye. What if something happened? God, how could she live with herself? How could she now, after—

"Elle!" John caught her around the waist, stopping her in her tracks. Elle struggled, trying to get around him, but his arms caged her in, squeezing her as she tipped out of panic and into full distress. "Elle, stop. It's okay."

"I have to— oh, god, what did I just *do?*" Trapped, Elle clung to John. She couldn't get her breathing under control. She couldn't think clearly. She couldn't—"I need to call her."

"Let her blow off some steam," John soothed. His hand stroked over her hair, giving her something to focus on. "Give it some time."

"But what if something—"

"Nothing's going to happen." His hand moved to her back, rubbing in patient, slow circles. "She knows how to drive. She'll be okay. Then you can call her in the morning, when you're both more level-headed."

Elle nodded. "Okay." He was right; of course he was. They both just needed time apart, time to—

You can't keep cowering behind him, Ellie.

Elle felt her body grow numb against John's. God, she *was* a coward. Letting him handle the brunt of her emotional game of pinball.

He held onto her, rocking her slightly, for so long she couldn't even tell the time anymore. Eventually, he must have realized she wasn't moving, because he bent down to pick her up, hugging her against his chest like a child. "Come on," he murmured into her hair. "Let's go to bed."

Elle lay against him in the dark in another one of his shirts, listening to his breathing even out. She couldn't fathom why he held her so tightly, knowing her the way he did. Her mom was right— eventually, he'd be disillusioned, and then he'd realize how badly Elle had been acting. She'd been manipulating him from the start, talking him into buying and doing things he never did, parties and decorations and *stupid* things. She'd moved in and overrun his home, his *family* home, and then tricked her way into his bed. God, she was a *monster*.

Tears began to slide hot little trails down her cheeks. How could she do this to her friend? To the man she loved more than anything else in the world? How could she be so cruel?

There was only one thing to do.

Elle slipped out of bed.

Mere moments later, she stood in her old bedroom closet, staring up at all of her moving bags with an ache in her chest. There were so many, all stored up where she thought she wouldn't need them, on the shelves at the top of the walls. She really *had* overrun poor John's house. He didn't deserve that.

It only took a few minutes for her to get garment bags down, to fill them with her clothing. A few more, and Elle started to branch out into her bedroom, gathering her books, her pictures, piling them on the bed—

"Elle."

Elle whipped around at John's voice, clutching a book to her chest. He stood in only a pair of sweatpants, frowning at her from just inside the doorway.

Shit. She hadn't been prepared for this. In fact, she hadn't been prepared at all. She had no idea what she was doing, only that—

"Elle," John said again, taking a deliberate step toward her. "What are you doing?"

"I…" She didn't bother answering. He knew. It was clear from his expression that he knew.

John scrubbed a hand over his face, letting out a ragged breath. "Come on, Elle. *Talk* to me." He took another step toward her, and she shrunk in on herself, clutching the book as a lifeline. "You said it yourself when we left the country club, Elle. I can't fix it if I don't know what's wrong."

"It's nothing you need to fix," Elle said, hoping her voice, at least, sounded calm. She set the book on the bed in a pile with the rest, and then, with nothing to occupy them, wrung her hands in front of her. "It's something *I* need to fix."

"By leaving?" Another step. If he were anyone else, she'd probably feel threatened by it, but with John— no. He would never hurt her.

But he might try to stop her.

Elle nodded. "My mom's right, John," she said, turning away. She could at least get things together while he was in here— and by doing so, have a reason not to look at him. She started to sort the heap on her bed into more manageable piles. There was no way he was changing her mind, now, anyway. "I *have* been using you. You welcomed me into your home, and I've overrun it. I've been selfish, and wholly unfair to you." With the words hanging in the air above her head, she realized just how selfish she'd really been. It solidified inside her, like a fully realized carving. "I can't tell you how sorry I am that—"

"Your mom is full of shit."

His voice was so close, Elle yelped, dropping the book in her hands. When she spun around, John was barely a foot away from her, fully scowling at her.

God, now she'd made him angry. *Great going, dumbass.*

"Do you think I do things for you because I expect you to pay me back?" He demanded. Elle stood stock still in front of him, too shocked to reply. "That's not what relationships are *about*, Elle. I do things for you because they make you happy, and seeing *you* happy makes *me* happy. You don't have to coerce me, or— or *seduce* me into doing things for you. All you have to do is *ask*."

Elle sucked in a breath. She'd been doing that, too. *God* . The realization made her face start to itch and burn with the threat of tears.

John took one look at her face and screwed his eyes shut."Do *not* try to turn that into an accusation. It wasn't."

"Then what was it?" Because it sure *sounded* like an accusation.

"It was *supposed* to convince you to loosen your iron grip on the shitty things your mom said— and *has* said, and *will* say— to you." His hands came up to grab her upper arms, not tightly, but enough to keep her in place. "Elle, I love you. I'm *in* love with you. I don't care about whatever things you think you've manipulated me into. You didn't. I would have done them anyway, just because *you* asked, and I would do anything to make you happy."

Swallowing, Elle just looked at him.

John stared into her eyes, and exhaled harshly. "You don't believe that, do you?"

She wanted to. She *wanted* to. More than anything. But—"I can't," she said, voice barely above a whisper. "I— it's not *fair* to you, if I—"

"Will you *please* forget about being fair?" John's hands slipped down, holding her elbows, now. "Elle, *please*. I don't want to lose you. Not because of your mom's misguided notion that I'll— god, what even was it this time?"

"Come to your senses and realize I'm a manipulative—"

"*Christ*." John rolled his eyes so hard, it was a wonder they didn't stick. "If it's not one stupid thing, it's another, with her."

"That's my *mom*," Elle said, leaning back out of his grip. He let her go instantly, without comment. "She loves me. She wants what's best for me."

"I'm sure she does, Elle," John said, "but that doesn't mean she knows what that is."

That—

That had never occurred to her. Not once.

Elle opened her mouth to counter it, but nothing came out.

"And," John continued, "that doesn't mean she knows how *I* feel. Or how I *will* feel. Because she may think she knows you—" His word choice wasn't lost on Elle—"but she *doesn't* know me. Not at all." With that, he turned on his heel, striding away from her.

Shit. *Shit.* He couldn't go. Not yet. This wasn't done— Elle had so many questions, so much she wanted to ask him, to *say*, to explain—

"Wait here," John said, throwing the words over his shoulder. "Don't move."

Well. Gaping, confused, and— yep, tearing up, Elle stood right where she was, rooted to the spot by her own shock.

This was— fine. Whatever was happening right now was... perfectly fine. The tears obscuring her vision, the way her chin trembled— all of this. Perfectly... perfectly fine.

Maybe John had realized what was happening, that Elle had no intention of continuing to force herself into his life. Maybe he realized, in all of his talking, that she had been doing just that, all this time. Forcing her way into his life, into his home, into his bed—

He came back in with something in his hand, scowling just as deeply as he'd been moments before. Elle lifted her gaze from the floor to look at him, but seeing his expression just sent her eyes right back down.

"This isn't how I'd planned this," John said by way of explanation. "Look at me, Elle."

Elle inhaled deeply, hoping her eyes were clear enough not to give her away, and then did as he asked.

John saw. Of course he did. He always did. Something in his jaw shifted in that moment, and then he held out his hand, and whatever was inside it.

It was a box. A small, black velvet box, that—

Elle gasped.

Oh. Oh— oh *no.*

"I wanted to… well," John started. "To do this better. Maybe more publicly, if you were into that. I wanted to talk about it first, because I didn't want you to really be surprised." He shook his head. "That's not the part that matters, though."

He knelt down in front of her like a knight before a queen, and for the life of her, Elle couldn't wrap her head around it. Was he— did he mean…?

He did.

John opened the box, and then just waited, holding it out to her in one of his enormous hands. It was a simple ring, a *beautiful* ring. She loved it, the second she laid eyes on it.

Oh my god.

"I don't care what your mother thinks is going to happen," John said, gazing up at her imploringly. "I care what *you* think is going to happen. If I'd thought you'd say yes to me, I would have proposed to you on Valentine's. Earlier, even. I knew I wanted to when I watched you at dress rehearsal, in that wedding gown you made."

Elle's heart stuttered in her chest. He'd been watching? She had been so caught up in her blocking and choreo that she hadn't even noticed him in the audience. Besides it wasn't a wedding dress, it was her—

Oh. Oh, *no.* Sarah had been right.

Elle felt some of her resolve crumble away.

Swallowing, John continued. "Elle, I love you. More than anything. I can't imagine my life without you in it." He looked at the box, then back up at her face. "I know I can't expect you to just…*stop* believing what Karen said, but I promise, I will do everything in my power to prove to you that she's *wrong.* I will never stop loving you, and I will never leave you. I want us to have a future together." His eyes were so *pleading,* so full of love and adoration, it took Elle's breath away. She clapped a hand over her mouth as the tears began to flow freely down her face. "Please, Elle. Can we try?"

She couldn't keep it together. Not for anything. It was as though John's words had blown open the part of her that wanted to save him from herself, and started filling her up with love instead, so bright and hot and *real* that, before she could stop herself, Elle burst into tears.

John reared back, clearly startled by the response, but she reached out to grab his hand, her other hand still over her mouth in a vain attempt to hold in her sobs.

"*Yes,*" she said, barely able to get the word out over her own bawling. "Yes, I—" And that was all she got, before a fresh wave of tears washed over her. Strangely enough, it felt like *relief.*

"God," John said. He leaned forward, resting his forehead against her belly. Elle threaded a hand through his hair, keeping him close to her— where he belonged. Where *she* belonged, touching him. "God, I— Thank God."

Elle's laugh was watery and tight, but it was there nonetheless. She just stood there, watching, as John pulled away and stood up, but when he reached for her hand, she was already reaching back.

"I had it sized for you," John told her. "I asked Logan to help."

This time, Elle's laugh was steadier. "He's going to be so mad he wasn't here for this."

"He'll get over it," John told her, pulling the ring from the box and throwing the box behind her, onto the bed. Then his eyes went wide. "Oh, god, I didn't even ask you—"

"Ask me," Elle told him, clutching his free hand in both of his. Her face was wet and red, she could barely breathe through her nose, and she couldn't care less. "Ask me now, John."

"Elle," he murmured, holding the ring at the tip of her finger. "Will you marry me?"

"Yes," Elle said, looking into his eyes. "Yes, John. I'll marry you."

When he slid the ring onto her finger, it was a perfect fit.

EPILOGUE

"Do you think Mom's gonna cry?"

Elle grinned up at her husband as she buttoned her pink cardigan. Her wedding set sparkled in the dim light of their bedroom, and she absently ran her thumb over the inside of it. Their wedding had been a little more than a year ago, now— their autumn wedding, with all the fiery red and gold and copper, with flowers and leaves and carved pumpkins. Elle still had the heads of her bouquet flowers in a display box down in the living room, surrounding pictures from their wedding. Everything had been so romantic and whimsical. All Elle really remembered, vividly, was John tearing up when he saw her at the other end of the aisle.

John himself pulled a blue cable knit on over his Batman tee shirt, then reached out to poke her nose with his knuckle. "Do *you* think she will?"

"I hope so."

Things had gotten better with Karen. They still had their moments— they probably always would— but it was easier, now, with Elle asserting her boundaries more often, more firmly. Therapy helped, but so did John. He was a constant reminder that she was stronger than her anxiety, but he was always there to help her through it, when it hit.

She picked up a box filled with presents, slim packages wrapped with pastel paper and pale yellow ribbons. "I hope your parents won't mind her outdoing them."

"I think they're prepared, after our wedding." He took the box from her and leaned down to peck her on the lips. "Don't hurt yourself, or Greg will have my hide."

"*Your* hide?" Elle teased, following him out of their bedroom. They passed both Logan's old room and her own, now unoccupied and preparing for bigger and better things.

"You *are* his favorite."

"I sure am." Two steps behind him on the stairs, she paused, glancing at their wedding photos on the wall. Gold framed snapshots of him in his sleek black tux, of her in the gown she had made. It was probably the only dress she liked more than her Belle ballgown.

Her favorite picture from that day hung at the top of the landing; a black-and-white photo of him holding her by the waist, up in the air, her dress trailing down below her. He hadn't even bothered to set her down before kissing her, the moment after the photo had been taken.

"I've got the pies," John said, setting them carefully into the box with the presents.

"Thank you, my love." Elle made her way the rest of the way down the stairs, pausing at the bottom step to kiss him as he passed. "I can hold that while you put your coat on."

"You, first," he told her, already opening the closet door. "It's pretty chilly out. I don't want you to get sick."

Elle laughed, but let him jostle the box onto his hip so he could get her coat out for her. He'd only grown more doting since their wedding. He helped her into her coat one-handed, and then carefully handed her the box so he could whip his own coat on. "I still stand by my original idea," Elle told him as he took the box back. "Greg wouldn't have minded sitting with Mom for one show. He handled her so well at the wedding."

"Ah, but how would she get her moment in the spotlight from the audience?" John's eye twinkled as he walked her to his car and held her door open for her. "This is more her speed." Elle just laughed in response.

With the box in the back seat, they started off toward John's sister's place for Thanksgiving dinner. Entwining her hand with John's, Elle found herself smiling. Things were *good* , now. They were *right*. Some days were still rough— maybe they always would be— but some days were diamonds, and those were the days worth waking up for, every morning.

"I hope she cries."

John laughed, squeezing her hand. Keeping his eyes on the road, he pulled it up to his lips to press a kiss to the back of it. Elle smiled at him with her heart swelling in her chest, placing one hand on the slight bump of her belly.